THE BARON'S INCONVENIENT BRIDE

LAUREN ROYAL
DEVON ROYAL

June 2021 Edition
SWEET BRIDES

THE BARON'S INCONVENIENT BRIDE by Lauren Royal & Devon Royal

Published by Novelty Books, a division of Novelty Publishers, LLC, 205 Avenida Del Mar #275, San Clemente, CA 92674

June 2021 Edition

Cover by Kimberly Killion

PUBLISHER'S NOTE: This is a work of fiction. Names, characters, places, and incidents either are the product of the author's imagination or are used fictitiously. Any resemblance to actual persons, living or dead, business establishments, events, or locales is entirely coincidental.

Learn more about the authors and their books at www.LaurenandDevonRoyal.com.

ISBN: 978-1-63469-180-2

MORE SWEET CHASE BRIDES BOOKS

For our new family,

the Dantos

ONE

Trentingham Manor, the South of England
August 1677

*H*E'D FORGOTTEN about her.

Well, maybe he hadn't quite forgotten about her, but he'd certainly put her out of his mind.

Well, maybe he hadn't put her entirely out of his mind, but he'd banished all thoughts of her to the outskirts. She was Ford's sister-in-law, after all, and an innocent, sheltered girl of fourteen. And Lord Randal Nesbitt was far too honorable to let a girl that young anywhere near his...well, thoughts.

But it had been four years since they'd last met at Ford's wedding. And now, Rand had just realized, Lady Lily Ashcroft must be eighteen.

A fetching, dark-haired, blue-eyed eighteen. A marriageable eighteen.

Marriageable? Having never really considered marriage in all of his twenty-three years, Rand found the notion jarring. Perhaps being in a chapel put ideas into a fellow's head.

Though truth be told, he hardly knew where he was or what was going on around him. All his awareness was focused on Lily standing beside him at the altar, her month-old niece cradled in her arms.

"Having now," the priest continued, sounding distant to Rand though the man stood right in front of him, "in the name of these children, made these promises, wilt thou also on thy part take heed that these children learn the Creed, the Lord's Prayer, and the Ten Commandments, and all other things which a Christian ought to know and believe to his soul's health?"

"I will, by God's help," Lily replied softly. Gently, gazing down at the babe she held close.

A smile curved Rand's lips. In four years she had changed, of course. But her gentleness, that unfailing sweetness, hadn't changed. Couldn't have changed. It was what made her Lily.

Ford Chase, Rand's friend—and father of the children in question—elbowed him in the ribs.

"Hmm?" Startled, Rand looked down at the month-old boy squirming in his own arms, its bald little head colored by the sun streaming through the chapel's stained-glass windows. Ford's son, he thought, surprised by a rush of tenderness. Rand's godson…or at least the tiny fellow and his twin sister would soon be his godchildren, provided he made it through their baptism.

"I will," he answered, echoing Lily's words.

"By God's help," the priest prompted.

"By God's help."

A few titters rose from the crowd, but Rand ignored them, shifting on his feet. Sweet mercy, he felt as though he'd been standing for a week. Mass, and then a lesson, and now this ritual at the font—delivering a two-hour lecture at Oxford wasn't nearly so exhausting. He suspected his knees were now permanently locked.

But even more than he wished to sit down, he couldn't wait to speak to Lily. Never mind that she'd barely noticed him. He'd scurried into Trentingham's grand, oak-paneled chapel at the last minute and had no chance to greet her before the ceremonies began.

The priest turned a page in his *Book of Common Prayer*. "Wilt thou take heed that these children, so soon as sufficiently instructed, be brought to the bishop to be confirmed by him?"

"I will." Rand and Lily said the words together this time. Their voices, he thought, sounded good together.

"Name these children."

The bundle in Rand's arms chose then to begin wailing. "Marcus Cicero Chase," Rand hollered over the squall.

"Rebecca Ashcroft Chase," Lily said more softly and with a smile, even though the girl's cries had joined her twin brother's, seeming to fill the chapel all the way up to its sculpted Tudor ceiling.

Whoever would have thought such tiny creatures could make such a huge racket?

The priest scooped water into his hand, letting it trickle through his fingers. It ran in rivulets down the backs of the two babies' heads and landed on the colorful glazed tile floor. "I baptize thee in the name of the Father, and of the Son, and of the Holy Ghost." He made crosses on the children's foreheads. "Amen."

Amen. It was over. Well-wishers crowded close. Still holding his bawling godson, Rand turned to Lily.

She was gone.

How could she have disappeared so quickly? Using his height to advantage, he peered over heads. But she'd vanished.

Nearby, Ford held little Rebecca and spoke with an older gentleman Rand recognized. Or rather, Ford was shouting at the gentleman, since the Earl of Trentingham, Lily's father, was hard of hearing.

Marveling that his friend looked so natural holding a baby, Rand jiggled little Marc uneasily. Rebecca had stopped crying, apparently content in Ford's arms, but in Rand's, her twin brother still howled.

Glancing around for help, Rand was relieved to see Ford's wife, Violet, moving close. When she reached for her son, Rand offered a grateful smile. But then he found himself oddly reluctant to hand Marc over. Loud little thing though he was, he smelled good and had a soft, warm weight.

When Violet took him, Marc quieted immediately. Resisting the urge to run his fingers over that fuzzy little head, Rand crossed his arms and leaned on one of the intricate carved oak stalls. "I assume you chose his name, Marcus Cicero, for the philosopher."

Violet bounced the babe in her arms, her brown curls bouncing along with him. She looked more motherly than Rand usually pictured her. Did children change people so much? "It was only fair," she said. "Ford had the naming of our firstborn."

"Nicky? Ah, Nicolas Copernicus," Rand remembered. "Well, I suppose it's a better choice than Ford's other favorite scientist."

"Galileo Galilei?" She laughed, her brown eyes sparkling behind her fancy gold-rimmed spectacles. "Yes, thank heavens Ford had already bestowed *that* name on his horse."

"And Rebecca? Who is she named after?"

"No one. I just like the name. And there's never been a major female philosopher."

"Yet," Rand added, knowing Violet hoped to publish a philosophy book of her own someday.

"Yet," she confirmed with a nod, clearly appreciating his support. She touched her husband's arm, claiming his attention. "We'd best be heading home," she said when he turned, "or our guests will arrive there before us."

When Ford smiled at her, Violet's return smile transformed her face. Perhaps she wasn't as pretty as her sisters, Lily and Rose, but she was lovely in her own way. A way that was enhanced by her obvious delight in both the occasion and the magnificent purple gown she'd donned to celebrate it.

Moreover, she made Ford happy. A sort of happiness that glowed from his eyes whenever he looked at her. Through six years together at university, Rand had never seen anything close to that look on Ford's face.

It was incredible how much his friend had changed.

Ford was still holding his new daughter, her tiny fist tangled in his hair. Giving in this time, Rand skimmed his fingers over Rebecca's dark curls. "They're so soft," he murmured.

Violet nodded. "All babies are soft."

"I wouldn't know. I cannot remember holding a baby before."

"Really?" She looked surprised to hear that.

Rand shrugged. "I was never around younger children save for my father's ward, who was five years old when she came to us."

"Well, someday you'll have babies of your own."

"Perhaps," he allowed. "I never say never. But should it happen, I can assure you it won't be any time soon."

Her laugh tinkled through the nearly empty chapel. "That's always what a man says just before he falls in love."

Ford rolled his eyes. "If you say so, my sweet." He turned to his friend. "Now, come along—I want to show you the water closet I built. It's much better than the ones imported from France."

Rand smiled as he followed his friends out the door. Perhaps Ford hadn't changed that much, after all.

TWO

"*W*HAT?" **LILY** demanded as her friend Judith Carrington pulled her toward a carriage. "What's so important you couldn't wait until we got to Violet's house to tell me? So important you nearly made me drop my niece, not to mention almost dislocated my arm dragging me out of there?"

Before climbing inside, Lily searched for her family in the crowd. Her father was easiest to spot, tall and trim with deep green eyes, his real hair still as jet-black as the periwig he wore for his grandchildren's baptism. Mum and Rose were both dark-haired and statuesque. They looked elegant in their best satin gowns, her mother's a gleaming gold and Rose's a rich, shimmering blue. Lily waved to them, then pointed at Judith, signaling that she would ride with her friend.

The Ashcrofts were a handsome family, in truth. Looking at them, one would never guess they were so eccentric.

Mum waved back distractedly, holding her two-year-old grandson, Nicky, as she busily ushered guests out the door to their waiting transportation.

Feeling Judith's hand on her back, Lily laughed and lifted

her peach silk skirts to duck inside the carriage. "What?" she repeated.

"Oh, just this." Even though they weren't ready to leave, Judith pulled the door shut. Then she settled herself with a flounce. "I'm betrothed."

"Betrothed?" Lily seized her friend's hands. "As in you're planning to wed?"

"Well, Mama is doing the planning. But it's ever so exciting. Come October, I'm going to be a married woman. Can you believe it, Lily?"

"No, I cannot believe it," she confessed, squeezing Judith's fingers. The third of her friends to marry this year. Yesterday they'd been children; now suddenly they were supposed to be all grown-up. "Who will be your groom?"

"Lord Grenville. Didn't your mother tell you she'd suggested he offer for my hand? Father says it's a brilliant match."

Grenville was wealthy, but thirty-five years old to Judith's nineteen. "Do you love him?" Lily wondered aloud. She hoped so. Judith was plump and pretty, but even more important, she was genuinely nice. A good friend who deserved happiness.

"We've met just twice. But Mama assures me we'll grow to love each other—or get along tolerably, at least." Her hands slipped out of Lily's, moving to worry the embroidery on her turquoise underskirt. "It will all work out fine, I'm sure of it."

"I'm sure of it, too," Lily soothed, wishing she were as certain as she sounded. Lily's parents had promised their daughters they could choose their own husbands, but she knew it didn't work that way for most young women.

Her family was different. The Ashcroft motto—*Interroga Conformationem,* translated as Question Convention—said it all.

The Carringtons, on the other hand, were as conventional

as roast goose on Christmas Day. Judith forced a smile and pushed back a lock of bright yellow hair that had escaped her careful coiffure. "Who was that gentleman who stood as godfather?"

Lily sat back. "One of Ford's old friends. Lord Randal Nesbitt."

"Wouldn't it be fun to be newly wedded together, have babies together?" Some of the color returned to Judith's cheeks. "You should marry *him*."

"Wherever did you get that idea?" Lily crossed her arms over the long, stiff stomacher that covered the laces on the front of her gown. "I barely know Rand."

"Rand?" Judith repeated significantly, and Lily blushed to be caught using the over-familiar name. But somehow she'd always thought of him as Rand, though she'd never realized it before. How odd.

"So what if you barely know him," Judith argued. "I hardly know Lord Grenville, either. And believe me, he doesn't look at me the way *Rand* was looking at you."

"Looking at me?" Lily echoed weakly. She'd hardly looked at him at all. She'd been focused on the cooing baby in her arms, her sister's first daughter. Her first niece. Nicky was great fun, of course, but now she'd have a little girl to play house with, to fix her hair, to—

"Upon my word, he didn't take his eyes off you the entire time." Judith's lips curved in an impish grin. "Watching him was more entertaining than the baptism."

Lily felt her face heat and wondered if Judith could be right—if instead of watching the ceremony, everyone had been watching Rand watch her.

But surely that hadn't been the case. Why would Rand be interested in *her*? The two of them had nothing in common. Her friend had seen something that wasn't there. "You just have the wedding fever," she said lightly, rubbing the back of her left hand. "Besides, if he's interested in anyone, I'm sure it's Rose. They share an interest in languages."

"Ah," Judith said with a tilt of her pert nose. "You know more about the fellow than you're willing to admit."

Ignoring that, Lily leaned to look out the window. But there was a long queue of carriages. They were going nowhere.

"Who's that?" her friend asked, following her line of sight. "The girl in pink, coming out of the barn with your brother?"

"That's Jewel, Ford's niece. Rowan and she have been friends forever."

"What sort of friends? And what do you suppose they were doing alone together in a barn?"

"Goodness, they're but children of ten! Your mind is too much on romance these days. Knowing those two, they were probably planning a practical joke."

"In a *barn*?"

Lily laughed at the expression on her friend's face. "I doubt there's an inch of Trentingham that hasn't seen one or another of their schemes. And Lakefield, too."

Judith looked likely to say more, but the door popped open and her mother poked her head in. "Were you leaving without me, dear?"

"Of course not, Mama." Judith scooted over to make room. "We just came inside to talk."

A large, jolly woman, Lady Carrington wedged herself beside her daughter and tucked in her voluminous coral skirts. Before her footman could shut the door, Lily's striped cat nimbly leapt inside.

Lady Carrington sneezed. "Shoo!" she exclaimed, waving an elegant hand at the creature.

"Beatrix," Lily said softly, "you cannot ride in this carriage."

The cat gave her a hurt look before hopping out.

"Much better," Judith's mother said as the door shut. She turned to Lily. "This afternoon, I'm hoping your father will advise me about flowers for Judith's wedding."

The Earl of Trentingham was nothing if not an expert on flowers. "I'm certain Father will fancy being consulted," Lily assured her.

The carriage began moving at last. "I've my heart set on yellow flowers," Lady Carrington told Lily, "because Judith looks best in yellow. But she wants to be married in blue. What color will you wear for your wedding?"

"Blue is nice," Lily said with a vague smile.

She wasn't ready to think about weddings, and most certainly not her own.

Rose was a year older—her wedding had to come first.

THREE

*W*HEN LILY entered Violet's house, Rose motioned her into the drawing room.

She nodded toward where Rand stood in conversation. "He keeps looking over here, Lily. He's spotted me." Tall and willowy, Rose made a pretty picture against the drawing room's soft turquoise walls—and well she knew it. She straightened one of her glistening chestnut curls and smoothed her deep-blue satin skirts. "He remembers me," she added confidently.

"Of course he remembers you—the two of you worked together translating that old alchemy book." Lily glanced in Rand's direction—or at least she intended no more than a glance. But it turned into more of a stare.

Was this really who she'd been standing next to all morning?

He was so...well, she'd thought him handsome when they'd first met. But he'd changed so much in the four years since Violet's wedding. Gone was the adolescent mustache. He'd grown taller, his physique lean and athletic. And his hair, a thousand mixed shades of blond and brown, was now longer than hers. She usually preferred young men with cropped hair rather than long, but on Rand, long looked glorious.

As though sensing Lily's gaze, he turned his head while still talking. For a split second, his intense gray eyes blazed into hers.

Or she thought they had. She blinked, clearing her vision. Now Judith had *her* imagining things.

"I've been dreaming about this day for weeks," Rose said, reclaiming her attention.

"The baptism?"

"No, you goose. Seeing Lord Randal again. Doesn't he look fine? Thank heavens he got rid of that mustache—" She broke off, startled by the ear-piercing wail of an infant. Two infants.

The cries grew deafening as their eldest sister approached, a twin nestled in each arm. "Violet," Lily called to her, "do you need—"

"Not at all," Violet said calmly. "Just putting them down for a nap." She whisked by with an air of efficiency and a nursemaid following in her wake.

"Poor Violet." Rose shook her head. "What a handful the twins are."

"They've had a lot of excitement today."

"I suppose." Rose frowned. "I hope twins don't run in Lord Randal's family."

Lily looked up at her in surprise. "Do you mean to marry him, then?"

"Of course. Ever since I danced with him at Violet's wedding, I've known we were meant to be."

Lily remembered that Rand had danced with her, too, at their sister's wedding. And then there was the fact that Rose lost her heart to every handsome male who crossed her path.

But Lily had to admit that Rand *could* be meant for Rose.

Good looks aside, they were well suited—the son of a marquess with the daughter of an earl. Rose's talent for languages would make her an especially fitting wife for an Oxford linguist. And Rand's unfailing patience and courtesy would come in useful with a wife as forthright as Rose.

Lily touched her older sister's hand. "I had no idea you'd been thinking about him all these years."

"Dreaming," Rose repeated on a sigh.

"Four years is a long time to dream." Lily took another quick peek at him, then smiled. "I suppose he *is* the memorable sort."

Rose cast her a sharp look. "You're not interested in him yourself, are you?"

"Of course not!" First Judith, now Rose? Was something in the air today? "Whatever would make you think that?"

"You said he's the memorable sort."

"That doesn't mean he's *my* sort. He's too tall for me." Lily drew herself up to her full height of five-foot-two. She'd barely come level with his chin. "Besides, why would he settle for me when he could have you? You two have so much more in common."

Glancing down at her, Rose snorted. "There's no such thing as a man who's too tall. Will you promise?"

"Promise what?"

"Promise me you won't pursue him. Promise me you won't get in my way."

The entire idea was so absurd, Lily laughed. "I promise. In fact, I'll do better than that. I'll help you win him."

"Would you?" Rose breathed.

"Of course. You're my sister. I love you, and I want to see you happy."

Rose's dark eyes actually misted. "You're too good, Lily. You want everyone to be happy."

"Is there something wrong with that?"

"Of course not," Rose said, and then in the next breath, "What will you do to help?"

Rose would be Rose, Lily thought with an inward smile. "Whatever I can. But you must do your part, too. And that means, for once, not pretending that your head is filled with pudding. I wish I could speak half the languages you do. You're educated and clever, and hiding that makes no sense."

"For Lord Randal, perhaps it doesn't, because he enjoys languages, too. But for other gentlemen—"

"For any gentleman. Why would you want one who doesn't value your strengths?"

"You don't understand men, sister dear. Most of them thrive on feeling superior." When Lily opened her mouth, Rose held up a hand. "But we were talking about Lord Randal, who isn't most men—" She broke off, her eyes widening. "Gemini, here he comes!"

As Rand approached, their mother seemed to appear out of nowhere—a habit Lily and her sisters found vexing. Mum gave him a brilliant smile. "Lord Randal. How very nice to see you again." Her brown eyes shone with genuine warmth. "We missed you at my first grandson's christening."

"She means Nicky, my godchild," Rose chimed in. "I shared the honor with Ford's two brothers."

"Lady Rose," Rand said with a polite nod before turning to Mum, a half smile curving his lips. "I was sorry to miss the occasion, Lady Trentingham, but I'm afraid I was in Greece."

"Greece!" Rose laid a graceful hand on her embroidered stomacher. "How marvelous. I would so adore traveling the world. I could make use of all my languages."

Lily did a little mental jig, delighted to see her sister doing as she'd suggested—as the entire family had been suggesting for years. For once in her life, Rose wasn't going to play the empty-headed flirt.

This is it, Lily thought. Her sister was at last ready to fall in love. Rose had spent years yearning and sighing over one after another of her suitors—who were drawn by the twofold attractions of her beauty and her inheritance—but Lily could tell she'd never been serious about any of them. In her own way, Rose was just a tenderhearted romantic. She was waiting for someone to take her breath away.

And if a fellow like Rand couldn't accomplish that feat, Lily didn't know who could.

Mum cleared her throat. "You'll remember Lily, my youngest daughter?" she asked Rand.

"Lady Lily." He gave a little bow, his eyes never leaving hers. Holding hers captive, like they had four years ago and again just a few minutes earlier.

In all of her eighteen years, she'd never seen another gaze like Rand's. It felt as though he could see right into her, yet not in an uncomfortable way...in a way that warmed and steadied her somehow.

She'd forgotten about that. It seemed she'd forgotten a lot in those four years.

Rose—bold Rose—reached to touch him on the arm. "Did you ever succeed in translating that alchemy book?"

"*Secrets of the Emerald Tablet*?" He smiled at Lily before shifting his attention to her sister. "Not yet. A fine puzzle it is, very time-consuming, and Ford said that with the sale of his watch patent there was no longer any rush."

At that, Ford broke into their little group. "You certainly took my words to heart," he said with mock outrage. "Four years is a bit longer than I had in mind."

"I'm here now, aren't I?" Rand countered. "And ready to finish it."

Grinning, Ford slapped his friend on the back. "Only because you have nowhere to live."

"That's not true. I have a beautiful new home."

"Half built."

Rand ruefully rubbed his forehead. "The hammering and sawing were driving me insane," he admitted.

"Rand has commissioned himself a house," Ford explained to the ladies. "It was supposed to have been ready by now, so he'd already given up his previous residence."

"And as a consequence," Rand added, "I've been sleeping in a construction site."

Rose nodded, her face a study in sympathy. "Where's your new home, my lord?"

"Please, call me Rand. And it's in Oxford."

"Rand has been made a professor of linguistics," Ford added.

Rose gasped. "A *full* professor?"

"At such a young age?" Mum's eyebrows arched. "That's very impressive."

Indeed it was, despite Rose's theatrics. Having met her fair share of academics through Ford and Violet, Lily knew it usually took decades to earn a professorship.

"It's merely a matter of determination and persistence," Rand told them, coloring faintly at the praise.

"You're being modest," Rose purred, favoring him with a wide smile—one Lily had seen her practice countless times in her dressing table mirror.

When Rand just shrugged, Lily took note of his lukewarm response. She'd have to get Rose to drop the old, coquettish act. It didn't seem to be meshing well with her new, intelligent persona.

"How long are you staying?" Mum asked him.

"My house should be finished within a week or so—"

"As long as it takes," Ford cut in, "to figure out whether the book indeed holds the secret to making gold. Now, would you all like to see the new water closet?"

"It seems to me," Rand said in the sort of needling tone only a fast friend would put up with, "it's taken you longer to build that water closet than I've spent on the translation." He turned to Lily's family. "I remember when his brother had water closets installed—"

"Colin," Ford clarified.

"My friend here was so envious. Said he'd design one for Lakefield in no time. That was what, six years ago?"

"Seven. Come see." As he talked, Ford led them out of the drawing room, threading his way through the many guests. "I've finished but one so far, and you're a fortunate man since it's connected to the room where you'll be staying."

Rand went with Ford up the square oak staircase, Rose hurrying to follow. Lily watched her sister's swishing skirts as she and her mother trailed everyone else up the stairs, a familiar striped cat scampering behind. Beatrix must have found another carriage to travel in.

Ford reached the landing and headed down the corridor. "Colin's water closets were imported from France."

"They must have been expensive," Rose said.

"Absolutely. But I examined his thoroughly, and they seemed a simple enough design to build myself. In fact, I thought of improvements."

"Of course," Mum put in.

She thought her son-in-law was brilliant. In fact, she'd originally told Violet that Ford was too intellectual for her. Funny how wrong she'd been about that, but it had been just as well. Mum was somewhat renowned as a matchmaker, and although Violet and Ford had turned out to be perfect for each other, if she'd tried to match them up, their marriage would never have happened.

The three Ashcroft sisters loved their mother dearly, but they were determined to avoid becoming yet another of Mum's touted successes.

Lily was watching, in fact, to see if Mum would try to match Rose with Rand. They were an obvious fit, after all, and at nineteen, Rose was becoming rather desperate. When their older sister Violet had turned but eighteen, Rose had pronounced her an official spinster.

But if Mum tried to push Rand on her, Rose would surely go looking elsewhere. And Lily would be honor-bound to help. The girls had a long-standing pact to save one another from their mother's matchmaking schemes.

Inside the guest chamber, everyone including the cat squeezed into a tiny room that Ford had hired a man to construct in the corner—while Ford was an accomplished inventor, he was less inclined to anything requiring sweat or a ladder. They all gathered around the water closet and peered down at it in wonder.

It was a padded box with a round opening in the top, rather like a close-stool. But instead of a removable chamber pot inside, there was a permanent alabaster bowl. "Back here," Ford pointed out, "this copper pipe leads down from it." The pipe disappeared into the wall. "The system works as a siphon."

They all nodded, since he'd explained siphons to them years ago, along with other scientific marvels.

"I suppose it empties into the river?" Rose asked, demonstrating her intelligence.

"It does. And there will be more pipes—eventually all over the house. I mean to put a water closet in every bedchamber. And my laboratory."

Leaning to pick up Beatrix, Lily hid a smile. Her brother-in-law all but lived in his laboratory.

Another pipe ran up from the back of the seat, ending at a tank affixed to the wall. "The water," Ford said, gesturing toward a third pipe that disappeared into the ceiling. "It's fed from a cistern on the roof."

"How does it work?" Lily asked.

"Well, first you use it—"

"No need to demonstrate that," Rose rushed to say.

"Of course not." Ford gave a good-natured roll of his eyes. While Lily suspected there'd been a time he'd looked askance at Rose's outspoken nature, he'd long since reconciled himself to her.

Rose was Rose, and all the family knew it.

"After you use it, you pull on this lever." Ford grabbed a handle attached to the tank. "It releases the water to wash the waste out to the river."

He pulled, and there was a rushing sound. Startled, Beatrix leapt from Lily's arms and streaked from the room.

Nearly bumping heads, everyone leaned over the alabaster bowl to watch the water flow down the pipe.

"Goodness," Lily said. "It's wonderful. There's nothing to take out, nothing to clean."

"As though you've ever scrubbed a chamber pot," Rose teased.

"Oh, hush." Lily playfully shoved her sister's shoulder. While it was true they had no lack of servants at Trentingham Manor, that was beside the point.

Used to their squabbling, Ford simply pushed back up on the lever. "When it's clean, you stop the water."

"That's it?" Mum asked.

"That's it," Ford said with a smile. "To deal with the, um, unpleasant odors in the pipes, I've curved the one below the bowl into an S shape. Clean water fills it and forms a seal."

Mum beamed. "Brilliant, as usual."

"Very convenient," Rand allowed.

The demonstration over, they all squeezed through the narrow doorway into the pale green bedchamber. Luggage— Rand's, Lily assumed—sat in a corner. "Why did you build the first one in here?" she asked Ford.

"I wished to make certain everything worked right before I started punching holes in the walls of rooms we regularly use." He waved them back toward the corridor. "Come along, now. I want to show you the pipes outside, and others are waiting for a demonstration."

"Everyone will want to see it, I'd wager." Rose maneuvered to descend beside Rand. "I wish they'd all leave. I cannot wait to use it."

Rand appeared to be smothering laughter.

Mum sighed but let the improper comment pass. "Me, too," she whispered to Lily as they followed the others downstairs.

"Me three," Lily whispered back.

Once outdoors, Ford hurried them through the garden and around the side of the house. Bright new copper pipe shone in the sun, making its way down the white wall before disappearing into the ground. A tidy trail of newly turned earth traced the pipe's path to the nearby Thames.

Amusement glittering in her eyes, Rose raised one perfect brow. "I see you've become handier with a shovel."

"Harry did the digging," Ford said, referring to his ancient man-of-all-work—and apparently either taking Rose's observation as a jest or failing to recognize her subtle sarcasm.

Probably the latter, Lily decided. Violet's husband *was* rather oblivious.

An orange kitten came up and wound around her legs, ducking beneath her skirts to tickle her ankles. With a giggle, she bent to fish it out. "This is all so very clever," she told her brother-in-law, smiling as she stroked the tiny creature's fur and felt it begin to purr. "Can you put some water closets in Trentingham, too?"

"And have pipes running down the outside of the house?" Now Rose's perfect brows drew together. "That wouldn't look well at all."

Mum shrugged. "I could accept the unsightliness for the convenience."

"Father would never allow it," Rose said.

To the contrary, Lily doubted their father would even notice—he rarely took note of much beyond his beloved flowers. If a thing didn't grow, he wasn't apt to pay it much attention.

"What's your kitten's name?" Rand asked.

Lily gazed down at the ball of fluff vibrating against her middle. "This isn't my kitten. I've never seen it before in my life." Still stroking the soft apricot fur, she looked up at Ford. "Is it yours?"

He shrugged. "Not that I'm aware."

Of course, Ford wasn't apt to pay much attention to anything that *did* grow, unless it was some sort of muck in a beaker in his laboratory.

"Cats just come to Lily," Rose told Rand.

He smiled. "They must be able to tell she's the nurturing sort."

Lily's cheeks heated. "I'm fond of animals," she said. "That's all."

"She's the *mothering* sort." Rose sidled closer to Rand.

"Rose," Mum said softly.

But that didn't deter Lily's sister. "A fellow doesn't care to be mothered," she murmured, laying a hand on Rand's arm. "Does he, Lord Randal?"

"I cannot speak for other fellows," he said, and left it at that. In keeping with the tactful wording, he gently extricated himself from her grip by crossing to his friend. "Ford, I do believe your other guests are getting impatient."

"And Violet asked if you'd freshen some of her floral arrangements," Mum reminded Rose.

Although Rose had a knack for turning flowers into

towering works of art—and enjoyed her hobby—she seemed reluctant to leave Rand's side. "Violet can wait awhile."

"Now, dear, that's not very sisterly." Mum smiled at the gentlemen. "Please excuse us," she said as she took Rose by the arm and led her off.

"I must give others the tour," Ford said and followed them.

And just like that, Lily found herself alone with Rand, wondering what she should say.

FOUR

*I*T WASN'T THAT Lily didn't know how to talk to gentlemen. No matter what Londoners might say, there was plenty of society to be had out here in the countryside. Lily could hardly remember a time when boys hadn't buzzed around her and Rose like flies. None of them had ever made her nervous.

But for some reason butterflies seemed to be battling one another in her stomach.

And Rand's piercing eyes seemed to see it.

With a nice smile, he gestured toward three oak trees hung with swings. Two children sat on a broad one built for a couple. "Is that your brother, grown so tall? He was an imp of six last I saw him."

"Rowan is still an imp, I assure you." Lily smiled back. Casting about for something else to say, she added, "The girl with him is Ford's niece, Jewel."

"They make a handsome pair." A frown appeared between Rand's eyes. "Do you think they're sitting rather close on that swing?"

Their raven heads *were* rather close together. But Lily

wasn't worried. "They're longtime friends. Rowan thinks of her as a sister—or a brother, more like."

The two children slipped off the swing and headed toward the house. When Jewel reached for Rowan's hand, he hid it behind his back. Watching, Rand laughed. "Apparently Jewel doesn't feel quite so sisterly towards the lad. And I reckon Rowan will wake up someday and notice she's a girl."

"And a pretty one at that."

"Almost as pretty as you."

Lily had received compliments before. But most young men were glib, flattery tripping off their tongues with little thought and many flowery phrases. Rand's words were simple and soft-spoken.

And he should be saying them to Rose.

Taken aback, Lily clutched the kitten tighter. The animal squeaked and leapt from her arms, landing by Rand's feet. It looked up at her with an injured expression before scampering away.

Lily stared down at Rand's black shoes, long-tongued with stiff ribbon bows. The heels were black, too, not red as was the fashion. Her gaze drifted up muscled legs to his trim waistcoat, noting his slate blue velvet suit was well-tailored but free of ribbons and baubles. Smart but not foppish.

Perfect.

When her gaze reached his face, he wore a grin full of meaning she couldn't decipher. Did he think she'd been ogling him?

Hang it, she *had* been ogling him. Why, she was acting like Rose!

To her great relief, he chose not to comment, instead motioning to where Jewel and Rowan made their way toward the house—by way of a stroll atop an eight-foot-high stone wall. "Is that wise?"

"Not to worry," she replied. "My brother is a monkey. Forgive me, but I'm after a turn in the garden..."

Though she'd meant to excuse herself, Rand turned with her toward the formal garden, a charming area divided by low hedges cut in geometric patterns, the flower beds dotted with cheerful reds, yellows, and purples. "Do you suppose Jewel is taking him to see the water closet?"

"Probably. I wouldn't be surprised if they're plotting a way to use it for a prank."

"I would hope not," he said. "I imagine they could make quite a mess."

She wrinkled her nose at the thought. Chamber pots were hardly appropriate conversational subject matter, no matter how new and fancy. "So you're staying with Violet and Ford until the translation is finished?"

"I'll be here for just a week or two, until my house is ready. Although I do hope to make good progress on the translation in that time." At the edge of the garden, he stopped beside a long table laden with food. "Would you care for some refreshments?"

Though Lily was famished after this morning's lengthy ceremonies, she hesitated, looking about. But Rose was nowhere in sight. "Yes, thank you."

He handed her an empty plate and took another for himself. "The house was supposed to be completed long before now, but the builder is an old friend, and you know how that goes—when something else comes up, it's always easier to put off a friend's job than a contracted client's."

"He doesn't sound like a very good friend," she observed.

"Quite the contrary. We've known each other since we were knee-high lads in dresses. It's just that Kit has recently taken on a demanding new client. Very powerful fellow."

"Oh? Anyone I've heard of?"

"You may have." Piling fruit on his plate, Rand cast her a glance. "Charles Stuart."

"Oh!" Lily giggled as she selected a wedge of apple tart. "I suppose, then, I can understand how another client might take precedence."

"When that client is the king," he agreed.

"Still, it's unfortunate you're forced to leave Oxford for the present." Though fortunate for Rose, she added silently. "Are all Oxford professors allowed to come and go as they please?"

"It's summer," he explained. "A four-month break. I usually travel the Continent, looking for lost languages"—he flashed her a lopsided grin—"but I thought I'd stay home this year and settle into my house."

She followed him into the garden, stepping gingerly since Beatrix had reappeared and was padding along with her, batting at her swishing skirts. "Yours sounds like an exciting life."

"I'm not sure I'd describe it as exciting, but I enjoy my life, yes. It's interesting and rewarding."

They skirted around a sundial, old but lovingly repaired. A few tables of various sizes were scattered about the garden, surrounded by chairs for the guests. Sitting with Lady Carrington, Lily's friend Judith waved in invitation, her golden curls gleaming in the sun. Lily waved back and started over, but Rand stopped at a tiny square table and pulled out one of the two chairs. "Will you do me the honor?"

"I..." There was no polite way to refuse. "Yes, of course." She seated herself carefully, sending Judith an expressive shrug. Judith winked and waggled her brows, obviously misunderstanding why Lily was with Rand.

That was something Lily didn't quite understand herself. It should be Rose here, she thought as Beatrix returned and leapt onto her lap.

"This striped cat is yours, if I'm not mistaken?" Rand took the chair opposite. "However did it find its way here from Trentingham?"

She found herself caught again in that astonishing gray gaze. "I'm guessing you don't know much about cats."

"My father raises dogs," he told her, taking two pewter goblets of wine from a serving maid passing by with a tray. "Big, mean ones who would eat your cat for breakfast."

Laughing, she pretended to cover Beatrix's ears. "Shush, you'll scare her!"

He laughed along with her, smiling another of his inscrutable smiles. "You're beautiful when you laugh."

She looked away, hoping he wouldn't notice her choking on a bite of tart. Ford was coming out of the house, leading another little group around to see the pipes to the river.

Swallowing the cinnamony apples and custard, she turned back to Rand. "Thank you, but I believe being nice is much more important than being beautiful. Although Rose is very beautiful," she added as an afterthought. "Don't you think so, my lord?"

"Rand," he reminded her. "And yes, Rose is indeed beautiful *and* being nice is much more important. But *you* are both beautiful and nice."

What on earth was she supposed to say to that?

He was impossible.

Her fingers went to the back of her left hand before she realized what she was doing and hid it beneath the table. Rose would love this sort of attention. The two were quite definitely suited.

A sparrow landed on their table, providing a welcome distraction. "Hello, Lady," she murmured and fed it some crumbs from her plate.

Watching her, Rand absently rubbed the ends of his

magnificent golden mane between two fingers. "Are you still hoping to build a home for stray animals?"

After all this time, he remembered her dream. "I am," she said, both startled and pleased, but also wondering if he thought her goal childish. She'd been a child when she'd chosen it, after all.

But he seemed to be taking her seriously. "Have you made plans?"

"Of sorts. I've come into my inheritance this year. I'm planning a simple building so as to have funds left to staff it for a number of years. I'm hoping to obtain donations as well. Eventually enough to keep running it once my money is depleted. And perhaps even build others."

"A solid strategy. Have you thought of having the building donated?"

"I'd prefer it built specifically for my purpose. To convert a house or other building could cost as much as starting from scratch."

He nodded thoughtfully. "Perhaps an architect would donate his services." His eyes twinkled, looking silver in the afternoon sun. "I happen to know one—"

"Uncle Ford!" Jewel came bounding out of the house, her pink skirts flying. "Uncle Ford! Something's happened with…"

Her words faded as she disappeared around the corner.

Rowan flew through the door next and darted after her, pink-cheeked to match her skirts, his mouth hanging open in something akin to horror.

Lily jumped to her feet. "They've done something," she exclaimed as Ford appeared at a run and dashed into the house, shouldering his way past all the guests hurrying out. "I knew it!"

FIVE

"I SWEAR, UNCLE Ford, we did nothing." Jewel held her skirts up off the floor while she turned in a slow circle, assessing the destruction. "Oh," she wailed, "look at my chamber!"

Rand gestured at his luggage sitting on the four-poster bed—as opposed to the floor, where it had been earlier. "I thought this was *my* chamber."

"Uncle Ford had it painted green because that's my favorite color. I sleep here when I visit. And now it's all ruined."

Ford poked his head out of the little room in the corner where he was examining his invention. "At least it's clean water," he pointed out defensively.

New water stains on Rand's luggage were the least of the damage.

The oak floor was sopping. The wet went up the walls, the water having apparently been deeper before escaping the chamber and making its way down the corridor and stairs. Most of the ground floor had flooded as well, including all of the beautiful, expensive carpeting that Violet had had specially woven.

But this room, where the disaster had originated, was by far the worst. The pale green bedclothes dripped, the air held a chill, the carpet felt soggy beneath their feet, and Lily suspected that mildew was setting in already.

"We did nothing," Rowan repeated. "We just came up to look, and when we opened the door—"

"Now, Rowan," Lily began, knowing her brother all too well. Especially when he was with Jewel. The daughter of an unapologetic prankster, Jewel had taught Rowan every trick she'd learned from her father. "Do you expect us to believe—"

"He's right," Ford broke in, apparently having finished his investigation. "It was the fault of my design—a problem with the tank mechanism." Looking rather pained to admit that, he ran a hand back through his long brown hair. "I expect it began flooding the moment I turned my back. I never considered…it never occurred to me…"

"Never say never," Rand interjected dryly.

Jewel went to the window. "Everyone else has gone outside."

"Of course, you goose." Rowan snorted. "The floor is wet all over the house."

"The women wouldn't want to ruin their fashionable satin slippers," Rand added, glancing down at the water-stained shoes on Lily's feet, visible since she was holding up her skirts.

"There are more important things than shoes," she pointed out. "Like Violet's carpeting. She's going to be furious."

"No, I'm not," Violet said, walking in with a squish-squash sound. She went on her toes to grace her husband with a light kiss. "I'm used to catastrophes," she declared with an exaggerated sigh. "Part and parcel of my marriage. Besides, we must only remove the carpets and spread them outside to dry. A few rain-free days and they'll be good as new."

"Are you sure?" Jewel asked dubiously.

"About it not raining? No," Violet said in her practical way. "But they *will* eventually dry. I'm afraid, though, that this room will be uninhabitable for a day or two, at the least." She cast Rand a regretful look.

"I can ride home," he assured her. "Oxford is but a few hours."

"Wait." Ford held up a hand. "What about the translation? There's no need for you to leave. We'll move someone. The nursemaids—"

"I won't have you upsetting your whole household," Rand interrupted. Unlike the sprawling mansion Lily lived in, Lakefield was a typical L-shaped manor house. Enough rooms to sleep the family, a few servants, and a guest, but that was all.

Ford crossed his arms. "Well, *I* won't have you leaving. Your house is a wreck at the moment."

A smile twitched on Rand's lips as he pointedly scanned the chamber. Lily bit back a laugh.

"Rowan!" Her mother's voice floated up the stairs. "Rowan, have you and Jewel—" A gasp chopped off her sentence as she stepped into the room. "Heavens, this is—"

"A blasted mess," Ford finished for her. "And my fault, not your son's."

"See?" Rowan said with a grin of vindication. "It's not my fault Lord Randal cannot stay here."

"It's nobody's fault." Rand strode to the bed, his shoes making a sucking sound as he went. "I should probably be home badgering Kit anyway, if the house is to be finished this decade." He reached for his luggage.

"Don't you want to finish the translation?" Ford looked frantic. "We'll find a place—"

"Lord Randal is welcome to stay with us," Mum interrupted with a smile. "We've more guest rooms than we know what to do with."

Lily's mouth hung open. Why, they hardly knew the fellow.

But apparently that made no difference to Mum. "You'll be close to Lakefield," she added. They were naught but a quarter-hour's carriage ride down the road. "By tomorrow, perhaps this room will once again be habitable."

Violet glanced around mournfully. "I doubt it."

Looking a bit dubious, Rand set down the luggage. "If I overnight at Trentingham," he said slowly, "I can return tomorrow and help put the place to rights."

"A generous offer," Ford said.

Violet pushed up on her spectacles. "There's no need for Rand to wrestle with soggy carpeting."

"The boards underneath must be dried, lest they warp."

"We have servants to do that sort of thing."

"But if we had extra help…" Ford pressed.

Violet rolled her eyes. "Rand can 'help' you in the bone-dry laboratory upstairs, huddled over that ancient alchemy text."

Her husband's expression made it clear that sounded good to him.

And so it was settled. Rand would sleep at Trentingham and return in the morning.

Lily supposed it was well done of Mum to offer the hospitality, but she hoped it didn't mean she was trying to match Rand with Rose.

That would ruin her sister's plan.

SIX

*T*RENTINGHAM Manor was teeming with family and friends who had come to attend the twins' baptism, so Rand's addition to the mix was clearly little imposition. But he was grateful for the countess's kind invitation. She seemed a true lady.

Although perhaps a bit overly attentive.

"Lily, dear," she said as they walked into the linenfold-paneled dining room for supper, "I'd prefer it if you'd sit beside Rand, since he isn't acquainted with our other guests."

Which would have made sense if Rose hadn't already planted herself on his other side.

"Lord Randal," Rose gushed, laying a hand on her chest, her fingertips suggestively grazing the skin revealed by her wide, fashionable neckline. "What a pleasure to have you as a dining partner."

"Rand," he corrected her. So far as he was concerned, *Lord* was nothing more than a reminder of his unpleasant childhood. He chose to think of himself as a professor now, not a marquess's son. "And the pleasure is mine," he assured her, meaning it. This civilized supper was far more agreeable than riding home to all the hammering and sawing at his house in Oxford.

"Cousin Rose." A gentleman on her other side begged her attention, waving a bejeweled hand at the floral arrangements—enormous vases of colorful posies that graced each end of the table, flanking a towering centerpiece. "Have we you to thank for these magnificent works of art?"

"Why, yes," Rose said warmly. "I'm pleased, cousin, that you're enjoying them." She turned back to Rand, fluttering her eyelashes so hard that he feared they might be spasming. "I love arranging flowers."

"They're stunning." They were. She had an artist's eye, a flair for color and balance. He turned to Lily. "Do you work with flowers as well?"

"Oh, no. I've no skill with plants."

Rose shook her head, as though she felt sorry for her poor, talentless sister. "She cares only for her animals."

As if on cue, a sparrow flew into the room and landed smack on the table, right in front of Lily.

"Holy Hades," Rowan said. "Not again."

"Rowan," Lady Trentingham hissed.

"Well, someone should shut the windows."

Rose fanned herself with a languid hand. "With all these people, it would be too hot if we shut the windows."

"Cut the hedgerows?" Her father nodded sagely. "Yes, I've asked the groundskeepers to start on the morrow."

No one looked confused or surprised. Apparently they were all well enough acquainted with Lord Trentingham to know that along with his passion for gardening, the man was half deaf.

"Excellent, darling," the countess said loudly, flicking a crumb off his cravat. She looked to Lily, who was busy feeding bits of bread to the sparrow. "Not at supper, dear."

Lily sighed. "Go, Lady." She tossed the gray-brown bird a final nibble. "Outside now."

Amazingly, the bird gobbled the last of its feast and then took flight, heading for one of the windows where a squirrel sat on the sill, seemingly watching the proceedings. With a flutter of feathers, the sparrow landed beside the squirrel with a pointed twitter. The squirrel chattered back, for all the world as if they were having a conversation.

Rand had never seen a wild bird that obeyed, let alone a squirrel that didn't run at the sight of humans. He turned to Lily. "You do have a way with animals."

"Oh, there's more to Lily than that," her mother informed him from down the table. "She plays the harpsichord like an angel."

Lily blushed. She looked fetching when she blushed. Not that he would make the mistake of telling her so—not again. *You're beautiful when you laugh...*he wanted to blush, too, just remembering his words. Had he ever in his life said anything so muttonheaded to a girl?

Well, he'd just have to redeem himself. Luckily, he now had an entire evening in which to do so.

His fingers itched to touch the tiny dent in her chin. "Will you play after supper?" he asked her.

"Eh?" the earl shook his dark head. "Everyone will stay after supper. They've all been assigned rooms, have they not, Chrysanthemum love?"

"Of course, darling." Lady Trentingham smiled her ever-patient smile. "And Lily will play," she told Rand.

"And I shall sing," Rose announced as she reached for some bread, grazing Rand's arm in the process.

By now it was obvious that she fancied him. He'd suspected as much four years ago, and apparently her feelings remained unchanged. Back then he'd felt flattered by her attentions, but now all he felt was uncomfortable.

Which was odd, to say the least. Rose was lovely—tall and willowy, with a flawless, creamy complexion, glossy deep brown locks, and eyes so mysteriously dark they could be mistaken for black. A classic beauty. And not an icy one. Though still as bold as ever, Rose had grown up. She was much kinder and warmer than he remembered.

But none of her warmth seemed to penetrate his skin. While on his other side sat Lily, scorching him like the Tuscan sun.

Chatting with the guest on her right, she seemed to sense Rand's gaze and turned slightly to meet his eyes, then looked away to continue her conversation.

"I should like to hear you sing," he told Rose, wondering if she had the voice for it.

Her slow smile revealed charming dimples. If she were one of Lily's cats, she'd have been purring.

And after supper, when she raised her voice in song, he was indeed impressed. Singing of love, her words floated through the air, rich and resonant.

But he found Lily's playing even more splendid. Despite the audience of various Ashcroft relatives seated decorously in the cream-and-gold-toned formal drawing room, Rand found himself rising and wandering toward the harpsichord.

While Beatrix dozed on her lap, Lily's fingers sailed over the ivory keys. She glanced up and smiled at him without missing a beat, and his mind went blank. Before he realized his mouth was open, he found himself harmonizing with her sister.

> "Go tell her to make me a cambric shirt,
> Parsley, sage, rosemary, and thyme,
> Without a stitch of a seamster's work,
> And then she will be a true love of mine."

Only when the verse ended did he notice that Rose had stopped singing to listen to him. His face burning, he nodded at her to take the next verse. Back and forth they went until the song ended and the chamber burst into applause.

Rand jammed his hands in his pockets, wondering what the two sisters must think of him, barging into their performance uninvited. He'd never done anything like this before. What could have got into him?

But Lily's eyes were shining. "Your voice is beautiful!"

His face went hot again. "Your playing is exquisite."

"I practice often." Her shrug was as graceful as her fingers. "It's a way to pass the time."

He nodded, a smile tugging at his lips. "I sing whenever I'm alone." Enjoying the admiration on her face, he reached to hit a key, letting the single note reverberate through the chamber. "I cannot play," he admitted.

"I cannot sing."

His smile stretched into a grin. "Play for us again, then, and your sister and I will accompany you. Together this time?" He looked to Rose, who nodded eagerly.

Lily thought for a moment, then the jaunty notes of "The Gypsy Rover" took air, and his voice rose along with it.

Rose waited until the chorus to join him.

"He whistled and he sang till the greenwoods rang,
And he won the heart of a lady."

Rand wished he really could whistle and sing and win the heart of a lady. And by the way Rose was gazing at him, she had a similar goal in mind. But though their voices blended perfectly, it wasn't she he was wishing to win.

They sang a third song, and a fourth, and then he lost count, relishing the way his words and Lily's melodies intertwined. Whenever she glanced up from the harpsichord and caught his eye, it seemed that he and she were the only ones in the room.

When the gilt mantel clock struck midnight just as another tune ended, Lily blinked and jumped to her feet, letting Beatrix tumble to the floor with an outraged *meow*. "Do you think it's time to retire, Mum?"

"Oh!" The countess stood as well. "Rose, you must come with me. We have yet to prepare a room for Rand."

Rose frowned. "I'm sure the staff has taken care of that."

"Not all our special welcoming details." With a gracious smile, Lady Trentingham turned to her assorted family. "I wish you all a good night." As they began drifting out, she addressed her older daughter. "Come along, dear. You'll need to find flowers for Rand's chamber."

"But Mum—"

"Come along," she repeated, more tersely than seemed to be her nature. "Lily, will you wait here and keep Rand company until his room is ready?"

"I need no flowers," Rand interjected.

"Nonsense. Rose?" Lady Trentingham moved toward the door, herding the last lingering guests along with her. "I'll be back in just a few moments!"

The chamber seemed so quiet after everyone had left. And Rand felt odd to find himself alone with Lily for the second time that day.

"Mum," he said, mostly to ward off the sudden silence. "That's a strange thing to call one's mother."

"I know." Still by the harpsichord, she sat again and resumed playing, an unfamiliar but soothing piece she seemed to know by heart. Beatrix reclaimed her rightful place on her lap. "You know that my father raises flowers. Droves of them. He named us girls after his favorites—surely you'll have noticed that—and Rowan after the tree. Mum's given name is Chrystabel, but he calls her Chrysanthemum...and we call her Mum for short." Her fingers stilled. "It's silly, I know."

"Keep playing." He leaned against the carved wood instrument and waited until she did. "I don't think it's silly. You must be a close family."

"We are."

Her matter-of-fact tone made it obvious she took that closeness for granted. But he wouldn't acknowledge the envy churning in his stomach. He'd long ago accepted that his family was happier without him. And life on his own was just fine. Better, in fact.

When Beatrix lifted her head, Rand followed her gaze to see a bird land gracefully atop the harpsichord.

"Hello, Lady," Lily greeted softly, her fingers still gliding over the keys.

Confused, Rand ran his tongue across his teeth. "Do you call all sparrows Lady?"

"No. I don't call most sparrows anything. But Lady is special."

"Do you mean..." He peered at the nondescript bird. "Is this the same sparrow that flew in at supper, the same sparrow you fed at Ford's house?"

"One and the same," she said, playing a little faster. "I raised her after I found her in an abandoned nest, and now she follows me around. She and Jasper."

"Jasper?"

"The squirrel."

She nodded toward the sill. Sure enough, a red squirrel sat there, gnawing on an acorn. Rand supposed it must be the same squirrel that had appeared at supper, although hang it if he could tell for sure. Like sparrows, one squirrel looked much the same as another.

To him, anyway.

Beatrix settled back down on Lily's lap, and Lady flew to

join her friend at the window. Jasper chattered, his bushy tail flicking up and down. Rand felt as if all the animals were watching him. Talking about him.

Under those three sets of eyes, he shifted uneasily. Surely he was imagining things. "Are you never alone?"

"Rarely," Lily said blithely.

That seemed peculiar, but then, perhaps it was Rand's love of solitude that was peculiar. In any case, he decided to ignore the animals as best he could. "What song is this?"

"Nothing, really. Just something I made up."

"You compose music, too?" Slowly he lowered himself to the bench seat beside her. "Is there no end to your talents?"

As she scooted over to make room for him, her fingers faltered, then continued. He smiled to himself, thinking he'd managed to fluster her. Was it the compliment, or his nearness?

He hoped it was the latter. Her nearness was certainly flustering him. Her nearness and her fresh, flowery scent.

Beatrix began to hiccup. "I'm not talented," Lily protested modestly. "Your singing is much better than my playing. I've never heard another voice like yours."

He knew he had a fine voice, but it wasn't a talent that had been valued in his family, so he usually kept it to himself. "Well, I've never heard anything like your music," he said. "So we're even. And I hope we'll play and sing together again."

At his words, her hands ceased moving for good. They went limp and dropped into her lap, eliciting an indignant cry from Beatrix, who leapt to the floor. In seconds, the cat had followed her animal friends out the window.

Lily cleared her throat. "If your room at Lakefield isn't ready tomorrow night, perhaps Rose will sing with you again."

She looked so earnest. He curled his fingers to keep from

reaching to touch that irresistible dent in her chin. "I don't care whether Rose sings with me again. As long as you play."

"Wh-what?" She shifted, turning to face him, searching his eyes with her wide blue ones. "But you and Rose sing together so beautifully. And she knows languages—not ancient ones like you do, but many modern ones, and—"

"I don't care about Rose," he clarified. "But you..." Was he really going to tell her? He rushed on before he could change his mind. "I've thought about you for four years."

The breath rushed out of her with a *whoosh*. Her eyes grew bigger and bluer in her lovely, fine-boned face. And when some invisible force seemed to draw the two of them closer, and his fingertips grazed her neck, he could have sworn her lips parted. He was near enough to feel the warmth emanating from her body, and as he leaned to close the rest of the gap, a happy little thrill warmed him from the inside, too...

Until she jerked away.

He blinked at her, feeling like he'd been doused in cold water. And realizing that her round-eyed, openmouthed expression wasn't a look of anticipation. It was a look of abject horror.

A look that made his hopes crumble to dust.

He felt sweet relief to hear her mother's voice approaching. Rand was desperate to escape to the solitude of his chamber.

But Lakefield's guest chamber had better be ready tomorrow, because one night at Trentingham had been more than enough.

SEVEN

$\mathcal{B}$EFORE LILY HAD a chance to gather her wits,
Mum and Rose appeared.

"Lord Randal's chamber is ready," her sister announced,
frowning to see them together on the harpsichord's bench.

"Rand," he corrected patiently.

He *was* patient, Lily thought. And good-looking. And brilliant. And if he wasn't quite the inveterate animal lover she'd
always pictured marrying, at least he'd never laughed at her
dreams. He'd even encouraged them.

But as quickly as these thoughts materialized, they were
washed away by a tide of guilt that made Lily leap from the
bench. *Marriage?* She was supposed to be bringing Rand
together with Rose, yet here she was snuggling up to him
herself and indulging in silly fantasies. How could she act so
selfishly? Only a lucky stab of conscience had saved her from
leaning in for a kiss, saved her from betraying her own sister.

And for what? One trifling kiss? Was a kiss worth the
price of her relationship with Rose?

Of course it wasn't.

Not that Lily could judge from experience.

Mum's lips curved in a smile. "Come, Rand. I'll show you the way."

He rose rather reluctantly and allowed Mum to lead him from the room. An uneasy silence descended in their wake. Lily dropped back to the bench.

Rose's dark eyes narrowed. "What were you doing with him?"

"Singing," Lily lied, shocked to hear the word pass her lips. She never lied to her sister. She never lied to anybody. "I mean, he was singing. I was playing. We were playing and sing—"

"All right." Rose waved an impatient hand. "As long as you're not after him. You promised he could be mine."

Despite that promise, Lily found herself bristling. "*He* might have something to say about that."

"Oh, I'm sure I can make him want me." For a nineteen-year-old who'd once claimed spinsterhood began at eighteen, Rose looked awfully smug.

"You know nothing about him. Have you even considered that there might be someone else he prefers?" *Like me,* Lily added silently.

What was she saying? She was acting like she meant to have Rand for herself, though that couldn't be further from the truth. Her own vanity was getting the better of her, and that simply wouldn't do.

She began an apology. "Rose, I'm—"

"Oh, stuff it, Lily," her sister said airily. "It's natural for you to be jealous, so I won't hold that against you. But just let me worry about Lord Randal's *preferences.* My new strategy of impressing him with my intellect along with the flirtation is already working. Why else would we have sung together all night?"

Lily refrained from repeating Rand's explanation: that it was her playing he admired rather than Rose's singing. "About the flirtation…"

"Lily, please. I do appreciate your assistance, but I know what I'm doing in that sphere."

"Of course you do," Lily said quickly, absently rubbing the back of her hand. Her fingers stilled when her sister's gaze settled on them.

Rose sank down to the bench seat beside her and placed a hand over hers. "No one notices," she said gently. "And it doesn't look bad anyway. After all these years, the scars are almost gone. Honestly—"

"I know." Lily reached to grasp both her sister's hands. A few narrow, faded white scars…so what if she wasn't perfect? Everyone made mistakes, didn't they?

And not everyone was blessed with such a loving, caring sister. Lily still couldn't believe she'd come so close to breaking her promise. She could never hurt Rose. She didn't want to hurt anyone. Or anything. Ever.

"Lily?"

Freeing her hands, she gave Rose a shaky smile as she raised them to the harpsichord. Her fingers moved slowly over the keys. Music always soothed her. Even when, like now, she chose a melancholy tune.

After a moment, her sister's pure, sweet voice took up the song.

> *"Alas, my love, you do me wrong*
> *To cast me out discourteously.*
> *And I have loved you for so long,*
> *Delighting in your company…"*

A fitting lyric, Lily thought with an internal sigh. Then she tried to look on the bright side. At least Mum didn't seem to be trying to match Rose and Rand.

They should be happy for small favors.

EIGHT

*R*AND'S BEDCHAMBER was filled with flowers. Artistic arrangements sat atop the bedside table, the clothes press, the washstand. He walked around the room, admiring each in turn, distracting himself by skimming his fingers over colorful, velvet-soft petals.

Rose obviously excelled at arranging flowers, and while Rand had been occupied with Lily—with repulsing Lily, to be more precise—it was clear Rose had been busy. And so had their mother, evidently, because the dressing table was lined with bottles of scent. *Her* hobby, Rand recalled, was making perfume.

No wonder her daughter smelled so delicious.

The small, clear bottles all looked the same—plain with silver-topped stoppers—but the liquids inside them were different hues, ranging from nearly colorless, to yellowish, to brownish. He lifted a bottle, opened it, and waved it under his nose. Finding the fragrance spicy and masculine, he dabbed some on his face, then sniffed his fingers. Shrugging, he took another bottle. More citrusy, this scent. He patted some on his jaw and decided he liked the first one better.

He shrugged out of his surcoat and tossed it on the bed, followed by his cravat. Despite the long day and the sort of bone weariness that naturally followed, he wasn't at all sleepy. Being here felt too strange. As did his, alas, unreciprocated feelings for a certain daughter of the house.

Absently humming a tune, he sat at the dressing table—a lady's dressing table, it was, much too delicate for his taste—and idly unstoppered another bottle. None of the specific ingredients were identifiable, but this one smelled like it could be used to season a pie. A Christmas pie. He watched himself in the mirror as he slapped some on both cheeks and tried to remember the last time he'd really enjoyed Christmas.

He didn't have fond memories of Christmas, so he moved on to the next bottle.

Fresh. Flowery. He was taken aback—it smelled just like Lily. Surely the countess didn't expect a man to wear such a feminine scent? It must have got mixed up with the bottles she'd intended to provide him. He found himself lingering over the concoction, inhaling deeply. There was something electrifying about the scent. Something that made him want to keep smelling it for…well, the foreseeable future anyway. Maybe the rest of his life.

Which was preposterous. He'd never been interested in marriage.

At least, he'd never thought he was. Dons, the teaching fellows at Oxford, weren't allowed to wed. He'd been comfortable in that position—under that restriction—for the past few years. It had made his choices easy. He'd hardly expected to become a professor so soon, although considering his steady advancement, he'd assumed it would happen eventually. Professors could marry, but that had always seemed so far in the future as to be unworthy of contemplation.

When he'd actually become a professor—the youngest in

his department's history—just a few weeks ago, he'd been too ecstatic to consider the secondary effects. Namely, the fact that he was now free to marry should he want to.

The chamber suddenly seemed overwarm. He rose restlessly and loosened the laces at his neck, untied his cuffs, rolled up his sleeves. Catching a glance of himself in the mirror, he halted. Implacable gray eyes gazed back at him.

Marriage had crossed his mind more than once today, rather uncomfortably. But whatever could have changed to make him suddenly picture himself with a wife...perhaps even children?

Could it be his new home? The place had, after all, five bedchambers. As he and Kit had drawn up the plans, had he been thinking, somewhere deep inside, that he might soon want to begin filling all those many rooms?

Sweet mercy, no!

Holding Ford's son might have triggered his parental instincts, but he was far too young to see himself as a father. Besides, he had no idea how to raise a child, no good example from which to work. He wasn't ready for such responsibility; perhaps he never would be.

That realization made him feel calmer. There were no big changes to be faced.

Now he could sleep.

When he finally drifted off in the soft feather bed, he could've sworn the faint, familiar strains of "Greensleeves" lulled him to sleep.

NINE

"**R**OSE, DON'T!" Lily pleaded in a whisper.

"Whyever not? It's a kind gesture to see to a guest's welfare." Ignoring her sister, Rose knocked on the door. "Lord Randal?" She raised her voice—and an Ashcroft's raised voice was no timid thing, living as they did with the half-deaf earl. "Lord Randal, are you quite all right? Will you be needing anything more this evening?"

Lily groaned, then sucked in her breath when the door suddenly swung open. There stood Rand, looking haphazard and half-asleep in nothing but a shirt and trousers. His sleeves were pushed up to reveal tanned forearms.

Though Lily ought to have been shocked by his state of undress, all she could think was, *How does a university professor acquire tanned forearms?* Weren't academics supposed to spend their days buried in books?

"Yes?" he said to Lily, despite her sister having been the original speaker. Jarred from her musings, she moved her gaze up to his face—way up, since he was so much taller—and once again found herself staring. He looked different in the meager candlelight, his features thrown into sharp relief.

She realized his wasn't a pretty face. His jaw was a dash too strong, his nose too long, his brows too heavy and straight. But there was something about those eyes, that smile…

She made herself release the breath she'd been holding. "I—"

"I only wanted to inquire as to your welfare," Rose hurried to put in.

"I'm quite fine," he said, moving to lean against the doorway.

A cloud of scent moved with him. Not a subtle cloud. "Have you been testing Mum's perfumes?" Rose wrinkled her nose. "I apologize, my lord. Evidently one of my mother's creations is less than pleasing."

Very tactful wording for Rose, Lily thought with admiration. She'd never seen her sister make such an effort at courtesy.

Rand waved a hand, releasing another burst of fragrance. "Oh, I've quite enjoyed the perfumes," he assured them.

"I expect you have," Lily said, biting back a smile. It wasn't a bad bottle, if she didn't miss her guess, but rather an unfortunate mixture of several. "How many scents have you sampled?"

"All of them," he said, rubbing his jaw, then sniffing his fingers. His eyes widened. "I suppose that wasn't such a good idea?"

"One doesn't mix fragrances. That's the perfumer's job," Rose informed him, sounding both intelligent and instructor-like.

A professor ought to admire that air of competence, Lily thought.

But he only shrugged. "I did it rather absently, I expect. My mind was elsewhere."

His gaze strayed to Lily's, perhaps implying where his mind had been. Could he truly have been thinking of her all this time? Regardless, it didn't matter. She'd made a promise to Rose.

"I...I must see to my animals before bed," she stammered, feeling her cheeks heat. Wondering whether that was due to his compelling eyes or her mention of the word *bed*, she hoped it was too dark for him to see her blush. "I expect you'll be wanting a bath before you sleep?"

Judging from the way Rand's lips curved—knowingly—he had seen. "I expect that would be wise." He rubbed his jaw again with a touch of self-consciousness.

"Go ahead, Lily," Rose said. "Your menagerie needs tending." She gave an elegant wave. "I'll be happy to see that Lord Randal gets his bath."

I'll bet you would, Lily couldn't help thinking, and something in Rand's expression told her he was thinking the same thing. "You're exceedingly kind," he said to Rose with a slight bow, "but please don't trouble yourself. I'm perfectly capable of seeing to my own needs."

Catching Lily's gaze, he smiled tentatively before shutting the door.

TEN

*S*HE'D OVERSLEPT. She never overslept. Moving to the last animal's bowl to fill it with fresh water, Lily yawned, still blinking away the cobwebs of a restless night— a night filled with dreams of silvery gray eyes and smooth, tanned skin.

She looked around the barn, happy that her chores were finished. The enclosures were clean; all the creatures had been fed, splints checked, matted fur brushed out till it shone. In comparison, she imagined *she* looked like something the cat had dragged in, but now that she was done, she would sneak back into the house through a servants' entrance to make herself presentable.

She set down the water pitcher and brushed straw off the plain green gown she'd thrown on upon awakening—then froze when she heard voices outside the barn.

"The knot garden is over there," Rose was saying sweetly.

"Ah, but your sister keeps her animals in here, doesn't she?" Rand's rich baritone was unmistakable. "I wouldn't mind a glimpse of them."

Or was it Lily herself he was hoping to glimpse? she wondered—then bit her lip.

She'd promised. She'd promised. She'd promised. How many more times would she have to remind herself? Wasn't her sister's happiness more important to her than a foolish infatuation?

Light flooded the dim, cavernous interior when the barn's double doors opened. As Rand and Rose stepped inside, Lily shoved her unkempt hair farther under the hat she'd jammed on her head to cover it. She managed to resist pinching color into her cheeks.

"Good morning," she said brightly.

Rand smiled. "Yes, it is."

Avoiding Rose's scowl, Lily knelt beside one of the pens to pet a fox cub.

"I've never seen one hold still before." Rand's footsteps crunched on the straw as he walked nearer and crouched close by. "They always run from people. They even run if they catch you watching them from a window."

"This one cannot run." She showed him the broken leg she'd splinted.

"But she doesn't seem frightened."

"He," Lily corrected. The small fox wagged its white-tipped tail. "And why should he be frightened?"

A spell of silence followed, filled only by rustling and the assorted noises of animals, as Rand tilted his head and studied her. "No reason," he conceded finally. "You're very gentle."

The tone of his voice made her go still. "Anyone can be."

"Not anyone." He stood. "What else do you have in your care?"

She rose and walked along the pens that crowded a corner of the barn, stopping where a spotted fawn nuzzled her with his nose. "Meet Timothy—"

"Timothy?"

"He looks like a Timothy, doesn't he? He lost his mother." Feeding the baby deer a handful of grass, she leaned to the neighboring pen to lift the cloth draping a deep basket. "And here's a rat—"

"A rat?" He stared at the creature in question, a fat, furry brown rodent that never failed to make her smile. "You would save a rat?"

"Randolph was hurt. But he's recovered quite nicely. I may set him free later today."

"To be eaten by a cat, no doubt."

"Not my cats. My cats are his friends. Besides, it would be cruel to keep him confined when he's well enough to roam." Timothy had finished his treat, so she wiped her hand on her skirts and moved to the next enclosure. "Over here I have a badger, but he's sleeping." She indicated a black-and-white snout poking out from a pile of old blankets. "They're nocturnal, you may know. And little Harold here is sleeping, too."

"A hedgehog?" Rand's eyes radiated amusement.

At the other end of the barn, a door opened. Lily's brother started in, then spotted them and began backing out.

"I'm finished, Rowan," she called. "You can come play with the animals."

"Maybe later." He slammed the door shut.

Rose laid a possessive hand on Rand's arm. "Shall we go see the gardens now?" she asked sweetly.

"Your father's gardens are quite extensive, aren't they? I really must be getting to Ford's house. I promised him help. If I might borrow a mount—"

"Of course," Rose said with a smile. "Our stables are much more impressive than this old barn. And I shall ride with you to show you the way."

"I think I can find Lakefield on my own."

No doubt he could, since Lakefield's lands bordered

Trentingham, accessible by both the road and the river. But Rose wouldn't be deterred. "I should like to come along. Perhaps I can help Violet. Twins can be a handful, you know."

Lily suppressed a laugh. Rose had never shown the slightest interest in helping Violet before. But it was good, she decided, for Rose to appear maternal. A gentleman looking for a wife would also be thinking in terms of a mother for his children.

"Well, then," Rand said easily, "we shall have a nice ride. You'll join us, Lily, won't you?"

"I—what?" she asked, taken off guard.

"Lily has yet to eat breakfast," Rose pointed out, having doubtless noticed her absence at the breakfast table. She did, at least, tactfully forgo mentioning that Lily wasn't properly groomed for a visit, either. Why, Rose was progressing by leaps and bounds. "She can join us later."

"Nonsense," Rand returned. "We'll wait. In the meantime, you wanted to show me the gardens?"

A smile lit Rose's eyes. Lily followed them out of the barn, turning toward the house while her sister led Rand in the other direction.

Mere seconds later, Rose's voice stopped her in her tracks. "Rowan Ashcroft, what on earth do you think you're doing?"

That sounded *very* maternal. Lily hurried around the back of the barn, arriving just in time to see her brother tug a thin wooden stick through a fold of paper, the friction producing a hiss. As the wood burst into flame, he looked up and gave a grinning answer to Rose's question. "I'm making fire."

The grin vanished as the sliver of wood burned close to his fingers. He dropped it with a yelp.

Rand strode forward to stamp it out. "What is it you have there?"

Rose brushed at her red satin skirts. "It doesn't matter,"

she said even more maternally. "He's well aware that he isn't allowed to play with fire."

Too maternally, Lily decided. It was one thing for Rose to display a love of children by offering to help Violet, quite another to scold like a fishwife. Especially considering Rowan was her brother, not her child.

"But what *is* it?" Rand bent closer.

Rowan handed him the paper. "It has phosphorus on it." If Rand looked surprised at hearing a boy of ten use such a word, Lily wasn't. Rowan spent hours every week in Ford's laboratory. "And this," he said, pulling another of the slim wooden sticks from his pocket, "has sulfur on one end. Ford's friend, a man named Robert Boyle, has discovered that the two together make fire. Phosphorus has a very low burning point," he added importantly.

Although Lily wasn't at all sure what that had to do with making fire, Rand nodded thoughtfully. "Brilliant. May I try?"

"Boys will be boys. And apparently men will be boys, too," Rose said in a tone Lily thought unwise.

Lily shot her a warning glance, then turned to her brother. "Did Ford give you these things?"

His face reddened. "He showed them to me. Mr. Boyle is thinking about selling them. It's a good idea, isn't it? I'm thinking he could make a lot of money."

"I'm thinking Ford would be unhappy if he knew you'd taken such dangerous things home." Her brother shuffled his feet. "I'm thinking," she added softly, "that Ford would feel terrible if you burned yourself because he made the mistake of showing you something interesting, believing you were old enough to know better than to play with it."

"I guess I should give the things back," Rowan muttered.

Rand drew the wooden sliver against the paper, smiling as

it sparked. "I'll return them." He reached out a hand. "Have you any more of the sticks?"

Rowan dug in his pocket, handed over a few more slivers, then turned and ran for the house.

ELEVEN

*A*N HOUR LATER, Rose banged on Lily's door. "Lily? Lord Randal wants to leave."

Lord Randal again. Dismissing her maid, Lily went to admit her sister. "May I suggest, Rose, that if you wish to win Rand, you might call him by the name he prefers?"

Rose shrugged. "I think Lord Randal has a nice ring to it. But I know you're trying to help, Lily, and I do appreciate it."

Lily wished her sister's words sounded more convincing.

"Are you ready?" Rose added.

"Nearly." Beatrix at her heels, Lily went back to her dressing table to fetch the hat that matched her blue wool riding habit. "Aren't you going to change?" she asked, eyeing her sister's elegant satin gown.

"I like this dress. I told Lord Randal I'd prefer to take the carriage."

"Oh." Lily set down the hat. "Shall I change, then?"

"Good God, why should it matter what you wear? I told you, he's growing impatient. Now, you must let him climb in first—"

"He's the man. He's going to hand us in."

"Just leave it to me. Then you must allow me to enter next so that I can sit beside him. You'll sit across."

"You're trying too hard." Beatrix jumped up onto the dressing table, and Lily stroked her fur. "Just be your usual beautiful, charming self—"

"I cannot leave this to chance," Rose interrupted. "Lord Randal is the only man I've ever truly loved."

From where Lily was standing, her sister's emotions ran more to desperation than love—though Lily felt guilty for thinking such uncharitable thoughts. "Whatever you say, Rose. I'll follow your lead."

Beatrix went with them and was first into the carriage. Rand, of course, insisted the ladies get in next. He settled himself beside Lily, and for a few awkward minutes, Rose alternately glared at her and aimed flirtatious smiles at him.

Rand appeared to be avoiding Rose's gaze, staring out the window instead. He hummed to himself, a tune Lily didn't recognize.

Suddenly Rose sniffed the air. "Sulfur," she said disapprovingly. Maternally. True, she was displaying her intelligence by recognizing the chemical, but hadn't she said men didn't care to be mothered?

Lily nudged her with a foot and gave a little shake of her head.

Apparently getting the message, Rose softened her expression into one of good-natured indulgence. "While you were waiting for us, did you play with the fire-making things? After you told Rowan you'd return them?"

Rand appeared anything but chastised. "What does Ford need with a scrap of paper and a few bits of wood? I'm sure he has more, and I think Rowan has learned his lesson."

Boys would be boys, Lily thought, then rushed to change the subject before her sister made the mistake of saying that again out loud. "How is it that a marquess's son became an Oxford professor?"

"Yes," Rose put in, "how on earth did *that* happen?" Lily heard a hint of disapproval in her tone, and hoped Rand didn't yet know her well enough to detect it.

"I'm a second son," he said simply, and left it at that.

But Rose couldn't leave well enough alone. "Surely your family would prefer to have you home?"

Rand snorted under his breath. "Not likely."

Sensing they'd touched on a sensitive subject, Lily tried to signal her sister to back off, but it seemed Rose was finished listening to her. "Do you not get along with them?"

"Not really." Impassive, his eyes remained on the world outside the window. "I couldn't wait to get away from home, and now that I've made my own way, I've no reason to return."

Rose's brow furrowed with genuine concern. "Were your parents unkind?"

"From what I can remember of her, my mother was very kind. But she died in a riding accident when I was six, and the marquess...well, suffice it to say that he showed more regard for his dogs than he ever showed me."

"He ignored you?"

"Unless I was in trouble."

A new edge in his voice made Lily's spine tingle. She imagined him young, fresh-faced, misbehaving...afraid. "Were you often in trouble?" she heard herself asking.

He shrugged. "Only when my older brother was nearby."

"Was your brother naughty like Rowan?" Rose asked.

"Rowan?" A strange expression passed over Rand's face. "No, he was nothing like Rowan."

Lily lifted Beatrix into her lap and hugged her. She had a hunch she didn't want to know more about this brother. With such unpleasantness awaiting him at home, who could blame

Rand for staying far away? Still, the thought of not seeing one's family for years and years...Lily couldn't fathom it.

She saw a loneliness in Rand that made her chest constrict. He was like one of her stray animals, abandoned, hurt, and forgotten. But a splint wouldn't fix Rand's hurts. Lily hated seeing his pain, but there was nothing she could do except be kind to him and wish for the best.

And, perhaps, help him find happiness with someone who loved him. With someone who would marry him and give him the sort of family he deserved.

With Rose.

TWELVE

O SOONER HAD the carriage door opened than Ford whisked Rand upstairs to the attic. "How was your stay at Trentingham?"

"Fine." Rand looked around at the chaotic jumble of scientific instruments that littered Ford's laboratory. "Is there nothing I can do downstairs, where the damage—"

"It's all being handled. I'm in the middle of something here—I'll be with you in a minute." Ford added a noxious-smelling substance to some cloudy fluid in a beaker. "Fine, was it?"

"Actually," Rand admitted, "it was rather awkward. Will the guest room be ready for me to sleep here tonight?"

Ford stirred the mess with a stick made of glass. "If you can live with a bare, damp floor."

"Bare and damp won't deter me."

"Very well, then." Ford nodded. "I must let this sit until tomorrow. Let me go get the book."

Rand plopped onto a chair and rubbed his face, feeling enormously relieved to be moving back here this afternoon.

Trentingham Manor was lovely, but at Lakefield he ran less risk of making an utter fool of himself.

He was no longer certain Lily found him repulsive—despite last night's scene in the parlor, she was acting as friendly and kind as ever—but that didn't mean he was comfortable living under one roof with two Ashcroft daughters. He felt much safer at Ford's house. More in control. Less likely to find himself seducing someone, being seduced, or saying something stupid.

I've thought about you for four years...

"Here it is," Ford said, setting the book on the table and taking a seat beside him.

"It" was *Secrets of the Emerald Tablet,* a small, brown leather volume that appeared to be of little consequence. Ancient and handwritten in a cryptic code, it looked like a simple diary. But it was much more than that. It was purported to hold the key to the Philosopher's Stone—the secret of how to make gold.

Ford had found the book years earlier and brought it to Rand to translate. When the task had proved a difficult one, they'd set it aside for a time. Now Rand looked forward to the challenge.

It would take his mind off...things. People. One person in particular.

"Awkward," Ford echoed thoughtfully, moving closer with a scrape of his chair. His laboratory was a homely space, huge but hardly luxurious, cluttered as it was with every toy a scientist and alchemist could desire. "Violet's mother is generally expert at setting her guests at ease."

"And her daughter is expert at upsetting them."

"Rose?" Ford chuckled. "She can be rather forward, but I assure you she's ultimately harmless."

"*Rather forward* hardly begins to define Rose. But I meant Lily."

"Lily? But Lily's so *nice*. What could she possibly have done to upset you?"

Rand just shrugged, not feeling up to sharing his humiliation just yet.

Besides, the question of what Lily had done to him—was doing to him—was still up for debate.

THIRTEEN

*D*OWNSTAIRS, LILY and Rose had joined their oldest sister in her cheerful turquoise drawing room. With the three of them together, it felt just like old times.

Almost. Violet, of course, was married now, and a mother of three herself. Although she lived close by and they got together often, Lily did miss the nights when they'd all gathered in one of their chambers, gossiping and giggling away the hours.

She watched Beatrix wander the room, poking her little black nose here and there as she searched for something familiar. Suddenly Lily wished for the old and familiar, too. "You should come home to sleep one night, Violet."

"At Trentingham?" Violet stopped pacing, which meant tiny Rebecca started snuffling. The babe seemed to prefer constant motion.

"I'll walk with her," Lily offered. She couldn't wait to get her hands on her niece.

When Rebecca was settled in Lily's arms, Violet dropped onto one of the turquoise velvet chairs. She lifted her spectacles and rubbed the bridge of her nose. "Why should I stay the night at Trentingham?"

"A sleeping party. It would be like the old days." As Lily walked back and forth with Rebecca, her gaze swept over little Marc asleep in a cradle. She smiled to see Rose playing with Nicky on the floor, his miniature English warship in fierce conflict with her Dutch one. "I know you rarely let your children out of your sight, but you *do* have nurse-maids. They could relieve you for one night, don't you think?"

Violet seemed to contemplate that odd idea for a moment before she grinned. "Perhaps I could find time to read a book."

"No," Lily said, then reconsidered. If solitary time to read was what her sister needed, she wouldn't deny her. "Of course you could read, if that's what you want. But I was thinking we could spend the night together. The three of us, like we used to."

Rose looked up with a wicked smile. "And read *Aristotle's Master-piece*?"

"Not that," Lily said quickly, remembering the hours they'd all spent together stealthily reading the scandalous marriage manual before Violet's wedding. She'd found *Aristotle's Master-piece* an uncomfortable combination of intriguing and embarrassing, and she hadn't been sad when the book moved to Lakefield along with her sister. "I just thought...I thought it would be nice to talk."

"Bang!" Nicky sailed his ship closer to Rose's. Beatrix's small head whipped back and forth, following the battle. "Bang, bang!"

"Quieter," Violet cautioned. "Your sister's sleeping."

Rebecca had nodded off in Lily's arms. Violet gazed at her daughter fondly. "Of course I'll come sleep at Trentingham. Someday soon. It will be great fun." Though she sounded enthusiastic, her brown eyes were filled with concern. "Is there something in particular you'd like to talk about?"

"Nothing special. Just…life."

Rose aimed a tiny Dutch cannon. "*I* want to talk about Lord Randal."

The one thing Lily *didn't* want to talk about. Though she dearly wished for Rose and Rand's happiness together, she couldn't help growing weary of her sister's gushing. She might be the sweetest of the Ashcroft sisters, but it made her want to gag.

"How many times," she said with uncharacteristic scorn, "do you suppose he's asked you to call him Rand?"

"Oh, about a million," Rose answered gaily. "But I like to think of him as a lord. *My* lord."

Lily mentally rolled her eyes.

"Has he shown interest?" Violet asked Rose.

Their sister's perfect nose went into the air. "He walked with me in the garden today. He's been very kind."

"Bang, bang!" Nicky yelled. "Auntie Rose, you're not watching. You're going to sink!"

"Quieter," Violet repeated—rather patiently, Lily thought, considering she'd probably heard her sister utter that word a thousand times or more.

Lily lowered herself to a chair slowly, so as not to wake the baby she held. "Still, he's hardly about to propose to you, Rose, and now that he's moving to Lakefield, things will only get more difficult."

Beatrix began hiccuping.

"That silly cat." Rose stood, abandoning her ship to the mercy of the English. She narrowed her eyes at Lily. "You made a promise. Do you mean to break it?"

Violet gazed with curiosity at Lily. "What promise?"

"She promised," Rose answered for her, "to help me win Lord Randal."

Lily swallowed hard. Hadn't she been helping? She looked to Violet for a reaction, but her sister's face was impassive. Her gaze shifted back to Rose. "Have you ever known me to break a promise?"

Rose appeared to give that some thought. "No," she said at last. "You always do the right thing." But she said it as though always doing the right thing were a character flaw.

And though it made no sense at all, Lily was beginning to think that might be true.

FOURTEEN

*A*FTER DINNER at Trentingham, Lily spent the afternoon tucked away in the drawing room, its thick oak doors shielding her from the chaos all around. Outside, the drive was crammed with carriages waiting to take friends and family home. Inside, uncles bellowed directions for packing and loading while children galloped about the corridors and nursemaids scurried after their charges.

But at the harpsichord in her family's cream-and-gold drawing room, Lily felt at peace. The ivory keys were cool and smooth beneath her hands, the music rising and falling in perfect, predictable patterns. There was something satisfying in letting notes on a page direct her fingers through familiar motions—motions that produced the same sounds and silences every time, without fail.

Music always made sense.

Lily knew she should join the others and say good-bye. And she would, soon. Just one more song and she'd be ready to face the confusion of the household. Two songs at the most. Well, maybe three, but the third would be on the shorter side—

The door opened, and her mother glided gracefully into the chamber. Mum waited for her to finish. "Dear," she began as the last note faded, "that was lovely, but you really should be—"

"I know, Mum." Lily rose, forcing her lips to curve in a smile. "I'll go make my farewells."

"That's my Lily." Mum smiled in return. "Aunt Cecily could use some help bringing Lucy and Penelope downstairs." Lucy and Penelope were Lily's small cousins, aged two and three. "I'm afraid all our servants are engaged with the luggage."

"Of course I'll help." With one last wistful look at the harpsichord, Lily quit the room and followed her mother upstairs, looking forward to hugging the two girls one more time.

But the nursery was empty. "Oh, well," Mum said cheerfully. "Aunt Cecily must have managed to wrestle the little rapscallions downstairs by herself. Come along, then." She turned back to the corridor.

Feeling like one of King Charles's tennis balls being batted back and forth, Lily followed. Then nearly bumped into her mother when she stopped before a door—the door to the room that had been assigned to Rand.

If Lily hadn't already known that, she would have figured it out by the singing that drifted from inside. Though the words were muffled, she recognized the same tune from the carriage this morning. Even muffled, his voice was gorgeous. It flowed through the gaps around the closed door, warm and rich like melted butter.

Mum knocked and called through the oak. "How do you fare, Rand?"

The door opened, and Rand stood there, a shirt dangling from one hand. "Very well, thank you," he said, stepping back into the room to toss the garment into his trunk. He looked, Lily thought, like he was relieved to be departing Trentingham.

Well, she was relieved, too. The less she had to watch Rose fawning over him, the better.

A frown on her forehead, Mum pointedly scanned the room. "Where is the maid I arranged for? Did she never turn up?" She nodded to Lily. "Perhaps you can assist Rand with his packing for a few moments."

"I—" Lily started.

"That's my Lily." Without waiting for her agreement, Mum turned to look down the stairwell. "Arabel!" she shouted. "Don't you dare leave without a bottle of perfume!" And before Lily could say anything, she was gone.

Lily sighed and entered the room, suppressing a smile when she saw Rand's sloppy method of folding breeches. "Let me help you with that."

"I can manage it myself, although I cannot fathom why the maid unpacked everything. I brought enough for a two-week stay, but not here."

"She wasn't privy to your plans." She took the garment and folded it neatly, thinking it felt a bit scandalous to be touching his clothes. "As soon as some of these people leave, more help will be available."

Lady and Jasper watched from the sill, holding a noisy conversation. "What could a squirrel and a bird possibly be discussing?" Rand asked rather peevishly, then didn't wait for her to answer. "I told Ford I'd be back in an hour. He wants to work some more on the translation."

"Ford will have to understand." She re-folded the last pair of breeches and placed the stack back in his trunk. "He can wait."

Rand snorted. "I suppose he's waited for four years. Another couple of hours won't kill him."

I've thought about you for four years...

Lily shook the words from her head. Last night ought to be the last thing on her mind right now.

She looked away as he came near to dump an armful of stockings in the trunk. Heat was rising in her cheeks, and her hands trembled slightly as they untangled the lump of stockings. If she meant to keep her resolve, she'd have to quash these feelings before they got out of hand.

"Rose is hopeless at packing, too, you know," she said conversationally. "You two truly have a lot in common."

"Are you disdaining my skill at packing, madam?"

She felt an instant of remorse before noticing the smile playing at the corners of his lips. An answering grin appeared on her own. "Are you alleging you have any, sir?"

What was it about him that made her so bold? She was hardly ever pert, not even with her own family. But with Rand, these things somehow tumbled out of her mouth.

"Why don't you show me, then?" He offered a clean but rumpled shirt. "Instruct me in the art of folding, o wise Professor Ashcroft."

Their fingers touched when she reached for it, and his hand was warm and much larger than hers. The shirt smelled like him, like soap and a hint of musk. Her skin prickled. Unable to meet his eyes, she looked down to see that he hadn't relinquished the shirt. In fact, he seemed to be using it to draw her closer, and try as she might to uncurl her fingers, they wouldn't do as they were told.

She barely had time to realize she was about to get her first kiss before it was happening. His lips met hers gently, feather-light, soft and warm as the finest whisper of down. But that whisper alone was enough to make her head swirl. Wanting to feel more, she rose on her toes to press closer.

Rose. She'd promised Rose. She couldn't do this.

Pulling away in a panic, she was horrified to realize the door was wide open. Why, anyone could have walked by and seen what they were doing! How could she be so stupid? Not to mention thoughtless, shallow, uncaring—

"I have to leave," she said, stumbling toward the doorway, nearly tripping over her own skirts. She was shaking all over.

Lady tweeted from the window, and Jasper answered with a chirp, alerting Lily to their presence. How long had they been watching? she wondered vaguely, but a hundred other questions and doubts stampeded through her mind, making her stomach want to rebel. How had she let this happen? How could she have betrayed her own sister?

And how in heaven's name would she ever forgive herself?

FIFTEEN

$\mathcal{I}$T WAS A WEEK later, when Lily was exercising her horse, Snowflake, that she spotted Rand running along the bank of the Thames.

He'd avoided her all that time. Or she'd avoided him. Or both—she wasn't sure. But now, riding toward him, her heart began to race…and it wasn't from the exertion of the gallop.

She slowed deliberately, both Snowflake's gait and her own breathing. She was determined to appear indifferent toward him, though she'd given up attempting to *feel* indifferent. Each day this week, Rose had contrived some excuse to visit Violet. And each day, when Rose had returned from Lakefield looking injured and disappointed, instead of sympathy, all Lily had felt was relief.

That's how Lily knew her feelings for Rand were real. They'd changed her.

And not in a way she liked.

But as Violet was always telling her—and anyone else who would listen—humans were rational beings, capable of rising above instinct and emotion to make their own decisions. And since Lily loved her family more than anything else on earth, she knew the rational decision was not to act on these feelings. Right and wrong might seem murky to her of late, but, for her own sake if not for Rose's, family loyalty had to come first.

Not that it was an easy decision. She hadn't forgotten that kiss.

Above plain buff breeches, he wore a loose white shirt unlaced and open at the neck, the sleeves rolled up past his elbows. Tied back into a queue, his glorious hair streamed on the wind behind him, shimmering in the sun. His unfashionably low-heeled boots pounded along the grassy bank in a rhythm measured and unceasing.

He ran, she thought, like a wildcat, lithe and sleek.

She knew the moment he saw her. There was a telltale stumble in that perfectly smooth motion. And a matching hitch in her heartbeat.

He stopped and leaned over, hands to bent knees, panting hard as he waited for her to ride closer. When she did, he straightened and looked up at her, using a hand to shade his eyes.

His face was flushed; his shirt clung damply to his skin. That piercing gray gaze swept her from her toes on up. When it met her eyes, searching, it seemed almost as though he were seeing her for the first time.

Holding her reins in one hand, she self-consciously smoothed her yellow riding habit with the other.

"Good day, Lily."

She swallowed tightly. "Good day."

"I'm finished running," he said, stating the obvious. But she had the oddest feeling that he spoke of more than exercise. Moving beside her white horse, he reached to help her down. "Will you walk with me? I like to do that after I run."

There was no harm, she supposed, in walking. But when his hands spanned her waist to ease her to the ground, they caused a disturbing jolt of sensation. And she felt his fingers rest there longer than necessary before he stepped back.

She deliberately looked away, taking Snowflake's reins and looping them over the branch of a scrubby tree.

A sparrow fluttered from the sky and alighted in the sparse foliage. Rand looked up, then raised a questioning brow. "Lady?"

"Yes. She thinks she's protecting me."

"She thinks I cannot defend you without her help?" His laugh sounded strained. "How dare she insult my masculinity."

To the contrary, Lily suspected Lady was acknowledging his masculinity—protecting her *from* Rand rather than in spite of him. But she certainly wasn't going to encourage him by saying so.

They turned and walked along the riverfront, settling easily into a comfortable tempo. Keeping far enough away from him that he couldn't take her hand, Lily focused on the water. Swans glided majestically, and faint laughter drifted from a river barge whose passengers were enjoying the summer sun.

"Do you run often?" she asked, then realized she knew the answer.

Here was the reason he looked so browned and sleekly muscled. Apparently not all academics spent their days locked away in research.

"Often enough," he said. "It helps me think."

Surprised, she turned her head to look up at him. "How can you think while you run that hard?"

"Not during." Wanting to explain, Rand met her gaze and smiled. "After. Like now. When my body is pleasantly worn-out and I can feel the breeze cooling my skin."

It had always done that for him, the running. It wasn't only the speed. It was the strain of pumping muscles, the sound of pounding feet, the delicious gulps of air rushing in and out of his lungs. The rhythm. It all combined to clear his head—to *fill* his head—leaving no space for worry or concerns. When he was running, he was only running.

And when he stopped, he could always think more clearly. Life seemed simpler. Problems seemed surmountable. Solutions seemed to materialize out of thin air.

But this time, when he'd stopped, Lily had materialized. And he'd thought, quite clearly, that he must be falling in love.

The realization had nearly made his burning leg muscles give way. His heart had hammered against his ribs. Was still hammering against his ribs.

He wasn't sure he was ready for love, wasn't sure it was meant for him. Wasn't he happy the way things were? He'd escaped his personal nightmare and made a life for himself. A good life, a comfortable life, a life in which he didn't have to answer to anyone.

A lonely life, a little voice whispered.

Lily watched Rand shake his head as though to clear it. " How long have you been at Oxford?" she blurted out.

"A decade—since I was thirteen. I couldn't wait to get out of my father's house, so I jumped at the chance to enter early. He doesn't approve of what I've become, but he cannot tell me what to do any longer."

"Did he expect you to assist him with his estates?" She knew that Rowan would do that someday, but it was different for Rowan—someday he'd be Lord Trentingham, while Rand would never be more than Lord Hawkridge's younger brother. "I can understand why you wouldn't want to do that, or live the life of an idle gentleman. You'd be wasting your talents."

"I've no idea what he expected, but I doubt he harbored dreams of keeping me home. My leaving for Oxford was the only thing we ever agreed on. The old goat was as happy to see the back of me as I was to turn it upon him."

He grinned as though that was supposed to be amusing, and she smiled in return. But she found it unbearably sad that he'd had to finish growing up by himself—and she sensed it made him sad, too.

No matter what, she'd always have her family and their support. She'd never realized how lucky she was. Rand had pursued his dreams, but he'd done it alone.

No one should have to be alone.

"How did it happen?" she heard him ask, and looked up to find his gaze fixed on where she was absently rubbing the back of her hand.

Swallowing, she hid the hand behind her back. "It doesn't hurt anymore, if that's what you're wondering. It happened long ago."

He stopped walking. "But how?" Gently, he retrieved her hand, and she was too embarrassed by its ugliness to protest.

She stared down at the thin white lines. The proof of her imperfection. "A cat. Not Beatrix. And it wasn't his fault—I was teasing him. I learned to respect animals after that. All animals."

"I cannot imagine you disrespecting anything."

Something in his voice made a nervous laugh bubble out of her. "I try not to," she said, "but I'm far from perfect."

"You're close enough to perfect for me," he said very seriously. His thumb drew circles on her palm, and she shivered. Her lips tingled with remembered sensation.

She licked them. "Rose..."

A puzzled frown appeared on his brow. "Rose? What about her?"

She hesitated. They were standing beneath a tree, and a flutter of wings heralded Lady alighting above them. But

Lily's sparrow friend couldn't protect her from her confusing feelings.

She suddenly felt very tired. Tired of lying, tired of resisting, tired of the excruciating guilt. She couldn't do it anymore. This tug-of-war had to end.

She pulled her hand away. "Rose is the reason I shouldn't be here with you, Rand. She wants you for herself."

"Ah, so you're being a good sister, is that it?" To her irritation, his lips curved in a smile. Did he take this for a jest? "Let me tell you, Lily, Rose may very well want me, and I'm sorry to hurt her feelings. But I want *you*."

He couldn't, she thought.

Maybe he did. But he just couldn't.

While Lady twittered, Lily took a step back. "You're so like Rose. You both sing, the languages..."

Her words trailed off. Lady flew to a lower branch.

Rand seemed to consider that line of reasoning for a long moment.

When he finally spoke, his tone was laced with quiet conviction. "Maybe I am like Rose. But I don't want someone like me. I want someone to *complete* me."

His words were so earnest, his relentless gray eyes so sure, that he melted her. When he moved closer, when his hand curled around the back of her neck, when he lowered his lips to hers...all she could do was give in.

And giving in felt entirely too *right*.

Slowly he backed her against the tree, his mouth gentle in the beginning, like it had been the first time. But when she felt the rough bark meet her back, his lips slanted, and she found hers parting, and then, well...

Lily knew about this kind of kiss—she was, after all, the youngest of three sisters. It had sounded rather messy and not entirely pleasant, no matter that she'd been assured otherwise.

There had been no need to worry.

Her eyes drifted closed and her hands crept into his hair, feeling its silky strands damp with his sweat. That should have been unpleasant, too, but it wasn't. He tasted of salt and somehow smelled clean and musky at the same time, and he overwhelmed every one of her senses.

"Lily?" he whispered against her lips. "I fear I'm falling in love with you."

Her eyes fluttered open.

"You cannot be," she said, numb with shock—and afraid it was the same for her. She tried to pull away, fought to gather her wits. This was wrong. "We...we haven't known each other long enough for you to know that."

"Four years."

"No," she argued, biting her lip. Tears threatened, but she blinked them back. This couldn't be happening. "Not four years. Not even a month. A couple weeks four years ago, and nine or ten days now. Most of them spent apart."

"Well, then," he said quietly, so guilelessly she knew he believed it, "it must have been love at first sight."

Love? The short word was far too big and real for Lily to manage. It made her heart knot and grow heavy in her chest. Blood pounded in her head, filling her ears.

If he loved her, Lily, then he'd never marry Rose, would he? What was the point of keeping her promise if Rose's hopes were destined to be dashed either way?

For one single moment, she wanted, more than she'd wanted anything in her life, to break a promise to her sister. Then she gasped, appalled that she'd even had such a disloyal thought. Her family meant everything to her. Rand's feelings didn't change that.

"I have to leave," she said, echoing her words from a week earlier. And she turned toward Snowflake and ran, Lady flying after her.

SIXTEEN

*F*OR THREE SOLID days, Rand did nothing but eat, sleep, work on the translation, and run. And think. And run and think some more.

At the end of that time, he still wasn't sure how—or even if—his feelings for Lily had turned from simple infatuation to something deeper. The mechanics of falling in love seemed cryptic, as elusive as the symbols in Ford's ancient alchemy book.

But Rand Nesbitt was a fellow who prided himself on his ability to figure things out.

Leaving Ford's laboratory for supper, he asked, "Do you believe in love at first sight?"

"No," Ford said flatly. "It makes no logical sense."

"Then you didn't feel…with Violet…"

"On first sight?" Ford's mouth twitched as though he were holding back a laugh. "Absolutely not. I thought her rather plain and more than a little odd. Though I cannot imagine why," he added thoughtfully.

Rand followed him down the winding staircase to Lakefield's cozy, burgundy-toned dining room, where Violet was waiting with their children.

She didn't look plain at all—she was practically glowing, as a matter of fact, as she handed one of the twins to a nursemaid. And as for odd, well, if that word didn't describe Ford Chase, Rand didn't know one that did.

When it came right down to it, who wasn't odd, anyway?

He took a seat and waited while a footman set a plate of chicken and artichoke pie before him. "Do you believe in love at first sight?" he asked Violet.

"Of course," she said. "But lust at first sight is more common."

A becoming blush touched her cheeks, making Rand suspect she'd experienced lust at first sight. He felt suddenly —absurdly—jealous, wishing her sister would feel the same lust for him.

Love. He'd uttered that frightening word, risked baring his soul, offered his heart in his hands…and had it rejected.

Lifting his fork, he shifted his gaze to Ford in an attempt to gauge his old friend as an inspiration for female lust. If he looked hard enough, he could almost understand why women might find Ford handsome, but truth be told, what he really saw was the gawky schoolboy he remembered from their first meeting at Wadham College.

This was a pointless exercise, he decided. But when he'd kissed Lily under the tree three days ago, she *had* kissed him back. At first, anyway. Perhaps that was reason enough to hope.

"Why are you asking?" Violet tucked a cloth under Nicky's chin, then pulled his plate closer and put a spoon in his chubby hand. "Do *you* believe in love at first sight?"

"I'm not sure," Rand said. He certainly hadn't until recently. Besides, his first sight of Lily had been so long ago. After all this time, how was he supposed to remember what he'd felt way back then? In the intervening years, he'd probably built her up in his mind.

And on such a flimsy basis, he now found himself envisioning a lifetime of wedded bliss. Pathetic.

Violet speared a piece of artichoke heart. "Of course, love —sustainable love—is dependent on more than physical appearance."

"Which is why," her husband said, "love at first sight is a myth."

"Not at all." Her voice took on the tone of a philosopher waxing philosophical. "Love occurs when something in one person recognizes something basic and true in another. To borrow a term from my mother's perfume-making, call it that person's essence. One would see this essence embodied in everything the other person does—those thoughts, actions, responses, and choices that go to display her values."

"One cannot see all of that at first sight," Ford argued.

"I beg to differ." Clearly enjoying this sort of debate, Violet waved her fork. "One person's essence responds innately to another's—it's not a conscious response, nor one that knows time. Upon meeting a woman, some part of you will notice how she moves, gestures, talks, smiles—how she carries herself in general. Her essence—not only her surface appearance." She focused back on Rand. "Take my sister Lily, for example."

Though the pie was delicious, swimming in rich gravy, Rand nearly choked. "Lily?" He shot a glance to Ford, whom he'd told about Lily in confidence. But his friend avoided his gaze, industriously cutting an already-small-enough bite of chicken.

"Just as an example." If Violet's expression might have revealed ulterior motives, she expertly concealed it while sipping wine. "Lily is beautiful, isn't she?"

Rand sipped from his own goblet. Lustrous mahogany hair, deep blue eyes, that delicate face and petite figure…

"I don't expect any fellow would argue with you about that."

"And perhaps most men would notice that first, but there's so much more to Lily. She makes beautiful music. She's also quite intelligent. One needn't be bookish to be intelligent."

"Did I ever say—"

"Those are all obvious things, but now let's look at her essence, those values we can see in the way she carries herself and behaves. She's nurturing and compassionate. People feel good around Lily, because she cares. She really cares, about everyone and everything. She's benevolent, she seeks harmony, and above all, she endeavors at all times to make the right choices. The sum of these is what makes her Lily."

"Her essence," Rand murmured.

"Yes!" Beaming, Violet set down her goblet. "And the sort of man who would recognize a kindred essence in Lily, most especially on first sight, would also recognize that she will someday make a wonderful mother." With that, her gaze lovingly went to her babies in their cradles.

And Rand was rendered speechless.

He wasn't sure he could even eat.

He was just getting used to considering love and marriage…fatherhood was another matter entirely.

SEVENTEEN

"*L*ILY, ARE YOU ready to leave?"

"Just a moment, Mum." With a sigh, Lily stroked Randolph's soft brown fur one last time. She'd put it off more than a week, but she knew what had to be done. Setting her jaw, she crouched to tenderly place Randolph on the grass.

Without so much as a thank you, the rat scampered happily into a flower bed.

Lily sighed again and fished Beatrix out from beneath her skirts. "May I bring her?" she asked as she rose.

"I suppose she'll contrive to come along either way." Mum sifted through the basket on her arm, checking that all her perfumes were in order. "But you must leave her in the carriage. You know cats make Lady Carrington sneeze."

Half an hour later, Lily stood on the steps of Carrington House with her mother and Rose. As Mum lifted the knocker, a sneeze resounded from inside.

"Beatrix is in the carriage," Lily said defensively. Glancing back to make sure, she saw a small black nose pressed to the vehicle's window. Jasper and Lady sat atop the carriage's roof, looking similarly innocent.

The door opened, and a butler ushered them into the drawing room, where Lady Carrington was waiting with coffee, expensive imported tea, and cakes. Judith sat on a sturdy carved chair, dabbing at her nose with a lace-edged handkerchief.

Mum set her basket on a table and raised the cloth covering. "Your usual blend," she said to Lady Carrington, handing her a bottle of scent. "And for you, Lady Judith, a new blend to celebrate your betrothal. More fitting for a lady of your status."

"It's spicier," Rose explained.

Judith's eyes widened. "Oooh, may I see?"

Lily brought the perfume to her friend, pulling the stopper out as she went. She waved the bottle under her own nose and smiled before handing it to Judith. "It smells lovely."

Judith dabbed a bit on one wrist and raised it to her reddened nose. "It does. Even all stuffy, I can tell. Thank you ever so much, Lady Trentingham."

"You're very welcome, dear."

Replacing the stopper, Judith stood. "Would you care to see the fabric for my wedding gown?" she asked Lily and Rose. "And the style? Madame left a fashion doll for me to show you."

They followed her up the curving oak staircase.

"I think the dress will be ever so beautiful," Judith said, pausing for a sneeze. "Heavens, I'm so excited about my wedding."

"You should be," Rose said somewhat wistfully.

The wedding dress fashion doll reclined in a place of honor against Judith's mauve pillows in her feminine room. "Isn't it lovely?"

"It is," Lily agreed softly. The doll's gown was palest blue with a wide neckline and golden ribbons crisscrossing the stomacher. The underskirt was cloth of gold.

Suddenly, quite unbidden, an image popped into her head —of herself wearing such a gown and standing beside Rand. The blue fabric brought out the hue in her eyes, which were fastened on Rand as she recited her vows in Trentingham's oak-paneled chapel. The golden underskirt shimmered, rustling when she moved...

"You're so lucky," Rose told Judith, snapping Lily out of her reverie.

She squeezed her eyes shut, then opened them with new determination. She ought to be picturing Rose standing beside Rand, rather than thinking disloyal thoughts.

Settling into the window seat, Judith sneezed again. "Pardon me," she said with a sniffle. Then her voice dropped a notch. "I'm lucky about the wedding," she mumbled, "but I'm worried about the wedding night."

Her heart aching for her friend, Lily forgot her own troubles. She sat beside Judith and took her hands. "You'll be fine," she told her with all the confidence she could muster. "All brides are nervous."

"Do you think so?"

"Goodness, I'm sure of it." She slanted a glance to Rose before looking back to her friend. "Do you believe in love at first sight?"

"Absolutely. But I've seen Lord Grenville, and—"

"I didn't mean to pry," Lily rushed to clarify. "I just wondered if you believed. In the abstract."

"Yes. Oh, yes." Judith had always been a romantic. "That's why I—"

"*I* believe in love at first sight," Rose interrupted. "I fell in love with Lord Randal the very first time I saw him."

Despite her worries, Judith grinned. "You fall in love with every gentleman you see."

"I do not," Rose protested. "Only the handsome ones. Like Rand."

Rand, Rand, Rand. Lily rose and paced back to the doll, staring at its pale blue magnificence. She would never feel right wearing a wedding dress before Rose was Lady Somebody.

"There are cakes downstairs," Judith said into the sudden silence.

Lily was all too happy to escape the discussion, but no sooner had they reentered the drawing room than Rose revived it. "Mum," she asked, "do you believe in love at first sight?"

"What nonsense," Lady Carrington said, her chins trembling with indignation. "Love grows between two suited individuals. It was that way for me, and it will be the same for my Judith and Lord Grenville." She brushed crumbs from her mouth and motioned her daughter closer. "Come here, dear. Have a cake."

Judith took two. Evidently her illness wasn't affecting her appetite.

"Mum?" Rose pressed.

Their mother set down her teacup. "I do believe in love at first sight," she said firmly. "I experienced it with your father."

Lady Carrington harrumphed.

"Of course," Mum continued undaunted, "dear Joseph took some convincing. I've yet to meet a man who believes in love at first sight."

Lily knew one. One who was trying to convince *her*.

"Nonsense," Lady Carrington repeated as she reached for another cake.

Mum smiled charmingly and changed the subject. "Have

you heard the latest?" she asked, lifting her cup. "Two more of my introductions are culminating in marriages. Lady Eleanor Randolph is betrothed to Lord Ducksworth. And you're not going to believe this." She paused to sip for effect. "I've managed to match the eternal bachelor."

Lady Carrington's eyes widened. "You don't mean…"

"Yes." Mum nodded proudly. "Lord Percival Newcombe."

"No!" her friend gasped, a cake halfway to her lips. "To whom?"

EIGHTEEN

"**J**OSEPH,**" Chrystabel said as she slid into bed beside him that night, "do you believe in love at first sight?"

Eyeing her warily, he set down his book. "Is this a trick question?"

"No."

"Then no. I don't believe in love at first sight."

"No?"

"Yes? Is yes the right answer? I've never thought about it, my love."

She laughed. He was such a man.

Chrystabel loved the nights, the precious hours spent alone with her husband in their thick-walled bedchamber. Here, where the sound of her voice competed with nothing but an occasional crackle from the fireplace, her Joseph could hear her perfectly.

He leaned to place a kiss on her forehead, then propped his book back up. "Does this have something to do with Lily and Rand? Are your plans not working out?"

She sighed. "I'm certain he's interested in her."

"Love at first sight?"

"Maybe. Do you remember how he looked at her, even four years ago?"

"No. I don't remember." He turned a page. "I'm not sure I noticed."

Of course he hadn't. He was a man. "Well, it was quite obvious he was drawn to her then, and it's even more obvious now. Surely you've noticed it now?"

"Not really."

"Even since I pointed it out?" she asked incredulously

He set his book aside and rolled to face her. "I have eyes only for you, Chrysanthemum," he murmured, brushing a strand of hair behind her ear. "Only you."

Half charmed, half exasperated, she snorted. "Well, Lily feels something for him, too—of that I'm sure. But despite all my efforts, the poor boy isn't making much progress. After I noticed Rand runs every day by the river, I told Lily that Snowflake needed some exercise, but—"

"Poor boy must not have my talents," her husband interrupted, then pressed a long, lingering kiss to her lips. "Are you sure he's good enough for Lily?"

"You're incorrigible," she said. But she didn't move away. "I told you, didn't I, that Violet said Lily promised Rose she'd stay away from Rand? Besides feeling bound to that ridiculous pledge, Lily is genuinely concerned for Rose. I can see it in her eyes, in her attitude. She's afraid to put her own happiness before her sister's."

"Give it some time, love. She'll come to her senses."

"But Rand's house will be ready soon," she fretted. "He'll be leaving."

"Give it some time," he repeated with another kiss. "If they're right for each other, he'll be back. You didn't win me in a day."

Oh yes, she had, she thought with a secret smile as she moved to blow out the candle, then tucked herself back in his arms. It just proved her finesse with men that he hadn't noticed.

NINETEEN

*O*NCE IN A great while, Rand Nesbitt found himself truly drunk. And though the deplorable condition invariably gave rise to next-morning regrets, it was also a jolly good bit of fun.

Sitting in Ford's laboratory, Rand stared at a nearly blank piece of paper. He blinked hard to make out the symbols, but they were just meaningless shapes. Unless... "That one on the end seems familiar." A shape sort of like an hourglass, except not really. Why, it almost looked like—

"It's a woman's figure!" Ford smacked the table. "A rather curvy woman, at that."

"I quite agree," Rand cried, and then proceeded to laugh himself silly. When he finished, he took another swig of brandy. "We've been here all night and translated only a single sentence," he said, finding himself fascinated, in an odd, detached sort of way, at hearing the slur in his own voice. "We'll never finish. You'll never make gold."

"What's a few more years when these words have been waiting for four hundred?" Ford reached across the cluttered table for the decanter, impressing Rand when he didn't knock over any of the assorted paraphernalia. He filled Rand's beaker for the third time.

Or maybe the fourth. Rand had lost count.

"So you're in love, are you?" Ford said.

"Maybe. Probably not. I cannot be sure." Rand paused for a sip, trying not to speculate on what chemical concoction the beaker might have held the day before. "I think so."

Topping off his own beaker, Ford nodded. "You're in love."

"She won't have me. It's that sister of hers. Rose." Rand took another sip—or rather a gulp that he'd intended to be a sip. "She keeps saying how Rose and I are more suited. Rose sings like I do. Rose can speak Italian." He shook his head. "As though that's what I'm looking for in a girl." Then another thought occurred to him—one that made the brandy seem to sour in his stomach. "What if she's only using Rose as an excuse? What if she's not attracted to me?" He *had* been sporting that wretched mustache when they'd first met; perhaps it had put her off permanently. "Or what if she won't have me because I'm only a professor? She lives in a mansion, after all, and I—"

"Lily's not like that," Ford rushed to interrupt. "She cares about her family. She cares about all people and animals. She does *not* care about living in a mansion."

Rand nodded—slowly, to keep the room from blurring—as he tried to believe that. He nearly succeeded. "Then why does she keep bringing up Rose?"

"Guilt," Ford said succinctly.

"Guilt?"

"Look, we all know Rose wants you—"

"Then why doesn't Lily?" Rand interrupted plaintively.

"Guilt," Ford repeated. Taking his time about it, he drained his beaker. "She doesn't want to steal you from Rose."

"Rose doesn't have me. Therefore Lily cannot steal me from Rose." Rand felt inordinately proud of that observation. "Those two statements make rational sense, don't they? And I'm a professor of linguistics, not logic."

"You're brilliant," Ford said dryly. "But you're forgetting something."

"What's that?" Rand asked, marveling at the way the words sounded once they'd left his mouth. *Whazzat.* Had he said *whazzat*?

"The way women's minds work. Or don't, as the case may be. Would you care for some more brandy?"

Rand held out his beaker. "I think I need it."

Ford refilled his own, too, then leaned back in his chair and stretched his long legs out in front of him. "Listen," he said, rolling the beaker between his palms, "it doesn't matter whether Rose has you. The salient point here is that Lily knows Rose is interested in you, and she's unwilling to hurt her sister by taking what Rose considers hers—never mind that you're not and never will be—because Lily is putting her sister's feelings before her own. She won't allow herself to marry—"

"Who said anything about marriage?"

"Hold your tongue and listen. Lily won't allow herself to marry before Rose, most especially to someone Rose wants for herself."

Rand sipped more brandy as he attempted to absorb that convoluted line of reasoning. In his current state, it almost made some sort of sense. "How on earth do you know all that?"

"Violet told me. And she also said that Lily made Rose some harebrained promise to stay out of her way, which further complicates matters."

"Did Violet suggest a solution?"

"She said it was hopeless. But that's where she's wrong."

Ford leaned forward, narrowing his eyes as he focused on Rand's. "Listen, my man. It's time for you to take your own advice."

Rand sat up straighter and then waited until the world stopped spinning around him. "Advice? About love? I'm not even sure I believe in it. I've certainly never given advice—"

"When Violet didn't want *me*, remember? You helped me devise a plan. And it worked."

"I did?" He blinked, trying to recall. "I must have been gloriously drunk."

"You were," Ford assured him. "Now, listen, because I'm far too masculine to say this more than once"—Rand gave a snort of disagreement—"at least, not without the influence of brandy. You told me I had to *show* Violet that I loved her, not just tell her so. I think you must do the same with Lily. As I said, she cares deeply for the wellbeing of all living things—including you. If she sees your feelings are stronger than her sisters', her sympathy for you will overcome her concern for Rose. And if she loves you back, she'll be free to make the right choice."

Rand ran his tongue around his teeth, considering the idea. "And how exactly do I show her?"

Shrugging, Ford tilted his head back and drained his glass, then smacked his lips. "That, my friend, is *your* problem."

TWENTY

*T*HE BURN OF overworked muscles. The sound of his own labored breath. The rhythm of his feet on the turf. All worked to clear Rand's mind...but disturbing thoughts insisted on creeping in anyway.

He'd stayed indoors yesterday, fuzzy-brained and out of sorts, the pounding in his head quite enough without the jarring beat of a run. He hadn't felt up to contemplating Ford's advice, either. It had been quite a while since he'd indulged in drink like that—for good reason. This recent bout would serve to ensure he drank moderately for another few years at least.

Still, he'd managed to make progress on the translation—enough, in fact, that he and Ford had come to the sad conclusion that *Secrets of the Emerald Tablet* held no secrets to making gold. Over the past few weeks, Ford had tested every formula Rand could find, with results ranging from hopeful-but-disappointing to all-out laughable.

Now there were no more formulas. There was no point in laboring to decipher what little was left of the text.

"I'm sorry," he'd told Ford when they'd closed the book last night.

"I always knew this was a possibility. Criminy, the mere idea of making gold was too good to be true. I'm sorry you wasted so much time on it."

Rand had shrugged, even that small movement hurting his aching head. "You know I'm always up for a good puzzle, and I enjoyed this one thoroughly. Besides, it gave me a sound excuse to escape all the construction. Kit should be finished by now."

Now there was no reason for Rand not to go home to Oxford.

Except Lily.

Today, sunlight sparkled off the Thames, and the fresh air felt good in his lungs. Pounding along the banks, his feet seemed to be saying, *show-her, show-her, show-her.*

He laughed at himself; what a pathetic case he'd become. His next breath was a huge one, drawn in through both nose and mouth, meant to cleanse his body and head. But with it came a faint scent that made alarm slither down his spine.

Fire.

He stopped and turned, scanning the horizon. There it was. Slightly inland and to the west, dark smoke puffing up to smudge today's clear blue sky.

Trentingham was over in that direction, he realized with a jolt of panic.

A moment later he was running faster than ever in his life.

ESTERDAY LILY had awakened with the sniffles and a scratchy throat, so she'd stayed home while Mum and Rose went out calling. Today, she'd awakened coughing and sneezing and could barely drag herself downstairs to tend to her menagerie. After completing her chores and nearly nodding into her breakfast, she'd crawled back into her night rail and collapsed into bed for a much needed nap, half expecting not to open her eyes again before dark.

But now she lay teetering on the brink of wakefulness, vaguely wondering what had roused her from sleep. She was tired, so tired her whole body ached, and she could tell from the color behind her closed lids that it was still midday. She rolled over, intending to drift off again, to seek more healing slumber—

Shouts. The stench of burning wood. Her eyes popped open, and she leapt from the bed and rushed to the window, her knees trembling.

Smoke billowed into the sky—light gray, dark gray, menacingly black—and below that, red and orange flames licked upward, rising from what looked like the soon-to-be-roofless barn.

Her animals were in there. Her heart racing, she grabbed a wrapper and struggled into it even as she ran for the door.

TWENTY-ONE

"**YOU CANNOT GO** back in there, my lord! It's about to collapse! They're only animals! Not worth your life!"

Rand ignored the frantic stable hand's warning, waving him toward the long bucket brigade bringing water up from the river. Coughing, he set down the badger and quickly scanned the small collection of dazed creatures.

The hedgehog, the fawn, a rabbit, a weasel...Lily had said she was planning to release the rat, and he prayed that she had, because he hadn't a chance of finding anything that small in the blinding smoke. But he'd seen a shadow in the grayness...the fox cub, he suddenly realized. The fox cub with the broken leg.

This one cannot run, he heard Lily say in his head. This one couldn't survive without him.

He'd originally raced into the blazing barn because he'd needed to make sure Lily wasn't in there. But once inside, he'd remembered her face, her gentle hands as she cared for her strays. He couldn't leave them to die. Not the ones he'd already saved, and not the fox cub, either.

To more cries of "No!" and "Stay back!" he charged once more into the conflagration. What air remained was hotter than his first two trips, and drier, searing his lungs. Flames thundered, their orange, white, and blue tendrils licking up the wooden walls. Billowing black smoke threatened to blind him.

He stumbled toward Lily's makeshift pens, coughs wracking his body as he peered through the haze, his eyes blurred with burning tears. Frantically he searched the enclosures, finding nothing. The blaze roared all around him, the sound filling his head, battering his senses.

Heat lashed him in scorching waves. He couldn't see; he couldn't breathe; he couldn't stay in here a minute longer.

This one cannot run...

He pictured Lily saying the words, kneeling beside a pen, *right there*. Sucking in acrid air, he reached down blindly, his fingers encountering soft, trembling fur.

And then he was on his way out, the cub a gasping, hot bundle in his arms, both of them searching for cool, healing air. Just as he cleared the door, a mighty crash sounded behind him, and for one terrifying moment he seemed surrounded by raining sparks.

Then there was light, and he could breathe, and someone was pulling the cub from his arms. "Oh goodness, oh goodness, oh goodness," someone cried, whacking him on the back. It made him cough more, and he tried to twist away, to run away, but he only stumbled. His eyes were still streaming and he couldn't see, but whoever it was followed him.

"You're on fire!" she screamed, and it was Lily's voice, and he stood still and let her beat upon his back until at last she stopped.

"Oh goodness," she said again and took him by the hand to pull him farther from the flames. They both collapsed to the ground. Rand rubbed his eyes, feeling grit, his head swimming in a haze of smoke and unreality.

He blinked until his vision cleared. He and Lily gazed at each other, ash and soot drifting around them and settling slowly to earth like a dark, eerie snowfall.

"You saved my animals," she whispered, quiet tears rolling down her cheeks.

"You saved *me*," Rand croaked through his raw throat. Still coughing, he reached a hand behind to touch his back, but it didn't hurt enough to be burned.

"It was your hair." Lily coughed, too. "Your hair was on fire."

He reached higher then, to the ribbon that bound the queue he wore when he ran, and it was still there—but the hair below it felt wiry and crumbled in his fingers.

"I'm sorry," she said, coughing some more.

He shrugged, still feeling dazed. "It hardly matters. It will grow back." They both coughed together. "Did the smoke get to you, too? Or are these sympathy coughs?" he said with a weak smile, then frowned, peering closer, finally noticing how she looked. "You're wearing a nightdress. You're ill, aren't you? Rose is at Lakefield now, as usual, but she failed to mention your illness. You shouldn't be out here—you'll catch your death."

Her cheeks flushed pink. She took the dressing gown clenched in her fingers—the one she'd used to beat out the flames—and draped it over herself. Once white, it was streaked gray and black from his hair. "You shouldn't be here, either," she said. "What are you doing here?"

"I was running and saw the smoke." His head cleared, and suddenly he realized the fire was still raging. "Go inside, Lily. Lie down. Your animals are safe." Even now, a couple of women were busy moving them to the stables. "I need to help here."

He pushed to his feet and came face-to-face with Lily's mother.

She laid a gentle hand on his arm. "You should go inside, too. You've done enough."

"But the barn—"

"It's hopeless, and the rest is under control."

Rand turned to see. Although the bucket brigade was still operating full force under the direction of her husband, the men weren't fighting the fire, instead drenching the surrounding area to prevent its spread. The barn itself—or what was left of it—was burning merrily despite their earlier efforts.

Lady Trentingham forced a wan smile. "It was old and needed replacing. So long as no one's hurt, it's no great loss. Come inside. I'll fetch some water so you can rinse off the soot." Without waiting for his agreement, she hurried toward the house.

His hands were coated in black, and he wanted to wash his face as well. He reached to help Lily rise. The sunshine was dimmed by the veil of smoke overhead, but not so much that he couldn't see a faint outline of her form through her thin white nightdress. He thought it wise not to mention that, however. She sneezed twice during their slow progress to the house and looked even worse than he felt.

Well, her poor red eyes and nose did, anyway. The rest of her was as lovely as ever.

By the time they stepped indoors, Lady Trentingham had a basin and towels set up in the drawing room. She ushered them both inside, handing Rand a clean white shirt and Lily a fresh dressing gown and a pair of shears. "I must see that ale is brought to the men—I'll be back to check on you two in a few moments!" she said before rushing off.

Lily hurried into the dressing gown and belted it tightly at her waist. Exhausted, Rand slowly unwound the ribbon from his hair, then looked down at his grayish shirt, noticing all the tiny black holes where sparks had singed it and marked his skin. Wincing, he began to strip it off.

Her mouth dropped open, but she didn't avert her eyes.

He paused, remembering he was supposed to win Lily by demonstrating the depth of his feelings. But surely a bit of temptation couldn't hurt, either?

Hoping she'd find him tempting, he pulled the shirt over his head and turned to the water.

TWENTY-TWO

*L*ILY'S GAZE WAS affixed to Rand's back, watching the way his muscles moved as he scrubbed all the black soot off his hands and arms, then his face and neck. She'd never seen a man's bare back, unless she counted Rowan's, but he was still just a boy. And Rowan's back didn't look like Rand's, either; it looked rather like her own or Rose's. Rand's tapered from wide shoulders down to narrow hips, and every muscle was defined beneath the dewy skin—sweat-dampened, no doubt, by the intense heat inside the barn.

Feeling her own temperature rising, she dropped onto a chair.

Drying his face with a towel, he turned. "Why did she give you scissors?"

"Hmm?" Swallowing hard, she tore her gaze from his chest and looked down to where her fingers, white-knuckled, gripped the shears. "I suppose she thought you'd want to cut off the burned part of your hair."

"Oh. That makes sense." His voice sounded husky—from the smoke, she imagined. But whatever the reason, his deep, guttural words seemed to vibrate through her bones. He tossed away the towel and grabbed her father's shirt. "Will you cut it for me?"

"Me? Cut your hair?" Her breath was coming short. He dropped the shirt over his head and tugged it into place. Though it was a bit small, it did cover him sufficiently.

She couldn't decide whether she found that a relief or a disappointment.

"Well, I cannot cut it myself, not and make a good job of it," he said reasonably, shoving the bottom of the shirt down into his breeches. "Most of it's on the back of my head," he added.

"It? Oh, your hair. Yes. I suppose it is." She began to clear her throat, but when that hurt, she coughed instead. "Sit down, and I'll do my best to cut it."

"I cannot." He indicated his filthy breeches and the cream-colored upholstery. "Can you stand?"

She did, though her knees felt shaky. Her illness must be worsening. Her arms felt weak when she raised the scissors and began snipping off the scorched hair. It smelled awful and looked even worse.

"I'm so sorry," she said from behind him, mourning the gorgeous mane.

He shrugged, the shirt stretching across his wide shoulders. "It was my only vanity. It's probably as well that it's gone. I'll have more time for my work now that I won't be caring for it."

He was obviously jesting, and she laughed at the mental image of a valet combing out Rand's hair and rubbing sweet-smelling oils into it, as Lily's maid did every night.

She was glad he wasn't angry. And her animals were safe. Her heart swelled as she carefully snipped. "Why?" she asked quietly.

"Why what?"

"Why did you risk your life to save them?" She watched his face in a big gilt-framed mirror on the wall. "You don't even like animals."

"I don't *dislike* animals, and I'd certainly never want to see any creature suffer. Just because they're not the center of my existence doesn't mean I don't care."

"Oh." It sounded so simple when he put it that way. So reasonable. So Rand. And she wanted to say that animals weren't the center of *her* existence, either. That though every life had worth, people—especially deserving people like him —were dearer to her than all else.

But she shouldn't be saying something like that, because he might get the wrong idea. And then she might be tempted to break her promise to Rose, and then—

"But if you want the real truth," he continued, "I wasn't thinking of the animals when I saved them. I went in looking for you, afraid you might be trying to save them yourself. And then, when you weren't there—" He swallowed, then grimaced and massaged his throat. "When I rescued those creatures, I was thinking of you, Lily, and how you'd feel if they perished."

She stopped snipping and began coughing again. It was one thing to have risked his life for her animals, quite another to have done it for *her*. He couldn't...she couldn't...

"Lily?"

"I'm almost finished." She cleared her throat painfully and made a few more cuts. But it was hard to concentrate, because she was afraid she'd just fallen in love.

She hadn't seen him in a week—a week she'd spent alternating between guilt-ridden tiptoeing around Rose and equally guilt-ridden daydreaming about Rand. A week in which she'd grown more certain of her feelings with each passing day, while her sister only grew more desperate.

By now it was clear to everyone but Rose that her cause was hopeless. Rand was never to be hers.

And Lily had a terrible fear that after this—this impossibly selfless, wonderful thing that he'd done for her—her own cause was similarly doomed. Just as the illness was draining her strength, Rand's kindness was eroding her resolve. She felt her supposed commitment to family loyalty weakening amidst an onslaught of powerful feelings. Gratitude, admiration, longing, and others too tangled to discern. Was Violet wrong about the human will? Was it only a matter of time before emotion overcame rationality?

When Rand suddenly turned and met her eyes, Lily had to lock her knees to keep them from buckling.

"Are you finished?"

"I think so." She sneezed, and then coughed, and then gave a long, deep, miserable sniffle. "Yes, I'm finished."

"You should go to bed, then. I'll walk you to your chamber."

"Rand, you cannot."

"Of course I can." He took her arm and began marching her toward the staircase. "You're ill and I'm exhausted. I can assure you nothing untoward will happen."

Truth be told, she was glad for his support as she trudged up the steps. Beatrix appeared and followed behind. "Thank you," Lily said primly when Rand had delivered her to her door.

"Go on, get in bed."

Supposing he wouldn't leave her alone until he saw her settled, she sighed and picked up the cat, then climbed under the covers, still wearing her wrapper. "Thank you," she said again.

Rand remained standing on the threshold. "May I come in?"

Lily's pulse skipped, and Beatrix began hiccuping. "That would be quite improper."

"Your mother left us alone."

"She does things like that. Mum has never been overly concerned with propriety." When she sneezed, embarrassingly loudly, Beatrix leapt to the floor. "At least so long as others are not around to observe."

"Ah," he said, "I remember. The Ashcroft motto. *Interroga Conformationem*, Question Convention." He glanced down to where Beatrix was ribboning between his legs, rubbing against his smudged boots. "What on earth is she doing?"

"She likes you."

"Why?"

Lily shrugged. "Why not?"

"I'm a dog person." In an attempt to get away, he sidled into the room, apparently forgetting that Lily hadn't granted permission. Bored by his disinterest, Beatrix scampered out the window to join Jasper on a tree branch right outside.

Rand immediately strode to the window. "There's ash drifting in," he said as he slammed it shut. When he turned, he stood stock still and looked around.

Lily followed his roaming gaze, trying to envision her bedchamber through his eyes while she dabbed her stuffy nose with a white-on-white monogrammed handkerchief.

A plush white carpet covered much of the dark oak floor. Her bed was hung with white lace panels and piled with plump white pillows. More white lace draped the windows. Her dressing table and washstand boasted white marble tops.

"It's very white," he finally said. From his tone, she guessed *white* actually meant something else. Immature, maybe. Babyish.

She blushed, then grimaced, knowing her cheeks now matched her red nose and eyes. She watched him wander to the mirror above her dressing table. It was framed, of course, in white.

He stared at himself, skimming his fingers along the bottom of his hair, which now ended short of his shoulders. "Do I look bad?"

"No. Only different. You...I suppose you could wear a periwig," she added, hoping he wouldn't, although most noblemen did.

He turned from the mirror. "Absolutely not."

She nodded, absurdly relieved. Even now, Rand's hair was too pretty to cover up, all those shimmering colors mixed together, strands of it sticking to his still-sweat-slicked brow.

Goodness, what was it with her and *sweat*, all of a sudden? The substance was wet and sticky and uncomfortable, and she'd never had any positive feelings toward it before! But there was something about a sweat-coated Rand that was just so...

Manly. There was no other word for it.

Lily chewed her lip. In point of fact, he was—damp or dry, long-haired or short—magnificent. So magnificent that her throat tightened just looking at him, and it was sore, so that made it hurt, and anyway, she couldn't tell him how magnificent he was, because that might give him the wrong idea.

He'd worried that she might have been in the barn. He'd saved her animals. She was afraid she might love him, for that and for so many other things, too.

What in heaven's name was she supposed to do now?

Nothing, she reminded herself savagely. She'd made a promise. One she wished she'd never made—was sorely tempted to cast aside—had already violated in spirit if not in letter—but a promise nonetheless. The fact that it was a foolish and battered promise did not diminish her obligation, nor minimize the damage she would cause to both her sister and herself by breaking it.

"I'm tired," she said, which was an understatement. "Could you possibly leave now?"

He didn't. Instead, he walked over, leaned down, and pressed his lips to hers. His eyes remained open, daring her to object.

She didn't. She melted immediately. He tasted of Rand and salt, but also of the smoke he'd encountered rescuing her strays.

When he drew back, he looked blurry, and she felt disgusted with her weakness. In a daze, she blinked her eyes to clear them. "I don't understand."

Completely uninvited, and apparently forgetting his stained breeches, he flattened white lace and sat beside her on the bed. "Understand what, my sweet?"

She blinked again at the endearment. "How can you want to kiss me when I'm ill and ugly and lying in this stupid white room?"

"You're not ugly." He grazed his knuckles along her heated cheek. Despite being overwarm, she shivered. "You'll always be beautiful to me," he said in a way that convinced her he meant it.

Unless she was simply delirious with fever. But his startling gray eyes looked perfectly sincere.

He'd said he was falling in love with her. She still remembered that. She'd been thinking about that all week, at times even getting angry—her, Lily, angry!—with Rose for so stubbornly standing in her way.

But Rose would never, ever forgive her...

"I missed you," she blurted out without thought. "This past week, I've missed you."

Rand's fingers stilled as he gazed at her in surprise.

Had anyone else ever missed him? Really missed him? He seriously doubted it. He had friends, of course—Ford and Kit the best of them—but they all had busy lives. They could spend months apart without truly missing one another.

For Lily to miss him seemed a great gift. An honor he could only hope to deserve.

"I missed you, too," he said after a moment, because he couldn't think of a way to put it better. He kissed her again, hoping his lips would tell her what he couldn't seem to put into words. Feeling the heat of her skin, he made it a brief kiss, but no less heartfelt.

"Rand?" Lily murmured weakly when he pulled away. Her eyes flicked open, squeezed shut. And then she uttered, "I'm sorry, Rose," in a pained whisper.

Refusing to register the rejection in her look, he brushed a damp curl from her forehead. "I'll come see you again tomorrow afternoon, Lily. I hope by then you'll be feeling better."

As he rose and quit the room, he remembered Ford saying he had to show Lily he loved her. And his unhelpful advice: *That's your problem, my friend.*

Closing her door behind him, Rand ran his tongue over his teeth.

If running into a burning building hadn't been enough, what else could he possibly do?

TWENTY-THREE

*T*HE NEXT DAY, Lily was feeling somewhat better and refused to stay in bed. Having always believed that looking better made one feel better, she chose a pretty periwinkle gown. When her maid dressed her hair, she asked her to wind silver ribbons through the curls to match the trim on her dress.

None of this, of course, had anything to do with the fact that Rand had said he'd be paying a call.

As her maid was finishing up, Rowan wandered in, looking much worse than she felt. His black hair stuck up in places, as though he'd been plowing his fingers through it, and his eyes appeared dark and haunted.

Lily nodded permission for the maid to take her leave, then turned to face her brother. "Rowan, what's wrong?"

"I'm just..." He came closer and began playing with a perfume bottle on the dressing table where she was seated. "Did you tell Father and Mum about the fire-making things I took from Ford's laboratory?"

"No, of course I didn't." She rubbed a hand over the back

of his head, smoothing his mussed hair. "That was between us."

His narrow shoulders relaxed, then tensed again. "How about Rose? Did Rose tell them?"

"Not that I know of. Why are you so worried about this? It was a mistake, and you learned not to take things, didn't you? Everyone makes mistakes."

The bottle made a rhythmic noise as he ran it back and forth on the marble tabletop, its gold painted designs glinting in the sun from the window. "I thought...well, I thought maybe Father and Mum would think I started the fire with the fire-making things. But I didn't have any of those things, I swear. I gave them all to Lord Randal, and I haven't taken any more from Ford's laboratory. Truly, Lily, I haven't." His hand stilled as he met her gaze in the mirror. "I...I just don't want anyone to think the barn burned down because I was playing with Mr. Boyle's fire-making things."

"Nobody thinks that. Has anyone said that to you?"

He shook his head.

"Nobody is blaming anyone for starting the fire. These things happen, and we're all happy that no one was hurt. It was an old barn that Father was planning to replace anyway."

He looked relieved—almost—before he resumed playing with the bottle, making circles this time. "You know what you said about making mistakes? How everyone makes mistakes?"

"Yes, everyone does." Goodness, did she know. She may have made the worst mistake of her life promising Rose.

"Well, I made one," Rowan said. "A really bad one. I thought something would be funny, but it wasn't. It went wrong, and it wasn't funny at all."

Her promise had gone wrong, too. Horribly wrong.

But knowing her brother, she was sure his mistake had

been nothing like hers. Lucky for him, he wasn't old enough to make such a monumental mistake. A mistake serious enough to ruin his whole life.

She put her hand over his, stopping the motion. "Was it a practical joke?"

Not looking at her, he nodded.

"Sometimes," she said, "we don't think things through before we do them." She hadn't thought at all before making that promise. Not for one moment. If she'd stopped to think, maybe she would have said no.

"But I feel terrible, Lily."

She raised a hand to turn his chin toward her, meeting his regretful green gaze. "If it was truly an honest mistake, you cannot let it make you feel so terrible. Just learn from it and act differently in the future. This mistake—did anyone get hurt?"

He shook his head violently.

"Then don't be too hard on yourself. You shouldn't suffer for the rest of your life because of one simple mistake."

"Are you sure?"

"I'm sure."

"Don't you even want to know what happened?"

"No. It's between you and your conscience," she told him, glad to find he had one. Her brother was growing up. Besides, it had only been a misfired prank. "Do you want to tell me?"

"No." He smiled, a true smile. "You're right. I shouldn't suffer for the rest of my life. I think I'll ride over to Benjamin's house and see if he wants to go fishing."

"You do that," she said. And with one more grin, he was off, knocking over the pretty bottle in his mad rush to leave.

She righted the blown-glass container, wishing she could right her own wrong so easily. Hers had been a simple mistake, too, an honest mistake. A promise she'd made impulsively, never guessing she'd come to regret it. How could she have known? What were the odds that the one gentleman Rose had ever seriously wanted would turn out to be Lily's perfect match?

The gentleman in question would be here this afternoon, and she hadn't the faintest idea what she'd say to him. But he wouldn't arrive for hours yet. Feeling restless but not up to anything strenuous, she decided to closet herself in the drawing room and soothe her nerves with some music.

When the gilt mantel clock chimed noon, Parkinson ushered her friend Judith inside.

"Keep playing," Judith said with a wave of one plump hand. She walked closer and brushed her fingers over a striking new flower arrangement that Rose had set on a small table beside the harpsichord. "What's this song?"

"I'm not sure." Her fingers flying over the keys, Lily smiled. "Rand hums the tune sometimes."

"It's cheerful."

"I thought if I could work out the notes, he might enjoy hearing it, whatever it is. He told me he would visit this afternoon, so—"

"Visit you in specific?" Judith looked delighted. "I knew there was something between you. Has he asked your father for your hand?"

"No!" Lily's fingers stilled, the abrupt silence a statement all its own. "You know I've been told I can make my own decision," she said quietly. "And besides, Rose claimed him first."

Judith sat beside her on the bench. "You look sad," she observed. "Do you wish *you'd* claimed him first, Lily?"

"Does it matter? Rose is older." Lily coughed. "I cannot wed before her."

"Nonsense. You can if you're in love." Judith pulled at a thread on her apple-green bodice while Lily coughed some more. "I would give anything to be in love with Lord Grenville."

Maybe Judith was right. If Lily truly loved Rand, should she suffer all her life because she'd made a simple mistake? What had she told Rowan?

But unlike Rowan's mistake where no one had been hurt, breaking her promise would hurt someone. Someone she loved dearly, even though she was cross with her now.

Lily gazed at her friend, tears welling in her eyes for them both. Then she gave an enormous sneeze—a sneeze that made the flowers beside the harpsichord quiver.

They both laughed as she pulled a handkerchief from her sleeve and noisily blew her nose.

"Lily," Judith said. "I'm so sorry I made you ill."

"It was worth it to see your wedding gown." Wiping her eyes, Lily smiled. "You're better now?"

"Much. I was really very ill for only a single day. The next day I was a little better, and the day following that, I was almost good as new."

"Well, I was very ill yesterday, and I feel better today, so tomorrow I shall be good as new, too."

"You're so nice." Judith's golden curls swished as she shook her head, her voice laced with admiration. "How do you do it?"

Lily shrugged. "I'm not all that nice." She didn't feel all that nice, not inside, not when she was deceiving Rose.

"Yes, you are. Most folks wouldn't be so charitable if a friend made them ill. But you're always ever so nice."

"It's the only talent I have, being nice," Lily said. "Violet is intellectual and ambitious, and Rose can speak half a dozen languages and create beautiful flower arrangements. I'm just nice." When her friend stared at her disbelievingly, she bristled. "It's what I am, Judith. If I wasn't nice to everyone, I'd be nothing."

"You're not nice to everyone," Judith argued.

"I'm not?" The two words came out faint and forlorn. Lily swallowed hard, ignoring her sore throat. "I try to be nice."

"You're not nice to *you*," Judith told her impatiently. "You put everyone else first."

"But that's the *nice* thing to do."

"You're so worried about everyone else's happiness, I think you forget about seeing to your own. Stop being so nice, and I think you'll be happier." Frowning, Judith glanced out the window. Her eyes widened. "There he is now."

"Who?"

"Rand." Judith blushed. "Lord Randal, I mean. Upon my word, he's handsome. What happened to his hair?"

"Did you not hear our barn burned? While he was rescuing my animals, his hair caught fire, and he had to cut it." Lily rose and went to the window, just in time to see Rand slide off his horse—and be greeted by her sister.

"He saved your animals? Oh, Lily, that's so romantic."

"It was very kind." She watched Rose laugh and take Rand by the arm, leading him toward the small redbrick summerhouse. Though he looked confused, he shrugged and went along.

Lily froze for a moment, feeling betrayed. By Rose? By Rand? Then she told herself not to be silly—Rose probably just wanted to show him something. Perhaps she was working on some flower displays in the summerhouse. And Rand certainly had no obligation to avoid Rose—not after Lily had repeatedly refused his suit.

Then Rose turned to say something to Rand, and Lily saw her face. Animated. Too animated for languid Rose.

"She's up to something," Judith said beside her.

Exactly what Lily had been thinking.

"Come along." Judith took her by the arm. Firmly. "We're going to investigate."

"Investigate?" Lily stared at her friend. "You mean *spy* on my sister?"

"She would spy on you in a heartbeat." When Lily didn't budge, Judith turned her to face the window. "Look. They're both gone. She's taken him into the summerhouse." She pulled on Lily's arm. "Come along. You cannot tell me you don't want to see what Rose is doing in there."

Since Lily couldn't honestly tell her that, she went. She felt like a sorry excuse for a sister, spying on Rose, but she couldn't seem to help herself.

By the time they made it outside, they were both running. When they stopped before one of the round summerhouse's four doors and Lily reached for the latch, Judith closed a hand over her fingers. "Wait," she whispered. "Listen."

"Judith!" Lily protested, her voice hushed but fierce. "There's spying, and then there is *spying*. I refuse to—"

And then she was *spying* despite herself—riveted in place by the conversation that drifted from inside.

TWENTY-FOUR

"I'M FLATTERED, my lady," Rand's wry voice came through the door. "But as it happens, I've set my sights elsewhere." He sneezed. "Pardon me. I seem to be coming down with something. Where are those flowers you wanted to show me?"

"Gemini! They seem to have disappeared." Lily heard Rose's practiced laugh, a tinkling, feminine sound. "Perhaps a kiss might compensate for the loss?"

On the other side of the door, Lily was so aghast she could find no words to express her feelings. "Poor Rand has caught my illness," she whispered irrelevantly.

"How is that?" Judith whispered back. As Lily blushed, her friend's pale blue eyes widened. "Oh, my word! He kissed you, didn't he?"

"Why should you think so? I caught your illness without kissing *you*."

"I can see it in your face," Judith declared. "You—"

"Hush. I cannot hear." Lily wondered if Rand and Rose were kissing.

No. Rose was talking. "I wonder," she mused in a speculative tone, "if the lady you've set your sights on has ten thousand pounds to bring to a marriage. It seems to me a mere professor could use that sort of money. A windfall like that would allow you to live the gentlemanly life you were born to."

Judith's mouth dropped open. "She must be desperate," she said over whatever Rand replied. "I cannot imagine—"

"Hush!"

"And I wonder…" When Rose paused, Lily imagined her trailing a fingertip down Rand's arm, as she'd seen her sister do with other young men. She was relieved when Rose continued talking. "I wonder what my father, who is out in his gardens as always, would do if he found the two of us alone in here, hmm?"

Lily gasped. "That's so unfair to Rand, threatening to trap him like that! She's the one who lured him in there!"

"Unfair to *him*?" Judith's whisper came through gritted teeth. "How about *you*, Lily? Is Rose not being unfair to you?"

"Rose would never hurt me on purpose! I'm certain she has no idea how I feel about Rand."

"Well, then, it's about time she found out," Judith said, and with that, she flung open the door.

Since Rand was opening it at the same time, Judith fell into his arms, landing with a thud against his chest. He took the time to steady her before stepping away. "Pardon me, my lady. I was just leaving."

"Thank you, my lord," Judith said dreamily.

Rand had that effect on women, Lily thought wryly, and followed her friend into the summerhouse. She cleared her sore throat. "Lord Randal Nesbitt, may I present my dear friend, Lady Judith Carrington?"

"I'm pleased to make your acquaintance," Judith said in a breathless tone that Lily found vexing.

"The pleasure is mine," Rand replied politely. "But I'm afraid I must take my leave."

"No." Apparently regaining her wits, Judith cast a glance to where Rose stood in the shadows. "It's Rose who's leaving." She marched over and took Rose by the arm. "Come along, Rose."

Rose planted her feet. "I'm not finished talking to Lord Randal."

Slender Rose was no match for Judith's solid build. "Oh, yes, you are." Undeterred, Judith hauled her out the door.

"You're supposed to be my friend," Rose protested loudly as she found herself dragged through the gardens.

"I *am* your friend." Judith's voice was growing fainter. "And as your friend, I insist on saving you from further embarrassing yourself."

Rose's reply was inaudible. Lily and Rand were alone. An expectant silence filled the cool, shaded summerhouse.

Rand sneezed.

"I'm sorry," they both said together.

He cracked a smile. "What are *you* sorry for?"

"I'm sorry you had to put up with my sister's nonsense."

"I'm sorry you had to overhear it."

"I'm sorry I made you ill."

His smile widened. "Ah, but I'm *not* sorry I kissed you."

"I'm sorry you're not kissing me now."

"I'm sor—what?"

He blinked and took a step closer, and Lily took a step closer, and they met in the middle.

Everything that had been holding her back had suddenly vanished, like the moon on a cloudy night. Something inside her had shifted. Never in her life had she been so angry with another person, much less with one of her own flesh and blood. She was too furious to think straight. How *could* Rose

—it was so completely shocking—she must be the most self-ish, underhanded—and to call him a *mere* professor—!

There was nothing *mere* about Rand. Not one thing. His form was towering and solid in her arms. His lips moved with devastating deftness over hers. He had the silkiest hair, the manliest scent, the kindest soul she'd ever known.

Rose didn't deserve him.

But Lily didn't want to think about Rose. Now that she could kiss Rand without so much as a twinge of guilt, all she wanted was to keep kissing Rand for as long as possible. Now that she could be close to him and touch him and taste him, untainted for the first time, she realized the truth.

He was all she wanted for the rest of her life. She was in love. And loving Rand was the most precious gift in all of God's creation.

A laugh bubbled out of her, the noise joyous to her own ears. Her heart felt light enough to escape her chest and float away. How giddy and strange she felt. Rose had put Rand in a very awkward position, and Lily had witnessed it, and somehow, that had changed everything.

Lily's laugh was a sound of pure, ringing happiness, a sound Rand hadn't heard from her in weeks—maybe ever. It was a sound he perceived not with his ears, but with his heart. Though it startled him out of their kiss, it brought hope.

Love. Ford was right, this had to be love. It wasn't a comfortable emotion—it was far too huge and overpowering —but it was there. And it wasn't going away.

Now Rand just had to figure out what to do about it. Marry her, despite never having pictured himself marrying anyone? He thought of her sweetness, her faith in him, the way she made him feel.

Her essence.

Then he pictured letting that essence slip through his fingers, and the choice was obvious.

Never say never, he told himself ruefully, and took her hand. Lacing his fingers with hers, he drew a deep breath.

"Have you seen my ironclad spade?"

They both jumped, then turned to see Lily's father standing in the doorway. She felt Rand had been about to say something important, and she was impatient to discover what. In haste and agitation, she scanned the dim summerhouse.

There was no spade. There wasn't anything in here, in fact, save the narrow wooden benches attached to the circular wall. "It's not here, Father. Why don't you ask the head gardener?"

"Hmm," he said. "I was hoping it would be in here. Perhaps I should ask the head gardener." Muttering to himself, he turned and left.

Rand sneezed, using his free hand to block it. "Pardon me," he said thickly.

"You *are* falling ill."

He waved that away. "Your father didn't hear your suggestion."

She shrugged. "If he hears one suggestion in ten, I consider myself lucky."

"He wouldn't have said a thing had he found me alone with Rose, would he?" Sounding incredulous, Rand raised their still-joined hands. "He didn't even notice I was here."

"Well, what did you expect? You're not a flower." Lily smiled up at him. "Now, what were you going to say before my father interrupted?"

He gave one of his inscrutable smiles in return. "Lily, can I ask you a favor?"

Her heart sped up. "Of course."

"Will you play me a song?"

TWENTY-FIVE

"**P**ARDON?"** Lily blinked, unsure she'd heard right.

"I want you to play a song. On the harpsichord. And I'll sing."

"Now?"

"Now. Right now. In your family's drawing room. Will you do that for me, Lily?"

She nodded, although she was confused. She'd been rather expecting—or perhaps just hoping—to hear a question of a different nature. But there was little Rand could ask that she would refuse.

He led her outside by the hand. In the fickle way of summer, the sky had clouded up while they were in the summerhouse. Beatrix, Lady, and Jasper appeared and followed them back to the house. Claiming he didn't want an audience, Rand maneuvered to get through the door without allowing them inside.

The animals went around and entered through one of the drawing room's windows instead.

Lily sat at the harpsichord and arched her fingers over the

keys, then hesitated. Her nose was running. She pulled the handkerchief out of her sleeve and dabbed.

"Go ahead," Rand said. "Blow."

Love, she supposed, meant being able to blow your nose in front of the man. So she did, even though she was no timid nose-blower.

It didn't seem to scare him away. In fact, in the middle of her blow, he sneezed again, and then he fished a handkerchief out of his pocket and blew his own nose, too.

"We're wrecks," Lily said, thinking it felt strangely wonderful to comfortably share an illness. She faced the keyboard again. "What do you want me to play?" She suspected the tune she'd been practicing for him wasn't what he had in mind.

He thought for a moment. "Do you know the one that starts 'Let's love and let's laugh'?"

Like many popular songs, it had no title, but she did know it. She nodded.

He leaned against the harpsichord. "Then play it, please."

When she did, he held her gaze as he began to sing.

"Let's love and let's laugh,
Let's dance and let's sing;
While shrill echoes ring;
Our wishes agree,
And from care we are free,
Then who is so happy, so happy as we?"

Although there were three more verses, he stopped singing. She played a few more bars and then stopped, too.

For a moment, the room was completely still, even the animals frozen like statues.

"Did you hear that, Lily?"

"The words?" she wondered.

"The words fit us, don't they? But no, I didn't mean the words. What did you *hear*?"

"What did I hear?" she echoed faintly, feeling bewildered. But her heart began pumping a little faster. "It sounded good. *You* sound good. You have a beautiful voice."

He stepped closer. "But my voice doesn't sound nearly as good alone as it does together with your music. It doesn't sound as complete. What I mean to say is…" His face colored slightly, but he pressed on. "I want that with you, Lily. I want you to provide the melody for my songs. And I, the words to your tunes."

She gathered he was talking about more than music. Her blood rushed even faster. She held her breath, afraid she might wake herself from this dream.

"Don't say anything," he said, still watching her. "Not yet."

Lady chirped in the window, and Jasper chattered, and Beatrix wound around Rand's legs.

Yet those intense gray eyes seemed to see nothing but Lily.

"I'm just a professor," he said.

Rose's thoughtless words had affected him. For a moment, Lily's anger returned full force. "Rand, you aren't *just* anything. Not to me."

He slid onto the harpsichord's bench and took one of her hands. "No, listen. I *am* just a professor. I live in a house. Once it's finished it will be a nice house, but just a house all the same, not a mansion like Trentingham. And it isn't perched on land that stretches as far as the eye can see. It sits in the middle of a town with other buildings all around it."

Was he asking her to marry him, or explaining why he couldn't? "I don't care—" she started.

He stopped her by squeezing her hand. "I'm a second son. I may have the word *Lord* in front of my name, but that's only a courtesy title. I'll never sit in the House of Lords like your father. I could attend court if I wished, and London balls, but the fact is, I don't. Or I haven't," he corrected himself. "I'm willing to go to such events if doing so would please you, as long as it's not during term time."

This *was* a prelude to a proposal. Her breath caught, making her cough in reaction. "I don't care," she repeated. "Rand, I—"

"I'm not finished." He coughed, too, then furrowed his brow, as though he was trying hard to remember everything he wanted to say. "You should know that I earn a good living. But you should also know that it's been years since the marquess supplemented my income."

"The marquess?"

"My father. But like I said, I do well enough." His gaze swept her gown. "I expect I can afford to clothe you in the lovely manner to which you're accustomed," he added in a teasing tone.

She smoothed her periwinkle skirts. "I'd wear sackcloth to be with you," she said quietly. "You just sang of love and laughter. Money cannot buy that. Besides, I do have a marriage portion. Three thousand pounds."

Three thousand pounds was a more than respectable dowry, considering the average shopkeeper earned less than fifty pounds a year. But Rand didn't look as though he cared, as though the money mattered at all.

At their feet, Beatrix began hiccuping, and he leaned to pick her up. "What of your animals?"

It was startling to realize she hadn't considered them, even more startling to see Rand—an avowed dog person—with her cat on his lap.

He absently stroked Beatrix's striped fur. "I do have a garden," he started; but then a corner of his mouth curved up in a half smile. "Well, I don't expect your father would consider it a garden, but I've a patch of land behind my house. I can ask Kit to toss up a shelter of sorts…but it won't be the grand animal home you've been envisioning."

The fact that he cared about her aspirations made tears prick her eyes. "It sounds perfect, enough for the strays I have now. And once I'm ready to use my inheritance…well, I always envisioned building here at Trentingham, anyway. I can hire local people to care for the animals." She knew there were plenty who would appreciate the work, and she'd be pleased to provide it. "Perhaps I'll be able to visit—"

"Of course you will. Oxford isn't far, and I expect you'll want to see your family often."

"A positive statement," she observed, risking a tiny smile. "Does that mean you're finished trying to talk me out of…"

She couldn't say the rest of it. He hadn't, after all, actually asked her to marry him. And the possibility was so shockingly new to her, she hadn't yet thought it over. So she let the words hang there, waiting.

It seemed like forever.

"Yes," he said at last. He shifted to face her and took her other hand. His palms were cool and smooth, and his thumbs traced her knuckles. Her gaze flicked to the scars, but she wasn't embarrassed by them just now. He cleared his throat. " Since I've apparently failed to talk you out of it, what do you say, my sweet? Can we make music together for the rest of our lives?"

He spoke with a lighthearted air, as though the words were nothing more than banter.

But his heart was in his hypnotic eyes.

Unlike Rose, Lily admired Rand's success in the face of his family's disapproval. That strength was one of the things she loved about him—through good times and bad, a wife could depend on a husband like Rand. But she knew him better than Rose did. She knew that beneath the self-sufficiency lurked a lonely little boy who needed someone to hold him.

Did she want to be that someone? Was she willing to do it at the expense of her sister? Could she, for the first time in her life, put her own interests ahead of another's?

She remembered Rose's behavior in the summerhouse and knew the answer was *yes*.

And she didn't even have to say it. He read her response in her eyes, and both joy and relief leapt into his.

Then their lips met, and she'd never imagined she could feel such happiness. He was magnificent, and he was all hers. He kissed her over and over, and she wished he would never stop.

When he finally pulled away, they just looked at each other and laughed helplessly, until they both started coughing. Which only made them laugh harder.

Life was perfect, even with a stuffy nose.

TWENTY-SIX

*W*HEN LILY AND Rand told her mother they had news for the family, her eyes sparkled with delight.

"Since your father's already in the gardens," she said, "why don't you find him and then wait by the twenty-guinea oak? In the time it would take me to explain why I want him to come inside, I can gather everyone else and meet you there." A wide smile on her face, she hurried off.

It didn't take long to find Father, who happened to be weeding a flower bed near the oak, using a hook and a forked stick. Lily decided to let him continue puttering.

She and Rand waited beneath the tree. "I should have told Rose first," she suddenly realized, knowing her sister was going to be devastated. A stab of sympathy took her by surprise.

Rand shot a glance to her oblivious father before slipping an arm around her waist. "Because of your promise?"

"You knew?"

His arm curved, drawing her closer. "Your mother would never forgive you if you told your sister first."

"True," Lily murmured, realizing a second truth: She didn't want to tell Rose first. She wasn't ready to face her own anger or her sister's.

"Lily?" He tilted her face up and touched a finger to the dent in her chin. "You're supposed to be happy right now."

"I am," she said and smiled.

They parted when Rowan hurried out to meet them under the gigantic oak. "Benjamin couldn't fish," he said with a pout. "Mum said you have something to tell us?"

"Yes," Lily said, "we do."

"So what is it?"

She tweaked his nose. "You'll have to wait for everyone else."

With a small huff of impatience, he leapt to catch the lowest bough that branched off the huge, twisted trunk.

"It's a big tree," Rand commented, looking like he didn't quite know what to say to Lily's little brother. She supposed that living at a university, he mightn't have much experience with ten-year-old boys.

"Zounds, it's bigger than big." Rowan swung back and forth, looking up at the cloudy sky through the canopy of leaves. "This tree has been here for more than three hundred years. And Father says we must never chop it down, even though it destroys the symmetry of his gardens."

"Symmetry." Rand raised a brow. "That's a big word for a lad your age."

Hauling his feet up, Rowan crouched on the big branch and began climbing. "I know," he said proudly, his voice drifting from above. "What does it mean?"

Rand and Lily both laughed.

"What's that?" Father demanded, noticing all of them at last. Lily laughed even harder, her amusement earning her a volley of coughs.

"It means balanced proportions," Rand said loudly enough for even her father to hear.

"Ah, symmetry," Father said. "You know, I've been advised to chop down this twenty-guinea oak for the sake of symmetry."

Amid more laughter, Rand moved closer to Lily's father so the older man could hear him better. Rand was patient with him, she thought. Not many young men would be.

Yet another reason to love Rand Nesbitt.

He raised his voice. "Why do you call it the twenty-guinea oak?"

Father smiled, always eager to answer that question, eager to tell the story that Lily had heard countless times. "A passing timber merchant once offered me ten guineas for the wood, saying it was quite the most enormous tree he'd ever seen."

"Ten guineas, not twenty?"

"I'm getting to that," Father said. "Well, the truth was, I'd been thinking of chopping the old boy down anyway, seeing as it impairs the symmetry of this garden. But I'm not one to act too rashly, you see, and so I told the merchant I'd like to think about his offer overnight. Next morning, bright and early, the fellow was at my door, increasing his offer to twenty guineas." Father waved the long, pointed tool in his hand. "I figured that if the wood's value could increase by a hundred percent overnight, the tree was an investment worth keeping."

Rand laughed out loud, and Father grinned. Lily was glad they seemed to get along. But her smile faded when her mother arrived with Rose and Judith.

The gray sky might be threatening a gentle summer rain, but Rose's expression looked like thunder.

Fresh sympathy tightened Lily's sore throat.

Rowan dropped from the tree. "We're all here now. What is it you were wanting to tell us? Is it something happy?"

It was, for her and Rand. Lily's emotions were riding a seesaw, and despite her confusion, her smile returned to her face. "Lord Randal has asked me to marry him."

Suddenly everyone was talking at once.

Mum threw her arms around her. "I knew it! Congratulations, dear."

"Can Jewel come to the wedding?" Rowan asked.

"No," their mother said. "Jewel is related to Violet's husband, not Lily's." She kissed both of Lily's cheeks, then pulled back and winked. "Even though I didn't arrange the marriage, I wish you every happiness." Not one to stand on ceremony, she turned into Rand's arms next. "Welcome to the family."

"Thank you," he said, hugging her back rather awkwardly. Lily gave him credit for trying, knowing her family could be overwhelming.

Rowan tugged on her gown. "Lily?"

She kissed his forehead, laughing when he blushed and pulled away. "Jewel may attend," she told him, "if her parents agree." She wanted her brother to be happy, too, and after all, it was *her* wedding. She ought to have a say in the guest list.

Her wedding, she thought in a daze. It still didn't seem real.

"What's all this?" Father asked.

Rand cleared his throat and raised his voice. "With your permission, sir, I'd like the honor of wedding your daughter."

"If you know my daughter well enough to wed her," Father bellowed back, "you know she's not about to ask my permission. None of my flowers ask me before doing anything."

"We can all hear, darling," Mum reminded him. But he

had Lily wrapped in a hug and wasn't paying attention. When he released her, he turned to shake Rand's hand.

"Well done," he yelled, and Lily just smiled and shook her head. If Rand could get through this day with her family, she reckoned he would learn to fit in just fine.

Judith tapped her on the shoulder, her pretty face lit up with a grin. "We're going to become old married ladies together!"

Lily gave her friend a hard hug, wishing Judith could be as happy about her own wedding. "Let's get married before we worry about growing old."

"Yes," Rose said, "*I'm* the one who's old."

Finally, having put it off as long as she could, Lily turned to her sister.

Rose's dark eyes were black with fury. "How could you?"

How could she *what*? Lily wondered.

What did her sister mean by those three words? How could she break her promise? How could she marry before her older sister? How could she steal the husband Rose had wanted? How could she be so selfish as to secure her own happiness?

All of it, undoubtedly, Lily thought with a resigned sigh. But while her heart grieved for her sister's pain, and she regretted her part in causing it, she refused to accept the guilt. In her view, Rose had forfeited whatever claim she had on Rand by her abusive treatment of him earlier that afternoon.

And though Lily loved her no less, and would forgive her in time, she would not reward her sister's folly with deference. Rose's misery was of her own making, and though it aroused Lily's compassion, she would not end that misery with a sacrifice.

Wanting to explain—in language softer than her present feelings, if she could manage it—Lily took her sister's arm to draw her aside.

Rose shook her off. "Don't touch me," she hissed, though she did move away from the others, closer to the oak. "You promised! You said you'd help, and then you told me to do the wrong thing on purpose." As she talked, she advanced on Lily, backing her into the oak. "I went to Lakefield every day to offer my assistance with the translation, but he wouldn't even see me." Her face was right in Lily's, her eyes flashing fire. "I always knew showing my intellect was the wrong way to get a gentleman worth having!"

The rough bark bit into Lily's back, and she hit her head against it, trying to gain some distance from Rose's venom. "No, it isn't," she protested. "It's the right way. Rand was just the wrong gentleman."

"Oh, and I'm supposed to trust *your* word?" With a huff and a swish of her skirts, Rose whirled away.

Shaking, Lily walked back to the others.

"I think we shall have a picnic tomorrow to celebrate," Mum was saying brightly. "With champagne."

Rowan made a face. "No champagne."

"You don't have to drink any," Lily said woodenly, rubbing her head where it hurt. She looked up at the sky and wished she felt more like celebrating. "It will probably be raining anyway."

"Nonsense," Mum said. "If it rains tonight, it shall be clear and beautiful tomorrow."

"A picnic sounds very nice." Shooting Rose a concerned glance where she still stood near the tree, Rand moved to take Lily's hand. "Thank you, Lady Trentingham. And I shall venture to invite your family to Oxford the day after, if you're amenable. Lily ought to see her new home, don't you think? I'll give you all the grand tour, and you can stay overnight. I've no furniture yet in my house, save in the one room I've been using to sleep, but a respectable inn lies directly behind it."

"An inn," Rowan breathed. "May we go, Mum?" He looked more excited about the journey than he had about the picnic—or the marriage, for that matter.

"We've stayed at an inn only once since Rowan was born," Mum explained to Rand, "and he was too young to remember." She smiled at her son. "Yes, Rowan, I expect that we can go. I should like to see where my daughter will be living. And Rose always enjoys traveling, don't you, Rose?"

She looked to Rose, but Rose wasn't there.

Lily turned just in time to see her march up the portico steps and slam into the house.

"I'll go after her," Judith said fretfully.

"No, I'll talk to her." Mum started toward the house, then paused to look back at Lily. "Don't worry, dear. You've done nothing wrong, but she's hurting now, and I can't say I really blame her. She'll come to terms with it sooner or later."

"I hope it will be sooner," Lily said in a small voice.

She loved Rand. But if her own sister couldn't be happy for her, could she be truly happy herself?

TWENTY-SEVEN

"**W**ELL, CHRYSANTHEMUM,**" Joseph said as she crawled into bed that night, "your daughter is betrothed as planned. Are you happy?"

"Happy? I'm not sure who's more miserable, Rose or Lily. Or me."

Rand and Judith had left. Rose had taken supper in her room. Chrystabel had spent over an hour trying to soothe her, then another trying to assure Lily that her sister wasn't lost to her forever.

Rain pattered on the window, spelling doom for her picnic, and a headache was brewing, relentlessly hammering her temples. She hated when everything didn't go as she'd planned.

"Move closer," Joseph said. "I'll rub your shoulders."

She did, snuggling into the feather mattress and sighing when his hands went to work. For a spell she just lay there, letting his fingers knead away her tension.

"Better?" he asked after a while.

"Getting there." The pounding in her temples was fading

to a mere annoyance. "I'm afraid Lily might change her mind."

"No, she won't." He rubbed circles on the small of her back. "She's in love."

"You finally noticed?"

Running his thumbs down her spine, he snorted. "I haven't the talent you seem to possess of discerning a person's feelings by the look in his or her eyes. I know she's in love because you told me."

"Ahh." The sound was half agreement, half bliss. "Lily is feeling very badly, though, that Rose is in pain. I'm afraid she'll break the betrothal because her sister is unhappy. Choose her relationship with Rose over Rand."

"Have you no sympathy for Rose?"

"Of course I do. She's my daughter, and I ache for her, never mind that she and Rand were all wrong for each other. I understand why she feels betrayed. And yes, her actions in the summerhouse were shameful, but I don't believe for a minute that she's truly that calculating. I fancy she sensed Rand slipping away and acted unthinkingly, out of desperation. Alas, our Rose never has been one to think before words leave her mouth. But she doesn't truly love Rand, and Lily does, which is why I'm worried that the betrothal...um...Joseph?" His hands had ceased their sublime services. "Might you continue just a *little* longer?"

He chuckled and resumed his task. "I was only scratching my nose. And try not to worry too much. I'm sure Rose will recover."

"Of course she will. She'll be after another gentleman within the week. Which is why I'm more concerned about Lily at the moment." She paused, listening to the soft rain. "I hope this unlucky rain ceases by tomorrow."

"Couldn't you just move the picnic inside? Perhaps to the

dining room, where civilized people usually eat?" His ribbing was as gentle as his fingers massaging her neck.

"Hmmph. Perhaps." She would have swatted her husband had she been at all inclined to move. "But the dining room is a much more intimate space than the gardens, and I fear asking Rose to share a table with the happy couple just now…while everything is still quite raw between them…"

"But shall Rose—darling, your shoulders have tensed up again—shall Rose even deign to attend? The occasion cannot give her much pleasure."

Chrystabel forced her muscles to relax. "She told me she'll not hide herself away and have Rand think her pining for him. She means to attend."

"Then perhaps we must disinvite her."

Chrystabel was horrified. "What, and shall we dress her in rags and cast her out in the lane while we're at it?"

"Your shoulders, Chrysanthemum. I wasn't suggesting expelling Rose from a family picnic—that would be indefensible. But what if it were a private picnic instead?"

"A private picnic?" Now Chrystabel grew thoughtful. "You mean to let Lily and Rand dine alone? Unchaperoned?"

"You let Violet and Ford meet unchaperoned before they wed."

"Yes, and look what nearly happened!" When Chrystabel had been stealthily arranging her eldest daughter's marriage, in desperation she'd allowed Violet to pay a late-night visit to Lakefield House. Thanks be to heaven, her daughter's reputation had ultimately come through unscathed, but it had been a close thing. "I'll not repeat my mistakes by risking another daughter's virtue. Though I've contrived to get them alone together for a few minutes here and there, the length of a whole meal is…however, perhaps there is a compromise…"

In silence she pondered a few more minutes while Joseph kneaded away. The last of her stiffness and discomfort had dissipated by the time she settled on the superiority of this new plan.

With renewed energy, she moved to kiss her dear husband. "I hope the rain continues tomorrow," she said with a sly grin, reversing her earlier wish.

Joseph chuckled. "That's my girl."

TWENTY-EIGHT

*T*HE SOFT DRIZZLE of the night before had given way to real rain today, but Rand borrowed Ford's old carriage and rode to Trentingham even though it was obvious there wouldn't be a picnic.

He was surprised when Lady Trentingham came to meet him, carrying one of the new umbrellas imported from France. As he climbed down, she stepped closer than he would have expected and held the contraption over both of their heads. "Come along!" she said. "My skirts are getting wet."

Obediently he walked beside her, feeling silly under the expanse of oiled canvas. Only women carried umbrellas— only wealthy women, come to that. Rich or poor, men wore hats and got drenched. "Where are we going?" he asked.

"To the picnic, of course." Both her hands clenched on the curved ebony handle, she hurried him through the gardens. "What with the disappointing weather, I decided to set it up in the summerhouse. I was nearly finished when I heard your carriage arrive. Here we are." She stopped before one of the four arched oak doors.

He opened it, blinking at the dimness beneath the dome. It was empty—of people, in any case. Though it was a bit hard to tell in the gloom of the dreary day, there seemed to be items inside that hadn't been there the day before.

"Go on in," she told him, shifting the umbrella to one hand to fish a little paper package out of her pocket with the other. She gave it to him. "Light the candles. I'll go fetch Lily."

As she went back through the gardens, almost but not quite running in her fashionable Louis heels, he unfolded the package and found a few more of Mr. Boyle's fire-making things. He drew one of the sulfured sticks through a fold of the paper and began lighting candles.

There seemed to be dozens of them spaced out on the benches along the wall. After nearly tripping over something in the center of the summerhouse, he decided to skirt the perimeter instead.

When he was finished, the little circular chamber was alight with a cheerful glow. Plenty enough to illuminate the "picnic" Lady Trentingham had set out on the benches. Platters of fruit, bread, sliced cheese, and sweets. A bottle of champagne and two goblets.

Only two?

He stared at them, puzzled, until Lily blew in through the same door, wearing a summery apricot gown that belied the rainy day.

Lily's mother stood on the threshold, the front of her umbrella dripping onto the bricks. "Well, then, will you two be wanting anything else?"

Rand glanced at Lily, but she looked as confused as he felt. "Where is the rest of the family?" he asked.

The countess waved a hand. "Sadly, there's not enough room." She didn't look particularly sad. "I didn't want you and Lily to miss your betrothal picnic, but the summerhouse is rather cramped, don't you think?"

"We could take everything into the house," Rand suggested.

"Heavens, no. It wouldn't be a picnic in the house."

He couldn't see why that should signify, but as this new arrangement was rather to his liking, he kept silent.

"All the doors are open," Lily said slowly, and Rand glanced around to see that all four entrances to the round structure were indeed flung wide. Passersby on any side would be able to observe their picnic.

"Yes, isn't the sound of the rain lovely? Well," Lady Trentingham concluded, retreating with a gracious smile, "pray enjoy yourselves! I shall pop by in a few minutes to see how you get on."

"Please don't trouble yourself," Rand began.

"It's no trouble," she said brightly. "Though I beg leave to excuse myself from the party, I mean not to neglect the guests of honor!"

And with that she was gone.

Removing his wide-brimmed hat, Rand shook his head, impressed by how artfully the countess had ensured their good behavior. "Clever woman," he muttered to himself.

"You'll get used to it," Lily chimed in, plucking a grape off a bunch.

Startled when something moved against his leg, Rand glanced down to see Beatrix winding between his feet. He looked about in expectation, and sure enough, found Lady perched up in the rafters and Jasper under a bench.

They would take some getting used to, as well.

Made uneasy by both the animal audience and the anticipated return of Lily's mother, Rand stood awkwardly for a moment. The only sound in the summerhouse was the rain tapping on the copper-domed roof and the gravel path outside. "Do you picnic in here often?" he asked at length.

"Never," Lily said, hesitating over a platter of strawberries. "It really *is* too small, as Mum said. When we entertain in the garden, though, we sometimes use it to shelter the food. And my sisters and I like to come out here in the summertime. It's a nice place to sit and read or play a game. If you open all four doors, the breeze flows through, yet it keeps the sun off our faces."

"Preserves your lily-white complexion, does it?"

She smiled at his play on words. "That it does." Finally settling on a strawberry, she turned to offer it to him. "Are you not hungry?"

Her thoughtfulness immediately dispersed all his uncomfortable feelings, and he accepted with pleasure. He couldn't help but be put at ease by Lily's sweetness. He popped the fruit into his mouth, found she had chosen well, and reached for another.

She laughed when he lifted the whole platter and took it with him to the middle of the room, where a handsome rug had been spread over the brick floor for their picnicking.

Taking a tray of bread and cheese, she joined him on the rug, tucking her legs beneath her with movements graceful as a swan. "When we were young, Violet and Rose and I could spend days in here. We used to take playing cards and lay them out end-to-end on the floor to divide the space into pretend rooms. Then we'd play house."

"Divide it into rooms?" Wiping strawberry-sticky fingers on his handkerchief, he eyed the small area. "They must have been minuscule."

"When you're tiny, even little spaces feel large."

He helped himself to a hunk of hard yellow cheese. "It sounds as though you had a happy childhood here at Trentingham."

"I did." She swallowed, concern darkening her eyes. "Was there no happiness in your childhood at all?"

"Oh, yes, until I was six. Then my mother died and my father...changed. Or maybe he'd been that way all along, but I hadn't noticed. Mother had always been attentive to me, perhaps taking my part...I was young...I don't remember." He shook his head. "I remember only how it felt after she was gone."

"Lonely," Lily said softly.

He nodded, thinking that loneliness was a feeling he'd carried with him far too long. But now, with her, it was gone. "I don't feel lonely now."

Her smile was a little bit sad. "Do you never see them, then?" she asked. "Your father and your brother? Or hear from them? Ever?"

"Not in several years." He'd thought that if he forgot about them the anger would disappear, but there were others at Hawkridge he'd done an all-too-good job of ignoring as well. Like the beloved foster sister who had followed him around with hero worship in her eyes. "But my father has a ward, a girl named Margery Maybanks who was brought to our home very young. She writes to me sometimes."

Not nearly often enough, and he missed her. Of course, that was his fault. Reading news of his family made ripples in the nice calm life he'd made for himself—so much so that he often went months before answering Margery's letters.

"Does she tell them about you, then? Does your father know you're now a professor?"

"Oh, he knows. According to Margery, he said that just went to prove I never belonged in the best circles."

Her heart leapt into her eyes. "I cannot imagine what it would be like if my parents weren't proud of my accomplishments. And my sisters and brother, too. That's what family is all about, why we need them around us."

"I've done all right without family."

"Because you didn't have one," she said stoutly. "But you will now."

Her acceptance meant the world to him. Gratitude formed a lump in his throat, and he was overcome in a most unmanly fashion. Embarrassed, he excused himself and rose to fetch the rest of the food.

Lily crumbled some bread for her animals while Rand delivered plates of cherries, sweets, and cold beef. Lastly he returned with the champagne, and she smiled, sitting back on her heels and dusting her fingers. "I thought you'd be deathly ill today. I was certain you'd send your regrets, and here you are, all recovered it seems."

Rand knelt on the rug, warily watching Jasper scurry over to claim his portion. "I'm surprised I fell ill at all, actually. You'll find I'm of a strong constitution—perhaps due to all the running."

"It's Beatrix you'll want to keep an eye on."

"Pardon?"

Before he'd grasped her meaning, a brown and white blur sailed over his left shoulder and pounced on the bread.

Lily laughed. "Share, Beatrix."

Though the cat's tail twitched in protest, she relented and let her squirrel friend approach.

The animals well occupied, Rand judged it safe to pour the champagne. He dropped a strawberry into Lily's and watched the drink fizz, remembering the first time he'd tasted this new beverage, at Ford and Violet's wedding. Where he'd also first danced with Lily...and Rose. "How is Rose faring?"

Lily accepted her goblet and took a big gulp, looking as if she needed it. "Rose is very angry with me."

"I'm sorry to hear that. Violet told Ford you'd never consent to wed me, for fear of hurting your sister." He raised his goblet in a toast. "I'm glad she was wrong."

They drank, solemnly, gazing at each other over the goblets' rims—and Rand berated himself for bringing up Rose. He wished he could kiss away the shadow over Lily's face, but his gaze darted to one of the open doors, leery of her mother's return.

To his surprise, it was innocent Lily who set down her champagne, leaned forward, and pressed her lips to his, rising on her knees to reach him. It was a slow, consoling kiss, though whether she was drawing consolation or offering it, he didn't know—with Lily they seemed to be the same thing. Tasting of champagne, she held his head in both hands, unexpectedly strong. Trying to kiss her back with all the tenderness he felt, he thanked God for sending her to him.

Rain pattered on the roof far above. "I love you," she said quietly.

"I know," he returned, his voice filled with wonder. Sweet mercy, how incredible to have never had love in his life—and then to suddenly have it. What a difference love made! In the space of a fortnight, his entire life had changed. As if years of shadow had given way to full sun.

He clasped Lily to him like some precious object, tucking her head gently under his chin. "When shall we be married?"

She gave a contented sigh. "Violet and Ford were wed two weeks after they became betrothed, and—"

"Two weeks?" His fingers played with a lock of her hair. "It won't be easy, but I suppose I can wait that long."

"That long? Mum has been complaining about the rushed wedding ever since. She wishes to make a proper job of it this time. Six months, she said—"

"Six months! You can't be serious."

He felt her smile against his chest. "Those were my words exactly. That is why I talked her into six weeks."

"Oh. I suppose six weeks is survivable."

"It will pass quickly enough. I'll be busy with wedding

plans, and you with your house. We'll be married before Michaelmas term starts in mid-October. And I hope that in the meantime Rose will come around…"

Her voice trailed off sadly, and she sat back on her heels, not meeting his eyes.

"You're not having second thoughts, are you?"

She took a minute to answer, a minute during which he neither moved nor drew breath. "No," she said at last. "Not really."

The words had come too slowly, too reluctantly. Rand's heart slammed against his ribs. "Lily—"

"I'm *not* having second thoughts," she repeated and then launched herself at him, knocking him back to the rug as she crushed her mouth to his.

He kissed her and laughed, sheer joy mixed with relief, keeping just enough presence of mind to steady the champagne bottle she'd nearly toppled…before losing himself completely in the sensation of her slight, warm body sprawled over his. He could have kept kissing her the whole afternoon, spectators or no.

Until he felt sandpaper rubbing his fingers. "What on earth—"

Lily giggled, a sound of pure merriment that drowned out the rain. "Beatrix, stop licking Rand's hand." Leaning on an elbow, she held up a bite of cheese, and the cat wandered over to take it with its delicate pink tongue.

At least it *looked* delicate. "I thought it would feel wet," he said. "And soft."

"Has a cat never licked you?" Lily's eyes danced, and Beatrix hiccuped.

"Does she always hiccup so much?" Rand asked.

"No. Or at least she didn't used to. She's been acting a bit odd lately. I suppose it's a good thing she stopped us, though." With a rueful glance at the nearest door, Lily sighed and sat up. "Are you still hungry? Try a nun's biscuit. They're my favorites."

Biting into the offered sweet, he tasted almonds and lemon and smiled. But beneath the smile, a twinge of uneasiness returned.

A nun's biscuit, of all things. Well, he hoped the image of chaste nuns would remind both Lily and himself that they weren't married yet, and ought not to be engaging in improper intimacies. It wasn't worth risking her parents' ire, on top of Rose's wrath.

Nothing was worth risking the wedding going forward as planned.

Lady Trentingham soon returned to an innocent scene of two young people munching on nun's biscuits. Lily was apparently back in all good spirits, and the sight warmed Rand from the inside out. He told himself there was no danger, that their feelings for each other were too strong to be foiled. Not her parents, nor Rose, nor the king himself could come between them.

But all of a sudden, six weeks seemed like a very, very long time.

TWENTY-NINE

*I*T TOOK THREE carriages to get to Oxford. A valet and two maids rode in the first, along with all the luggage. The second conveyed Father, Mum, and Rose. And the third held Rand and Lily, with Rowan, evidently, as their chaperone.

Rand sat beside Lily on one of the two upholstered benches, holding her hand. Across from them, Rowan chattered, excited about his first trip to Oxford.

"You've never been?" Rand asked.

"Never."

"Neither have I," Lily added.

He squeezed her hand, praying she would be pleased with the town and with his house—anything that might add to her satisfaction, and hopefully help outweigh the less pleasing consequences of their betrothal.

Though she might have found more enjoyment, Rand thought, had Rowan shut his mouth for thirty seconds in a row sometime during the journey. He was a nice enough child, but spending several hours trapped in a small space with the lad was sufficient to convince Rand he wasn't quite ready to be a father.

When children came along, he was certain he'd love them as much as he loved Lily. But he was just getting used to the idea of being a husband; he felt woefully unprepared for fatherhood as yet.

Especially if all children talked as much as Lily's brother.

"Do you know," Lily said, dragging his thoughts back to the conversation, "we've never been much of anywhere besides London and the area that surrounds Trentingham. Oh, and Tremayne, but not for years."

"Tremayne?"

"A castle and lands our family owns near Wales. We stayed there during Cromwell's Protectorate, and again in '65 when the Great Plague was a threat. Now that Grandpapa has passed on and Father become the earl, Rowan is Viscount Tremayne."

"Are you?" Rand asked Rowan, smiling when Lily's brother nodded and puffed out his narrow chest. "Well, then," he told the boy, "you're certainly more important than I. I'm a mere lord."

"You're important," Lily protested.

Rand waved that away, though secretly pleased. "Have you never been out of Britain, then?" he asked Rowan.

"No."

"None of us have." When the carriage jounced in and out of a rut, Lily jostled against Rand. "Where have you been?"

"Rose said he's traveled a lot," Rowan chimed in importantly.

Rand shrugged. "I've been lucky to spend time on the continent. Spain, France, Italy, Greece..." He turned to Lily. "I'll take you those places, and more."

Rowan was gazing out the window at the unfamiliar countryside. "Rose said Lily won't be able to talk to anyone."

It was obvious the boy had no idea his words might sting. Rand wrapped an arm around her. "I'll be happy to communicate for your sister."

Lily watched out the window, too. She rubbed the scars on her hand, determined not to let Rose's spite spoil this special day. As they descended toward Oxford, the grazing land gave way to water meadows, and now the road was peppered with charming houses, each with a lovely, well-tended garden.

Rand began humming, that same old tune she'd heard before, somehow both quiet and cheerful at the same time. Lily's mind drifted, and she touched her fingertips to her lips, imagining them tender and a little bit puffy like they'd been yesterday after kissing Rand. Though surprised by her own daring at the picnic, she was glad she had…well, pounced on him. Remembering what it had felt like to go to him, to *make* him want her instead of just *letting* him want her, was far more pleasant than her other preoccupations. She'd gone to sleep last night with one hand on her mouth and awakened that way, too.

As they crossed a river to enter Oxford, she smiled at a beautiful square bell tower built of mellow stone. "It looks so old."

"Charmingly old, I hope." Rand's fingers tightened on her shoulder. "I hope you won't mind living here."

"It's lovely," she breathed.

"We're on Magdalen Bridge, and that tower is part of Magdalen College. It was built by Cardinal Wolsey. Every May Day since 1501, the college's choir ascends the tower at dawn to greet the coming of spring with hymns."

"Oh," she said, "I imagine that must be spectacular." Beyond Magdalen, they passed through the low-arched East Gate, and then they were within the city wall, its battlements interspersed with turrets. Towers of Oxford's many other colleges rose to punctuate the horizon, monuments to centuries of education.

Among the huge buildings of the university, townspeople lived and worked in smaller homes and shops under steep, sloping roofs. Few people walked the streets, but those that did looked prosperous, unlike in London where the poor slept in the gutters. "It's a quiet town in the summer months," Rand said, "but it will be bustling come October, full of students in their billowing black gowns."

"Can we climb all the towers?" Rowan asked, bouncing on the seat.

"Not *all* of the towers, but certainly one or two," Rand promised. "I'll take you all on a walking tour later."

Following instructions Rand had given the coachmen earlier, they turned onto New College Lane, a narrow street that ran between New College and Hart Hall. Behind a small rectangular courtyard, his new house rose three stories, the left side still cloaked in scaffolding.

"Here we are," he said, somewhat unnecessarily given that their carriage had stopped behind the other two.

The door opened, and the driver lowered the steps. Upon exiting, Rand waved at Lily's parents, noting that they looked a good deal more cheerful than stormy-eyed Rose.

He swallowed, hoping he could shield Lily from the worst of her sister's ire.

Looking lovely in a cornflower blue traveling gown, Lily stepped out and stared up at the rows of Palladian windows. "It's very big!"

"Did you think I'd expect Lady Lily Ashcroft to live in a cottage?" he teased. But he breathed easier knowing she so far approved of her home-to-be.

When Rowan emerged and made a beeline for the scaffolding, Rand reached a quick hand to grab the boy's arm. "No, you don't."

"Holy Ha—I mean zounds, I just wanted to climb it."

"It isn't safe," Rand said firmly, then turned back to the rest. "Come, let's see if the architect is at hand. I'll introduce you all—and find out why he hasn't finished as promised."

A workman came out the front door, burdened with two buckets of paint. He smiled and bowed awkwardly. "Lord Randal."

"Henry. How goes the job?"

"All but done. Mr. Martyn should return soon. He was called away—"

"Of course he was," Rand interrupted. "Isn't he always?" With a short laugh, he waved the man and his paint toward the scaffolding and ushered Lily's family inside the house.

Even though Kit was off-site, the interior swarmed with industrious men, a testament to the architect's deft management. "The house is designed in the classical style Kit favors," Rand explained as he led the Ashcrofts through an impressive entry and into the first chamber, a drawing room where a man was noisily installing a marble fireplace surround. "I admired many homes like this while touring Italy, so when he started sketching elevations of what he had in mind, we found ourselves in complete accord."

"It looks different," Lily's mother observed. "Plainer than other homes, but somehow more elegant, too."

"Kit and I designed it together." Rand clearly loved this house; Lily could hear the pride in his voice. "I wanted the decorative elements understated, not so grandiose as in most new homes today. And Kit has an eye for grace and balance."

"Come along!" Rowan yelled.

A bundle of energy after having been pent up in the carriage, he directed a whirlwind tour through the main rooms and the kitchen—no matter that he didn't know where he was going. Upstairs, he led them all on a merry chase down a narrow hallway between the five bedchambers.

"We designed the house with corridors," Rand explained, "so there's no need to go through one room to get to another."

Since the master bedchamber was the only room in the house with any furniture, their footsteps and voices echoed in the empty spaces. To Lily's remorse-tinged-relief, Rose remained quietly withdrawn, trailing the rest of the group with disdainful eyes. When Rowan had finished racing in and out of every chamber, he slid down the slick new banisters to the bottom. The others followed more sedately and gathered in the entrance hall on the ground floor.

"It's beautiful." Lily hugged herself and smiled, looking slowly around the square, high-ceilinged room. She loved all the architectural details, the niches built into the walls, the light that streamed through the many large windows to brighten the interior. Rather than being covered with heavy, dark paneling or a riot of intricate carving, the walls were smooth plaster.

"All white," Rand pointed out with a grin. "Like your bedchamber."

"You've seen Lily's bedchamber?" Rose asked pointedly, breaking her long silence.

Lily blushed and avoided her family's eyes by looking up at the classic coved cornice around the ceiling. "Will the walls be staying all white?" Her voice came out squeaky.

"I don't expect so. My last lodgings came furnished and decorated in a style that never quite felt like home, but I hadn't any idea how to fix it. For this one, I was planning to hire someone to choose fabrics and furnishings and wall coverings. But now that I have you—"

"She'll leave it all white," Rose interrupted.

"Rose," Mum started.

But then someone walked in, silencing Rose more effectively than her mother ever could.

Lily turned to see what had captured her sister's attention. Or rather, who. Dressed in deep blue velvet with white linen and crisp lace, the gentleman was tall, lean, and had the carriage of someone used to being in charge. His hair was black, his eyes a unique mixture of green and brown.

"My house is still unfinished," Rand said without preamble, but Lily could tell he wasn't really angry. His long-suffering sigh was just for show. "What might be your excuse this time?"

"Will King Charles do?" the gentleman asked, a lazy smile curving his lips. Those unusual eyes narrowed. "What happened to your hair?"

"A fire," Rand said without elaborating. He turned to Lily's father, raising his voice. "Lord Trentingham, may I present Christopher Martyn, distinguished recipient of the Procrastinating Architect Award."

Lily's father smiled vaguely; then his ears seemed to perk up. "*The* Christopher Martyn?"

Mr. Martyn bowed. "At your service, my lord."

"Atchur—?"

"Lord Trentingham is hard of hearing," Mum said warmly as she reached to pull Rowan down from a ladder. "You'll need to speak up."

But apparently Mr. Martyn didn't need to speak at all. Father stepped closer. "I'm looking for an architect to design one of those newfangled greenhouses—"

"Lord Martyn is busy," Rose broke in loudly. "Working for the *king*."

"I'm not a lord, my lady. Just plain Mr. Martyn. Although Kit will do."

Rose looked very disappointed to hear that, and Lily took perverse pleasure in thinking her sister couldn't call the man *lord* against his wishes. Having decided she didn't always have to be nice, it seemed she was turning out to be rather bad.

But it felt better than she'd expected.

Rand performed the rest of the introductions, and then, while Kit took over explaining the details of the building, he drew Lily aside.

"What do you think?"

"I think Rose likes your friend Kit."

"That's not what I meant." He tapped her on the chin. "What do you think of the house? Will you be able to stand living here?"

Feeling wickeder by the minute, Lily pretended to consider. "I saw only one master chamber. I'm not certain that's acceptable."

He looked a bit startled. "When the plans were drawn up, I was expecting to live here alone. But it's a large enough room, don't you think? Wouldn't you rather share—"

"Let me see," she interrupted. "You're asking me to give up living with my moody sister in the dull countryside and move to this bustling, sophisticated town...hmm...and then I'll have to sleep with you every night." Watching his alarm turn to amusement, she grinned. "It sounds perfect."

"What about your menagerie?"

"Though I've yet to see the garden, I'm sure it will do fine." Perhaps it wouldn't be ideal, but it would be much, much better than living without Rand. Even suffering her sister's ill temper was better than living without Rand.

Why hadn't she been able to see that all along?

"Are you certain?" he pressed, moving closer. He ran his hands up her arms until they were resting on her shoulders.

Out of habit, she shot a glance to Rose, but she really, truly didn't care what her sister thought. She, Lily, deserved happiness, too. "I've never been more certain of anything in my life."

Rand looked like he wanted to pull her against him and kiss her then and there. And she wouldn't have minded, even right in front of Rose.

But Kit interrupted. "Oh, Rand, you have some mail."

Rand was still gazing at Lily. "Later, Kit."

"One thing looked important. A missive from Hawkridge."

That succeeded in seizing his attention. He jerked his head around and gaped at Kit. "You can't mean—from my father?"

THIRTY

"THE MARQUESS never contacts me," Rand protested, sounding dazed.

"Never say never," Lily said softly.

And Kit burst into laughter.

"What?" she asked, half distracted by Rand's distress but unable to ignore his friend's reaction. "What's so amusing?"

"That's Rand's saying. He's been dogging me with that phrase ever since we were wee lads."

"I think my mother used to say it," Rand said absently. "Where's this letter?"

Kit nodded. "I've been collecting your mail as it comes in. I'll get it."

"I expect we should all go upstairs to my bedchamber." Rand led the way while Kit went off to fetch the mail. "It's the only room where we can sit."

Even there, the seating was lacking. Rose took the single chair at his desk, while Rand waved the rest of them toward his enormous bed, a heavy oak four-poster with hunter green hangings. "I'm sorry there are no other chairs," he said, settling himself on a carved wooden chest. "All my furniture is in storage, and in any case, it needs replacing." He forced a smile. "I'm hoping my new wife will help with that."

"I'll be honored to." Lily sat beside him. "And I promise not to choose white."

"Nothing white?" Rose looked suspicious. "Nothing at all?"

"White isn't a good color for a home with children," Lily said, feeling her cheeks flood with heat. Why had she mentioned children? What a thing to speak of while her parents perched on her future marital bed!

She was grateful to Kit for entering just then with a stack of mail, drawing everyone's attention back to the mysterious missive.

Rand flipped through the letters and slowly pulled one out. "Here it is." Forgotten, the rest of the mail fluttered to the floor.

Kit bent to collect it. "You didn't believe me?"

"I was hoping you were wrong." Rand shrugged as he broke the seal. A big, black one. Then he just sat there with the paper in his hands. "Word from the marquess cannot be good."

Lily scooted closer. "Perhaps it's not from him, Rand. Could it be from your friend, his ward?"

"She doesn't use the Hawkridge seal."

"Does your brother never write?"

"He has nothing to say to me." He stared at his name on the front. "No, this is the marquess's writing."

At last he unfolded the paper. As he scanned the single page, an expectant silence descended on the room. Impatient, Lily leaned to glance at the letter. The writer had a heavy hand. The ink was dark and decisive.

She looked up to Rand. His face matched the plain white walls, all the color drained, his eyes lifeless.

"What is it?"

Both his hands dropped to his sides, the paper dangling from one. "My brother Alban is dead," he said disbelievingly. "At the hands of another man."

The air left Lily in a rush. She had some idea that Rand and Alban had never got along, but they were still brothers. She could only imagine how the news made Rand feel. Unsure what to say, she reached for his free hand and quietly laced her fingers with his.

"I'm so sorry," Mum murmured.

"What—" Father started.

"Hush, darling." Mum patted his hand. "Rand's brother has died."

Rand shook his head as though to regain his senses. The paper crackled when he waved off the sympathy. "He and I weren't close, so condolences are unnecessary." When he turned to Lily, his deep gray eyes held pain that belied his words—unless it was not grief, but an older pain jarred to the surface. Not for the first time, she wondered what had happened between Rand and his brother when they were children. But now was not the time to ask.

Silently he offered her the letter, and more silent moments passed while she examined its contents. Biting her lip, she finally looked up. "You're now your father's heir."

"You're going to be a marquess?" Rose looked between him and Lily, her eyes flashing with envy. "The Marquess of Hawkridge? And what are you now that your brother is gone?"

"Baron Newcliffe," Kit said. "But none of that matters."

Rose's expression said it mattered quite a bit, as well as displaying scorn that a commoner like Kit wouldn't think so.

Releasing Lily's hand, Rand stood and began pacing. "I've no wish to be a marquess. Or even a baron. I like being a professor."

"You may not have to give that up, Rand. Or at least not

right now." Lily watched his agitated movements, feeling helpless to soothe him. He looked like a penned animal. She suspected that if it wouldn't be so impolite, he'd leave Kit and her family here and set off running through the streets. "How old is your father?"

"Only fifty-two," he admitted. "And last I heard, healthy as a horse."

"Well, then…"

He gestured to the letter on Lily's lap. "He commands me to move to Hawkridge. He expects me to leave the position I've worked hard to earn and scamper home to help him run his infernal estate." He scowled. "I'll spend my days fiddling with account books and extorting rents and dancing attendance on the king—as if I've nothing better to do with my time!"

"That's not all there is to managing an estate," Lord Trentingham said gravely.

Rand finally stopped pacing. "Beg pardon, my lord. I'm sure you're right. But it's still not the life I want for myself. I'm happy with my life here…" He turned to meet Lily's gaze. "I'm even happier now you'll be here with me."

Mum rose from the bed and touched his arm. "Then go tell him that you mean to stay."

"Defy my father?" he asked, perhaps surprised to receive such advice from another parent.

But Chrystabel Ashcroft was no ordinary parent. "Yes, Rand, defy him if you must. You are a man grown; he cannot force your obedience. But try to reason with him first. A son owes a father that much."

"I owe the marquess nothing," Rand grumbled. "But I suppose I cannot ignore his summons entirely."

"Indeed," Lily said gently, "you cannot. But you don't have to go alone."

"Good heavens," Mum cried, turning on Lily. "You are not thinking of going with him?"

"Why not?" Lily's brow knitted in genuine confusion. "As Rand and I are to be married, this matter will affect my life, too. Besides, shouldn't I meet Lord Hawkridge before the wedding?"

Rand grimaced. "If I have my way, you'll never meet him at all."

Lily rose and moved close to him. "Rand..." Much as she loved and admired him, his attitude toward his family was one area she thought could see improvement. Especially now that his father was the only family he had left.

Glancing at her own dear parents, her heart ached for him. "Of course I want to meet your father," she told him. "He's part of what made you the man I love."

"Whatever I've made of myself, it was despite him, not because of him." Rand's eyes were hard as steel. "Trust me, Lily. The farther you stay from Hawkridge, the better."

"Gemini," Rose sneered, "is your father such a troll you fear he'll send your bride packing?"

"Rose!" Mum admonished. "That's *quite* enough from you."

Lily was so angry, she couldn't even look at her sister.

Rand reclaimed her hand. "I'll only be gone a few nights," he said in a consoling tone. "Come, let's enjoy the rest of the day. Did I not promise you all a tour of the town?"

Lily gave him a pointed look. "Isn't your father awaiting your arrival?"

"The letter was written early last week; he can wait another day."

Searching his eyes, she saw the steel in them soften. She turned to her mother. "Mum, may I *please* go?"

Mum's mouth pinched with regret. "I wish I could give my consent. But you two are not married yet, and it would be highly improper for you, Lily, to stay at Hawkridge unchaperoned, much less travel all alone with a single man." She nodded to Rand. "*I* know your betrothed is a gentleman, but I've your reputation to think of, too."

"Then come with us," Lily begged. "Chaperone us if you must."

Mum glanced from Lily to Rand to her husband, looking thoughtful. Lily's heart swelled with hope—then lurched when sounds of a crash reached them from below. Knowing her brother, Lily looked about the room in panic. "Where's Rowan?"

Mum lead the charge downstairs, but Lily, nearly as frantic and more nimble, outpaced her. She flew out the front door and found Rowan sprawled on the ground, splattered with white paint from a bucket lying nearby, its contents splashed all over the bare dirt yard. Above him, the scaffolding tilted at a crazy angle.

He pushed to his feet—or rather, he tried to. "Ouch!" he hollered and collapsed back to the dirt.

She rushed to kneel beside him. "Is it your ankle? Rand told you the scaffolds weren't safe!" She tugged off his boot.

"Ouch, it hurts!" Tears sprang to his eyes. "This is God's reckoning for my stupid mistake; I just know it."

Gently she probed his ankle, looking for indications of a break. "Yes, you really should have listened to Rand," she said sympathetically.

"No—ouch!" he wailed. "I'm talking about the barn! I told you about the joke going wrong, but I didn't have Mr. Boyle's fire-making things. It was a mistake," he finished weakly.

"A mistake? You set it? You set the fire?" Anger made her voice shrill. They'd talked about mistakes, but she'd never realized...but she *should* have realized. She liked to think she was smart enough to put two and two together. She'd been too focused on her own problems, her own mistakes, her love for Rand and her promise to Rose.

"Rowan!" Mum called as she raced outside. "What happened? You're covered in paint!"

Rowan just stared at his sister, tears leaking out of his eyes. Eyes that silently willed her to keep his secret.

When he didn't say anything, Mum shifted her attention to Lily. "Is he hurt? Or is it something else?"

Lily watched Rowan swallow hard. Inside her, a sense of duty battled with sibling loyalty. By not telling Mum, was she as good as a party to the crime? The fire was a serious thing, not some minor offense like straying too far from home on a fishing outing with a friend. Rand and her animals could have perished in that fire. Or someone else.

But in the end she held her tongue. Rowan knew he had done wrong, and he was sorry. And he was certainly paying for his mistakes now. She nodded to let him know his secret was safe.

"It's his ankle, Mum." Lily's voice held no anger now; only sympathy. Once the shock wore off, she suspected, her little brother would be in a good deal more pain. "I think his ankle may be broken."

THIRTY-ONE

*A*FTER A ROUND of hysterics from Lily's mother—
which her future son-in-law found rather gratifying,
for he was relieved to discover the formidable woman *did*
occasionally suffer from bouts of human weakness—Lord
and Lady Trentingham gratefully accepted Rand's offer to
send for one of his colleagues, a Wadham College lecturer
and physician.

Rand scribbled a note while Kit and Lord Trentingham
brought the sniffling boy inside to the master bedroom.
Almost as sore as his ankle was Rowan's disappointment at
missing the tour of Oxford and not getting to climb any
towers. His parents both decided to stay behind and see to
the patient, and so it happened that the two young men and
two Ashcroft sisters set out as a foursome to explore the
town. They left the others playing a game of draughts in the
huge oak bed.

Rand shook his head at Lily. "I thought you said he was a
monkey."

"I should have said he's an accident-prone monkey. He's

done worse to himself, though. He'll be back on his feet in no time."

"King me!" Lily heard Rowan yell as they quit the house, much later than they'd originally planned. She imagined her family's raised voices echoing through the home on top of the construction noise, and was thankful she would be elsewhere for the next few hours.

Their walking tour started at Wadham, where Rand had begun his years here at Oxford. The college was on Parks Road, around the corner and down one street from his house. "You really live in the center of things," Lily remarked.

"We will, yes." Clearly trying to set his troubles aside, he took her hand as they all crossed the smooth green lawn toward Wadham's elegant facade. "I hope you'll like it here."

"I love it already. This town feels so peaceful and alive, all at once."

"Wait until it's teeming with students." He nodded to the porter at the stone-vaulted gateway. "Good afternoon, Dickerson."

"Afternoon, Professor Nesbitt."

Rand led the party into a graveled quadrangle. "Do you not go by Lord?" Rose asked.

He groaned. "Far too pretentious. Besides, I *earned* the title Professor."

"But now you're a baron."

Lily saw Rand's jaw set. "Here, I'm a professor."

It seemed he was determined to keep it that way. Not that Lily minded, but she wondered what sort of a struggle he'd be up against at Hawkridge. And she could tell from the tenseness in his body that in spite of his valiant effort to ignore the letter, he was worried about it, too.

She looked around the quadrangle at the stately stone buildings, built in Oxford's traditional Gothic style. All was quiet now, but she smiled as she pictured students hurrying to meet with their tutors, young Rand and Ford among them. "The architecture matches the old colleges, but somehow it looks new."

"Only Pembroke is newer," Kit said. "Dorothy Wadham built this college in 1610."

Rose made a noise of surprise. "A woman built Wadham? I thought Oxford was strictly for men."

Rand nodded. "It is—even the servants in the colleges are all male. But as Nicholas Wadham's widow, Dorothy carried out his wishes. There are portraits of them both in the hall and statues just outside it. Come, I'll show you."

Gravel crunched beneath their feet as he led them across the quiet quadrangle. The figures made a striking composition framing the door, King James on one side and the founders on the other. The statue of Nicholas Wadham was holding a model of the college.

"He never actually saw it," Rand said. "They began building after his death." He tugged open the heavy door. "Go in. The hall is beautiful."

While the others went inside, he held Lily back, leaning close for a short, sweet kiss that left her feeling light-headed. "I think we're going to be very happy here," he murmured.

"I think so, too...if we get to stay." Lily felt his arm tense beneath her hand. "Are you certain you'll be all right traveling to Hawkridge alone?"

"I must be, since I've got no other choice." He sighed, pulling away slightly. "I own it won't be pleasant. But you heard your mother—I'm grown now, and my father can no longer force his will upon me."

Though she couldn't argue the truth of his statement, Lily knew that parents tended to have ways of influencing their children. She also knew Rand was harboring a great deal of resentment that might cloud his judgement where his father was concerned.

She squeezed the tense arm, wishing she could be by his side when the meeting took place. His muscles relaxed, and she let him walk her inside. Passing an entrance screen of exquisite Jacobean woodwork, she gawked at the hall's great hammerbeam roof before her gaze dropped to the portraits of the founders. Nicholas Wadham wore a tall black hat, Dorothy a flattish cap and an uncomfortable-looking neck ruff. "They look formidable," she said.

Kit smiled. "Considering all the pranks they've witnessed over the years, I suspect they're disapproving."

Rose rotated in a circle, taking in the solemn stained-glass windows and the long rows of tables with candelabras spaced down their middles. "I cannot picture Ford here."

"He came three times a day," Rand assured her, "dutifully wearing the required robe. Ford Chase was never one to miss a meal."

Rose nearly smiled, and Lily noted with pleasure that her sister hadn't uttered a spiteful word since the start of the tour. Could she possibly be thawing? As they exited the hall, Lily saw Kit slanting Rose a sharp, appreciative look. Well, she always had been a beauty, so long as she wasn't scowling.

Rand took them to the chapel, so they could see its magnificent east window depicting Jonah's whale, then turned to lead them out of the college.

"What's this?" Rose asked, stopping by an unassuming door to stare at four lines of lettering crudely carved into the wood.

Rand smiled. "When King Charles slept in that room one night, the Earl of Rochester wrote that."

"He didn't." Sounding wickedly intrigued, Rose read aloud.

"Here lies a great and mighty king,
Whose promise none relied on.

He never said a foolish thing,
Nor ever did a wise one."

Their collective laughter rang through the empty quadrangle.

"Was the king angry?" Lily wondered.

"To the contrary," Rand said, "he found it quite amusing. He claimed his words were his own, while his deeds were those of his ministers."

In high spirits, they left Wadham and walked the unpaved streets. Lily already loved this city, a city so steeped in tradition that new buildings were built in old styles. She nearly burst out laughing when she noticed Lady flitting along from tree to tree, then glanced around and found Beatrix stalking them in the shadows. She decided to keep quiet about that, given that Rand was uneasy around her constant companions. But her heart sang to see that her animal friends would be comfortable here in Oxford, too.

Of course, that was assuming she and Rand ended up living here.

"The Sheldonian Theatre," Kit announced. They all stopped to gaze up at the cupola atop its domed roof. "A friend built it," he added, sidling closer to Rose. "Christopher Wren. His first large public building."

Rose failed to look impressed with either the building or Kit's friendship with the celebrated architect. "I've met Mr. Wren," she said. "He attended my sister's wedding."

Seemingly undiscouraged, Kit tried the doors and looked disappointed to find them locked. "The ceiling inside is amazing."

Rand nodded. "It's painted to look like the sky."

"But that's just ornamentation." Kit leaned against the double doors. "The ceiling itself is a wonder of advanced construction, designed with no columns to spoil the view. An apparent defiance of gravity, because Wren contrived all the weight to be supported from above."

"It's a beautiful building." Lily paced its columned front, trying to focus on the tour and put tomorrow out of her mind. "What is it used for?"

"Ceremonies, mostly." Rand caught up to her and took her hand. His palm felt cool and dry. "Matriculation, graduation, and the like. And the university's printing presses are housed in the basement."

"Can you see," Kit put in, "the street-level windows that let in light? Wren greatly values natural light. He told me he based this building on the Theatre of Marcellus in Rome."

Despite her unease, Lily didn't miss the admiration in Kit's voice. Or the touch of longing. "Have you seen the Theatre of Marcellus?"

"Sadly, I haven't." He gave a self-deprecating shrug. "I'd be thrilled to study the great buildings on the Continent, but I'm afraid I'm hopeless with foreign tongues. I have nightmares of never finding my way home."

"Rose has an excellent head for languages," Lily told him.

Her sister swung to glare at her. If looks could kill, Lily thought, she'd be deader than the sculptured heads on the railing around the building.

And things had been going so well. Lily bit her lip. "What's that?" she asked, pointing at a random object in a graceless bid to smooth things over.

"The Tower of the Five Orders," Kit enthused. "It's the most unusual structure in all of Oxford."

He led them through an archway, a short tunnel through a plain building, and into an open quadrangle. The buildings surrounding it were more imposing than the austere exterior would suggest. Many doors gave entrance, each with a Latin inscription in gold letters on a blue background.

Rose turned slowly, translating them all. "Grammar and

history, logic, rhetoric. Music, arithmetic, geometry, astron-
omy. Philosophy." And at the far end, "School of Medicine,
School of Law, School of Theology."

"Those three are the superior schools," Rand explained.
"Before attending any of those, one must pass each of the
other schools first and receive his Master of Arts."

Kit wandered closer to Rose again. "You *are* good at
languages."

She shrugged, but looked pleased. Kit was making
progress, Lily thought. Flattery was one sure way to Rose's
heart.

He cleared his throat as he looked to Lily. "You asked
about the tower." It was a wondrous sight in the otherwise
rather sobering surroundings. "The Five Orders display the
different styles of classical architecture, distinguished by
differing columns, bases, and pedestals. From the bottom to
the top, oldest to newest, we have Tuscan, Doric, Ionic,
Corinthian, and Composite."

Rose looked more interested than Lily would have
expected. "Who is sitting up there?"

"The statue? King James. Can you see that he's holding a
book? The Bodleian Library is behind you—it receives a copy
of every new book ever published. As for the rest of the
building…"

Lily listened with half an ear as Kit talked about the
Gothic carving and pinnacles. Bells began ringing from the
various towers of Oxford's many colleges, their chimes all
different yet harmonious. A beautiful sound. A sound she
looked forward to hearing day after day, night after night,
when she lived here with Rand, alone in their lovely, brand-
new house.

For both their sakes, she hoped everything would work
out so they could.

As though sensing her thoughts, he moved closer. When

he took her hand again, she felt his thumb drawing circles on her palm, making her shiver. He smiled, not an inscrutable smile but one full of gentle teasing and unbridled affection. A smile that made her long to stay with him in this enchanting town forever. No matter what happened, she knew Oxford would always hold a special place in her heart, because it was so special to him.

He deserved to stay here. He'd already lost one home, one family. How unfair that a second home should be ripped from him, too. Lily wished passionately for Rand to build bridges with his father, but was it worth giving up everything he'd built here?

And yet, how could he have both?

THIRTY-TWO

HE ALLEY THAT separated the Spotted Cow inn from Rand's property was dark and narrow. Lily clutched her cloak tighter around herself and glanced up at the clouds covering the moon.

It's only fifty feet, she told herself. Should anyone approach you, Beatrix will draw blood with her claws, Jasper will nip off the poor soul's toes, and Lady will peck out his eyes. Just go.

She made a run for it, careful of her footing on the slippery cobblestones, and arrived on his doorstep without incident. The house was dark and silent. She slammed the knocker against the big oak door, then waited, clutching her satchel and shivering in the damp, chilly air, until it finally creaked open.

"Lily?" Clearly baffled, Rand opened the door wider, then blinked as her three animal friends scampered in past him.

The expression on Rand's face was priceless. The rest of him looked delicious, his hair tousled from sleep, his body wrapped in a dark brown brocade dressing gown tied loosely at his waist.

"May I come in?"

"Oh." He blinked. "Of course." Holding a candle with one hand, he wrapped his free arm around her shoulders and drew her inside. As he shut the door, he eyed the assorted creatures. "How on earth did they get to Oxford?"

"I told you, they follow me." She placed her satchel by the door and drew back her hood.

"They follow you," he repeated dryly, as though that explained nothing at all. "What are *you* doing here?"

"I must speak with you." She had the sudden urge to slip her hands beneath his silk dressing gown, but that was so shocking an idea that she instinctively moved from his grasp.

He looked suddenly grim. "Lily...if this is about Rose, please do not—"

"It's not about Rose," she interrupted, her teeth chattering.

"You're cold." He moved closer again and rubbed her arms and back with his free hand. "Then you're not here to break our betrothal?"

"Beg pardon?" Distracted by the sensation of his hands on her, she took a moment to grasp his meaning. "Goodness, of course not! Is that what you want?"

"It's the last thing I want," he said, then met her lips with his and proved it. She melted into his sleep-warmed body.

Her lids were drifting closed when she glimpsed the light guttering and quickly reached to steady the candle. A moment more and he would have dropped it, possibly burning down his brand new house. She smiled against his lips, pleased that she could make him lose his head the same way he did hers.

"Maybe we should go to your bedroom."

"*Beg pardon?*" His eyes got so wide, the whites were visible all the way around.

"No, not for *that*." She giggled. "Just to talk. It's the only place we can sit down, remember?"

"Ah. Indeed." He cleared his throat, and Lily choked back more giggles. "Well, then...shall we?" He raised the candle and motioned her toward the stairs.

They went up side by side, Rand holding the candle low to light her path. "I cannot believe you're here," he said, shaking his head. "Who ever thought sweet, saintly Lily Ashcroft would dare sneak out for a midnight rendezvous?"

"Is that how you see me—saintly?" They reached the top of the stairs and turned down a corridor. "Of late, I've acted anything but saintly."

"Lily," he began in a troubled tone.

"No, it's a good thing. I think. I cannot be the nice girl all the time. At least that's what Judith says."

"Judith sounds like a good friend." Rand had left his bedroom door open, and he ushered her in before following and closing the door.

It was brighter and cozier in here, with a cheerful fire in the hearth. Like the rest of the house, the chamber smelled of new wood and paint. Rand lit a branch of tapers near the four-poster bed, then set his candle on the desk. Lily's eyes glanced off the bed with its disarrayed green counterpane, and she was grateful to see Rand setting the desk chair before the hearth and gesturing for her to sit.

As she settled herself, he warmed his hands at the fire, then leaned against the mantle. "So what would you like to talk about?"

She began without preamble. "I'm coming with you to Hawkridge."

He sucked in his breath, opened his mouth to speak, closed it, then hesitated. Finally, "Has your mother volunteered to chaperone us?"

"No," Lily admitted. "She might have done, but now she won't leave poor Rowan. But I don't care. I'm going with you anyway. This journey is far more important than my reputation."

He belted his dressing gown tighter around his waist. "I'm not sure your mother would agree."

"She certainly would not—thus I prefer not to give her a choice in the matter. If we leave tonight, we'll be at Hawkridge before my family realizes I'm gone. By the time they catch up to me, we'll have already met your father, and they may drag me back to Trentingham in chains if they like."

"I don't know if this business can be concluded in a single meeting."

"Then I'll figure out something later. Please, let's just get there. We've only a few hours until sunrise."

Rand's hand jerked, as if he'd meant to swipe at his hair and then remembered most of it was gone. "You'll add running away from your family to your list of un-saintly acts?"

Lily didn't flinch. Right and wrong weren't always clear, but in this case she had no doubts. She'd pledged herself to Rand, and he to her, and now they would face life's challenges together. "I'll do it for you," she said simply. "For us."

His expression softened—a bit. "I can handle the marquess on my own. Truly, I'll be fine. I won't pretend I'm not dreading it, or that I won't miss you. But I'll not have you subjected to that awful place."

"Why?"

He frowned, looking into the fire. "Why...what?"

She could tell he was faking, was trying to avoid the question. "Why is Hawkridge so awful? Why do you hate your father and brother?" She chewed her lower lip, knowing these answers would be hard for him, but also knowing she needed to hear them. "What did they do to you, Rand?"

He stared into the fire for a long time.

"Rand?"

He still didn't look at her, but he did begin to speak. "It's hard to explain. They didn't...*hurt* me exactly. Well, my father beat me when he thought I misbehaved, but no worse than any child receives from his parents."

Lily privately disagreed, but she knew her family was unusual in that respect. She didn't interrupt.

"Most of my punishments were due to Alban, though. He transgressed and the blame fell on me. I could never convince my father that Alban was the guilty party. He was the exalted heir, the one who could do no wrong. And I was just..." His voice trailed off.

"Just what?" Lily asked gently.

Rand shook his head. "I don't know. The marquess hates me, but I've never known why."

"I'm sure your father doesn't hate you—"

"Oh, yes, he does. I've always been able to see it on his face." Rand's voice sounded hollow, and Lily judged it best not to dwell on the point.

Just then, Beatrix vaulted onto her lap. Lily let out a yelp, having forgotten the animals' presence, but she was soon comforted by the cat's warm, vibrating body. Stroking her soft fur, she looked back to Rand. "And what of Alban? Did he seem to hate you, too?"

"Not particularly. At least, not more than he hated most people. He was just evil."

Lily's hand paused mid-stroke. "Evil?" Though she was careful not to betray any skepticism in her voice, the assertion sounded far-fetched to her. Surely few people in the world were truly evil. "Are you certain his *intentions* were evil? Perhaps the two of you were simply at odds, and he behaved selfishly, as most children do—"

"No, Lily, he was evil. He did things to people—and animals, too. He liked to hurt them."

Lily shivered at the thought. She could scarcely imagine a

relation of Rand's intentionally causing harm. It didn't seem possible. Could he have misunderstood? He'd been very young…

"Rand, I—"

"It's all right," Rand cut her off. "The marquess never believed me either." His tone was brusque, but she could hear the hurt underneath. "If you had read Alban's journal, though, you'd have been convinced."

"You read his private journal?" No wonder the Nesbitt brothers hadn't gotten along! If she'd read her sisters' journals, or Rowan's, they'd be out for her blood.

Not that any of them kept a journal, but that was beside the point.

Rand had the good grace to blush. "Yes, but only because I was hoping to expose him."

"To get him in trouble?"

"Well, he deserved it. And I didn't precisely *read* his journal," he said, a bit defensively. "I transcribed it."

"What do you mean?"

"I decoded it. He wrote in secret languages he invented. Because his writings were so incriminating."

"And you broke the codes?"

"Every one he could devise." Rand gave a bitter laugh, and Lily got the distinct impression this was the only part of his childhood he looked back on with any satisfaction. "Alban was flummoxed. Eventually he had to stop journaling." Rand sobered. "One good thing came of it, though—I realized I had a skill for puzzling out languages. That aptitude allowed the marquess to gain me early entrance to Oxford, and he was nearly as happy for it as I."

"He must have been proud of you," Lily said hopefully.

"Not in the least. He was just grateful to see the back of me. The last time I visited was when I became a fellow, and he could hardly look at me. A Nesbitt, working for a living. He thinks me a disgrace."

Lily wanted to protest, but now she hardly knew what to think. She was having a hard time imagining the Nesbitts by Rand's description. Could they truly be as frightful as he remembered?

Did she want to find out?

She licked dry lips. "Thank you for telling me all of this. It means a lot that you trust me enough to confide in me."

He crouched before her chair and took her hands, making Beatrix drop to the floor with an indignant mew. "I told you so you would understand why you cannot come with me. Hawkridge is not a nice place to visit. Especially for someone as sweet and gentle as you."

Lily wasn't sure she was all that sweet—not anymore— but she couldn't deny that the name of Hawkridge now filled her with a certain amount of dread.

His hands slid up her arms, his thumbs stroking the sides of her neck. He kissed her forehead, though she'd have preferred her lips. "Now *you* must trust *me*. I know how to deal with the marquess, and I won't let him deprive us of the life we've planned together—the life I promised you. I'd never let anything come between us. You know that, don't you?"

His face was gilded by the firelight when he finally found her mouth with his, his fingertips dancing on the delicate skin of her cheeks. The doubts swirling in her mind were quickly drowned beneath a wave of tender sensation.

Never say never, a little voice in her head whispered. But this time, she kept it to herself.

THIRTY-THREE

*T*HE NEXT MORNING, Rand stopped by the inn's common room to make his farewells and give Lily a chaste peck on the cheek. Noticing his hair was damp from recent washing, she suspected he'd gone for an early morning run.

Then she looked closer and realized he must've made time for a visit to the barber, as well. His hair was properly trimmed and his cheeks fresh-shaven. He'd dressed himself in a dove gray velvet suit much finer than the wool suits he normally wore. Was he hoping to impress his father?

Well, his efforts were certainly working on Lily. He looked so tempting that she had to clasp her hands behind her back to keep them to herself.

"How far are you going?"

"Only a couple of hours downriver from Trentingham. I'd accompany you all as far as the mansion, but..." He gestured toward the chaos that was Lily's family and servants preparing for their leave-taking. They were far from ready.

Lily nodded her understanding. "If Hawkridge is so near Trentingham, I wonder that I never met you before Violet met

Ford. I thought I'd been to every house within a day's driving distance with my mother and her gifts of perfume."

"There were no women at Hawkridge," he reminded her. "My mother died before you were born."

"But surely your father entertains."

"Not since the death of my mother. Even Christmas at Hawkridge is a rather dreary affair, more of a duty to the servants and tenants than a real celebration."

"It does sound a bit dull," she allowed. "Did no children ever visit Hawkridge, then? How did you make friends?"

"It wasn't easy. If Kit hadn't lived so nearby, I likely wouldn't have had any friends at all."

"No wonder you enjoy the bustle of Oxford." She gazed up at him. "I enjoy it, too. Thank you for bringing me here. And my family. We all had a lovely time."

"Up until I received the blasted letter and Rowan fell off the scaffolding."

"It was nice after that, too," she protested.

He shrugged, then grew thoughtful, running his tongue over his teeth. "You're right," he said. "The afternoon went very smoothly, once your mother calmed down. Your parents don't seem angry with Rowan."

"Events occur. You take them in stride."

Rand snorted. "My family didn't. Your parents also don't seem upset that you're marrying a professor."

"You're a baron now, too."

"But I wasn't, and they never seemed to care."

"They trust my choice. Besides, they admire you and what you've done with your life."

He smiled, and something seemed to shift in his eyes, in his posture. He looked more content than he had in days. "You have a wonderful family," he said with fervent warmth.

"My father is half deaf, my mother is an unrepentant

gossip, my brother thinks tricking people is a laudable achievement, my sister loathes the very sight of me—"

"They're wonderful," he repeated firmly, and she was secretly pleased. If he was learning to appreciate her imperfect family, perhaps there was hope for him reconciling with his own.

THIRTY-FOUR

*R*AND WAS LONG gone by the time the Ashcrofts were set to depart. A valet and two maids had had to stuff the family's first carriage with a surprising amount of luggage, considering they'd left home for just one night. Then there was the matter of conveying Rowan downstairs and settling him in the second carriage with his parents, as Mum wished to watch over him during the bumpy journey. This left Lily and Rose alone in the third carriage.

The ride was predictably quiet, each sister staring out opposite windows. Lily sat with Beatrix in her lap, barely seeing the scenery and certainly not enjoying it. Between her concern for Rand and the tension with Rose, her stomach was tying itself in knots. She wished she could say something to lighten the mood. She wished they could be as close as they used to be.

But they were nearing Trentingham and she still hadn't worked up the courage to speak when the carriage bounced over a particularly deep rut. Lily was sent careening into Rose, and Beatrix tumbled to the floor with an angry shriek.

"Sorry, Rose!" Lily gasped, scrambling off her. She rubbed

her forehead where it had bumped Rose's shoulder. "And my apologies to you, too, Beatrix."

Picking herself up with as much dignity as she could muster, the disgruntled cat curled up in the furthest corner of the carriage, her back turned to Lily.

Lily must have looked forlorn indeed, because Rose finally spoke. "She'll forgive you." Tidying her hair, she jerked her head to indicate Beatrix. "She's just nursing her pride."

Lily knew that; in truth, she'd been wondering whether *Rose* would ever forgive her, not Beatrix. But she was so happy they were talking, she didn't much care what was said.

Now, how to keep Rose talking?

Flattery, of course, was the obvious choice. "Kit admired you yesterday. Did you notice?"

"Of course," Rose said haughtily, arranging a plump, dark curl over one shoulder.

"Did you admire him?"

Rose shrugged. "He's handsome enough. It's unfortunate he's not titled."

Lily frowned. "He's a successful architect. Goodness, he gets commissions from the king himself! I imagine he can afford to live in a grand style. Why should it matter that he's not titled?"

"Of course it matters. Violet is a viscountess, and you— soon you'll be a baroness and eventually a marchioness. Why should I settle for less?"

"You're the Earl of Trentingham's daughter, which means you could marry a guttersnipe and you'd still be Lady Rose. Besides, if you're in love with the man, it's not settling."

"Well, I'm not in love with Kit, am I? I've just met him, and I've no intention of getting to know him better when he's not what I want." Rose averted her gaze, looking out at the rolling countryside.

End of discussion. Lily could swear she felt the temperature in the carriage drop.

So much for growing closer.

A few minutes later, Rose surprised her sister by speaking again. "Why are you even here?" She kept her gaze on the view.

Lily traced the scars on the back of her hand. "What do you mean?"

"I mean, when you sneaked out of your room last night, I figured you meant to abscond with your betrothed to Hawkridge."

Lily's jaw dropped. "You knew I sneaked out?"

"Of course." Lily could hear the scorn in her voice. "My room was next door to yours. What did you think, the walls were ten feet thick?"

"No, I just—" Lily swallowed hard. "Did you tell Mum and Father?"

Silently, Rose shook her head. It had begun raining outside, and the carriage passed by a flock of wet, bedraggled-looking sheep. When the last of the herd was out of view, she turned to Lily, her eyes dark and unreadable. "I know that you won. I'll never like it, but I do know it. And I don't intend to put myself in your way."

Lily looked at her hands, unsure of her response. This seemed like progress—didn't it?—but her sister's voice held no trace of understanding or affection. She'd almost rather have Rose's contempt than this cool, businesslike acceptance.

"Why did you come back?" Rose asked again.

"He didn't want to take me with him. He said Hawkridge isn't a good place for me."

"Do you think he's right?"

Lily shrugged. She didn't know what to think. "Maybe."

Rose moved across the carriage to sit beside her sister. "Then you have to go," she said strongly.

Lily's head jerked up. "What?"

"If you marry him, sooner or later Hawkridge will be your home. You can't run away from that. You must go there and show that you belong—with him, *and* at Hawkridge. You mustn't begin a marriage with doubts."

"Do you really think so?" Lily was astonished to hear Rose offering words of support, but they did agree with her own views. She'd let Rand go alone because it was what he wanted, and she wouldn't presume to tag along uninvited. But that didn't mean she'd felt it was for the best. "It's too late, anyway," she said with a sigh. "Rand's already gone, and I've no one else to travel with. Mum won't take me until Rowan's ankle is mended, and by then Rand will probably be back."

"What about Violet?"

"With two newborns on her hands? She wouldn't leave them if the King himself commanded it."

Rose heaved a sigh that put Lily's to shame. Resignation seemed to age her features. "Then I suppose I'll have to go with you."

"*What?*" Lily's screech made Beatrix jump. "Why would you do that?"

"What other option is there? You cannot go alone." Lily opened her mouth, but Rose continued, "I know what you're going to say, and yes, it's true that an unmarried sister is not an ideal chaperone. But I'm better than nothing, and you said yourself Mum won't leave Rowan until he's mended. By the time she learns our whereabouts, there'll be nothing she can do."

"'By the time she learns our whereabouts'?"

Rose almost smiled. "I have a plan."

Lily wanted to laugh, thinking it sounded an awful lot like the plan she herself had described to Rand. Perhaps the two sisters were more alike than they'd realized.

But then her amusement faded as doubt flooded in. She searched Rose's eyes carefully, but their black depths betrayed nothing. "Why are you doing this for me, Rose?

Looking solemn, Rose touched Lily's arm, a fairly affectionate gesture for her. She wasn't the cuddly type. "I've been angry with you, Lily. And I haven't quite forgiven you yet." A hint of warmth seemed to creep into that cool tone of voice. "But you're still my sister."

THIRTY-FIVE

*W*HEN THE ASHCROFTS arrived at Trentingham, the girls immediately asked their mother's permission to visit Violet and the twins. Mum raised a brow, perhaps wondering at the abrupt restoration of Lily and Rose's friendship, but only bid them return in time for supper.

Then came Rose's role: sweet-talking Tilney, the young coachman who'd written her sonnets when she was sixteen, into readying a carriage and bringing it round to the end of the drive, where they could meet out of view of the mansion.

Meanwhile, Lily withdrew to her bedchamber to pack a fresh case; they'd be traveling light since they couldn't ring for a footman without risking discovery. She was seated at her white dressing table, scribbling, when a light knock came at the door and Rose entered, hauling her own reduced luggage. "Nearly finished?" she puffed.

"Finished." Lily placed the note on her bed, praying it wouldn't be found until she and Rose failed to turn up for supper.

Hiding their small cases beneath their cloaks, the girls quit the house by way of the back door, then made a dash for their father's orchards. Staying under tree cover made for a round-about route, but it was far safer than cutting through the garden, where they'd be exposed to all the west-facing windows. Lily grew hot and out of breath, but they made it to the end of the drive soon enough, and without incident.

Except for the fact that their mother stood beside the carriage, chatting amiably with Tilney.

"Mum!" they both gasped, exchanging a panicked look.

Lily wiped sweat from her brow. "Are you off on a visit, too?" she asked in what she hoped was an airy manner.

"No," Mum said pleasantly. "I was simply telling Tilney here that he ought to meet the blacksmith's niece down in the village. She's visiting from Kent, you know. Lovely girl."

Tilney looked embarrassed, though not displeased.

"Well, we'd better be off," Rose said, making a show of glancing at the sun. "It's only a couple hours until supper time."

But Mum didn't budge, and she was blocking the carriage steps. "What's that you're carrying, my loves?"

The sisters exchanged another look. "Gifts," Lily improvised. "Toys for Violet's children. We did some shopping during our walking tour yesterday."

"Exactly," Rose put in.

"Oh, how darling! May I see?"

"Um..." While Rose's cheeks slowly heated, Mum reached into her pocket and pulled out Lily's note.

Lily's case slipped from her fingers.

Mum turned to Tilney. "Would you be so good as to give us a moment alone?" When he was out of earshot, she looked back to her daughters. "I never imagined you would lie to me about something like this," she said quietly.

Lily glanced up to see her mother's eyes lingering on her,

expressing particular disappointment in her youngest daughter. The sweet one. The good girl.

Or so she used to be.

Perhaps being bad wasn't such a good thing, after all. She certainly didn't feel good right now. Her eyes were itchy with threatening tears, her insides squirming with remorse.

When her daughters still held their silence, Mum sighed. "Well, I can see you're bent on going to him, Lily. I just wish you'd felt you could tell me so yourself."

Lily's eyebrows shot up. Her mother couldn't mean... "You're letting me go?"

Mum gave a rueful laugh. "You've got two working legs and a cunning mind, so I can hardly stop you. I'll not have you traveling alone, however. I'd take you myself if Rowan didn't need me, but..." She frowned. "Rose, are you certain you don't mind accompanying her?"

"Of course not." Setting down her case, Rose flexed her fingers. "It was all my idea."

"Was it?" Mum looked taken aback, then thoughtful. "All right, if you're sure," she said finally, and shifted to regard both of her daughters. "I feel terribly queer sending Hawkridge uninvited guests, but I trust Rand will take care of you—and see you safely home should the marquess take exception. You two will doubtless mind your manners"—here her eyes lingered on Rose—"and be gracious to your host."

"Yes, Mum," Rose muttered.

"And in return," their mother continued earnestly, "you must both promise that you'll talk to me from now on." Eyes softening, she reached to tidy one of Lily's curls. "I'm not thrilled about this little excursion of yours, but it's still a thousand times better than your running away. You must know that? That the very last thing I want is to drive my children away from me?"

"I do know that. I do." Lily swiped at her damp eyes. "I'm sorry, Mum. I don't know what came over me."

Her mother smiled. "Love makes us do foolish things sometimes."

Lily nodded gratefully.

"Now, where did Tilney get to?" Mum put two fingers in her mouth and whistled, and the coachman appeared at once. "Will you kindly drive us back to the house?"

"What?" Lily dropped the case she'd just picked up.

"Have you changed your mind?" Rose demanded.

Mum laughed and ushered them into the carriage. "We're only returning to get the rest of your luggage. I expect you to represent Trentingham creditably." She winked at Lily. "I hear Hawkridge Hall is very grand, and you'll want to be looking your best."

THIRTY-SIX

*M*UCH SOONER than he would have liked, Rand found his carriage turning away from the Thames and rolling up the wide drive to Hawkridge Hall.

His gaze swept over the three-story redbrick building. Although its symmetrical H shape was typical of houses built this century, the house was atypical in size and appointments. And the marquess spared no expense to keep it that way. The windows had been replaced since Rand moved away, now the new sash style with double-glazed glass. The mansion was the height of contemporary fashion.

But it sickened him. He had few happy memories of this place.

He was climbing out of the carriage when the mansion's arched front door swung open to admit a maid and a footman. With a bow and a murmured "milord," the footman took charge of Rand's luggage.

"Welcome back, Lord Randal." The maid curtseyed and touched a hand to the white cap that covered her gray curls.

"Nurse Etta?" Rand blinked in shock. His old nurse had been demoted to a housemaid.

"You'd best follow me." Though her voice was kind, her eyes wouldn't quite meet his. "Lord Hawkridge awaits you in his study."

Of course the marquess wouldn't come out to greet him.

"I know the way," Rand said quietly, knowing any trace of pity in his voice would shame the old woman. He couldn't quite manage to smile, but left her with a polite nod and made for the house.

Inside, he was surprised to discover he still recognized most of the servants bustling about Hawkridge's imposing great hall. Friendly faces turned to him as he passed, and he acknowledged them with as much cheer as he could muster —which unfortunately wasn't much. Pausing at the entrance to the study, he steeled his nerves and entered.

The man behind the desk looked up. His body stiffened beneath his jet-black velvet suit, and his mouth thinned into a hard line. "What took you so long? Your brother is already buried."

Just hearing that tone of voice, Rand felt, for a moment, like the small boy who'd always quavered in the face of his father's disfavor. The frosty gray eyes missed nothing, assessing him as they used to—and with no more approval. If Rand had harbored a foolish hope that the loss of the marquess's elder son would make him look anew at his younger one, those dreams were dead.

Never mind how carefully he'd dressed this morning; Rand felt slovenly under that gaze. For that moment he was ten again, thirsting for the man's love, willing to do almost anything to gain his acceptance. But whatever he'd tried had always been for naught, and today was no different.

And he wasn't that small boy anymore.

"I was unavoidably detained," he said evenly, and offered no other explanation. While the desk sat on a raised dais toward the back of the study, the only other chairs were on the lower level. Rand took one, though he hadn't been invited. Looking up at his father this way used to make him feel contrite and insignificant, but he'd come too far to fall for the man's tricks.

The old goat harrumphed, his face shadowed beneath his luxuriant periwig. He was one of the few men Rand knew who wore a periwig every waking hour of every day, even tucked away out here in the countryside. Rand crossed his arms, bracing for his father to make mention of his uncovered, chopped-off hair. Then he chided himself. They'd been apart too long for the man to recognize the difference. Or he hadn't noticed. Or he simply no longer cared.

Or all of the above.

The marquess wasted no time on preliminaries. "Your brother, as you know, had been betrothed since childhood to Margery. I swore to her father they would marry the day she turned one-and-twenty. That happens to be next week. I intend for you to fulfill that pledge."

Rand felt as though the air had been knocked out of him. He closed his eyes for a moment, then forced them open, a failing attempt to appear unruffled.

Margery. How could he have forgotten how these developments would impact Margery?

"Where *is* Margery?"

"In London. I sent her to obtain a proper wardrobe for mourning. She returns tomorrow." The marquess lifted a quill, pristine white lace falling back from his wrist. "I expect you to greet her as befits a husband-to-be."

"I cannot." Rand had washed his hands of the marquess long ago. He wasn't responsible for the man's twenty-year-old agreement. "I'm sorry for Margery, but—"

"My honor is on the line," the marquess continued as if Rand hadn't spoken. "And the family wealth is at stake."

Looking toward the heavens for patience, Rand waved an

arm, the gesture encompassing the grandiose opulence that was Hawkridge Hall. "I cannot imagine how the family wealth could be in jeopardy."

For once, his father looked almost uncomfortable. "I've never had any reason to discuss family finances with the likes of you. But you may as well know that I mortgaged the Hawkridge lands to raise funds for Charles."

Rand knew he meant Charles I, not the current King Charles, and that the funds had gone to support the king's side in the Civil War. The money would have been lost along with the battles, but William Nesbitt had been and still was a loyal Royalist. That he'd done such a thing was hardly surprising.

But his next words were.

"We were on the verge of ruin when Margery came into our lives."

Margery. Rand pictured her young upturned face, her delicate features framed by the palest blond curls. Between her sporadic letters, he hadn't thought of Margery often— he'd avoided thinking of anything at Hawkridge for years— but when he had, they'd been fond thoughts. He thought of her much like a sister.

Never, ever as a potential wife.

The marquess dipped the quill and began signing papers while he talked. "As Margery's guardian and eventual father-in-law, I've managed her extensive lands along with Hawkridge's for twenty years. The loss of those lands and income would be devastating, leading to eventual bankruptcy."

One of Rand's hands reached up to find the ends of his once-long hair, then fisted and dropped to his lap. "Surely you exaggerate."

"I do not." The marquess flipped a page.

Rand knew the man's half attention was calculated to

make him feel worthless, but it wasn't going to work. He wouldn't *let* it work.

"If you don't marry Margery," his father continued, "her land will be lost to us, and all of Hawkridge will suffer." At last, he looked up. "All, Randal."

All.

Not only what was left of the family, but the old family retainers. Etta and the other servants. The tenants, the villagers—everyone who depended on Hawkridge for their livings.

Rand knew his father was preying on his sympathies. His father bore no great concern for the people—he worried for himself, and himself alone. But that didn't make the entreaty any less effective.

Fortunately for Rand, the choice had already been made. The marquess may have made a pledge to Margery's father, but he, Rand, had made a pledge to Lily, and that meant his honor was on the line, too. Though he feared for the future of Hawkridge's people, they would just have to find another way to save the estate.

"I'm not marrying Margery."

The marquess's quill paused in its scratching. "Have you heard what I've said?"

Rand rubbed his palms on his velvet breeches. "Yes, and I regret that I cannot assist in this matter, but I'm betrothed to another. Lily's father is an earl, and she has a dowry of three thousand pounds—"

"Three thousand wouldn't begin to make a dent in Hawkridge's needs." Parchment crackled when he flipped another page. "You will wed Margery."

Rand rose from his chair and stepped onto the dais. "I will wed Lady Lily."

The marquess finally looked up, his mouth twisted in

profound disgust. "No matter the lousy chit's pedigree, you'll wed her over my dead body."

Rand heard blood rushing in his ears. He leaned forward over the desk, thankful it made such a big, solid barrier between them. Because had the desk not been there, he feared nothing could have prevented him from fastening his hands around the old goat's neck. Rand drew breath, but before he could get a word out, an aging footman entered the room.

"Forgive me, milord," the footman wheezed, bowing to the marquess, "but were you expecting more callers today?"

THIRTY-SEVEN

"*I*S LORD HAWKRIDGE expecting you?"

When Lily hesitated, Rose stepped forward with her nose in the air. "We're here at Lord Newcliffe's invitation." In her Louis heels, she had a couple inches' height over the butler—and she clearly wasn't afraid to use them. "You may take us to him directly."

"There's no need for that," said a familiar voice, and Lily turned to see Rand crunching toward them across the gravel. When he reached them, she instinctively took his hand. It had been a long and emotionally draining day. Though she and Rose seemed to have reached some kind of truce, their second carriage ride today had been just as uncomfortable as the first. She'd never felt more in need of Rand's reassuring presence.

But after giving her fingers a polite squeeze, he let go. "Lily," he said in an odd tone. His eyes flicked to Rose, registered surprise, then settled back on her with an expression of...something else. Something that made her stomach clench.

He clearly didn't want her here.

Well, she hadn't exactly been expecting a welcome parade, considering he'd told her not to come. But nor had she imagined a reaction like this. Was he merely annoyed that she'd defied his wishes? Or was it something worse?

When he leaned close to her ear, she winced, anticipating a rebuke. His warm breath tickled her skin. "Sweet mercy, am I glad to see you."

She broke into a smile, her knees going weak with relief—until she noticed the man standing behind him.

He resembled Rand, except he sported an elaborate periwig, deep frown lines, and eyes that were closer to flint than silver. Those eyes examined her from head to toe, taking in the gown her mother had helped her pick out, lovely pale green velvet with a white underskirt and little white rosettes dotting the bodice. The dress struck a balance between demure and sumptuous, perfect for impressing a snobbish, fusty old nobleman—or so they'd thought. Suddenly Lily feared she looked repulsive.

"Well?" Lord Hawkridge narrowed his eyes. "Who on earth are you?"

Looking stunned, Rand set his jaw and wrapped an arm around Lily. "This is Lady Lily Ashcroft, the Earl of Trentingham's daughter. My betrothed."

The frown lines deepened. "What is *she* doing here?"

"My lord," Lily said in a steady, respectful tone, "I'm from good family, and I am in love with your son."

Lord Hawkridge's expression didn't thaw. "Then you will make him an excellent mistress," he snapped.

"That's enough!" Rand growled dangerously. "You will be courteous to my guests."

"Your guests?" His father barked a laugh. "They cannot be thinking of staying the night."

Rand tightened his arm around Lily. "Lily is my

betrothed, and Rose will soon be my sister. If they go, so do I."

After a moment's thought, Lord Hawkridge apparently decided this wasn't a battle worth fighting. He beckoned to a rather elderly housemaid. "Put them in the Queen's Bedchamber, Etta. For now," he added ominously.

When his cold gaze fell again on Lily, she stared back with all the steel she possessed. Rand was a warm presence at her side, and she felt bolstered to sense Rose at her back. It was amazing what a common enemy could do to help mend fences.

Lily narrowed her eyes at the old man, just as he'd looked at her. *Let him do his worst.*

THIRTY-EIGHT

"**D**O YOU LIKE your room?"

Lily whirled to see Rand in the doorway, directing servants bearing her and Rose's trunks.

"The chamber acquired its name," he told the sisters, "shortly after it had been redecorated for a visit by Queen Catharine. It is also—by no coincidence, I believe—as far from my own chamber as physically possible."

"Mum would approve," Rose said primly, testing a richly embroidered chair.

Lily ignored her. "The room is magnificent." She wasn't surprised the queen really had graced the Queen's Bedchamber, for it certainly looked like it had been decorated for royalty. Even Lily, whose own family home was worth gawking at, found this chamber astonishing.

The enormous state bed, hung with costly cloth of gold, sat on a raised parquet dais behind a balustrade in the French style. Great poufs of ostrich feathers crowned each of the bed's four posts. The ceiling was elaborate painted plaster-work, the furniture gilt wood. The walls were hung with rich tapestries, and the marble fireplace boasted gilded crowns over the chimneypiece and on the piers.

But above all, the position of the room demonstrated its status. Beyond its windows, as in a royal palace, the gardens and avenues spread out in perfect symmetry, from this, the exact central vantage point.

Rose stood at one of those windows, examining the view with a critical eye. "Father's gardens are much more impressive," she remarked.

Lily blushed for her, but Rand only chuckled. "I hope you'll tell the marquess so."

Along with the other priceless furnishings, the Queen's Bedchamber contained a lovely rosewood harpsichord. No matter the marquess's intentions in bestowing the chamber— and Lily had no doubt he'd meant to overawe his guests with a sense of his wealth and power—he really couldn't have assigned her to a more perfect room. The thought made her smile.

Not to say that she was comfortable here. Just knowing the unpleasant Lord Hawkridge lurked somewhere in the mansion was enough to make her wish herself home. "Have you spoken with your father already?" she asked Rand as soon as the servants had left.

"A bit." He dredged up a smile—a weak, obvious effort. "I'll tell you about it later. I need to think. I need to…to go off by myself. Sometimes I do that."

"All right. Where are you going?"

"I just need to run."

"I'll come along—"

"Alone, Lily. I'll be back soon. I promise." He took a step closer, leaning in to meet her lips.

Rose cleared her throat.

Rand paused, frowned, then settled for kissing Lily's forehead.

She bit her lip, slanting a look at her sister. Rose stood at the gilt dressing table, re-pinning her hair with an air of innocence.

"Will you be all right here for a bit, Rose?" Lily asked "I'm going to walk Rand out of the house."

Rand lifted a brow, then shrugged and turned toward the door. Lily followed him into the adjacent antechamber, where he peeled off his surcoat and cravat. After draping them over a fashionable japanned chair, he began rolling up his sleeves as he strode from the room, leaving her to hasten after him.

Lily hadn't taken him for a moody sort of fellow, but then, she admitted to herself, in truth she hardly knew him. But she knew she loved him. And if he needed some time to himself, how could she begrudge him that?

She followed him from the chamber and down the massive oak staircase, another feature of the mansion that had clearly been built to impress. Beneath the handrails, pierced wooden panels were carved with armor, cannons, muskets, spears, and lances. Trophies of war, their details highlighted by gold and silver leaf.

A display of force and power.

Lily quickened her pace. "Can you at least give me a hint? Is he demanding you leave Oxford to live here?"

She watched his shoulders tense beneath the thin white cambric of his shirt. "That minor detail hasn't even been discussed yet." He sighed and stopped to wait for her. "He's forbidden our marriage."

Though her heart leapt into her throat, she ordered herself not to panic. Lord Hawkridge couldn't really prevent them from wedding, could he? They would wish for his blessing, of course, but as a last resort, they could always elope. Especially given that Rand seemed to care little for his inheritance.

As he resumed his descent, she reached for his hand. "Why?"

"My brother was to wed my father's ward, a girl named Margery Maybanks. I told you about her, didn't I? The marquess expects me to honor that commitment."

"Would you not make a poor substitute? She loved your brother, not you."

A short, harsh laugh tore from his throat. "Oh, I doubt she loved Alban. Aside from my father, I'm aware of no one who did." At the bottom of the staircase, he headed across the great hall toward the front door. "Margery's father saved the marquess's life in the Battle of Worcester, and the marquess promised him a boon. A few years later, on his deathbed, the man made his claim: that the marquess raise his motherless young daughter here and marry her to his heir on the day she turned one-and-twenty."

A footman opened the door, and they stepped out. After the dark tones that dominated the mansion's interior, Lily blinked in the sunshine. "And now you're the heir." She tugged on Rand's hand until he stopped and turned to face her. "Can you refuse?"

"I *have* refused. But…there's more."

"What—"

He hushed her with two fingers on her lips. "Let me think, Lily. I'll return soon." He bent to replace his fingers with his mouth, but after a quick kiss, he ran off around the corner of the house, his boots loud on the cobbled pavement.

His gait looked determined. She followed slowly, rounding the corner in time to see him cross a lawn and disappear into a tangle of trees. A wilderness garden, perhaps. It seemed to be more planned than the woods that bordered Trentingham, with man-made paths cut through it.

She would honor his request for solitude. She had little interest in the gardens, and should he look back, she didn't want him to think she was tailing him. Instead, she wandered around the perimeter of the house, vaguely following the sounds of barking dogs.

On the west side of the mansion she found a yard, bordered by several small buildings. A bakehouse, a still-house, a washhouse, a brewhouse, a dairy. She peeked in the diamond-paned windows of the last, seeing milking pails, pans, skimming dishes, and strainers. Inside, a young woman was bent over a cheese press. She straightened and gave Lily a puzzled look, then offered a tentative smile. Lily thought she would have been pretty if her face weren't covered in smallpox scars.

As she walked away, her fingertips went to her own smooth skin. Would Rand still love her if she succumbed to the pox?

She rubbed the scars on the back of her hand, telling herself not to be silly. She would love him no matter what disfigurement he might suffer, for better or worse, as the marriage vows said. And when she locked her eyes on his, she knew, for a fact, he felt the same.

Behind the dairy, another fenced yard was teeming with the dogs she'd heard earlier. Despite her worries, a grin spread on her face. She gathered her skirts to climb the rails.

"They're dangerous," someone said, not unkindly.

She turned to see Etta, the older woman who'd shown her to her room. Etta bore smallpox scars as well, but not nearly as many as the milkmaid, and her large green eyes and curly gray hair made Lily think she had probably been lovely as a young woman.

"I've been sent to look for you," Etta explained.

"By whom?"

"The marquess. He wishes to know your whereabouts."

"Well then, tell him I'm playing with the dogs," Lily said, amazed at her own boldness.

Why, Rose would scarcely recognize her. Loving Rand had awakened her newfound strength.

A smile twitched at the corners of Etta's mouth. "If you won't mind my saying, my lady, nobody plays with those dogs."

Lily turned and looked again. They were huge dogs—mastiffs—and there were more than a dozen. But she'd never met a dog she didn't like. Or even more important, one who hadn't liked her.

"Well, then," she said blithely, "it's about time someone *did* play with the poor creatures."

And ignoring Etta's gasp, she bunched her skirts and climbed over the fence.

THIRTY-NINE

*W*HEN RAND RETURNED from his run, he headed straight for his old room to wash his face and change his shirt. Then he went in search of Lily, and was dismayed to find the Queen's Bedchamber empty but for Rose napping on the opulent golden counterpane.

Not for the first time, he wondered why Rose was playing chaperone here. The Oxford excursion had seemed to take the edge off her fury, but she was still clearly hostile toward her sister. Why would she agree to do a favor for her?

Impatient to find Lily, Rand retreated to the antechamber, grabbed his surcoat off the chair, and shoved his arms into the sleeves. He slipped his cravat back around his neck and strode over to a massive gilt-framed mirror to tie the neat knot his father had always required of him. In his rush, his fingers refused to cooperate.

"Trouble, my lord?"

The mirror reflected a woman poking her head through the doorway.

"Hmm?" He turned and, seeing it was Etta, experienced an absurd rush of nostalgia. She'd aged, of course, and she was newly scarred since he'd last seen her, though not too badly. She seemed shorter than he'd remembered. But the placid green eyes were the same.

Those were eyes one could count on. He hadn't thought about Etta in years, and he felt a wave of shame for that. But he hadn't wanted to remember the people here who'd cared for him.

The people who could be hurt if he failed to figure something out.

"Oh, please don't call me *my lord*, Nurse Etta. You're supposed to call me Randal in a stern tone of voice."

When she laughed, it wasn't an old lady's laugh—it was the one he remembered from his childhood. Nurse Etta may have been stern when it was required, but most times she had been kindly and good-natured.

"Then don't call me Nurse Etta." She came close and took over tying the cravat. "My word, that makes me feel as though I'm still responsible for you three young hellions." She smiled up at him, looking much like the younger woman he remembered, despite the smallpox scars. "I've been plain Etta for years."

"How did that happen?"

"Why so disapproving?" Finished, she patted his chest and stepped back. "When Margery grew into a young lady, I faced the choice of finding another household with small children elsewhere, or taking a different position here. Your father was kind enough to let me stay on."

He'd never expected to hear the words *your father* and *kind* in the same sentence, and his expression must have shown it.

"Circumstances change, Randal," she added in that old Nurse Etta tone of voice. "It's up to us to accept them and move on."

He suspected those words were directed to him and his

current situation, but he didn't want to hear them right now. "I'm looking for Lady Lily."

"A lovely young woman." She took out a cloth and rubbed at a smudge on the mirror. "She's outside playing with the dogs."

"What dogs? You cannot mean…no…"

She plumped a pillow, then looked up. "Yes. The marquess's dogs."

That was worse than learning Lily was with his father. His heart pounding, Rand headed outside at a run.

But when he reached the enclosure, he told himself he should have known better. He stood for a moment just watching. Lily was fine, if covered in dog slobber. In fact, she seemed to be in her element.

She had a fawn-colored dog fetching a short stick and a brindle dog playing tug-of-war with a longer one. Two more dogs seemed, miraculously, to be waiting their turns for attention. Another few were simply ignoring her, but that in itself was a wonder.

Some of the hounds stood as tall as her shoulder, and they were all trained to fight, bred mainly for their fierceness. Except the marquess, everyone on the estate was terrified of the beasts, Rand included.

Thinking it might be more dangerous than running into a burning barn, he climbed into the enclosure and wove his way through the excited animals to Lily.

She glanced over at his approach, then focused on the brindle dog. "Let go," she commanded. The canine dropped his end of the stick, ending the playful tug-of-war.

Rand was unsurprised. Animals always seemed to listen to Lily. "Thank you for your patience," he said, drawing near.

She shrugged, clearly still unhappy that he'd run off. But she seemed unwilling to make trouble, either. She tossed the shorter stick and watched the fawn-colored dog chase after it. "I understand," she said quietly.

Hurrying back with the wood, the mastiff sideswiped Rand and made him stagger. The mass of these beasts was amazing; not a one of them weighed less than he did. "This isn't really safe," he told her. "They're very aggressive."

"Balderdash. They were starving for attention." With a swipe of its huge pink tongue, the hound licked her smack on the face. She tossed the stick again. "You should put some thick, knotted rope in here. They'd enjoy playing with it, chewing on it. And that tree is a hazard." She waved toward one corner. "Those apples are exactly the right size to get lodged in their throats. I'm surprised none of them have choked."

He shifted on his feet. "I'm sure my father knows what he's about. He's been breeding the monsters for years."

"Monsters? I thought you said you were a dog person."

He felt himself turning red. "These don't count. I prefer the small, fluffy sort."

Reclaiming the stick from between the dog's big teeth, she appeared to be suppressing a laugh. "Have you ever had a small, fluffy dog?"

"No. But I used to look at these and wish for one."

"They can be meaner than these. We shall have to try to locate a sweet one for you." She dropped the wood to the ground and finally met his gaze. "Are you ready to tell me the rest?"

"Can we get out of here first?"

"I suppose." She patted a couple of hounds on their heads before bunching her skirts in a hand. As she climbed the fence, the dogs began howling. When Rand went to follow, one beast whacked him with its tail, a stinging blow he half suspected was deliberate.

He probably deserved it.

When they were safely beyond the fence, he took Lily's face in both hands and kissed her, relieved when he felt her lips cling to his. "I'm sorry for running off," he told her. "It's a bad habit."

Apparently having forgiven him, she smiled. "I hope it's your worst."

"Oh, it is, I assure you. Other than this one oddity, I'm a perfect companion."

"*Those* are perfect companions." She gestured toward the dogs. But her tone was teasing.

Feeling better than he had since arriving, he slipped an arm around her waist and walked her into the gardens. "I'm glad you've made friends here already."

She smiled. "I feel much more at home with them. Not that Hawkridge isn't lovely," she added quickly, turning to admire the mansion.

Rand couldn't help thinking she'd probably rather live here than in Oxford. Surely most ladies would prefer a grand estate on the bucolic banks of the Thames to a smaller house smack in the middle of—

Who was that?

Rand peered at the facade, thinking he'd glimpsed a face in one of the windows…a window near the center. But it was gone so quickly he couldn't identify the person, or even be sure of what he'd seen.

"Hawkridge shows no signs of damage," Lily remarked. "Yet your family supported Charles in the war, did they not? How is it that the mansion escaped Cromwell's wrath, and so close to London, no less?"

"We have my mother to thank for that. Publicly, she was great friends with Oliver Cromwell and went so far as to entertain him here. Privately, she was an important member of the Sealed Knot."

"What was that?"

"A clandestine organization that aimed to restore Charles to the throne. The members had secret names; my mother was 'Mrs. Gray.' When I was very young, she traveled to the Continent several times as a courier. Many letters went back and forth, always written in code."

"Ah, I see where you inherited that talent for deciphering codes."

He grinned. "My mother even concocted an invisible ink that they used. In the Sealed Knot letters, Cromwell was 'Mr. Wright.' While on the surface she supported him, all along she was plotting his downfall."

"She must have been quite a woman."

"She was smart and principled and beautiful. And I suppose she made this home beautiful, too," he added, knowing, in a detached way, that it was. "But I don't want to live here."

"I, too, would prefer to live in Oxford," Lily assured him, sounding sincere. "Your house is much more modern, so simple and classic. And empty. I'm so looking forward to filling it over time, making it ours." She frowned. "That is, if your father...well, I suppose if he has his way we won't wed at all, so it hardly matters where he'd want us to live."

"I don't care what my father wants, Lily. I won't give you up for anything. *Anything.*"

She nestled closer, and he didn't even mind the dog slobber getting on his best coat. "Tell me the rest. Your father pledged to marry Margery to his heir, and now *you* are his heir. What else?"

He began walking her down a path. "Margery's a commoner, but an heiress. She inherited a vast estate. Land that my father has been managing for twenty years."

"And?"

"He claims that Hawkridge will bankrupt without the income from that land. He said he was close to losing everything when Margery came along. He mortgaged Hawkridge to the hilt to support Charles during the war."

"Would he have?"

"What?"

"Risked his estate for the king?"

He blinked. "Of course. Did your father not do the same?"

"It was my grandfather at the time. And no." Her father's daughter, she plucked dead leaves off the hedges as they walked. "Grandpapa sent money, but no more than he felt he could spare. And he never went off to fight, nor did he send his son. While we waited out the war and Protectorate at Tremayne, they were both right there along with us. Grandpapa always said he valued family above the monarchy."

A different way of thinking, but Rand liked it. "I suspect the marquess would have called him a coward. But if *he* hadn't gone off to war, he would never have been indebted to Margery's father. And I wouldn't be in this mess today."

"*We* wouldn't be in this mess," she corrected gently. "We'll find a way out together."

In that moment, his affection for her increased tenfold. He couldn't remember when anyone had stood by him so unconditionally. In order to persevere, he'd always needed to find the will within himself. But now he could depend on—lean on—Lily. Those narrow shoulders were deceptively strong.

In the shade of a spreading tree he stopped, gathering her close and touching his lips to hers. "I love you, Lily Ashcroft," he murmured against her mouth.

"And I, you." Her hands slipped under his coat, and she leaned back to look up at him. "What else? There's more, I can tell."

"You're a dangerous girl." He chuckled and kissed her on the nose before sobering. "The maid the marquess assigned to you, Etta…"

She frowned and took his arm to resume walking. "She's a kind sort."

"She used to be my nurse, and yes, she's very kind." He hadn't expected to find anything he cared for here at Hawkridge. Or anyone. "She—and others—made my childhood here bearable."

A bee buzzed over their heads, then flew off. "You worry for them," she said with the sort of compassion that made her Lily. "Not for your father, not for Hawkridge the estate, but for Hawkridge's people."

"The old family retainers."

"And the tenants and villagers, too, I imagine. There must be dozens of people who depend on Hawkridge for their livelihoods."

"Hundreds." Stopping again to pull her close, he buried his face in her fragrant hair. "Oh heavens, Lily. As much as I don't want to jump to the marquess's command, as much as I cannot imagine giving up my hard-won professorship, as much as I cannot stand to think of losing you—absolutely *won't* consider losing you—"

His voice broke.

"You also cannot imagine letting all these people down," Lily finished for him, drawing back.

Holding his gaze, she caught his hands in both of hers. His eyes were murky with devastation, but she knew he hadn't given up on her yet—though he might not know it himself.

"There must be another way," she said. He was so solid. Immovable. He'd always be there for her. "Besides meek acceptance of your father's dictates, there *must* be another way."

Clearly wanting to believe her, he nodded—but not with anything like confidence. "I meant what I said. I won't give you up for anything. But I ran, and then I walked, and yet I couldn't think—"

"There's my marriage portion." She drew him to sit beside her on a wooden bench.

"I told him about that," Rand admitted, looking guilty.

"As you should have. It will be yours as soon as we wed."

With a gentle hand, he pushed her hair off her face. "I don't feel as though it necessarily should be. I didn't earn it. Everything else I have, I've earned."

"It's the way the world works, Rand. I vow, you're one of the few gentlemen I've met who wouldn't run to the altar for that sort of money." Yet more proof he was special. "What did he say?"

"He said, and I quote, it 'wouldn't make a dent in Hawkridge's needs.'"

She nodded, unsurprised. Three thousand pounds was a respectable sum for a dowry, but a man of the marquess's stature wouldn't face bankruptcy for a lack of that amount. "Do you expect an additional ten thousand would make a difference?"

He blinked. "Ten thousand?"

"My inheritance. I've told you about it, remember? Grand-papa left me ten thousand pounds—"

"*Ten* thousand pounds?" The look on his face made her realize she'd never mentioned the amount, only discussed what she planned to do with it. "I never thought about...I remember now that Violet was left that much money, but she's the eldest...it never occurred to me..."

Sudden understanding stole over his expression.

"Is *that* what Rose was talking about that day in the summerhouse?" he said, looking incredulous. "Her inheritance? I assumed she was counting on her dowry and planning to wheedle the rest out of your father. I never for a minute believed she'd actually deliver on such a sum."

"Not even Rose makes promises she cannot keep," Lily said, feeling a fresh stab of guilt when she remembered her own broken promise. But it was a little stab, because she knew she and Rand belonged together, and because she also knew that whatever sorrow her sister had suffered was inconsequential compared to what was now at stake. "Yes, we were each left ten thousand pounds. We can give it to your father, to save Hawkridge, and then we'll be able to marry."

Rand looked stunned. "You had plans for that money. You were going to build a home for stray animals. And use the rest of your funds to run it for many years."

She swallowed a lump in her throat. "So I'll find another way," she whispered. "I love animals, but I love you more."

His eyes grew suspiciously glossy. She'd never seen a man cry. She wanted to reach him, but the difference in their heights was more pronounced sitting. Feeling daring, she moved onto his lap and took his face in her hands, kissing his eyes, his nose, his cheeks. His arms came around her and clasped her to his chest.

After enjoying his warmth for a while, she asked, "How much is Margery's fortune?"

"I don't know. Maybe more. But if the marquess cannot save Hawkridge with thirteen thousand pounds, he's not the man he pretends to be." When he kissed the top of her head, she felt his lips curve into a smile. "It should certainly keep Hawkridge from ruin and set it on the road to recovery, and then I'll be able to persuade him to bless our marriage."

"What if Margery wants to marry you?"

"Beg pardon?" A strangled laugh escaped him. "Believe me, what my father wants and what Margery wants are two very different things. We grew up together, like brother and sister. Besides, with her fortune, she can find herself a much better husband. Someone important."

"You're a baron," she reminded him. "And someday you'll be a marquess."

"But at heart, I'm a professor." His finger found the dent in her chin. "That you would give up your inheritance to be with me..." His voice grew rough again. "It's overwhelming. I don't deserve you, but—"

That being utter nonsense, Lily raised her head to silence him with another kiss. Their lips moved together in a slow, shivery dance that drew all her awareness to this one moment in time, this one speck in all of existence. She would never get enough of this, enough of him. If he was wrenched from her...

Her brain refused to finish the thought.

FORTY

"*Y*OU OFFERED YOUR inheritance?" Seated at the elaborate gilt dressing table in the Queen's Bedchamber, Rose was incredulous. "But what about your animal home?"

Lily shrugged. "It's not as important as Rand." At Etta's command, she held her arms away from her body so the maid could arrange her sleeves into artful puffs.

Rose made a disapproving noise. "And what of this Margery? Aren't you worried about her?" Dipping her finger into a little cosmetic pot, she leaned close to the mirror and reddened her lips.

"Rand thinks she will be our ally in this matter. She has no wish to marry him."

"What makes him think so? He's handsome, rich, and now titled. And weren't they childhood playmates? She could have been loving him from afar all this time."

Lily was surprised to hear a little snort of laughter escape Etta, who had seemed a very reserved sort of woman. When Rose glared at the maid, she quickly refocused on her task.

"Well, Rand seems to think it unlikely that Margery harbors any feelings for him." *And Etta seems to agree*, Lily added silently. "In any case, we'll know for certain tomorrow morning, when she's due back from London."

Rose looked skeptical but said no more. Finished dressing, the two girls made their way down to the dining room in silence.

Like the rest of the house, the chamber was beautiful. Lily had glimpsed an enormous, lavish banqueting hall upstairs, but this room was much more intimate.

Rand escorted them in, an Ashcroft sister on each arm. The ladies' heels clicked on the two-toned parquet floor. Lily stopped to run a hand over the patterned design on the walls, surprised to find it was gold stamped on brown leather. "It looks like gilded wood!" she exclaimed.

"The leather is supposed to absorb the smells of food."

She'd never heard of such a thing. "It's lovely."

"All of Hawkridge Hall is lovely," Rose said, but not as though she were happy about it.

"It's a lovely prison," Rand muttered darkly.

In opposition to the prison that was Hawkridge Hall—a prison designed and paid for by his father—the Oxford house was one-hundred-percent Rand's. A symbol, Lily suspected, of his hard-won independence. Kit had told her that he and Rand had spent months designing it before the cornerstone was laid, because Rand had wanted every square foot to be perfect. And it was.

When Lily saw Rand's eyes widen in alarm, she swung around to see his father. "Oh! Good evening, my lord."

"My lady," he grunted. "Shall we be seated?"

Lily wondered how much the marquess had heard as they all took their places at the oval cedarwood table, the marquess seating himself at the opposite end from his son.

There were eighteen matching caned chairs around the

table in this "family" dining room, and in Lily's opinion, a family sat together to better enjoy each other's company. At least *her* family did. Mentally shaking her head, she took a chair beside Rand rather than one in the middle—then pretended not to notice when two footmen had to scramble to move her table setting.

Being not so nice was feeling better and better.

Supper was an awkward affair. Rose was chiefly engaged in ogling the Nesbitts' solid gold plate and staring daggers at her younger sister. Meanwhile, Lord Hawkridge was dressed in black mourning and seemed offended that Rand was not. Lily still cherished hopes of getting father and son to reconcile, but other than a few minutes of desultory conversation about the marquess's beloved mastiffs, she couldn't even get them to speak. The party sat mostly in silence punctuated by the clinking of Hawkridge's custom-designed silverware.

Though the house was magnificent, there was something about it Lily didn't like. Something dark and forbidding. Maybe it was the deep colors on the walls and all the somber, oak-framed paintings. Maybe it was the studied formality. Or maybe it was just that she'd never been anywhere before where she'd felt so very unwelcome.

When the meal finally drew to a close, Rand pushed back his chair. "Lily plays the harpsichord beautifully," he said as a sort of invitation.

"I have work to do," the marquess replied and left the room.

Rand didn't look sorry to see the back of him. "Rose?"

Her chair scraped the parquet as she stood. "I'm going to bed," she said flatly.

Lily's eyes followed her out. "I don't understand," she said quietly, shaking her head. "This morning she seemed... well not quite *friendly*, but at least civil."

Rand covered her hand with his. "Give your sister time. It's still been less than a week since our betrothal."

"Goodness, has it? It feels like a lifetime." She sipped wine from a Venetian glass goblet. "Have you told your father about my inheritance?"

A footman entered to clear the table, and Rand cleared his throat. "Would you care to walk in the gardens?"

Holding her tongue, she went with him outside.

He led her through the more formal gardens and into an area of grass walks lined with hornbeam hedges and field maples that enclosed many small, private gardens. The late-night summer sun was sinking, but not yet so low that she couldn't see and appreciate the beauty of the individual compartments, each of which contained not only a variety of rather wild-growing plants, but also a surprise. Some hid copies of famous statuary, one offered a sundial, and another a cozy bench for two. The one Rand led her into held a tiny round gazebo.

A narrow seat curved around the inside. The structure was so small that when they settled across from each other, their knees touched.

Rand reached to take Lily's hands. "We won't be overheard here. He has spies."

"Spies? I don't think—"

"You always look for the good, sweet Lily," he interrupted. "And you don't know him," he added, leaning close to press his lips to hers. The air was taking on a twilight chill, but the kiss warmed her all the way down to her fingers and toes.

She struggled to pull herself together. "When are you going to tell him he can have my money?"

Lady flew into the gazebo's opening and landed at their feet, but Rand didn't seem to notice, let alone recognize the bird. His jaw tensed. "I'll tell him tomorrow. After I talk to Margery."

It was the first hint she'd seen that he suspected this might not all work out as planned. Suddenly she didn't feel so deliciously warm. She felt numb.

What if Margery wanted to marry him? Rand had said Margery had been raised right here at Hawkridge. With him. Was it such a stretch to believe she might have come to love him?

He was, after all, utterly lovable. Generous and caring, strong and successful, self-sufficient where it showed, but with that lost little boy hidden inside. What woman could truly know him, as Margery must, and not wish to wrap him in her arms and heal that little boy?

And with both Lord Hawkridge and Margery against her, would she, Lily, stand a chance?

She tried to search Rand's eyes, but the light was failing outside, and here in the gazebo it was even darker. "What if she wants to marry you, Rand?"

"She won't."

"But what if she does?"

He scooted around the circular bench until his thigh rested against hers, feeling warm even through their clothes. "I'm marrying you. No matter what the marquess wants. No matter what Margery wants. I love you. You, Lily." Rand slid a hand into her hair and tilted her head until she met his eyes. "We're going to marry and live happily ever after. I promise."

She hoped so, and when he kissed her, she believed him for a moment. But when he stopped, she couldn't help wondering if he was wrong.

Her life so far had been happy and uneventful, like one of the baskets Rose used for flower arrangements, perfectly woven. Was this where it would unravel? Was losing Rand the price she would pay for disregarding her sister's feelings? For breaking a promise? For being selfish instead of nice?

"Now," he said, his tone changing to one that implied the matter was settled, "since the others are uninterested in entertainment, will you play the harpsichord for me alone?"

FORTY-ONE

*L*ILY LEARNED there was a second harpsichord in the north drawing room. Inlaid with different colored woods, it was even more beautiful than the first.

"Johannes Ruckers," she breathed, reading the name painted above the keyboard.

"You know him?"

"Not personally." She grinned at the mere idea. "But Flemish harpsichords are said to make the most beautiful music, especially those built by the Ruckers family."

"Try it," he said, seating himself in a breathtaking chair that was gilded, silvered, and painted in marine colors to suggest dolphins sporting in the ocean.

She sat on the petit point stool and ran her fingers experimentally over the keys, enjoying the rich sound of the rare instrument. A small smile curved her lips as she launched into the tune she'd been practicing.

Rand smiled in return, tapping a toe in time to the music. Until he bolted out of the chair. "Where did you learn *that*?"

She continued playing. "I taught it to myself. Worked it

out, I mean. As a surprise for you. It's the tune you often hum, isn't it?"

"Do I?" His lips twitched. "Perhaps I do, from time to time."

He hummed along for a few bars, then leaned an elbow on the harpsichord and set his chin in his hand. His head was nearly level with hers, his eyes commanding her to look up.

"What?" she asked.

He grinned. "Do you know the words?"

"Does it have words?"

"Most assuredly."

"Well then, sing them, won't you?"

"Start over at the beginning," he said with an enigmatic smile.

When she did, he began singing.

> *"Come my honey, let's to bed,*
> *It is no sin, since we are wed;*
> *For when I am near thee by desire,*
> *I burn like any coal of fire."*

She couldn't care less where she lived, she thought dreamily. Hawkridge, Oxford, a hovel...if only Rand would sing to her every night, she'd be happy all her days.

Wait...

Lily's fingers stilled as she gasped. "Is this song about—?"

There was a mischievous glitter in Rand's eye. "Are you scandalized?"

Lily felt heat rush to her cheeks. "Whoever wrote a song about *that*?"

"Anonymous. He writes a lot of songs." Grinning, Rand reached around her to hit a key. "You're pink. I like you scandalized."

She giggled. "Where did you learn such a song?"

"From a book."

"A *book*?" What a sheltered life she'd led. "Someone wrote this down?"

"Oh, yes, and hundreds more. The book is called *An Antidote Against Melancholy.*"

"And you own a copy?"

"Not myself, but I have a friend with an extensive library." His eyes sparkled with undisguised mirth. "Would you like to hear another song?"

Lily hesitated. She had to admit to feeling intrigued, but...

She must have had a terrified look on her face, because Rand burst out laughing. "I can see you've heard enough for one night. Perhaps the book would make a good wedding present, hmm?" He wiggled his eyebrows suggestively.

The playfulness suddenly drained out of her. "If we make it to our wedding."

"Of course we will." He rose, pulling her up with him. "Tomorrow I'll talk to Margery, and then to the marquess. And then we'll reclaim our lives. I want no part of this." He waved an arm, encompassing the mansion, the estate, the title —everything.

"I just want you," she said. "No matter who or where you are. Professor, baron, marquess, Hawkridge, Oxford...I don't care. I care only that we're together."

He searched her eyes for a long, solemn moment, and then he yanked her against him and crushed his mouth to hers.

This was what mattered, she thought wildly—this pull, this overwhelming need. This longing to share hearts and lives. *Where* was just a tiny, insignificant detail.

Then she ceased thinking at all. She stopped thinking and just kissed Rand, for a minute, or an hour, or maybe...

"Lily," a strangled voice said in her ear, "what on earth are we doing?"

Startled from the kiss, she froze. Rand's surcoat was in a

heap on the floor, and her hands held bunches of his shirt—where she'd been pulling it out of his breeches. Shocked, she let go and stumbled back until her legs hit the stool. "I...I don't..."

"It's all right," he soothed, tucking his shirt back in. "We just got a bit carried away."

"A bit?" She sank onto the stool, trying to catch her breath. "It's *not* all right, Rand. Kissing when we're weeks shy of our wedding day is one thing, but right now we can't know for sure if we'll *ever* be married."

"What are you saying?"

She bit her lip, gathering her thoughts. "I don't think we should be close right now. It feels wrong. What if things don't work out for us?"

"I'll never let that happen."

"Never say never," she quoted softly.

The light went out of his eyes.

They were silent a while, their breathing sounding harsh in the still room.

"No," he said at last. "This time I say never."

FORTY-TWO

"OW IS HE?" Joseph asked, looking up from his book.

Sighing, Chrystabel lowered herself to the plush stool at her dressing table. "Brave, but not a particularly gifted actor. The ankle was obviously still paining him, so I gave him some sack to help him sleep." She began preparing herself for bed.

"You're fretting, Chrysanthemum. I can hear it in your voice." Joseph removed the reading spectacles his son-in-law had given him this past Christmas. "Don't be such a mother. Rowan will be fine."

"Hmm?" Chrystabel dipped her fingers in a bowl of lavender water, then dried them on a clean cloth. "Oh, I grieve for poor Rowan's discomfort, but it's not him I'm fretting over. Lily—"

"Is with Rose. I'm sure they both arrived safely at Hawkridge."

"Indeed, that's just it." Dampening the cloth, Chrystabel began to wash her face. Was it her imagination, or were those hollows under her eyes? "Lily is off with her betrothed unsupervised, and, given the way his son speaks of him, I can hardly trust Lord Hawkridge to have a care for her reputation."

"If you're so concerned, why did you let them go?"

"I didn't feel I had a choice. Lily was clearly determined, and we *did* raise our daughters to make their own decisions. But now I wonder if I was rash." Chrystabel heaved another sigh. "Meanwhile, I cannot account for Rose's part in this at all. I'm very much mistaken if she's forgiven Lily, yet she claims to have volunteered to bear her company."

Looking thoughtful, Joseph chewed on one end of his eyeglasses frames—a new habit that secretly drove Chrystabel wild. "Are you suggesting that Rose may have some other agenda?"

"No—maybe—I don't know." She turned from the mirror to meet her husband's eyes. "I don't like to think her capable of deliberately sabotaging Lily's happiness, but she's definitely hiding something from me."

"Darling, she's your nineteen-year-old daughter. *Of course* she's hiding something from you."

Chrystabel almost smiled.

"In any case, haven't we learned by now that interfering in their squabbles only makes things worse? They're good girls; they'll sort it out. Hopefully before one of them maims the other."

Now Chrystabel did smile. "You're right, of course. Lily is tougher than she looks, and Rose has a good heart underneath. I must let nature take its course." The smile faltered a little. "And I must do my best to trust that Lily's and Rand's own integrity will keep them chaste."

"Right you are." Joseph put his book and eyeglasses aside. "Now come to bed. You've hardly paid me any notice all day, you're so solicitous of our son. You must convince me you like me better than him."

FORTY-THREE

*R*AND HAD A restless night.

His mind kept turning over all the possibili-
ties, all the ways their plans could go awry. When he'd left
Hawkridge at thirteen, Margery had been only ten. Visits
during his university years had been sporadic and infrequent
—he'd preferred to spend school breaks with Ford's family
when possible. His last time home, he'd been seventeen and
Margery not yet fifteen.

He'd known Margery the child. He'd been acquainted
with Margery the girl. But Margery the young woman was a
stranger.

What if he were wrong? What if Margery the woman *did*
want to marry him? She'd lived under the influence of the
marquess all these years...

Something shifted at the foot of the bed. At first he was
alarmed, but then a warm little weight settled across his feet
and began vibrating.

Of course Beatrix had found her way to Hawkridge. Ordi-
narily her presence would have bothered him, but tonight it
made him feel like Lily were here.

Soon after, he finally drifted off, a ghost of a smile on his face, his head full of the tune she had learned for him.

~

*L*ILY SAW NO indication that anyone's mood was improved the next morning. Lord Hawkridge had breakfasted early and closeted himself in his study before the others came downstairs. And Rose's surliness made Lily wish she'd done the same. Would every meal here prove an ordeal?

She and Rand were about to rise from the dining table when they heard a vehicle roll up the drive. Excusing themselves to Rose, who was still picking at her saltfish, they hurried outside to meet it.

As they stepped onto the cobbles, a footman swung the carriage door wide, and an oval face appeared in the opening.

Dressed in black mourning, Margery looked dazed. She was a pale young woman, ethereal almost, and Lily imagined that her recent ordeal had made her even more so. It wasn't every day a woman lost her betrothed to violence.

Lily could hardly conceive of how she'd feel should such a thing happen to Rand. To be planning a life and have it snatched from her so suddenly...well, she was certain she'd look pale, too. Margery currently stood in the way of Lily and Rand's happiness, and Lily had been half expecting to resent her on sight. But now she could feel only sympathy.

Even in her grief, Margery was beautiful. Her hair, so light it was nearly white, framed her face in perfect curls. Her flawless skin looked translucent, and her eyes were a startling deep green. Set off by her pale loveliness, they looked huge. And very, very disturbed.

Lily's heart went out to her...until the woman spotted

Rand and her delicate face lit up. Then Lily's heart plunged to her knees instead.

Rand helped Margery down the carriage steps, where she promptly burst into tears, wrapping her arms around him and burying her face in his shoulder.

Lily stood by while the love of her life awkwardly patted her rival's back. "Margery. Ah, Margery."

"Randy," Margery choked out, gripping him harder.

He'd told Lily that Margery hadn't loved Alban, but it was obvious she did love Rand. Watching them together was more than Lily could bear. She tapped him on the shoulder. "I'll be playing with your father's dogs."

"Lily—"

"No. You need to talk. If I'm not with the dogs, look for me down by the river."

Resolutely she walked away, hoping she wasn't walking out of Rand's life.

FORTY-FOUR

"**R**ANDY."

Despite the worried look on Lily's face, and Margery's obvious distress, Rand smiled at her use of the childhood name. Life might have been miserable back when he was known as Randy, but it had also been simpler. And this girl had never been part of the misery.

"Margery." He squeezed her shoulder, feeling responsible for her happiness, the same way he'd felt when she came to Hawkridge as a small girl. "Whatever's wrong, we'll make it right."

It seemed the old bonds were still there, like with so many others on the estate. How could he have ignored them all these years? And if the worst came to transpire, could he walk away again, abandon them in their need?

He wasn't sure he could.

"Shall we go inside?" he asked her.

With an obvious effort, she controlled her tears. "Is your father at home?"

"He's in his study."

"Then no. I'm not ready to see him. Can we just walk?"

"Of course." One arm around her shoulders, he drew her toward the gardens. As they rounded the corner of the house, his gaze drifted toward the dog enclosure, but he didn't see Lily.

Heading toward the grassy paths where he'd walked with Lily last night, he sighed. He wouldn't lose her. That was unthinkable. But for now, he had to concentrate on Margery. She needed him, too.

"I'm sorry for your loss," he began carefully.

"Alban?" To his shock, she all but snorted. "I'd never wish death on a man, but I cannot pretend to miss him." She dashed the wetness from her eyes.

"Then...you're not crying because of him?"

"Heavens, no." She took a deep breath, looking better already. Some color was returning to her cheeks. "Alban was cruel. Surely you remember how he was as a boy." She shuddered, perhaps remembering things that Rand would rather not know. "I never wanted to marry him."

"Then why did you agree?"

"It was my father's last wish. Not that that stopped me from begging to get out of it. But Uncle William would hear none of it."

The marquess wasn't really her uncle, but she'd called him that since her girlhood. To Rand, it had always sounded too friendly a name for the old goat.

In a sheltered area between two rows of trees, she stopped. "Randy..."

When she hesitated, he turned to her and smiled. "No one calls me that anymore, you know."

Her own smile was wan, but there. "Shall I call you Professor? Or, oh, how could I have forgotten? My lord baron." She executed an absurd, formal curtsy.

"Rand will do," he told her, glad to see the old Margery peeking through all the misery.

"Rand, then," she repeated, growing serious again. "I shall try to remember, but you'll have to remind me if I forget. Rand...I...are you aware that Uncle William expects me to marry *you* now?"

"He's told me as much," he answered, suddenly apprehensive.

She resumed walking, absently trailing one hand along a hedge as she went by. "Who was that girl with you?"

"Lady Lily Ashcroft, the Earl of Trentingham's daughter."

"She's very beautiful."

"I think so." He watched her elegant fingers skim the leaves. Margery was beautiful, too, but in a fragile sort of way. She was taller than Lily and not as fine-boned, but Margery would never allow dogs to slobber all over her. She wouldn't climb fences or laugh at bawdy songs, either. Margery could be a saucebox, but beneath it all, she was a very proper young woman.

Well, she'd been stuck at the Marquess of Hawkridge's household all this time, Rand reminded himself. It was a wonder she had any spunk left in her at all.

She stopped again. "Why is Lady Lily here?"

"She...ah...well, when I received the summons from the marquess, it said only that—"

"Are you in love with her?"

He met her gaze. There was no sense in lying—the truth would surely be obvious anyway. "Yes," he said. "I am."

"Thank goodness."

He blinked, nonplussed. "Pardon?"

"I don't want to marry you, Randy. I mean, Rand." A small smile curved her lips, then faded. "I didn't want to marry your brother, and I don't want to marry you. I love you like a sister. Not a wife."

"You have no idea how relieved I am to hear that."

"Oh, I imagine you're just as relieved as I am to hear it

from you." Turning to walk back toward the house, she slanted him a sidelong glance. "Did you truly believe I love you that way?"

"I didn't think so," he said. "But I wasn't sure, and many wed for alliance, not love, and the marquess wanted—and Lily worried—"

He stopped, humiliated to find himself babbling.

When a student babbled, he accused the ninnyhammer of being unprepared. Which Rand was, at the moment. Woefully unprepared to deal with this—love, pressure from his family, responsibilities he'd never wanted nor thought would be his...all of it.

They reentered the formal gardens, the gravel crunching beneath their shoes. "Well," he said in an attempt to lighten the mood for both of their sakes, "you cannot blame me for wondering if you might, after all, be besotted. I did, if you'll remember, grace you with your first kiss."

That earned a good-natured smirk. "I don't remember 'grace' being an applicable description. And if I recall correctly, it was *your* first kiss as well. You seemed to be concerned about going off into the world an inexperienced man." Her green eyes perhaps a bit more lively than before, she glanced over at him. "Have you gained any experience, Randal Nesbitt?"

"Oh, in the past ten years I've kissed a lady or two. And you?"

"Besides your loathsome brother at his insistence?" She looked as though the memory made her gag. But then her features softened. "I'm in love with Bennett Armstrong."

"Bennett Armstrong?" He frowned, trying to remember. "Is he not a scrawny boy of twelve?"

In spite of her despondency, a little chuckle bubbled up. "He was when you left at thirteen. He's twenty-two now. And not scrawny, I can assure you."

The warmth in her voice told Rand she had the same feelings for Bennett that he had for Lily. Or a likeness of them, anyway. He had a hard time believing most people lived with these strong emotions.

He attempted to picture a grown-up Bennett Armstrong. "His father is a baron, yes?"

"Bennett is the baron now. His father died when the smallpox swept through the county. Three years ago, that was."

That explained Etta's new scars, and the ones he'd seen on other old family retainers. "You never wrote me about the smallpox."

Margery shrugged. "I didn't think you'd care."

He *hadn't* cared, not then. Guilt ate at his insides.

"Bennett is a wealthy baron," she continued. "His father left him gold and estates. I'm certain my own rich but untitled father would have been pleased to see me happily wed to such a gentleman, no matter that Bennett won't be a marquess like Alban. Like you," she corrected herself. "Yet I argued with Uncle William until I was blue in the face, and he refused to let us marry." As they drew closer to the house, Margery's feet dragged. "And now there's the complication…"

She seemed reticent to continue. He stopped her with a hand on her arm. "The money? He told me about that. The way the marquess sees it, this is a matter of honor and finances. Love doesn't figure into the equation."

"Money doesn't figure into it, either." She frowned. "I told you, Bennett is a wealthy man. With land, and—"

"It's not your wealth the marquess is concerned with, but his own."

They'd reached the edge of the garden, and Margery plopped down on a bench. "What do you mean?"

"Didn't he discuss this with you?"

"No. You think he'd deign to explain himself to a woman? He prefers to be dictatorial. It's how he gets his jollies."

With a sour laugh, he sat beside her. "You're not wrong about that," he said and explained about Hawkridge's dependence on her property and the repercussions of losing that income.

"No wonder he didn't want to admit it!" Margery burst out when he was finished. "He kept mumbling about honor and the promise to my father. And now, of course, since it happened, he has the perfect excuse to refuse Bennett—"

"Lily," Rand interrupted her, "has a solution for Hawkridge's finances."

"Does she?" Margery blinked. "But that doesn't solve—"

"She has an inheritance. Ten thousand pounds. Plus another three thousand from her marriage portion. That ought to be enough to set the marquess on the road to solvency, and then everyone can wed whomever they want."

Margery toyed with her black skirts. "No, Randy," she started.

A booming bark drew their attention to the river. In the distance Rand saw Lily toss a stick, and a big, wet mastiff jump into the water to retrieve it. Beatrix sat nearby, placidly watching. Apparently the monsters didn't eat cats, after all.

"What are you looking at?" Margery asked.

"Lily." The hound scrambled up the bank and shook violently, spraying her with water that left big dark splotches on her light blue gown. He laughed aloud. "She's playing fetch in the river with one of the marquess's dogs!"

The sight of her, being so very Lily, lightened his heart. She caught him watching and waved. Waving back, he turned to Margery. "I must go tell her you want Bennett, not me. She'll be so happy."

"Rand—"

"Don't worry, Margery." She looked so distressed. "We'll

make it right." Sudden impulse made him lean and give her a quick, chaste kiss on the lips. "For old times' sake," he said lightly, rising from the bench. "Was it better than last time?"

He was gratified to see the ghost of a smile return. "Perhaps. But not as good as Bennett's."

"No? I'm not sure whether I'm happy to hear that or gravely insulted." He grinned. "I need to talk to Lily; then we'll speak with the marquess."

He started off.

"Wait, Rand, there's more—"

But he was already walking away, and Lily had spotted him. Whatever else Margery wanted to talk about could wait.

FORTY-FIVE

*T*HE SMILE FROZE on Lily's face.
       He'd kissed Margery. On the lips.

He'd walked with his arm around her, too. Lily knew that, because although she'd been playing with the dog, she'd kept half an eye on Rand and Margery the entire time.

Or at least while they were visible. For a while they'd disappeared into the hedge- and tree-lined gardens. Had he kissed Margery there, too? In the little round gazebo where she and Rand had kissed last night?

He was going to marry Margery.

As Lily watched him come closer, she decided she wouldn't make a fuss. Because she was nice. Because his father wanted it this way, and if all the parties agreed, there was no point in fighting fate. Because Margery had known Rand nearly all her life, while Lily had known him just a few weeks.

Then suddenly she was in his arms, and she wondered how she could have thought any of that. His mouth was on hers, fervent and possessive, and she slipped her hands inside his open surcoat, pressing herself close. Her heart raced; the blood rushed through her veins. And it was the same for him, she was certain.

Nothing had changed between them.

By the time he pulled away, her senses were spinning, her knees wobbly and weak. And although he was smiling, he looked as shaky as she felt. His heart was in his extraordinary gray eyes, there for her to see.

Perhaps fate would tear them apart, but it was clear as the cloudless sky that it wouldn't be because Rand's feelings for her had changed. And although she wanted an explanation for why he'd kissed Margery, she wouldn't ask, because she didn't want him to know she'd doubted him.

Still smiling, he brushed at his dripping coat and plucked his damp shirt away from his body.

The sight of that shirt molded to his chest made her swallow hard. "I'm sorry," she said. "I'm afraid Rex has soaked me through." The dog was panting at her feet. She bent to grab the stick and tossed it arcing over the water, watching the mastiff gleefully splash in to fetch it.

Looking every bit as gleeful, Rand swung her back to face him. "It's all right. I'll happily risk more wet to kiss you again." And she was happy to oblige, but this kiss was short and light. "Margery doesn't want to marry me," he said with an even wider grin.

She felt like singing—though she wouldn't subject him to that, of course, not for all the gold in England. "Oh, Rand—"

"What do you think you're doing with my dog?"

They whirled to see the marquess storming down the path to the river. Beatrix scampered up a nearby tree to join Lady and Jasper where they sat on a branch, chattering nervously. Lily's heart pounded.

"Don't worry," said a whispered voice; Margery had sidled up behind them. "He might bellow like a bear and insist on his own way, but he's not a man to do physical violence."

"I beg to differ," Rand said tightly, making Lily wince to think what he must have endured.

As his father drew near, he looped an arm over her shoulders, a clear message of possession. The tall, formidable marquess stood before them and glared down into Lily's face. "Well?"

Although Lily had always been nice, she'd never been shy. "I was only playing with Rex, my lord. He seems to enjoy it."

"Rex?"

She shrugged. "He needed a name. I assure you, I've done him no harm."

He whistled to the dog, which obediently ran over. "His name is Attila," he said, grabbing the chain around the animal's neck. "And like the rest of my mastiffs, he's a valuable fighter. He'll sell for a top price once he's fully trained— that is, if he doesn't die of a chill first." His fist was white-knuckled on the links. "My dogs do not play."

Lily drew herself up to her full height of five-foot-two. "Perhaps they should. As they don't seem to get a lot of human attention, some toys would be a welcome addition to their enclosure. Knotted rope, as I told Rand." Rand's hand tightened on her shoulder in warning, but she ignored it. She refused to be intimidated by the man she hoped would be her father-in-law. "And you'd do well to uproot the apple tree in there—the fruit is of a size to be a choking hazard."

Surprisingly, Lord Hawkridge looked thoughtful if still fierce. "These dogs are meant to accompany soldiers at war. They get plenty of human attention when I train them—to kill. But perhaps some toys might not be amiss. Knotted rope could well promote fighting amongst themselves, which would help keep them in shape."

It wasn't exactly what Lily had in mind, but it was something. And he was no longer ignoring her.

He turned his attention to Margery. "When did you arrive?"

She exchanged a look with Rand. "Moments ago, Uncle William."

"Good. We'll talk over dinner. It's long past time we settled your betrothal and marriage. Come along and make yourself presentable."

He swung on a heel, taking Margery's arm to pull her along with him, the dog trotting on his other side. Lily stared at Lord Hawkridge's stiff, retreating back. Margery needed to make herself presentable? Lily had rarely seen someone so pristine. She glanced down at her own water-and-mud-stained skirts with dismay.

Rand came around to face her and lifted her chin with a hand. "You did well," he said admiringly.

She fluffed at her filthy blue gown. "If he believed Margery needed grooming, he must think I'm a veritable fustilug."

He pressed a kiss to her lips. "He wasn't looking at you; he was listening. Miraculously. And he only said that to Margery as an excuse to drag her off. He doesn't want us talking and figuring a way around his plans." Another kiss. "Little does he know that we already have."

Lily was cautious of celebrating too soon, but she drew hope from his words. "How long until dinner?"

Rand glanced at his pocket watch. "An hour." Tucking it away, he shrugged out of his surcoat.

She nodded. "I'll just have time to bathe and change."

"And I'll just have time for a run." He handed her the coat. "Take this inside for me, will you?"

"You're going for a run? Now?"

His fingers, working the knot in his cravat, stilled as he met her gaze. "It's just a run, Lily. I like to do that. To—"

"To think. I know."

Then why did she feel shut out?

Not understanding, he smiled as he handed her the lace-trimmed linen. "Thank you. I'll see you at dinner."

All through her bath Lily told herself that Rand's running didn't equate to running away—at least not from her. By the time Etta laced her into a fresh peach gown, she almost believed it.

FORTY-SIX

"**J**EROME, YOU** may leave us now. And inform the others they are not to enter the dining room unless I ring."

The aging footman bowed and backed away, his face betraying relief. Rand watched the marquess pick up his fork and stab a piece of buttered and sugared turnip. The staff was still wary of his father's moods, he thought with an internal sigh. If employment were easier to come by, he imagined most of the old-timers would have left long ago.

"Now," the marquess said, looking pointedly at Rand and then Margery. "You're both here. It's time to seal this betrothal and get on with our lives."

"My lord," Lily started.

"No." The man waved his fork. "You're not part of this family, my lady, and there is nothing you can add to this discussion."

She shared a look with Rand, then set to silently picking at her food.

Seething, Rand lifted his goblet. "You're wrong," he said tightly. "Lily does have something to contribute—an inheritance that she's prepared to put at your disposal in exchange for your blessing on our marriage. Ten thousand pounds, plus her dowry, which brings the total to thirteen. I believe that adds quite a bit to this discussion."

Regardless of the fact that it was an enormous sum of money, the marquess barely blinked. "And where do you suppose that leaves Margery? Your foster sister, promised to my heir on her father's deathbed?"

"Free to marry Bennett Armstrong." Rand sipped smugly.

The marquess's fork clattered to his plate. "Bennett Armstrong!" he bellowed, his face turning red. "How dare you utter that name in my house?"

Feeling Lily shudder beside him, Rand reached to squeeze her hand.

What color was left in Margery's cheeks had vanished. "Uncle William—"

"Am I to understand," he interrupted her in a low, dangerous voice, "that you *still* wish to marry that boy?"

Her lower lip quivered. "Uncle, you don't know him. He's a good man—"

"He's a *murderer*!"

Rand's jaw dropped open. "Murderer?"

Margery turned glistening, sorrowful eyes on him. "I tried to tell you earlier."

"Bennett Armstrong is a murderer?"

"No!" Margery cried at the same time the marquess snapped, "Yes!"

When Lily gasped, Rand tightened his hold on her hand. But his gaze was fixed on his father.

"He murdered my son and heir," the marquess seethed, "and I intend to see him hang."

FORTY-SEVEN

"BENNETT IS NOT a murderer!" Margery burst out. "He did it in self-defense!" She turned to Rand, looking frantic. "Alban came after him in the first place."

But all Rand could absorb at the moment was that Margery's sweetheart had killed his brother.

No wonder his father was dead set against the match—it would effectively make him father-in-law to his son's killer. Rand couldn't blame him for abhorring the thought, no matter the whys and hows of Alban's demise.

"My son," the marquess said, pointing his knife at Margery, "was not a man capable of killing. *Your paramour* murdered him in cold blood. Of course the blackguard would feign innocence." He bared his teeth. "Surely even a besotted, addlebrained female like you can see through his lies?"

"Alban *would* kill," she shot back. "I saw him kill, time and time again. A rabbit, a lamb. My very own cat when she pounced on him as he was trying to force himself on me."

Lily hid her face in her hands.

"It's Bennett who's incapable of killing without just provocation," Margery added hotly.

The marquess bristled. "And he doubtless considered someone determined to wed his bride as 'just provocation.'"

"Stop it, both of you!" Rand broke in. "This squabbling gets us no closer to the truth." Ignoring his father's thunderous expression, he asked in a calm, reasonable tone, "Was there an inquest?"

"Yes," Margery crowed, "and the bailiff made no arrest—because the accused is innocent."

"You foolish girl." Her guardian's eyes blazed. "It came down to his word against a dead man's. Unhappily, there wasn't enough evidence for an indictment. But there will be soon. I've offered a hundred pound reward for information confirming his guilt."

Lily looked up at that. "A *hundred* pounds?"

"You cannot!" Margery gripped the table, her voice rising in panic. "Uncle William—"

"I certainly can. And I have. The messengers were sent out yesterday morning."

Margery's eyes filled with tears. "Then Bennett's as good as dead."

Rand couldn't find it in himself to disagree with her. To do so would be a lie. A footman wouldn't earn a hundred pounds in ten years, let alone a groom or coachman or maid. For that kind of money, someone would come forward with incriminating evidence, truthful or not.

The marquess wielded a lot of power in this small piece of England, and if he meant to see the fellow hang, Rand had no doubt he would see it done.

Plainly seeing the truth in Rand's eyes, Margery let out a pathetic moan and rose from her chair, rushing to kneel at the marquess's knees. Her black gown pooled around her. "I beg you, Uncle William, don't do this. I'll have no will to go on should Bennett die. Let him live long enough for me to prove his innocence."

"Impossible," his father snapped, "given that he's guilty."

She gazed up at him, the tears overflowing, making tracks down her pale cheeks. "Then you'll be killing me along with him."

Just then, she looked entirely too capable of doing herself in, and Rand watched, amazed, as his father's features softened with compassion.

But it wasn't long before they hardened again. "The blackguard must pay for murdering my son." His calculating eyes darted from Rand to Margery. "And if you two are thinking of trying something…"

Rand raised his hands in a gesture of innocence. He wasn't yet certain which version of the events he believed, although admittedly Margery had the better measure of Alban's character. Still, he felt the need to look Armstrong in the eye before making any kind of judgement.

But as usual, the marquess took it for granted that his youngest son was up to no good. "I'll be sending a contingent of men to keep Armstrong under house arrest. The killer is not going anywhere."

A bell sat by his elbow, and now he raised it and jingled it fiercely, as though venting his frustration on the dainty sterling silver trinket.

"Jerome!" he called, and the footman rushed in.

In moments, it was done. A dozen men were on their way to surround Bennett Armstrong's home.

An hour later, Rand, Lily, Rose, and Margery were on their way there, too.

FORTY-EIGHT

*L*ORD BENNETT Armstrong's house was smaller than Hawkridge Hall and Trentingham Manor, and from the mishmash of styles and the way the house sprawled this way and that, Lily surmised it was older than Hawkridge and Trentingham as well. Sections looked medieval, other parts Tudor, still other portions modern. But regardless of all that, it was obviously the home of a wealthy man.

Each of the three doors had one of Hawkridge's men assigned to guard it, and two more men were posted on every side of the house—in case Lord Armstrong tried to lower himself from a window.

At first, the guard at the front door refused their party entry. But Rand remembered the fellow, and soon he was pumping his hand and asking after his wife and children. The man seemed to have a bit of a soft spot for Margery as well, and after she swore up and down that they weren't there to break Lord Armstrong out, he agreed to admit them into the dark, paneled interior of the house.

The Ashcroft sisters followed behind, Rose looking

thoughtful and Lily feeling hopeful. Though her future with Rand was still uncertain, she was beginning to glimpse a possibility of reuniting him with his father. Today she'd seen flashes of warmth in the marquess's treatment of Margery—albeit faint flashes, but clearly there was a heart somewhere beneath his unpleasant manner. Getting Rand to acknowledge that fact wouldn't be easy, but the longer they were here, the more obvious it became that he still had strong ties to his childhood home and its people. Father and son both cared for Hawkridge, and if they could work together to save it—with Lily's money and harmonizing influence—they just might find themselves being a family.

But first they had to face the troubling matter of Bennett Armstrong. From a quick, whispered conference outside Hawkridge's stables, Lily knew Rand suspected Lord Armstrong was innocent. Lily hoped he was right, as such a lucky outcome for Margery would clear her own path to marrying Rand. But like him, she was reserving judgement.

Luck had not been on their side of late.

The baron's butler directed the four visitors to a study, where they found the accused gentleman writing a letter.

"Bennett!" Margery streaked across the chamber and threw herself at him. "Oh, Bennett, Uncle William means to see you hang!"

"I know, love." He held her face in both his hands, looking haggard and afraid. "I was just writing to my uncle with instructions of what to do should that come to pass."

"Oh, Bennett—"

Her speech was cut off when he crushed his mouth to hers, kissing her as though he would never let her go. Margery cooperated fully, clinging to him like a fragile, desperate vine.

Rand's jaw dropped. "Apparently she's not as proper as I thought," he whispered to Lily.

"Hmm." She slanted him a glance, thinking that was a bold accusation after what had nearly happened between them last night.

The two lovers didn't part until Rose loudly cleared her throat. Lord Armstrong looked up with widened pale green eyes, apparently startled to find there were others present. "Randy? Is that you?"

"I'm called Rand these days." He strode forward to shake the fellow's hand. "And this is my betrothed, Lady Lily Ashcroft, and her sister, Lady Rose."

Lily curtsied, trying to dredge up a smile. "Lord Armstrong."

Although his gaze didn't pierce her soul like Rand's did, he was quite good-looking. He managed a weak, embarrassed smile in return. "Pray pardon our...um...enthusiasm," he said, stepping away from Margery, though he kept hold of her hand.

"Oh, Bennett." Margery's bottom lip quivered. "I'd hoped that after the inquest, Uncle William would come to his senses. But if anything, he's become even more determined."

"I've seen evidence of that," Bennett muttered, glaring at the guard stationed outside his window.

"He's offered a hundred pounds for information that leads to proving your guilt."

"Blast him." Sinking back into his bulky wooden chair, Bennett squeezed his eyes shut and pressed Margery's hand to his lips. "That's that, then," he said shakily, lowering her hand. "You know, I thought I was prepared for this. But I suppose one never really is."

Her cheeks wet, Margery sagged against the desk.

Lily's heart constricted at the sight of such despair. "Is there no way to prove your innocence?" She didn't know him, most especially whether or not he might be innocent, but he clearly loved Margery.

Bennett just gave a helpless shrug. "There were no witnesses."

Rand began pacing. "Tell me what happened."

"I was hunting and, as sometimes happens, had become separated from my companions. Alban rode up almost immediately, as though he had been following and waiting for such an opportunity. He dismounted, pointed a pistol at me, and accused me of plotting to steal his bride."

Rand paused and leveled him with a stare. "Were you?"

Bennett looked to Margery for help. Wiping her face, she met Rand's gaze. "Your father wouldn't allow us to marry, so we were planning to elope. But I've no idea how Alban could have found out."

"Alban had his ways," Rand said darkly. "So then what happened?"

Bennett's swallow was audible from across the room. "I dived off my horse to knock the gun from his grasp, and it went off. Then he drew his sword, and I panicked. Alban was known for his swordsmanship, and he wasn't looking for a duel of honor—he'd made it clear he wanted me dead. I swiped a stout branch off the ground and bashed him over the head. He went down like a sack of flour."

Rand still paced. "And he was dead."

"Dead as a doornail, I'm afraid. I didn't mean to kill him —I could have shot him if I'd wanted that. I was hunting and had a musket, after all. But I wasn't sorry. He didn't deserve Margery—he treated her abominably." Despite the strength of his words, Lord Armstrong's eyes skittered away guiltily.

Apparently he *was* sorry…about something, anyway.

"Don't you see?" Margery straightened and went over to Rand, halting him with a hand on his arm. "It was self-defense. If he hadn't done Alban in, Bennett would've been dead instead."

"But how to prove it?" Lily asked.

"I don't know." Margery looked around the room pleadingly. "But you must help me find a way. You all must."

Lily looked to Rand with a question in her eyes, and he nodded his agreement. Rose's face was impassive, but Lily could tell from the way she was leaning forward in her chair that she, too, felt sympathy for the young couple.

"Of course we'll help," Rose said softly.

FORTY-NINE

"**WE CANNOT HELP.**" Rose fluffed her wine-colored satin skirts as Etta attached the matching stomacher. "I feel sorrow for Margery, but I fear there is no solution. The baron will hang."

"There *is* a solution." In fact, Lily was planning to set to work on it this very evening. Seated at the gilt dressing table, she chose her jewelry with extra care. If she was to have any hope of influencing the marquess, she'd have to exceed his exacting standards of female elegance. "Lord Hawkridge must be made to see reason."

Rose snorted. "He'll sooner see a goat rise up on its hind legs and perform ballet."

"Now, now," Etta said on a chuckle, "you mustn't speak so of his lordship. He can be a hard man, but he is not entirely without reason."

Holding a sapphire bob up to one ear, Lily examined herself critically in the mirror. "What reason could he possibly have for the way he treats Rand? For despising the good son and revering the bad?"

Etta laughed again. "You've bested me there, milady—his

lordship is certainly guilty of misjudging his children. But then, we all have our blind spots."

"Blind spots?" Lily's gaze shifted from the mirror to Etta. "How could he miss the fact that Alban was a monster?"

The woman grimaced. "We all wish to think well of our children."

"Except in Rand's case," Rose said dryly.

"Lord Newcliffe is a special case." Etta straightened a final ribbon and stepped back. "Lovely. Are you pleased with your appearance, milady?"

But Rose was peering at the maid instead of her reflection. "Special how?"

Etta hesitated, scrubbing her clean hands in her tidy linen apron. "The new baron was a troublesome child at times," she said finally.

"Perhaps as a boy he got up to a bit of mischief," Lily protested, thinking of him pilfering his brother's journal, "but that should hardly matter now. Now he's a respectable, honest, hardworking young man—a man anyone should be proud to call Son."

"And how," Etta said quietly, "would his father have come to know that?"

Lily frowned, realizing Lord Hawkridge had spent just a handful of days with his son in the past decade. Because Rand had left. "But he wanted Rand to leave," she said, mostly to herself.

The older woman shook her head. "It's not that simple. I don't mean to say his lordship treated Randal fairly...but he wasn't *entirely* without reason."

When she said no more, Rose pouted. "Vagueness is worse than silence. I suppose you refuse to tell us exactly what Rand did to upset the man?"

"Heavens, look at the time," Etta said pointedly, though

she carried no watch. "His lordship does not look kindly upon late supper guests."

Lily hastened to fasten her earbobs and dab herself with scent. She would have to do.

Walking down the corridor, Rose cast Lily an appraising glance. "You look especially pretty."

"Thank you," Lily said in surprise.

"It was an observation, not a compliment. Do you imagine a fancy gown will impress the marquess into changing his mind about Lord Armstrong?"

Lily coughed, then cleared her throat. Her sister was far too shrewd for her comfort. "It cannot hurt, can it?"

Rose shook her head. "You'd do better to stay out of it, Lily. Lord Hawkridge would make a formidable enemy."

Lily rolled her eyes, a gesture she'd learned from Rose. "Am I supposed to merely stand aside while he hangs an innocent man? Not even try to help?"

That earned her a snide look. "Lord Armstrong may not have murdered Rand's brother in cold blood, but do you really think he's innocent?"

"You don't?"

Rose shrugged. "He's hiding something. Couldn't you tell?"

Lily tilted her head. "You cannot mean…you don't think he *deserves* to hang?"

"Of course not!" Rose's horror seemed genuine enough. "I'm just trying to show you that you're out of your depth here at Hawkridge. You cannot be sure of Margery's or the baron's true motives, and yet you're challenging a powerful nobleman on their behalf. And all this just to marry Rand? A man who, in the end, may very well cast you aside and marry Margery instead?"

Lily stopped dead at the bottom of the stairs. "Why should he do that? They love each other like brother and sister, not husband and wife. Even if—heaven forbid—Lord Armstrong cannot be saved, Margery would—"

"Then Margery will have lost the only man she loves like a husband. Will the distinction make much difference to her anymore?"

"I don't know." Lily couldn't even contemplate what it would be like to have Rand ripped from her, his life cut short like Bennett's very well might be. It hurt too much. "But the distinction will still matter to Rand. He cares for her, but he loves *me*."

"Undoubtedly," Rose said in a flat tone, "and he's honest and upright and should have a whole fleet of ships christened in his name."

Lily planted her hands on her hips. "I couldn't have said it better myself."

"Then what will Mr. Honorable do when he sees the vulnerable girl he grew up protecting left heartbroken and alone? Leave her at the mercy of her callous foster father?"

Lily opened her mouth. She closed it. She ran her fingers along the scars on her hand, thinking.

"Come, Lily," Rose went on, "you've seen the two of them together. The way they charmed that guard at Armstrong's house. And earlier today, they kissed—"

"How do you know that?" Lily demanded. "You stayed behind to finish breakfast."

"I finished." Rose shrugged. "Then I decided to take some air."

Lily narrowed her eyes. "You want me to doubt him. You seem to want me to go home, though you were the one who urged me to come here. Why?"

Rose crossed her arms, as if she were cold. "I'm telling you what I see. When I brought you here, I didn't know it would be so complicated. I thought it would be...manageable."

"And now you believe I cannot manage?"

Rose shrugged again.

"And you're not trying to sabotage my relationship with Rand because you still want him for yourself?"

For a split second, Rose looked like a statue of a vengeful goddess. She was still with cold fury. Then she was gone, without a word, so quickly that Lily hadn't yet decided whether she regretted making the accusation.

After the ugly argument, Lord Hawkridge didn't even show himself at supper. Claiming a backlog of work due to Alban's loss, he'd rung for a tray in his study instead.

Rose silently fumed all through supper, and afterward, when the four young people passed the evening hours in the north drawing room, she sat with her nose pointedly buried in a book. Lily played gentle tunes while Rand and Margery sat nearby puzzling over Lord Armstrong's fate. In spite of herself, Lily watched them closely, Rose's words of caution echoing in her mind. Every so often, Rand would catch her eye and smile, and she'd get that melty feeling inside and feel reassured. What did Rose know, anyway?

Rand had said it himself: He'd never let anything keep them apart. Ever.

It had grown quite late, and all four of them were yawning when Lord Hawkridge appeared in the doorway. Lily's fingers stilled on the keys, leaving an expectant silence. Rose looked up from her book.

"No matter what you believe," the marquess said, addressing himself to Margery, "I have raised you like my own daughter and care for you as though you were. Your pleas haven't fallen on entirely deaf ears."

Lily saw Margery's heart leap into her eyes. "Yes?" Rand asked when his foster sister appeared unable to speak.

The marquess swung his harsh gray gaze on him. "I have a plan to spare her paramour's life."

"Thank you, God," Margery breathed. "Thank you."

"Thank *me*," Lord Hawkridge snapped. "The truth is I know better than to make this offer. You should be thankful I have a soft heart."

Rand flinched, clearly struggling to suppress a retort.

Margery rose, her black skirts trembling as she slowly approached the doorway. "What is your plan, Uncle William?"

The marquess straightened. "On your twenty-first birthday, one week hence, you will wed my son."

"Oh, no—"

"Oh, yes. Should the two of you fail to marry, your paramour will hang. Should the wedding take place, I shall see that he is granted a commutation of sentence and transported to the colonies instead." He paused, drawing breath. "May God forgive me my weakness," he said, closing his eyes briefly before he turned and strode from the chamber.

As one, the rest of them released their breaths. Lily tried and failed to swallow past a new lump in her throat. No longer pretending indifference, Rose gaped at Rand and Margery, clearly waiting to see what they would say.

"This is unconscionable," Rand gritted out.

Margery's face was even paler than usual. A pure, bloodless white. "We must marry," she whispered, casting Lily a stricken glance. She focused back on Rand. "We must marry to save Bennett's life."

FIFTY

MARGERY TOOK a few faltering steps toward Rand, then dropped to her knees at his feet. "We must marry." She hid her face in her hands. "We must."

Wearing a dazed expression, Rand reached for her shoulders and raised her to stand. "There must be another way."

Lily wasn't aware that her whole body was shaking until she noticed the harpsichord emitting sour, erratic notes. Snatching her hands from the keys, she wrapped her arms around her middle, trying to hold herself still.

Margery finally lifted her head and searched Rand's eyes, her own green eyes frantic. She gripped his hands in both of hers. "But will you? To save his life? Tell me you will. From my earliest memories, I looked up to you, Rand. You were my big brother who could do no wrong. You won't let me down, will you? Tell me you'll marry me to save Bennett's life."

Though a muscle in his jaw twitched, he nodded. He didn't even look at Lily—perhaps he couldn't bring himself to. "I won't doom a man to die. But there must be another way."

Tears streaming down her face, Margery hugged him, hard. Then, muffling a sob, she ran from the room.

Lily released a long, shuddering breath. "Rand—"

She cut herself off upon noticing her sister lingered nearby, as if she wanted to say something. But then Rose seemed to change her mind and quietly excused herself.

Now only Rand and Lily remained. "I've never seen Margery this selfish," he began, his gaze moving from the empty doorway to meet hers. "She didn't for a moment consider how I'd feel about this marriage. Or you."

Lily clenched her teeth to stop their chattering. "I'd feel the same way if your life were threatened. I'd ask anything of anyone."

After a moment of thought, he nodded. "I'd do the same for you. But there must be another way for Margery and Armstrong. I won't lose you."

She hugged herself tighter. "Someone's life is at stake."

"There must be another way."

It was becoming a litany, one she dearly wished she could believe. "Does your father truly wield such power?"

"I'm afraid so." Rand came to her side and began rubbing her arms. But she wasn't cold. "The farther you go from London, the less provision you'll find for due process of the law. If the Marquess of Hawkridge wishes Armstrong dead, he can make it happen. Is it not the same for the little area of the world where your father is the lord?"

Reluctantly she nodded. "I suppose it is. But I've never seen him wish anyone dead. Life at Trentingham is usually peaceful." A peace she hadn't expected to miss, a peace she'd even equated with boredom at times.

Oh, to live again that blessed, boring peace.

"Life at Hawkridge has never been peaceful," Rand said ruefully, helping her to her feet. "But I hope to take you away from here to where we can live in peace. Soon."

Neither of them felt like speculating on the strength or frailty of such a hope. Though Lily's shaking had subsided, her heart had begun pounding a slow but forceful beat, rattling her bones. *Ne...ver...say...ne...ver...say...*

"Lily?"

They'd stopped in front of the Queen's Bedchamber. All that awaited her inside was darkness and her sister's spiteful turned back. In that moment, she'd have given almost anything to be at Trentingham, curled up in her own cozy bed with Mum and a cup of chocolate. When she'd been little and had nightmares, Mum would always bring her chocolate, and then the scary things would go away.

This wasn't going away.

When Rand's arms came around her, she tried to pretend they were Mum's. But they weren't. They were the arms of the person who had hurt her, and knowing why he had to hurt her—and understanding he was doing the right thing—didn't make it hurt any less. Still, she savored his familiar warmth and breathed in his musky scent. Dimly she realized he must not have had time to bathe after this morning's run. She didn't mind. It just made him smell more like Rand.

We're going to get married and live happily ever after, he'd promised.

That had been a stupid promise to make. Just like her promise to Rose.

Rand held her a long time. When he finally pulled away, he first pressed the lightest, tenderest kiss to her forehead. "It's not over," he whispered against her skin, his chin feeling scratchy.

Lily nodded, then turned and entered her chamber. Rand was right, in the strictest sense; she hadn't lost him yet. But for the first time since the day he sang to her and proposed, Lily felt real fear.

Oh, she'd had her niggling doubts and worries, but in her

heart she'd always trusted they'd find a way to be together. Even if Rand's father had proved intractable, they could still have eloped. Hang the consequences. They could have survived without the marquess's blessing.

They could not survive with a man's blood on their hands.

And short of an angel descending from the heavens, Lily knew of nothing that could end this nightmare. Not even chocolate. It was obvious to her now that Lord Hawkridge could not be reasoned with—the unveiling of his cruel, fiendish 'plan' had proved his lack of humanity. Etta had been wrong about the man.

The room was nearly pitch black but for a few dying embers in the fireplace. Lily could just make out Rose's face, turned toward Lily's side of the bed. She usually faced away. She must have flipped over in her sleep.

Or perhaps she'd somehow sensed their sisterly bond deepening, now that they had something new in common: They both knew what it felt like to lose Rand.

Had Rose felt then what Lily was feeling now—or even a fraction of it? Absently tracing her scars, Lily wondered if Rose had hurt so deeply. Because if so, she thought she could forgive her all the turned backs and cold shoulders in the world.

FIFTY-ONE

*I*N HIS SMALL chamber, Rand sat on the bed to tug off his boots. *There must be another way,* he repeated to himself over and over as he pulled off his stockings and crushed them into balls that he threw across the room with a rage he hadn't felt since he'd last lived in this wretched house. He shrugged out of his surcoat and yanked at the cravat at his throat, throwing those across the room, too. He wished he had something to break, but his chamber had been stripped of all but the furniture some time in the ten years between when he'd left for Oxford and now.

There had to be another way.

He was loosening the laces on his shirt when a soft knock came at the door. Thinking it must be Lily, his heart gave a little hitch. He hurried to open the door.

Margery stood there instead.

She was still wearing the dull black gown, the clothes Hawkridge had forced her to purchase in London to show the proper respect for his dead son. Her eyes red-rimmed, she twisted her fingers together. "There's something else I need to tell you."

Though her tone sounded dire, Rand just sighed. "Come in, Margery."

He shut the door and led her to sit on the room's only chair, attempting to appear sympathetic. It wasn't that he didn't care, but he'd had about all the anguish he could take —and despite her obvious distress, he couldn't imagine anything that could make this situation ever worse.

Until he heard her next words.

"Rand, I…I'm with child."

"Sweet mercy!" He dropped abruptly to sit on the bed.

He was too shocked to know how to react. Sympathy for her predicament, censure for her misdeeds, and anxiety for her health all occurred to him at once. How could prim and proper Margery have done something like this? Margery, his baby sister Margery…

"I know what you're thinking, Randy." The very picture of misery, she laid a hand on her still-flat middle. "It was a horrible mistake. That is, well, *it* wasn't horrible. *It* was very nice—" At Rand's appalled expression, she turned red and lowered her gaze. "But afterwards," she began, then stopped and shook her head. "I was only a little nervous at first. It was just one time, and there isn't always a baby, you know. But then I would sit in church every Sunday, unable to think of anything else but my wickedness, and then I began noticing the signs—"

"Spare me those particular details, if you wouldn't mind," Rand said quickly. Living among academics, including those who studied medicine, he was familiar with the common symptoms of pregnancy—and he did *not* need to associate them with his baby sister.

"I'm sorry." Margery's eyes filled with tears again, and Rand's sympathy began to win out over his other instincts. "We didn't mean for it to happen! Truly. It's just—" Her voice broke, and she took a moment to gather herself. "We just got carried away," she finished in a whisper.

Remembering last night in the drawing room, Rand felt his skin prickle. He and Lily had been alone. Alone in a luxurious room with music, candlelight, and emotions running high. Anything could have happened between them. Why, something almost *had* happened! He ought to be down on his knees giving thanks for their lucky show of restraint—for Rand suspected it was only luck that had kept Lily from suffering his poor foster sister's fate.

Though he could not condone Margery's behavior, in light of his own close call, sympathy was definitely carrying the day. Temptation was a difficult thing to resist. Perhaps Lily was right that they ought to keep some distance until—*until*, not unless—their marriage was settled. The thought of having to decide between preserving Armstrong's life or Lily's well-deserved reputation, plus the reputation of Rand and Lily's unborn child…

Well, Rand couldn't say what he would choose. It was a far worse dilemma than the one he faced now—which was to say, unfathomable.

Apparently seeing his expression soften, Margery continued less timidly. "No one else knows about the babe except Bennett. It's why we'd planned to elope. I tried to obey, Rand, truly I did, but I just couldn't marry Alban knowing I carried another man's child. Alban was…he would have killed it," she said flatly.

Nausea threatened, but Rand fought it off. "Well, he cannot kill it now," he said in a way he hoped was soothing.

"But I still…" She swallowed hard. "Oh, Randy, I know it's a lot to ask, but will you—" She gave a violent sniffle. "Will you raise it as yours?"

For what felt like the hundredth time today, Rand was stunned.

"We can hope it's a girl," Margery rushed on, "so it won't be your heir, and—"

"We're going to find another way." Rand's head was suddenly throbbing. "It won't matter if it's a boy or a girl, because the child will be raised by its father."

"But *what if?*" Evidently she was quite past clinging to that hope. "Uncle William is planning our wedding for seven days hence. What if we're forced to marry? Will you raise this child as yours? I could have hidden it from you, tried to make you believe it *was* yours, but—"

"You're not like that, I know." Margery had obviously made mistakes, but he knew she would never try to deceive him.

And he also knew there was no chance he'd ever fall for such a ploy, because if, heaven forbid, he was forced to wed her, he wouldn't be sharing her bed.

He could never bring himself to share a bed with anyone but Lily.

Margery stood and threw her arms around him. Slow tears trailed down her pale cheeks, leaking from eyes that looked hopeless. "*What if*, Rand? Will you be a true father to this child?"

"Of course I will," he said simply, because there was nothing else he could say.

But he would find another way...because there was nothing else he could do.

Nothing.

FIFTY-TWO

*S*TILL STARING AT the spot where the final ember had winked out in the fireplace, Lily huddled beneath the covers of her giant state bed.

Although Beatrix nestled against her and Rose snored softly nearby, she'd never felt so alone in her life.

Was she fated to be alone forever?

There must be another way, Rand had said over and over, as though he could make it so by repetition alone. But Lily was unconvinced. It seemed that no matter what solution they came up with, his father would shoot it down.

For a long time she lay awake, stroking Beatrix's downy fur and watching the unfriendly shadows cast on the walls by tree branches blowing in the wind. Rand had no love for this house, and as much as she always tried to look on the bright side of things, she couldn't help but think that in this case he was right. Although it was beautiful, there seemed something sinister about Hawkridge, something that made her skin crawl. She didn't feel safe here.

She hugged herself for a long while, praying for exhaustion to overtake her. Then she climbed out of bed and slid a wrapper over her night rail.

A few minutes later, she knocked softly on Rand's door.

He came to answer, wearing just breeches and a shirt that was open at the neck and cuffs. He looked as sleepless as she.

"Rand?" Feeling shy and nervous, she fingered the end of her long plait. "May I sleep here?"

He gathered her close. "I thought we were trying not to tempt each other, in case it turns out...well, you know," he finished lamely.

A heaviness settled in Lily's heart. She stared down at his bare feet. No matter what he said over and over, he wasn't convinced that everything would end well. Or else he would be inviting her in, no questions asked.

Feeling like she had nothing to lose, she raised a palm and placed it against his chest, inside the open placket of his shirt, where his bare skin was brown and warm. "Rand..." Shutting her eyes against the pain in his, she went on tiptoe for a kiss. Though his mouth on hers felt achingly familiar, the melting sensation didn't bring the relief she was seeking.

It failed to make her forget that, barring a miracle, he would soon be married to someone else.

He reached blindly to bury his fingers in her hair, deepening the kiss until the melting turned into a searing heat tinged with the bite of brandy. A tiny moan escaped her throat as she wondered if this was the last time their lips would move together, the last time she'd feel his warmth spread all the way out to her fingertips and toes.

Finally, with a strangled sound, he broke the kiss and swung her up into his arms.

She gave a yelp of surprise. "Rand, what on earth—"

"We'll only sleep, Lily." He deposited her on his small childhood bed and looked down on her, gently finger-combing her hair into a halo around her head. "Perhaps if we stay together, we'll both be able to sleep."

Her big blue eyes blinked up at him, red and swollen but still impossibly beautiful. "I know we shouldn't, but just now I cannot bring myself to care." She bit her lip, and he noticed her mouth, too, was red and swollen—but from kissing instead of crying. "Will the staff realize I'm here?"

He lay down beside her, pulling her slender form against him. "I'll walk you back before first light. We've a couple hours yet." Regardless of what he'd said, he wondered if he would be able to sleep at all with her in his arms, feeling like heaven. He'd be a wreck tomorrow.

It would be worth it.

Feeling limp and exhausted, he lay perfectly still, holding her close and smelling her hair. As she drifted off his eyes remained open, staring up at the underside of the serviceable blue canopy overhead. No Queen's Bedchamber, this—no silk for Rand Nesbitt at Hawkridge Hall. His room was barely more than a closet.

"I don't like it here," she whispered into the silence, though Rand had thought she was asleep. "This house. I cannot sleep here alone."

"But you're not alone. You're with Rose."

"With Rose I am still alone," she said sadly.

"Stay with me, then," Rand murmured in her ear. He snuggled closer still, burying his nose in her soft curls. "And tomorrow, I'll take you home."

FIFTY-THREE

*R*AND SET THEIR luggage by the carriage and, leaving two outriders to deal with it, headed into the house to fetch Lily and Rose.

"You'll be back, I presume? A week from yesterday?"

Rand pivoted to see the marquess standing outdoors, holding two dogs by their chain collars. "Yes, I'll be back," he forced through gritted teeth, hoping against hope that he'd be arriving with a solution to this dilemma.

"Sit," the man told the dogs. "Stay." He climbed the steps to Rand. "Margery told me you're willing to wed her in order to save Armstrong's life. She's very grateful."

Rand had nothing to say to that.

"Son," the marquess started—and when Rand visibly flinched, his father sighed. "I suppose I deserve that. I just wanted to say I'm pleased that you're willing to do the right thing and marry the girl. It's admirable, considering you had other plans."

Rand consciously unclenched his jaw. "Lily is more than plans; Lily is my life. And your approval means nothing to me. I don't seek admiration from the man who's despised me all my life."

With that, he turned to head upstairs, but the marquess caught his arm. "I'm...I'm sorry for that." Rand's jaw dropped—had the word *sorry* just passed his father's lips? "I was thinking, last night, about you and Alban and Margery."

"And how you treated the two of them better than me?"

"Yes," he bit out. "I did. I'm not proud of it, but there's the truth. I always blamed you for your mother's death. Whenever I looked at you, I was reminded, and—"

"Her death? However did your twisted mind come up with that? I wasn't even here when she died!"

"Exactly. You'd run off somewhere, as was your habit in those days. She died searching for her precious younger son."

Rand felt like all the air had been sucked right out of him. *Run off, as was your habit.* "She died searching?"

"She raced off on Queenie, her favorite mare. The animal failed to clear a fence. Broke two legs and had to be put down. Your mother broke her neck."

"I..." Afraid his legs would give out, Rand retreated in search of somewhere to sit. The backs of his calves finally bumped into a hall chair, and he collapsed onto it.

He stared at the black-and-white floor between his limp, spread knees. "I just came home and she was...gone. You told me it was a riding accident, but you never said..."

The marquess followed him, looking down on him. "No point in telling a boy of six," he said in clipped tones. "If I was wrong to blame you for her death, at least I wasn't callous enough to accuse you out loud."

Rand looked up. "No. Instead you ignored me, mistreated me, drove me from your home—"

"And you managed to survive regardless. And"—the marquess shifted on his feet—"to make something of yourself."

Rand Nesbitt's many accolades meant less than nothing to the Marquess of Hawkridge. "Not something you'll ever approve. In the world where I belong, I'm called Professor, not *my lord*."

His father's jaw tightened. "You're a baron now and will someday be a marquess. That's another matter we need to discuss. Which we will, just as soon as you wed Margery and set up residence here."

"I have no intention of living here. I'm not in such a hurry to put myself back in range of your disapproval and abuse."

"I've made my apologies," the marquess muttered. He glanced through the open door. "I've dogs to attend to."

"By all means," Rand said, waving him off.

The old goat always had valued his dogs over his son.

FIFTY-FOUR

*T*HE RIDE TO Trentingham was awkward.

Rand was subdued while Rose was silent altogether, leaving Lily struggling to keep up a civil chatter more or less on her own. The worst of it was that for the first time since the baptism, she found herself wracking her brain to find anything to discuss with Rand. Their ease with each other was gone, their relationship changing already.

It was only two hours between the estates, yet the time passed like the carriage's wheels were mired in mud. Though Beatrix rode inside, her warm softness on Lily's lap failed to provide any comfort. When they finally rolled up before the manor, she couldn't wait to get into the house.

Just inside the door, Mum met her and wrapped her in a hug. "That was a short visit."

Lily clung to her mother for a moment, inhaling her familiar floral scent. "It felt like a lifetime." When she pulled away, she looked around as though seeing her home for the first time. So light and bright, the staircase off the entry fashioned of classical white balustrades instead of heavy, dark carved wood. The atmosphere warm and loving, not cold and full of resentment. "It's good to be home."

Concern flooded her mother's brown eyes. "Do you not like Hawkridge Hall? Will you not want to live there?"

"Oh, Mum, it seems I won't be living there even if I did want to!" Here, finally, was someone who cared. Lily had felt invisible at Hawkridge Hall—no, worse than invisible. A burden to Rand and *persona non grata* to everyone else, including her own sister. "Things have changed—"

Spotting Rand standing in the doorway, she broke off.

"Rand." Though Mum smiled at him, the expression in her eyes said she knew something was wrong. "How very nice to see you again. You'll stay for supper, won't you? Or does your father expect you back at Hawkridge this afternoon?"

"No," he said dully. "I'm going home to Oxford for a few days."

"The sun sets late this time of year, so you can stay for dinner, then, at least."

He shrugged as though he didn't care. "I'm going for a run," he said to Lily, already struggling out of his surcoat. "I'll be back in a while."

"No," she said. "Oh, no."

As he turned and walked away, Mum laid a gentle hand on Lily's arm. "I can see that things didn't go well with his father. Leave him be, dear."

"No." Lily started toward the door. "I've let him be quite enough. I'll be back and explain later."

"Lily!" Mum called.

But she was already out the door and down the steps.

FIFTY-FIVE

"**W**AIT!" **LILY** called.

But Rand didn't, even though she was sure he'd heard her. To the contrary, he shoved his coat and cravat into the carriage and then began to run, putting more distance between them.

She hurried past blue and yellow flower beds in her high Louis-heeled shoes. Hoping she wouldn't twist an ankle in the soft grass, she wished she hadn't dressed so fashionably this morning.

The shoes and the lavender gown with the heavy over-skirt had been a final, half-hearted attempt to impress her future father-in-law. If she wasn't so forlorn, she'd laugh at herself for her characteristic optimism. The fact was, there was nothing she could do to make Lord Hawkridge like her. He was bent on his son marrying Margery, and that was that.

He'd probably sent up a cheer when he saw her climb into the carriage and ride away.

There was Rand, crossing the bridge to the other side of the river.

"Rand!"

Thanks to living with her father, Lily knew how to make her voice carry. But although Rand stopped running, he didn't stop altogether, instead pacing determinedly along the far bank.

Hopping on one foot and then the other, she pulled off her shoes and left them jumbled on the daisy-strewn lawn. Then she picked up her skirts and ran—across the grass, over the bridge, along the path with the river on one side and grazing fields on the other.

Her face heated and her lungs burned. She developed a searing stitch in her side. But she wouldn't stop running.

She would never give up on Rand Nesbitt.

In the woods beyond, she spotted him in the distance and pushed herself to close the gap. "Rand," she called breathlessly.

He slowed, stopped, and turned, looking defeated. "You'll cut your feet," he said in a dead voice.

Panting, she looked down to the forest floor, littered with twigs and leaves. Her silk stockings were torn, which was no surprise, but she hadn't noticed when it happened.

"I—don't—care," she said between gasping attempts to catch her breath. She bent at the waist, hugging the pain in her side. "All I care for, Rand, is you."

If she'd hoped he'd melt at those words, she was disappointed. "Sometimes," he said, "I need to be by myself. Can you not leave a body alone?"

"I've tried that. It hasn't worked."

"I need to think. I cannot think."

She straightened and met his gaze. She had something she needed to tell him, and she knew he needed to share something, too. A piece of the puzzle was missing—the piece she suspected had made him run. "We can think together. Maybe two heads are better than one."

His jaw tensed as though he were forcibly holding back

words. He crossed his arms, shutting her out. His gaze drifted up to the canopy of leaves overhead.

The solitude he wanted would solve nothing. "I'm staying here, Rand. I won't leave you. Do you hear me?" She shouted it to the trees. "I won't leave you, no matter what your father says!"

Slowly he lowered his eyes. "Do you believe in fate?"

"I believe you're *my* fate."

"Lily, my sweet." He shook his head, reaching for her. "Come here."

His arms felt so good around her, so solid and sure. He kissed her, kissed her until she was more breathless than she'd been from running, until she felt boneless and light-headed. He put one-hundred-percent of himself into the wordless promise of that kiss.

And she knew, without a doubt, that whatever it was that made him run away, time after time, had nothing to do with her presence burdening him. Perhaps he simply didn't know how to share. He'd spent so very much of his life on his own.

Well, she'd show him how. Two heads *were* better than one, two hearts even stronger.

When he finally drew back, she searched his intense gray eyes. "What happened? It's something else, isn't it? Besides Margery and your father's ultimatum?" He tried to look away, but she moved to the side, keeping her gaze locked on his. "What happened?" she repeated. "What new disaster has arisen to pile on top of the others?"

He sighed, looking reluctant to confide in her.

But at least he didn't run.

With both hands, she propelled him toward a large stump and pushed down on his shoulders until he sat. "Talk to me," she said, reminding herself of her mother.

Leaves rustled overhead, and a sparrow fluttered from one branch to another. Lady had found her way back home.

Jasper blinked his little squirrel eyes at them, then darted up a tree. Lily rubbed her scarred hand and examined her ruined stockings, waiting.

"The marquess," Rand said at last, "has revealed he had an excuse for the way he's always mistreated me."

"You were a child. There was no excuse." But then a flash of insight made Lily wonder if this was the 'troublesome' incident Etta had mentioned.

Her curiosity piqued, she had to redouble her efforts at appearing patient. The last thing she wanted was to scare him off.

"He blamed me for the death of my mother."

"What?" She dropped to sit beside him. "I thought it was a riding accident."

"Yes, but I never knew the circumstances. It seems, as a child, I had a habit of running off." He paused as though waiting for her to agree or to chide him. When she didn't, he went on. "I was six when it happened. She couldn't find me and went out looking."

"Then fell off her horse?" Lily asked quietly.

"And broke her neck."

"Oh, Rand." Sensing his grief, she shifted to face him and wrapped her arms around his shoulders. "It wasn't your fault."

"I'd disappeared."

"You were six. You weren't responsible for her accident. It could have happened another day, another time—"

"But it didn't." The guilt rolled off of him in waves. "It happened when I ran off. I killed her."

With a hand on his chin, she turned his face to hers. "No. You're not to blame."

"My father thinks I am. I left her, and she died. And look at me. I'm still running off and hurting the people I love."

She offered him a wan smile. "I believe I just put a stop to that. And Rand, you didn't kill her. Your father saying so doesn't make it true. You were six years old. Events happen. This one was tragic, but you cannot believe it's your fault."

"My father believes it."

"Not really," she argued. "Or he'd have voiced that blame aloud long ago. And he never did, did he? Or you would have known that's why he was cruel to you."

He appeared to consider that for a moment, and Lily felt a little of the tightness ease from his body. "You won't convince me the old goat is good," he finally said.

"No, and I wouldn't try. His treatment of you was unpardonable, but perhaps natural, for all that. He was hurting—"

"Hurting?" Rand interrupted in a tone of patent disbelief.

She nodded. "He must have loved her very much to react in such a strong manner, even if it was wrong."

"Love? I cannot picture the man in love. I doubt he even believes in such a fine emotion."

She decided to drop that for now. "Regardless, he was wrong to treat you poorly. Not only because you were—are—his child, but also because—"

"I was only six," he finished softly, as though really hearing that for the first time.

"Yes, you were only six."

An invisible weight seemed to roll off his shoulders, and he sat there a long while, silent, leaning his forehead against hers.

"I need time to think," he said at last, pulling slightly away.

"About your mother?"

He shook his head, a slow, mournful motion. "About Margery. I cannot marry her, loving you. I cannot. But the baby—"

"The baby? *What* baby?"

"She's with child," he said miserably. "Margery is going to

have the baron's son. Or daughter. It wasn't intentional. She claims she and Armstrong got carried away. Just once."

Shock and dismay swirled in Lily's stomach and made a lump rise in her throat. But having seen Margery and the baron together, she had no trouble imagining the two of them getting carried away.

She swallowed hard. "How do you feel about her being with child?"

"My baby sister is having a baby—she did what it takes to have a baby." Rand's mouth twisted ruefully. "I honestly don't know how I feel about that. And...she asked me to raise it as my own. If we can't find a way for her to wed Armstrong, that is."

"And you agreed, of course," she said softly. Picturing Rand raising another girl's baby made Lily's stomach continue roiling, but she was determined to maintain an outward calm. "Because what else can you do? The child oughtn't to be punished for its parents' indiscretion."

"Yes, I agreed," he admitted. "But I confess, as much as I can't picture myself wed to Margery, I find that when I think of raising her child...I don't mind. Which is odd."

"You're far too generous to refuse an innocent babe a good home. Why should you think it odd?"

"Because until very recently I found the thought of raising *any* child abhorrent. But now, when I close my eyes..." He did so, and a little crease appeared in his forehead. "I see a little girl with big blue eyes and dark curls." He opened his eyes. "Our daughter."

Lily's heart skittered. "I see a boy. A gray-eyed boy with long, dark gold hair."

His lips curved in a half smile. "Twins. They run in your family, don't they?"

Despite everything, she had to laugh. "If you'd seen my sister heavy with twins, you wouldn't wish that on me.

Besides, it's Ford's family that runs to twins. Surely you know he's a twin himself."

"Ah, yes. Kendra." For a moment, Rand looked far away, lost in the past. Then the faint smile faded from his face. "One child, twins, triplets—I don't care, so long as they're ours. More than anything, Lily, I want you to have my children."

"I want that, too, so very much." Instinctively, Lily's hand moved to her middle. Then it fell back to her lap. "But that would mean...not only Bennett Armstrong..."

Rand nodded stiffly. "Armstrong condemned to death, Margery tarnished as a fallen woman, and her child branded a bastard. Could I live with myself, having caused all of that?"

Of course he couldn't; he wouldn't be Rand if he could. The lump was rising in Lily's throat again. "There must be another way," she said, using his words. "You're right—we both need to think."

He put his bigger hand over hers. "Not now. I'm sorry, but I must go to Oxford. I need more clothes, and other—"

"I didn't mean you're never allowed to go off alone. You'll think in Oxford, and I'll think here."

By unspoken agreement, they rose and began walking in the direction of Trentingham—without hurry this time. Rand took her hand. "After Oxford, I must go back to Hawkridge. Armstrong said he was hunting with a party; one of the other men might have seen something. Or someone else. If need be, I will interview every soul in a ten-mile radius. If there exists any evidence to exonerate the baron, I will find it."

Leaves crunched beneath Lily's stockinged feet, and when a twig snapped with a loud *crack*, Rand swept her up into his arms. She linked her hands behind his neck. "I shall come and help you."

She saw the telltale hesitation, felt the slight tightening of his arms before he decided to come out with it. "Let me talk to my father first. You'll be but two hours away, and I'll come for you, I promise, once I'm convinced my father will be civil." His gray eyes pleaded for her to understand.

And she did understand, but it was frustrating to feel so helpless. Yet she was secretly pleased that he meant to confront his father at last, just as the marquess had finally, after all these years, confided in his son. Why, it was almost as if they were beginning to see each other as human beings.

"Trust me on this, sweetheart," he added softly.

"Very well. But if I think of anything that could help, anything at all, I'll come to you," she warned him as they emerged from the woods.

In the soft grass that lined the banks of the river, he set her on her feet and pressed his lips to her forehead. "I wouldn't want it any other way," he murmured, the words a warm promise against her skin. "We're in this together. Never doubt that, my love."

FIFTY-SIX

*D*INNER WAS A subdued affair.

Bacon tart was usually one of Lily's favorites, its flaky crust and sweet almonds contrasting with the salty meat, but today she only picked at it while she and Rand recounted the details of their predicament to her parents.

Mum looked very sorry that she'd let her daughters go to Hawkridge, although as Lily pointed out, their absence wouldn't have changed anything.

"It would have spared you some discomfort, dear," Mum said.

But that didn't matter to Lily. The reward for that discomfort had been more time with Rand—precious time that could turn out to be their last.

Afterward, Lily saw him out to his carriage. "If you think of anything," she told him, "anything at all—I want to know. And if I think of anything, I'll send word to you in Oxford."

"I may not be there long enough for word to reach me. Fewer than six days remain until the wedding. I mean to get back to Hawkridge well before that to begin investigating."

"Then stop here on the way. Please. It won't cost you but

half an hour, and I may have an idea—"

She broke off when his lips descended on hers.

The kiss was fierce, desperate. It made her mouth burn and her senses reel wildly. She knew, without a doubt, that she would never find this with anyone else—and the truth cracked her heart.

When he finally broke the kiss, he shut his eyes and clasped her to him, so hard it almost hurt. "Lily, this cannot be the end for us. It just cannot."

"It won't be." Gingerly extracting herself, she brushed her lips over his one last time. "You'll stop by on your way to Hawkridge?"

He opened his eyes and nodded.

"Then I'll see you in a few days," she said, suspecting those days would be the longest of her life.

Rose, however, wasn't going to let her mope around.

"I think tonight we should have our sleeping party," she said when Lily reentered the house.

Lily rubbed her face. "So you're speaking to me again?"

Her sister only shrugged and looked away, her expression contrite.

But Lily smiled, knowing this was Rose-speak for *I'm sorry.* She reached to squeeze her sister's shoulder. "I'm so glad. That we're speaking again, I mean. And Rose, I know I said some hurtful things last night, and I'm s—"

"They were true."

"Pardon?" Lily's brows snapped together. "But I accused you of—"

"Sabotage, yes. Just listen, and please don't interrupt, or I might lose my nerve." Rose took a deep breath, leaning against the balustrade as if for support. "I convinced you to go to Hawkridge because I wanted to break your betrothal. I was…very angry with both you and Rand. So when he seemed to fear introducing you to his ghastly father would put you off the marriage—a more than justified fear, I might add—I decided my best chance was to get you to Hawkridge Hall, one way or anoth—"

She broke off as two footman appeared, carrying between them an enormous silver tureen. And moving at a snail's pace. Glancing about, Rose dragged her sister into the drawing room. Too mired in confusion and disbelief to protest, Lily sank onto the nearest couch. She saw Beatrix slip through the door just before it closed, and felt absurdly glad for the presence of a friend.

Rose remained standing, nervously toying with the bows on her sleeves. "Once we arrived at Hawkridge," she went on, "nothing went as planned. The marquess was even worse than I'd hoped, but somehow you weren't afraid of him. I saw you stand up to him over the dogs—"

"You were spying?"

"Observing," Rose said haughtily. "Anyway, you were stronger than I'd expected. *I* certainly wouldn't have stuck by Rand. Can you imagine having that beast for a father-in-law?"

Lily just looked at her.

"Oh, right. I suppose you can." Turning away guiltily, Rose drew another deep breath. "After that, I realized having you at Hawkridge wasn't working in my favor. What you accused me of…you were right. I was trying to convince you to give up and go home, hoping that without your influence, Rand would succumb to Margery's charms and his father's coercion. But Lily," she rushed to add, "I didn't say anything that wasn't true, did I? You really *didn't* have a prayer of changing the marquess's mind, and Rand *is* too good to abandon Margery, and—"

"That makes it so much better," Lily said flatly. "My own sister was trying to destroy me *and* the love of my life, but at least she didn't tell a fib."

"Yes, *was*. I *was* trying to hurt you. But now I'm not. I've changed my mind."

Lily just shook her head. After an incredibly draining few days, she seemed to have no emotions left, not even anger. "Why should I believe you?" she asked wearily.

"Because I know I was wrong, and I'm so very, very sorry. Last night, when that beastly man came up with his horrid offer, and I saw what it did to you—to all three of you. You were so devastated, I can't even describe it. Devastation like that is something I've never felt. Not even when Grandpapa died, and I loved him more than anyone in the world." Her dark eyes filled with tears.

Lily bit her lip. "The way I love Rand is different from loving Grandpapa," she said gently.

"I know. Now I know. Lily, I never wanted to hurt you like *that*. I never want to see that look on your face again."

Lily gave a wan smile. "I'm afraid you may have to, unless Rand somehow manages to dig up proof of Lord Armstrong's innocence."

If he truly *was* innocent...but she had to believe he was. It was the only chance she and Rand had.

"If there's anything I can do to help..."

"Thank you."

For several minutes, the only sound in the room was Beatrix roaming atop and around various items of furniture, occasionally pausing to lick herself.

Eventually Rose cleared her throat. "So...am I forgiven?"

Lily thought about it. "If *I'm* forgiven."

Relief dawning on her face, Rose hurled herself on the couch to wrap Lily in a hard hug. "I don't deserve you," she said in a sniffly voice.

Lily hugged her back. "You've got that right," she replied, startling her sister into a laugh.

FIFTY-SEVEN

*A*FTER A LONG visit with Rowan in his bedroom, where he was more or less confined until he could manage the stairs, Lily changed into a more comfortable gown for supper. She didn't need to impress anyone here at Trentingham.

As she reached the bottom of the staircase, she saw Violet coming in out of a light drizzle. "I didn't know you were joining us tonight," Lily exclaimed happily, running to kiss her on the cheek. It seemed ages since she'd seen her eldest sister. "Where are Ford and the little ones?"

"At home, pouting." Violet removed her spectacles and wiped the spatters of rain with a lace-edged handkerchief. "But they can survive one night without me. I wouldn't miss your sleeping party for the world!"

"My what?"

The front door swung wide again, and a cloaked figure entered, drawing back its hood. "Lily," Judith cried, "what a sensational idea! Thank you so much for the invitation."

"What invitation?" Lily said as a footman took her

friend's cloak. "I'm sorry, Judith—and it's lovely to see you—but I have no idea what you're talking about."

Her face fell. "But I received a message this afternoon. Was it a mistake?"

"I got one, too," Violet put in.

"What message? I didn't send any messages."

"Then who did?"

Voices from above drew their notice to Rose descending the staircase, carrying a vibrant flower arrangement in a Delftware vase. "Fruit, nuts, bread, and cheese," she was saying to her maid. "And see if Mrs. Crump will bake nun's biscuits, since those are Lily's favorites. We'll need it all brought to her room at nine o'clock."

As her maid hurried off to alert the cook, Rose arrived at the bottom of the stairs, smiling wide behind the blooms. "Violet, Judith! I'm so glad you both could attend."

"Attend what?" Lily demanded, wondering if she were going mad.

"Your sleeping party, you goose." Rose braced the vase against one hip so she could wrap her older sister in a one-armed hug.

"*My* sleeping party?"

"Well, I've handled the preparations, but it was your idea, remember?" Rose's dark eyes filled with concern. "You said Violet should come over to sleep. And I thought you would like to have Judith, too, since she's your best friend."

"But—tonight?" Lily didn't want to be rude, but the last thing she needed just now was a party. Tonight she just wanted to crawl into her bed, curl up, and think hard about how Bennett Armstrong's innocence could possibly be proven.

A flush touched Rose's cheeks. "You told Rand that two heads are better than one. Well, four would be even better, don't you think? Perhaps tonight we can hit upon a solution."

Though she still wasn't sure she felt up to what Rose had planned, Lily was touched. "Thank you," she said, "for caring."

"Gemini," Rose said, hefting the vase, "you're my sister. Of course I care. Now, I must get this arrangement to the supper table. I made it specially for tonight—won't it cheer up the dining room?"

As Rose bustled away, Lily looked after her in wonder. She'd never seen her sister so industrious—nor half so thoughtful.

A soft drizzle continued outside, turning the world gray and dismal to match Lily's mood. The whole story was told again to Violet and Judith over supper. By the time they all made it up to Lily's room for their sleeping party, laden with a decanter of wine and the refreshments that Mrs. Crump had prepared, Lily was exhausted to the point of numbness.

She collapsed crosswise on top of her white coverlet. "I'm afraid you're going to have my party without me."

Violet set down a bowl of fruit and reached a hand to help her sit. "I'm sure you're tired," she said sympathetically, settling beside her on the bed. "But we have a mission to accomplish."

Even in her state, Lily couldn't help but notice the faint circles under her oldest sister's eyes. "You look rather tired yourself."

"Two babies will do that to you," Violet said with a tender smile. But it faded as she watched Lily lay a hand on her abdomen. "You'll have children, too, Lily."

"We just have to put our heads together and come up with a brilliant idea," Rose said as she sat herself on Lily's other side.

The three of them against all the injustice in the world.

"I think I've missed something, Rose," Violet said,

swinging her feet back and forth. "Why all of a sudden are you willing to help Lily wed Rand Nesbitt?"

"Baron Newcliffe," Rose corrected, her cheeks reddening. "And as to why…well…" She darted a questioning glance at Lily, who made a locked lips gesture, indicating her silence. Rose looked relieved. "Seeing them face so many obstacles to be together made me realize I'd never loved him like that. I only wanted him because he's handsome."

"And titled," Violet reminded her, leaning across Lily to send their sister an arch look.

"Well, that, too. I *do* want someone of consequence, you know. But Lily and Rand—they belong together."

"Thank you," Lily whispered, hearing truth in Rose's words even though it wasn't the whole story. How bittersweet it was to have her sister finally approve at the same time her betrothal was falling apart.

Seated at Lily's dressing table with a platter of bread and cheese, Judith stopped eating long enough to release a languid sigh. "You and Rand are so romantic."

Lily eyed her friend thoughtfully. "You look happy."

"I am." Judith's pale blue eyes shone. "I've spent some time alone with Edmund—I mean, Lord Grenville—"

"You'd never been alone with him?" Rose interrupted.

Buttering bread, Judith blushed. "Well, it's not exactly proper, I know, but Papa managed to talk Mama into allowing it. I was so very unhappy, not really knowing Edmund and thinking I might never come to love him."

Lily began filling four goblets with wine. "So what happened?"

Judith looked up, her cheeks flushed with wonder. "He's ever so marvelous. The sweetest man. I cannot imagine why I expected to fall in love at first sight. It takes getting to know someone, don't you think? What a gentleman looks like doesn't matter as much as what he's like inside."

Rand, Lily thought, was marvelous both inside and out. She would never find another like him.

She handed Judith a cup. "So what is Lord Grenville like inside?"

"Thoughtful. Kind. He answered all my questions and listened when I answered his. He loved his first wife dearly, but he was ever so sad that she couldn't give him any children. More than anything, he wants children. And I...I want to give them to him."

"Have you considered," Rose asked, "that the failure to have children might be due to some lack on *his* part?" It was just like Rose to say out loud what others would only wonder silently. "After all," she added, "he's thirty-five." She said *thirty-five* as though the fellow were likely to topple over and die of old age at any moment.

"That's not so ancient!" Judith burst out defensively. Lily's sister blinked, clearly taken aback, but Judith went on. "Do you know, Rose, that someday you will be five-and-thirty, too? And for your sake, I hope by then—"

She broke off, leaving the rest of the sentence unspoken. But they all knew what she'd been about to say.

I hope by then you'll have found a husband.

"Well," Rose said stiffly. "I hope for *your* sake that Lord Grenville's childlessness wasn't due to his own shortcomings in the marriage bed."

"Rose," Violet groaned, raising her gaze to the heavens.

"I think," Judith said just as stiffly, "I can safely reassure you on that count. He's a *very* good kisser." A hunk of cheese halfway to her mouth, she paused and glanced around as though waiting for a reaction. "Are you not scandalized," she finally asked no one in particular, "that I allowed him to kiss me?"

Lily laughed. "No, we're not scandalized. As a matter of fact, Mum always advised us to kiss a man before assenting to marriage. After all, it's a lifetime commitment, so it's a good idea to ascertain your compatibility in that area."

"Oh," was all Judith said.

In fact, Lily thought she looked a mite disappointed they didn't think her a fallen woman.

"I'm so glad you're happy," she told her. "I imagine that now you're really looking forward to your wedding."

"Oh, yes," Judith breathed.

Lily wished she had her own wedding to look forward to instead of dreading Rand and Margery's. Five days now. While she was thrilled for Judith, for some reason her friend's newfound happiness made her own situation seem that much more miserable.

Judith handed her a nun's biscuit. "Have you kissed Rand, then?"

Lily nodded, biting into the sweet almond and lemon treat.

"She may have done more than kiss him," Rose said, waggling her brows.

Feeling her face flood with color, Lily gasped. "You have no reason to believe such a thing."

"Haven't I?" Rose countered. "This morning—" She stopped, gaping at Lily's face.

Which was a picture of outrage.

Rose must have seen her return to their chamber this morning, Lily realized. Was she really going to spread tales about her late-night excursion? Just a few breaths after Lily had allowed her to gloss over her own indiscretions?

Rose's dark eyes widened as she got the message. "Gemini, I was only jesting."

Lily brushed sugary crumbs off her skirts while she thought of a way to quickly change the subject. "Remember that song I was practicing for Rand? The one he's always humming?"

"What of it?"

"It has naughty words. And there are others, too. A whole book of them."

"A book?" Rose sat forward eagerly. "Did he show it to you?"

Lily shook her head. "He doesn't own a copy. He said he read it in a friend's library."

"And you believed him?" Rose rolled her eyes. "That's the oldest—"

Violet cleared her throat. "Could you mean *An Antidote Against Melancholy*?"

"Yes," Lily said, reaching for her wine, "I think that was the title."

"Then I believe Ford is the friend in question. I've seen that book in our library." Biting into a strawberry, Violet looked quite unconcerned. "It *is* naughty," she added with a grin.

"Let's send for it," Rose suggested. The glitter in her eyes belied her solemn tone. "It sounds educational."

Violet laughed but scribbled a note to Ford. They sent a footman to deliver it and instructed him to wait and bring the book back. "Now," she said, "while *we* wait, we must solve the problem at hand."

Lily went over the whole story again, all the painful details. Then they tossed around ideas. But every solution proposed, no matter how promising at first, turned out to be flawed, impossible, or downright ludicrous.

As it appeared more and more that Lily's situation was hopeless, the suggestions became fewer and farther between, until an hour later they'd fallen into a heavy silence.

Violet slipped off her spectacles and rubbed her eyes. "Faith, we're a woebegone bunch. This is supposed to be a party. We'll discuss this again later, but for now, let's see if the songbook has arrived."

Soon they were in the drawing room, giggling, the book propped up on the harpsichord where they could all see the words while Lily read the music.

"Play this one, Lily," Rose said, her dark eyes wide. She began singing.

"My mistress is a mine of gold —
Would that it were her pleasure
To let me dig within her mould
And roll among her treasure!"

The Ashcroft sisters laughed, but Judith just sipped her wine, looking bemused. "I don't understand. Dig within her mould?"

"He means the woman's...you know," Rose said.

Judith looked even more baffled. "I'm not certain I do know."

"Truly?" Rose asked incredulously. "I vow and swear, you must read *Aristotle's Master-piece* before you get married."

Now Judith gasped. Although she knew the Ashcroft sisters had all read it, the book was considered scandalous. A desperate look in her eyes, she turned to Violet. "You're married. Tell me."

Lily was relieved that she wasn't the one asked to explain.

While a pink-cheeked Judith learned the facts from Violet, Rose flipped pages in the book. "This one seems amusing," she said when Violet was finished. "'The Comical Dreamer.'"

Lily set the book back up on the harpsichord and began to play. This time they all sang together, even Judith.

"Last night a dream came into my head,
Thou wert a fine white loaf of bread
Then if May-butter I could be,
How I would spread,

Oh! how I would spread myself on thee!"

By the final verse, they had dissolved into giggles. Lily clutched her stomach—she couldn't remember the last time she'd laughed so hard. Despite everything, she was having fun.

"Sh-shall we," Judith gasped, "sing another?"

FIFTY-EIGHT

*C*HRYSTABEL SMILED to herself when she heard the opening notes of "The Lusty Young Smith." It was one of her favorites.

Stretched out beside her on their bed, Joseph couldn't hear the words filtering through the thick stone walls. "What's that they're singing, Chrysanthemum?"

"Oh, I cannot make out the tunes." She sipped from her goblet of wine. "I'm just happy that Lily is enjoying herself."

He'd die if he knew. Joseph liked to think his daughters were much too ladylike for bawdy fun, and she wouldn't be the one to disabuse him of the notion. "I'm sure the others are just trying to cheer Lily up. And doing an excellent job, from the sound of it. It was good of Rose to plan the sleeping party. Thoughtful, don't you think?"

Setting down his empty goblet, Joseph nodded. "Perhaps Rose is finally growing up."

"Perhaps she is." Chrystabel finished her own wine and sighed. "Our children are *all* growing up."

"Too fast," he agreed. His green eyes turned troubled. "About Lily—"

"I'm concerned, yes. Worried sick, truth be told. Should Rand not find a way out of this, Lily will be left devastated."

"Especially if anything untoward happened between them at Hawkridge," he added anxiously.

"Oh, nothing did, thank heaven." Turning to face him, she reached to caress one whisker-roughened cheek. "I suppose I should have told you, but it never occurred to me that you were worrying, too." She always expected him to be oblivious to such concerns, like other men. But sometimes he surprised her. And he did love his children very much.

That was only one of the many reasons she loved *him* so very much.

He frowned. "How do you know? A mother's intuition? Because I've told you before, my love, you cannot tell these things just by looking—"

She laughed, a sound of amusement mixed with relief. "I know because I had Parkinson write to his aunt at Hawkridge, a woman by the name of Etta. Her return letter arrived with the coachman, bearing assurances that the staff saw nothing. And the staff see *everything*."

Diplomatically, Chrystabel omitted the part about Lily spending a night in Rand's bedchamber.

They *had* only slept, after all.

FIFTY-NINE

*H*ALFWAY TO OXFORD, rain had begun falling, turning the roads to mush and Rand's journey to a snail-paced nightmare. He'd arrived home and trudged through the empty house to the one furnished room, his bedchamber, where he'd promptly fallen into bed and passed a restless night.

Morning found him in a foul mood. Another day gone and no closer to finding a solution. He scrubbed up and pulled on some clothes, then opened his door, intending to inspect the house.

A measuring tape in one hand, Kit stopped and turned. "Rand. When did you get home?"

"Last night. Late." Rand rubbed his aching head. "How is the job progressing?"

"Haven't you noticed? It's all but done."

"Is it?" He followed Kit along the corridor, peeking into beautifully finished rooms. "My apologies. You've worked wonders."

"I've been here since you left. Amazing how a few days onsite will motivate craftsmen to work." He grinned, then suddenly frowned. "Hey, Rand, you're going to break your teeth."

Rand consciously relaxed his jaw, which had been clenched to the point of pain.

"What's got your dander up?" Kit asked.

"The mental image of my father at Hawkridge, planning a wedding for five days hence."

"I thought you wanted to get married."

"To Lily, not Margery Maybanks."

"Margery?" Kit's green-brown eyes widened. "Margery! Why on earth would he want you to marry Margery?"

Rand sighed. "It's a long story."

"Best told over a tankard of ale, I'd guess. Come along. It's a bit early yet, but the King's Arms is always open."

≈

"*C*HIN UP, DEAR," Lily's father bellowed across the table.

"You cannot give up hope," Mum added more gently, pointedly handing Lily a spoon. "There must be something that can be done."

"Rand. Rand will have to come up with something." Unable to eat, Lily pushed her dinner around on her plate and sighed.

The lighthearted camaraderie of last night was gone. In the wee hours of the morning, the young women had all giggled their way upstairs to share Lily's big bed. It had been a tight fit with four instead of three, but worth it for the comfort she'd felt, surrounded by people who cared.

Today she could find no comfort. They'd awakened too late for breakfast and spent most of dinner revisiting all their useless suggestions, reviewing them with Father and Mum.

No one had any new ideas to contribute, and Lily's predicament seemed more hopeless than ever.

"Violet? Are you ready to come home?" They all looked over to see Ford had appeared in the doorway. "Did you have a fine time?"

Violet gave him a wan smile. "We did last night." She pushed back her chair and rose. "While I go get my things, Lily will fill you in on what's happened. Perhaps you'll see a solution we haven't."

But even Ford's brilliant mind had no new solution to offer. He was in agreement that absolving Bennett Armstrong was their only option. "Maybe one of the other hunters witnessed the confrontation," he suggested. "Or someone else. Just because no one's come forward—"

"Rand is planning to interview everyone in the vicinity." Lily bit her lip. "But I'm afraid if anyone knew anything, they'd have come forward long before now."

Ford looked thoughtful. "Not if they were afraid of facing the marquess's wrath. He clearly doesn't want to hear his son was at fault."

"That's true," she said, reluctant to succumb to the thread of hope that suddenly tugged at her heart. "A different way to look at this. He did, after all, offer an enormous reward for information that would prove Lord Armstrong guilty. Perhaps people are reluctant to approach him with anything that would prove the opposite."

Her father nodded sagely. "It's wise to keep on top of it."

Judith reached for more bread. "She said 'the opposite,' Lord Trentingham. Someone could be frightened to bring Lord Hawkridge evidence that proves the opposite."

"Eh?"

Evidently giving up, Judith slathered butter on the bread. "You must trust Rand, then," she told Lily, taking a big bite. The solemn atmosphere had failed to curb her appetite. "You love him, and you have to believe he won't give up until he finds proof."

Yes, Rand had promised they would find a way. After giving Judith a shaky smile, Lily turned to Ford. "Thank you. You've given me hope."

"It was nothing. Just another way to look at a solution that had already been proposed—nothing has changed."

While that was true, Lily was holding as tight as she could to that thin thread of hope. For the first time since she'd awakened this morning, she felt able to breathe.

Violet returned, her satchel in one hand and *An Antidote Against Melancholy* in the other. "I'm ready."

"Why did you want that book?" Ford asked.

As her gaze flicked to their parents, Violet flushed a delicate pink. "Oh, I just thought it might help Lily." She took his arm. "Come along. I cannot wait to see Nicky and the twins."

"What's the book called?" Mum asked.

Having failed to escape, Violet forced a smile. "*An Antidote Against Melancholy*. Lily was feeling a bit melancholy last night, you see, and—"

"Oh, then would you mind leaving it here? I expect she may feel a bit melancholy again the next few days."

"We already read the whole thing," Violet said, clutching the book possessively.

"Well, then." Mum was nothing if not persistent. "Leave it here for me. I adore helping people, as you know, and it seems to me I could learn a lot from a book called *An Antidote Against Melancholy*."

Lily suspected Mum would learn more than she anticipated. In specific, she'd learn her daughters weren't quite the innocents she imagined. And if she could judge by her sister's face, Violet was thinking much the same.

Looking amused, Ford pried the book from his wife's hands and set it on the table. "Here," he told his mother-in-law with a grin that would do any fiend proud. "I hope you and Lord Trentingham will enjoy it."

As Mum smiled and reached for it, he hustled Violet from the room, laughingly ignoring her protests. Rose and Lily exchanged frantic looks.

Their mother lifted the front cover.

"No!" Lily cried, her hand shooting out to slam the book shut. "Sorry, I...I just felt a bit of melancholy coming on, and, um, certain passages might be, you know, helpful. To reread. Some things are better the second time, you know. So, um, can I keep the book a little longer?"

"Of course." To Lily's great relief, her mother relinquished the book without a fight. "Judith, dear, would you please pass the sugar bowl?"

Judith obliged, and Mum spooned sugar into her coffee, humming a simple tune as she stirred.

It was only when she noticed Rose's mouth hanging open that Lily realized the tune was "The Comical Dreamer."

SIXTY

BY THE TIME Rand told the whole story, he and Kit had long since finished dinner and were nursing tankards of ale.

Last night's rain had ceased, but the day had dawned depressingly gray. The dark paneling inside the King's Arms made it dreary, and the crackling fire near their table did little to warm the room or lighten Rand's mood.

"Of all the rotten things your father has ever done to you, this wins the prize." Kit shook his head. "Margery. Is she all grown-up, then?"

"Very much so. She's nearly twenty-one, and a beauty, too. But I cannot imagine myself married to her."

"For all intents and purposes, she's your little sister." Looking thoughtful, Kit signaled for another round. "Margery was always very sweet."

"I'd say you're welcome to her, but I'm afraid Bennett Armstrong would have something to say about that. Especially considering she's carrying his child."

Kit blinked. "On top of everything else, she's with child?"

"Yes, and she's asked me to raise the babe as my own."

"You will, of course, should it come to that." Kit knew Rand inside out. "But we must find a way to fix this." He paused, musing as he drained his tankard. "Skinny old Bennett, huh?"

Despite the gravity of his situation, a ghost of a grin materialized on Rand's face. "He's not skinny anymore. I wouldn't challenge him were I you. Remember, he's killed once already, even if it was in self-defense."

"True, but I cannot bring myself to feel sorry that he did. Alban was..." Seemingly at a loss for words, Kit shook his head. A serving maid set down two fresh tankards, and he flipped her a coin. "I still remember that day Alban found us down by the river. He was angry at you for some reason—"

"I'd read his journal."

"Ah, that was it. Anyway, I thought he was going to kill us both. I've never run so fast in my life." He shuddered at the memory. "I say, do you suppose Alban may have kept journaling all these years?"

"Sweet mercy, I wish." Rand took a deep swallow of ale. "That occurred to me, too—what better evidence of his intention to kill Armstrong than a confession in his own hand? But my brother stopped writing years ago, when he realized he'd never devise a cipher I couldn't break."

Kit snorted. "Trying to encode secrets in a house with Rand Nesbitt—madness. The fool should have found a better hiding place."

"Pardon?"

"I said he should have—"

"—found a better hiding place," Rand repeated slowly. He ran his tongue over his teeth. "What if that's exactly what he did?"

Kit frowned. "I must've had one ale too many. What are you—oh!" He sat up straighter. "Perhaps he began hiding his journals instead of encoding them?"

"Perhaps. He did seem rather determined to record his... well, the journals called them 'experiments,' but I always thought of them as sins. I never understood his writing obsession. Though, in hindsight..." He grimaced.

"What?"

Tasting bile rising in his throat, Rand washed it down with more ale. "He always had certain entries marked— usually the worst ones—and those pages were faded and creased, as if he'd handled them more frequently. I didn't think anything of it as a child, but now I wonder...I suspect he returned to them often, to reread them. Relive them."

Kit's only response to that was a generous swig from his tankard.

They both nursed their ales for a spell, lost in thought. Kit finally broke the silence. "If he *was* still journaling, where would his writings be hidden?"

"I have no idea. But finding them is the best hope I've got." Rand drained his ale and stood. "I must collect some things, talk to some people. I'll leave for Hawkridge at dawn."

Kit rose, too. "I'm coming with you. Your house can wait."

SIXTY-ONE

*R*AND **SHOWED UP** in Trentingham's entry hall days before Lily thought he would, and the moment she saw his face, she knew he had a new plan. Even from the top of the stairs, she could see hope shining in his eyes.

Her heart leapt in response. Without a thought for her sister standing beside her, she lifted her skirts and ran down and into his arms. "You've thought of something, haven't you?"

"I have, yes." He kissed her enthusiastically before continuing. "There's no guarantee, of course, that it will work out, or that even if it does, the evidence will convince the marquess, but—"

"I say," Kit Martyn interrupted from the doorway, "spit it out already, man."

"Yes," Rose yelled down the stairs. "Go on, tell us." She started down to meet them, moving much more daintily than Lily had. "I'm likely to die of curiosity. We've all been wracking our brains for a solution—my sisters and I and our friend Judith—and I want to hear what you've come up with that our superior female minds missed."

Rand laughed. "It's Alban's journal."

Lily's brow crinkled. "I thought you told me he stopped writing?"

"I thought he had. But it's possible he simply began using a very good hiding spot. If that's the case, all I have to do is find it, and I'd wager his plans to kill Bennett Armstrong will be written there in his own hand. No matter how much the marquess wants to believe in his innocence, it will be impossible to refute that."

"If Lord Armstrong is telling the truth," Rose put in.

Yes, if, Lily thought. But he'd seemed so sincere. And she had to believe him, because proving his innocence was the only chance she and Rand had.

"Finding the journal could work against you instead of helping," Rose pointed out. "If it's found and there's no mention of ill will towards the baron, your father will take that as proof of Alban's innocence. Even should witnesses come forward, the journal will give him an excuse to disbelieve them and keep the noose around Armstrong's neck, so that Rand and Margery will be forced to submit to his will."

It was an intelligent observation. Annoyingly intelligent. And depressingly true, but Lily couldn't think about that now.

Hope had taken flight and refused to be grounded.

She clutched Rand's arm. "Do you really think you can find the journal?"

"For all we know, it could be sitting in plain view in his bedchamber." Rand crossed his fingers. "After all, it's been many years since he had to contend with my snooping. But otherwise, I'll turn the house upside down if need be."

"And inside out," Kit added. "I'm going along to help."

"Thank you," Lily said, impulsively giving him a hug. "I'm going, too."

"Lily." Rand stared at the oak-planked floor for a moment, then raised his gaze to meet hers. "I came to tell you my plans as I had promised, not to take you with me. Before I left, the marquess specifically instructed me not to bring you back."

Although she wasn't really surprised, Lily felt crushed. Had Rand's father hated her that much?

"Nonsense," said Rose. "The Ashcroft motto is Question Convention, and Lily will do as she likes. You cannot leave her here languishing while you men have all the fun. Besides, she could very well notice something you miss. Women's minds work in different ways than men's."

"Truer words were never spoken," Kit put in dryly, but Lily noticed him eyeing Rose with approval. "She's right, Rand. Lily should come along. We'll need all the help we can get."

"But I never—" Rand started.

"Never say never." Kit raised a dark, meaningful brow. "Didn't you declare your father was done dictating your life? Ten years ago."

Rand's shoulders went back. "My concern is for Lily, not myself. She's going to suffer a rather chilly welcome."

"Then I'd best bring my cloak," she said, smiling when Rose laughed.

"Wait!" Their mother appeared out of nowhere as usual. "Where do you suppose you're off to?"

Apprehensive of letting her daughter intrude where she was unwelcome—and where, moreover, she'd been miserable —Mum at first refused to let Lily go. But earnest explanations from Rand and impassioned pleas from Lily slowly wore her down. Eventually it was decided that the three would travel on horseback for the sake of haste, then return to Trentingham overnight rather than trespass on Lord Hawkridge's grudging hospitality.

Though Mum had granted her consent, Lily could see she was still anxious about the plan. She hated causing her mother strife, but she knew—and she'd figured it out for herself this time—that her place was at Hawkridge, with Rand. The intent behind Rose's words may have been malicious, but the words themselves rang true: If she wanted to belong at Hawkridge, she needed to *be* at Hawkridge.

In fact, Lily couldn't wait to leave, even knowing the marquess would be furious to see her. It felt good to do what was right instead of what was nice.

And it felt even better to be doing something to remedy her misfortunes instead of sitting here feeling frustrated while the hour moved ever closer to Rand and Margery's wedding.

SIXTY-TWO

$\mathcal{L}$ILY QUICKLY CHANGED her gown for her blue riding habit, and an hour and a half later, they arrived at Hawkridge Hall.

As they rode up the path from the river, Lily stared at the massive mansion. "It doesn't *look* evil," she said thoughtfully.

Rand leaned from the saddle to smooth her hair. "It won't be," he promised, "just as soon as we've exposed Alban for what he was."

"Goodness, I hope we can find that journal."

"We will. We have to."

The stables were around the back. As they headed in that direction, past the dog enclosure, Lily gasped.

"Oh, my heavens!" She slid from the saddle and hit the grass running. "Rex!"

Gaping, Rand watched her scale the fence. By the time he dismounted and caught up with her, she was kneeling in the dirt, her hands on either side of one very agitated mastiff's head.

"Hold him like this," she ordered without looking up. Rand leaned down to comply, not a simple task since the animal was violently pawing at its face. It gasped and gulped, its stomach pumping as though it was trying to vomit.

Lily reached for the dog's mouth and pried it open, ignoring all the foamy saliva that dripped from the canine's black lips. Rand struggled to hold the animal still while she pulled out its long tongue.

"Up!" she yelled, her fingers moving the tongue this way and that. "I need to see!" Kit leapt to help, angling the mastiff's head toward the sun while Lily peered down its throat. "I knew it!" she ground out through gritted teeth, calm and determined although she was clearly livid.

Heedless of the animal's sharp teeth, she reached back into its mouth. But she couldn't grasp whatever was choking the poor creature.

Only a whimper betrayed Lily's distress. After that, she was all action. She stood and, leaving the dog's front paws on the ground, went around to lift him from behind. Though the canine was easily twice her weight, she managed to raise both his legs. But she was too short to get them up high.

Rand and Kit both jumped to help, taking one hind leg each while Lily knelt again by the dog's head. "Come on, Rex," she pleaded. "Cough it up. Shake him!" she told the men.

They did, holding him up like a wheelbarrow, but though the dog jerked and made choking sounds, the object still remained lodged.

"Dear me," Lily moaned, panting as though she could breathe precious air for the animal. "Set him back down."

With the flat of her hand, she administered three sharp blows between the huge creature's shoulder blades, but nothing happened. Finally she leaned over its back, wrapped her arms around its middle, and squeezed so hard her face turned red, pressing up on its belly with both fists.

All at once, a slobbery red apple came shooting out of its mouth.

"Oh, Rex!" The dog collapsed to the ground, and she hugged him around the neck, laying her cheek against his sweaty coat. Tears poured down her face. "I thought I was going to lose you!"

The other dogs came closer to investigate, barking loudly and poking at Rex with their noses. Though he was clearly exhausted, Rex turned his head and licked Lily's face, a big wet swath of pure love.

She laughed, and Rand smiled, his own eyes embarrassingly damp. His legs felt shaky, as if he'd run miles. He was speechless.

Kit spoke for them both. "That was incredible, Lily."

She hugged Rex even harder. "It was only what had to be done."

"No," came another voice, one filled with admiration. "It was an amazing display of quick thinking." Rand turned to see his father unlocking the gate. The marquess walked right over to Lily and reached down a hand. "Thank you for saving Attila. I need to get rid of that apple tree."

Lily was too nice to say she'd told him so, but her lips curved in a smile that made Rand's chest thump. She unwound her arms from the hound's neck and allowed the marquess to help her rise.

As soon as she moved away, the other dogs pressed even closer. Lily brushed at her less-than-pristine riding habit. "Perhaps, my lord, you should take him into the house for a while. He needs some time to recover, and out here he will get no rest."

"My dogs are not allowed in—" the marquess started, then apparently had second thoughts. "An excellent suggestion, Lady Lily. Will you come with us and help me get him settled?"

Rand watched, aghast, as his father and Lily headed for the house, the dog walking gingerly between them.

After a moment, he and Kit exchanged glances and began following. "He didn't even ask what she was doing here," Rand whispered.

"He didn't notice me at all," Kit said dryly. "He had eyes only for your lady."

"He's grateful at the moment. It won't last."

Kit shook his head. "She's won him over."

"Perhaps," Rand conceded, although it seemed more likely his father was temporarily bewitched. Lily, after all, was very good at casting spells, especially where Nesbitt men were concerned.

But regardless, he'd best not forget that nothing had really changed. "This doesn't mean he'll assent to my wedding Lily instead of Margery."

"No," Kit agreed. "We still need to find that journal."

In the back parlor, Lily settled Rex-Attila by the fireplace and requested a blanket. Without questioning her, the marquess rang for a footman and asked for one to be brought. Lily knelt by the dog, murmuring soothing nonsense while the marquess looked on, a bemused expression on his face.

When he finally looked up, his features hardened. "Christopher," he said, apparently noticing Kit for the first time. "It's been years."

Kit nodded an acknowledgment. "Since Rand left for Oxford."

"What brings you here now?" the marquess asked rather suspiciously.

Before Kit or Rand could answer, Lily spoke up from where she knelt on the floor. "We've come to find Alban's journal," she said clearly, although they had all agreed they would claim they'd come to discuss Rand's marriage and then perform their search on the sly. "Rand is of the opinion that it could clear Lord Armstrong's name."

To Rand's surprise, his father didn't respond with one of his characteristic explosions. "My son hadn't kept a journal in years."

Rand's stomach dropped to somewhere in the vicinity of his knees, but Lily seemed undaunted. "Are you certain, my lord?"

"I knew my son," he said shortly.

Rubbing his dog's back, she gave a graceful shrug. "Well, it couldn't hurt for us to look, could it? You wouldn't mind, would you?"

Her tone could melt butter in a snowstorm, not to mention a man's heart. In his current mood, Rand's father was no exception. "Go ahead," he said. "But it's a waste of time. Even should you find my son's writings, I'm certain there will be nothing in them that would exonerate Margery's lover." His gaze on Lily was almost apologetic. "My lady, I appreciate your care for my dog, but you cannot marry Randal."

"I understand, my lord," she said softly. But as she rose to join Rand and Kit near the door, her eyes looked as determined as ever.

Rand appreciated that determination more than words could say. As they turned to leave, he took her arm. "We'll get Margery to help, too."

"She's not here," came his father's voice behind him.

More than a little concerned, Rand swung back. "Where is she?"

The marquess waved a hand, apparently unaware that his son had assumed the worst. "In Windsor, with Etta. They went to choose fabric for her wedding gown."

As the vision faded of Margery locked in a dank dungeon somewhere—not that Hawkridge Hall had one—Rand's shoulders slumped with relief. "They'll return soon, then?"

"First thing tomorrow morning."

"They're staying overnight to choose fabric?"

"And fittings or some such. They were to visit a seam-stress. I gave them leave to stay the night at an inn, since they seemed to think it would be dark by the time they finished. I know nothing of these female things."

The man knew nothing of Margery at all, Rand thought incredulously. His foster daughter wouldn't care what she wore to be wed against her will. Rand would lay odds Margery was spending the night with Bennett Armstrong—and he wasn't surprised her old nurse had conspired to arrange it. The two had always been thick as thieves, women in a household run by men. In fact, Margery was likely the reason Etta had decided to stay after her nursemaid days were finished.

The men standing guard over Armstrong had all been at Hawkridge for years, and Rand had already seen proof of their loyalty to Margery. He doubted it ran deep enough to allow an escape—a betrayal of that magnitude would likely mean execution—but he suspected they'd turn a blind eye to an overnight visit.

By all appearances blissfully unaware, his father stroked the dog's head. "Now be about your business. The sooner you give up on finding this journal, the better. You need to prepare for your wedding. To Margery," he added with a glare.

Refusing to rise to that bait, Rand turned and walked away. There was no point in arguing now.

When he'd found what he was looking for, it would be a different story.

SIXTY-THREE

*T*HE MOST LOGICAL place to start, of course, was Alban's suite.

Unlike the single small chamber that had been Rand's refuge during his childhood, the marquess's heir had had three rooms to call his own. They began in his bedchamber proper, a darkly paneled room that sat between the other two and provided entrance to them all.

"Cluttered as ever," Kit remarked when they walked in.

"Nothing's been touched." Rand paused on the threshold. "It's as though he still lives here."

"He hasn't been gone that long," Lily said gently. She skimmed a hand thoughtfully over the unmade bed. "Perhaps his death is still too fresh for the housekeeper to deal with."

"I doubt that." Rand crossed to his brother's dressing table and opened a drawer. "I cannot believe Alban changed enough to curry favor with the staff, even in ten years. He was ruthless in both his expectations and treatment of them. I reckon they're as relieved to be rid of him as anyone." Finding nothing but a neatly folded stack of cravats in the drawer, he slid it closed and opened another. "If this room is undisturbed, it's my father's doing."

Ignoring a frisson of unease, Lily inspected a pile of books on Alban's night table. "What did his journals look like?"

"Nothing in particular, at least back in the day. Whatever blank books he could find."

All the books on the table had titles on their spines, so Lily assumed they weren't journals. Just to make sure, she began opening them.

"I remember this," Rand breathed, pulling something sparkly from a drawer full of stockings. "My mother wore it all the time."

Lily moved closer to see. It was a beautiful oval pendant made of white gold, with many small diamonds set into a delicate filigree design accented with black enamel. "Goodness, it's really quite lovely. Do you think your father gave it to her?"

"Maybe," Rand said as he slipped it into a pocket. "I wonder if he knows Alban had it."

Rather than checking the obvious places, Kit lay down on the floor and stuck his head beneath the red brocade bed skirt. "There's a box under here," he said, pulling it out.

It was long, large, and shallow, made of wood with a heavy, locked hasp. "The journal must be in there," Lily said, amazed that they'd found it so easily. "Where do you suppose we can find the key?"

"Where would you keep a key?" Rand asked no one in particular. Or perhaps he was addressing his brother's ghost.

"Behind the headboard?" Lily suggested.

Rising to his feet, Kit rubbed the back of his neck. "Maybe under the mattress."

"No," Rand said. "Alban was more clever than that. It will be in this room, but not anywhere that typical."

He began methodically lifting objects while Lily checked

the headboard and Kit looked for a key tucked into the ropes that supported the mattress. Both of those places revealed nothing.

"Aha!" Rand set down a Blue Willow jar that he'd found on the mantel. He held a wad of cotton that had concealed the key inside.

His fingers shook as he worked the lock.

Please, Lily prayed silently, let this be it.

But when Rand raised the lid, the box wasn't filled with books. Instead it held an astonishing array of knives.

Lily stared in horror. "Is that dried blood?"

"Alban never was very tidy." Rand's gesture encompassed the general condition of the room. "Chilling, isn't it?"

Lily nodded and swallowed hard, her gaze still fixed on the jumble of sharpened steel. Curved blades and straight, serrated and smooth, double-edged and honed to a deadly point. "Perhaps we have no need to find the journal now. This should convince your father that his eldest son had no good in mind."

A short, harsh laugh rent the air. Kit's. "I expect not. Alban's love of hunting was well known."

Rand nodded. "He rarely carried a firearm, either. Alban liked to kill with his hands. I'm surprised he even tried to shoot Armstrong, although I suppose that goes to show his desperation to see the fellow dead." He released a pent-up breath. "No, I'm afraid this proves nothing except that my brother was fascinated with knives. I doubt the marquess will find that news startling."

"It seems he was fascinated with killing, too." Lily shivered, imagining all the creatures that had died at his hands. While she had no qualms about hunting for food, somehow she knew he'd had other reasons. She looked up and met Rand's eyes. "I believe Lord Armstrong. The man who owned this collection wouldn't hesitate to murder."

"We still must find his journal to prove it."

But a careful, exhaustive search of the bedchamber revealed nothing. They spent an hour combing Alban's dressing room—reaching into his pockets made Lily's skin crawl—and another turning his sitting room upside down.

Nothing.

Kit plopped onto a red-and-gold-striped chair. "We're missing something."

"There's no desk in here," Lily said. "Where did he write?"

Rand began pacing. "In his bedchamber. At his dressing table. Didn't you see the quill and ink?"

"But the drawers there were filled with accessories, not paper."

"Alban didn't write letters," Rand said peevishly. "He wrote only in his journals."

"No," Kit disagreed. "I think Lily is on to something. Perhaps at fifteen, when you left home, Alban wrote only in his journals. But he died at twenty-five. Surely he was involved in some of the estate work by then. Did he not have a study?"

Rand gave a weak shrug—a shrug that alarmed Lily, because it suggested he might have given up. Could Lord Hawkridge have been right that Alban had stopped journaling? The thought was so distressing she was afraid to voice it aloud.

"This is the sum total of Alban's rooms," Rand said dully. "Perhaps he shared the marquess's study."

But Rand's father was *in* his study when they went there to search. He looked up from his paperwork, impatiently tapping his quill on the desk as he swept all three of them with a cold gray gaze. "I can assure you," he said curtly, "you will find nothing of Alban's in here."

Lily deliberately smiled, a smile she suspected would

have done Rose proud. "My lord, I'm certain that your son, as your heir, would have assisted you in the tasks of running your estate—"

"Of course he did. He was never a man to shirk his duties." Lord Hawkridge's eyes swung toward Rand, as though to say he *was* one to shirk.

Lily felt her hackles rise. Rand had had no choice but to make his own life—not if he'd wished to survive. And though his life would be changing now, he certainly deserved time to grow accustomed to the idea.

Besides, she could see no need to rush. Lord Hawkridge appeared almost indecently healthy for a man of his age, not that he was elderly to begin with. Fifty-two, Rand had said. And for all they knew, he could live to be a *hundred* and two.

She forced her lips to remain curved in that smile. "Did Alban do that sort of work with you here in this study?"

"Of course not. I told you, there's nothing of Alban's in here. He converted part of the library into a study for himself." With that, he looked down and scribbled something on one of the papers in front of him.

"Converted part of the library," Rand muttered as they trooped upstairs. "I suppose his own three rooms weren't large enough."

Their footsteps sounded muffled on the woven rush matting that covered the floor of the long gallery. Gilt-framed family portraits lined the lengthy chamber, hung on dark, gilt-trimmed panel walls. Noticing one in particular, Lily stopped.

The painting showed a younger Lord Hawkridge standing behind his seated lady, who held a white kitten on her lap. Her blue eyes looked kind, and Lily liked her on sight. The marquess's eyes looked...happy, she decided in surprise.

He must have been very much in love.

Lady Hawkridge wore a lovely pink dress and the beautiful

diamond pendant Rand now had in his pocket. "I see your mother did love that necklace," Lily said with a soft smile.

Rand nodded. "Maybe this picture is why I still remember it."

Beside that portrait, another young man gazed from a canvas, a man Lily guessed to be Alban. He resembled Rand, except his hair was darker, his expression cooler. His eyes, however, of indeterminate color, looked so cold as to make his smile seem warm in comparison.

There was, of course, no portrait of Rand.

"Professors do not rate paintings," Rand said dryly beside her, apparently reading her mind.

She looked back to the picture of his parents. She could almost see the woman's graceful fingers stroking the silky, purring cat. "She looks very loving," she said of his mother.

"She was. The only love I ever received."

"Not the only," Lily said quietly, and Rand squeezed her around the shoulders.

Kit had gone ahead through the library and into a small room beyond, where a massive desk took up most of the space. Upon entering, Rand immediately moved behind the desk and began opening drawers.

Kit was already pulling books off the shelves. "These are deep," he said. "There's another row of books behind the first." He gestured to the opposite wall. "Lily, you can start over there, and we'll meet in the mid—"

She was heading over to do as he suggested when she heard his indrawn breath. She swung back. "Have you found them?"

"I think so."

Behind the books he'd removed sat a long row of multicolored spines, none of them marked with titles. As he drew one out and opened it, a grin spread on his face.

"Yes, this is a journal. An older one, from 1664. Now we just need the most recent."

Her heart racing with renewed hope, Lily pulled out another and flipped open the cover. "I cannot read it."

"It's in code," Rand told her, standing over her shoulder.

"Oh, right." The dates, at least, weren't encrypted. She turned pages, noting this one ran from mid-1668 to early 1669. "And you got in trouble for breaking the codes."

"Did he ever," Kit confirmed with a wry grin.

"When I translate the latest journal," Rand said, "it will get us *out* of trouble. Let's find it."

But though thirty-odd journals crowded the shelf, none of them were the most recent. They looked behind the books on all the other shelves, floor to ceiling, but there were no more journals to be found.

An hour later, when they'd closed the last cover of the last book in the small room, Lily dropped onto a chair. "What now?"

Rand's jaw set. "We search the rest of the house."

"It's gigantic! And one small journal could be anywhere… if it even exists."

"It exists," Rand forced through gritted teeth. "My brother didn't record his deeds for twenty-four years and then suddenly stop."

Lily felt as though her emotions were on a swing. Down and then up. Up and then down. Dejection settled in for now. "It could take days. We could still be searching when the priest shows up to marry you."

"Lily." Rand came over and took her face in both hands, raising it for a soft kiss. "We will find it, and when the priest comes, he will be marrying *us*." He looked to Kit. "We may as well start here in the main library."

That lofty, two-story chamber was easily eight times the

size of Alban's study. Lily took one look at the endless shelves and felt like weeping.

This would never do. She had to regain her spirits, had to do her share of this enormous task. Rand wasn't giving up, and she couldn't, either.

But after the excitement of the discovery and the disappointment that had followed, she couldn't face starting over just yet. "I'm going to check on Rex," she told the other two. "I'll be right back."

Downstairs, she hugged the huge mastiff around his neck, tightly, as though she could draw strength from his big, warm body. After all, he'd survived a harrowing ordeal and, from the looks of it, come out none the worse for wear. When he licked a slobbery path across her face, she laughed. "All right, then. I'm going to find that journal."

Feeling immeasurably better, she rose, then froze, staring at the dog. "I wonder..." she whispered, then took off at a run, heading back to the library.

SIXTY-FOUR

*E*TTA IN TOW, Margery ran into Bennett's study and smiled when he bolted up from his desk. "What are you doing here?" he gasped.

They met halfway, his mouth divine on hers, the kiss wild despite her old nurse's presence. Her fingers twined into his long dark hair, and his arms went around her to clutch her close. When he finally came up for air, she was breathless. "I told you I'd come to you again, didn't I?"

"Well, yes, but—"

"I've been combing the countryside for witnesses. Rand had promised to do that, but then he took off for Oxford and has yet to return." She ran her hands up and down Bennett's back, frantic to touch him, to feel the muscles beneath his thin shirt, to convince herself he was here, he was real, he wouldn't die, that somehow they'd end up together. "I cannot just sit in my uncle's house and pray anymore. I have to *do* something. I have to find someone who saw Alban come after you."

His hands clenched on her waist. "I feel so helpless, stuck here in this prison. All I can do is write letters." His gaze flicked to the papers littering his desk. "Letters and more letters," he said, looking back to her, his green eyes laced with despair. "But I know no one with influence greater than the marquess's. No one who can save me."

"Did you get *my* letter? The one where I explained Uncle William's promise to spare your life if I marry Rand?"

The look in his eyes—misery—told her he had. "Do you suppose you could come to love him?" he asked, his voice so harsh she pictured each word being forced through his throat.

"Not like this. He's my brother—"

"Then you cannot do it. I won't allow you to sacrifice your life for mine. You'll be unhappy all your days."

"Not as unhappy as I'd be if you were *dead*." She wasn't going to let him argue this point. "I'm going back out—I just stopped here to tell you what I'm doing. If God has heard my prayers, I'll find someone able to vouch for your innocence. Either way, I'll be back tonight."

"Tonight?" She saw his shoulders tense. "Margery, no," he said in a lower tone, darting a look at Etta. "We cannot take that risk. We lost our heads once, and look what happened. I ruined you, and now I can't even—"

"You didn't ruin me," she cried.

Eyes widening in alarm, he cast another mortified glance at her old nurse.

"It's all right, Bennett, she knows everything. Now, stop saying that you ruined me, because we both know the truth— if anything, *I'm* the one who ruined *you*."

Margery had never thought of herself as a person driven by lust. Until she met Bennett. If meeting Bennett had turned her world upside down, their one night together had realigned it in the most perfect, awe-inspiring form imaginable. Though she felt remorse for her weakness and for tempting him to share in it, in truth, she couldn't quite bring herself to regret that night. Not anymore. Because if the worst came to pass, it was all she'd have left of him: the memory of one precious night, and the piece of him now growing inside her.

She swallowed hard. "I'll stay in a guest chamber with Etta if you wish. Uncle William thinks we're staying overnight in Windsor to order a wedding gown—as though I would care what I wore to wed Rand. Sackcloth would do." She snorted. "For all his power, my uncle can be staggeringly blind to a woman's wiles."

"He's a man," Etta put in with a nod of her curly gray head. "His wife could outwit him just as easily. A crafty woman she was, although she loved him too well to play him the fool very often."

Margery had seen a loving side of Uncle William in the past, but right now she found it hard to summon loyalty. "Am I wrong, Bennett, for going behind his back?"

She'd warred with herself for days. Perhaps Rand's mother had been the crafty sort, but Margery had always prided herself on her honesty.

Until Bennett.

Now she was hiding a pregnancy and sneaking off to meet her lover, and she couldn't find it in herself to feel guilt for either dishonest action. But she was also contemplating ruining two other lives to save Bennett's, dooming both Rand and Lily to loveless futures...and that sparked enough guilt to make her dive under the bedcovers and never come out.

One of her hands left Bennett's body and went to her own belly as she prayed her child wouldn't suffer for the sins of its mother.

"No, you're not wrong," he murmured in answer to Margery's earlier question. "Hawkridge is behaving unreasonably. He claims to love you, yet he plots to deprive your child of its father."

One of his hands slipped from her waist to cover her

fingers. She wished he could feel their child move, but even she hadn't felt that yet. It was too early. Were it not for Etta having noticed the signs, she wouldn't even know she was carrying a babe.

And yet she knew in her bones that Bennett's child grew under her heart. And she could only be joyful for it.

"Uncle William doesn't know I'm with child," she said softly. "Because it wouldn't make a difference. And should the unthinkable happen, I would want him to believe the child is Rand's."

The last word was said with a sob—a sob Bennett smothered with his mouth. Heedless of Etta watching, they both poured themselves into the kiss.

It wouldn't be their last, Margery consoled herself when they finally parted. They still had tonight.

But what of all the many, many days and nights after that?

SIXTY-FIVE

"I HAVE AN idea!" Lily shouted as she burst back into the library. "Maybe Rex can find the journal."

Up on a ladder, Rand turned to look down at her. "Rex? You mean Rex the dog, otherwise known as Attila?"

"Yes, Rex the dog. And no, I haven't gone mad. Animals have a keen sense of smell, you know."

Kit's lips twitched. "I didn't realize journals were smelly."

Lily was so hopeful, she only laughed. "Alban's would carry a specific scent. Come, let me show you what I mean."

Rand and Kit exchanged a dubious glance but followed her out of the library.

On their way through the long gallery, Lily glared at Alban's image. He wasn't going to come between her and Rand and their happiness. Rex wouldn't let her down.

Downstairs in the back parlor, Lord Hawkridge was examining the mastiff. When they walked in, he looked up from where he was kneeling—a very unlikely position for such a dignified gentleman.

Lily liked him the better for it. There was always hope for a man who loved animals.

He smiled, an expression that sat rather oddly on his face. "Attila appears to have fully recovered, Lady Lily. I'm very grateful. My thanks to you."

"I would do my best for any living creature, but you're quite welcome. He's a special dog. In fact, I'm wondering if I might borrow him for a while."

He rose to his feet. "Gratitude extends only so far, my lady. Attila lives here."

Rand spoke up. "She doesn't mean to take him away. Only to use him to help find the journal."

"He's a fighter, not a hunter." A more skeptical look had never graced a man's face. "And there's no journal to be found."

Rand crossed his arms, appearing ready to do battle, but Kit cleared his throat. "It's a harmless enough request from one who has done you such a favor. Attila will stay in the house. The exercise will do him good after his ordeal."

"Exercise is all he'll get—he won't be finding any journal. But I suppose it's harmless enough. So long as he stays indoors. I plan to keep him inside overnight."

Lily beamed. "A kind and wise decision, my lord." She snapped her fingers. "Rex, follow me."

"His name is Attila," the marquess called after them.

She led Rand, Kit, and the dog across the marble-floored great hall and through to Alban's suite. Once there, she patted the bed. "Up!" she commanded, and the huge animal landed where she wanted—with a leap that made the bed ropes groan.

Rand grinned. "My father would kill you if he saw this."

"Nonsense. Your father adores me. I saved his favorite dog." She grinned in return, stroking the animal's stiff fur. "Kit, would you run to the kitchen and fetch some meat? Cut into cubes, if possible."

He made her a mock bow. "By all means. Even the exalted

marquess believes you walk on water, so your wish is my command."

As he marched to do her bidding, she giggled. In spite of everything, she giggled. "This is going to work, Rand. I know it."

Holding one bedpost, he leaned to press a kiss to her lips. "Don't get your hopes up, will you? Even if we find a recent journal, I'll have to translate it, and we'll have to hope it turns out to be incriminating. And *then* we'll have to convince the marquess it says what I claim it does—unlikely to be a simple task—and that such evidence merits freeing Bennett and allowing Margery to wed him. We're a long way from victory, sweetheart."

"But we're about to take the first step. I feel it."

When Kit returned with a bowl of meat, she took Alban's fancy silver inkwell and held it to Rex's nose. "Journal," she said clearly.

"That's not a journal—" Rand started.

"Hush. I'm going to have him smell journals, too, and I don't want to confuse him. One word for a scent is enough." She fed the dog a piece of meat, then waved the inkwell beneath his nose again. "Journal. Journal." She fed him more meat, then snapped her fingers. "Down. Come along. You, too," she said to the gentlemen.

Rand barked, eliciting a hoot of laughter from Kit as they followed her.

She hurried back upstairs to the library and through to the small room beyond, Rex trotting by her side. Once there, she took down a stack of Alban's journals. "Sniff, Rex. Journal." She opened one and held it under his nose, then another and another. Each time he sniffed a page, she fed him another reward. "Journal. Journal."

Kit and Rand just looked at each other and shrugged.

After the dog had sniffed a dozen different journals and

received a dozen treats, Lily leaned to look into his eyes. "Journal. Find another journal. Now, Rex. Go."

Without hesitation, the mastiff bolted from the room.

They all ran after him.

Back downstairs, through the great hall, into Alban's bedchamber. By the time they caught up, the three of them were panting harder than the dog.

"Journal," Lily reminded him.

He went straight to the silver inkwell.

She released a strangled laugh. "Good, Rex." She fed him a piece of meat, holding the inkwell out to Rand. "Will you take this out of here? He'll never find anything else with this in the room. It smells too strong."

"Does it?" Kit wondered.

Rand waved the inkwell beneath his friend's nose.

"Whew." Kit blinked. "It does stink."

Rand smelled it himself. "Tannin, and something else I cannot identify. I'd forgotten Alban mixed his own ink. Plain lampblack and linseed oil wouldn't do for his exalted works."

He set the inkwell outside the room, shutting the door for good measure when the mastiff looked after it longingly.

The three of them watched him sniff all around the chamber.

"This isn't going to work," Kit said. "There isn't an inch of this room we haven't looked in or over or under."

"Give him a chance," Lily said. She set the bowl of meat on the mantel. "Journal, Rex. Find a journal."

Rand gestured toward the night table. "He hasn't noticed all those books."

"He's not searching for books. He's searching for a scent. Those books weren't handwritten by Alban, so they don't smell of his ink."

Rex trotted into the sitting room, sniffed around there, and came back.

"Perhaps," Rand said, "we should lead him to some other chambers. Ones we haven't searched yet."

"Give him a chance," Lily said.

Rex sniffed all around the bedchamber again, jumping on and off the bed twice in the process. The coverlet slid to the floor, and Kit bent to pick it up. "He's—"

"Give him a chance," Lily said.

Rex examined the dressing room. Thoroughly. Lily walked to the doorway and watched. "Journal. Journal. Rex, find another journal."

Returning to the bedchamber, the dog sniffed around once more. Then he stopped before the marble fireplace and sat on his haunches, gazing into it.

He barked once.

The three humans looked at each other.

"He's done," Kit said. "He didn't find it."

Refusing to believe that, Lily knelt by Rex's head. He licked her cheek, then looked back at the fireplace and barked.

"He thinks it's there," she said. "In the fireplace."

Rand lifted a poker and stirred the cold ashes. "Nothing. There's nothing here."

"Maybe Alban burned it," Lily whispered, afraid that if she said the words out loud, she might somehow make them true.

"Maybe." Rand set the poker back in its wrought iron stand with a final-sounding *clunk*. "I suppose he might have, if he were worried enough that someone might find it."

Disappointment fisted Lily's heart. She stepped toward Rand, toward the comforting heat of his body, the comforting circle of his arms.

Would this be the last day she ever felt that comfort?

Rex barked again. And again. And again, gazing at Lily as

though he was trying to tell her something but didn't have the words.

"He thinks it's in there," she said with a sigh. "It must have burned."

"No." Kit walked across the room, then back, staring at the fireplace. He poked his head into the sitting room, then looked again at the fireplace. "There's space behind there."

"What do you mean?" Lily asked.

"Empty space. Maybe a hiding place. I cannot believe I failed to notice it immediately. Can't you see the proportions are off, in both this room and the next?"

"We're not architects," Rand said dryly, but with a fresh note of hope in his voice. "How do we get to this space?"

Kit began feeling around the paneling above the mantel-piece. "There has to be a latch, or a lever, or something…" He moved to the side, running his hands down the wood to the floor.

And there it was. A little *snick* reverberated in the room, and a panel swung open.

Lily stepped in first.

A secret room. No, a space. It was tall as a man but no more than three feet deep. Just wide enough to step into and access the area behind the fireplace, a nook so dark she couldn't see her own hand in front of her face.

She heard the soft hiss of a flame being struck. Rand stepped in holding a candle, illuminating the hidden space and its shelves.

Shutting her eyes in horror, Lily turned away.

But she'd seen what was on the shelves. Traps of all sizes, some with steel teeth large enough to capture a man. A bloody saw. Well-used rope. Cuffs. Whips.

And a lone, leather-bound journal.

Rand reached for it and hurried her out, closing the door with a *bang*.

Taking the candle from Rand, Kit reopened the panel, peeked in, and slammed it shut again.

Lily's limbs shook. "What—what were all those things for, Rand?"

"I'm not certain I want to know. But I imagine this journal will reveal all."

"Will you show your father that space?"

He was silent a long moment. "No. Not unless I have to. Not unless the journal fails to reveal Alban's plan to kill Armstrong, or the marquess refuses to believe my translation."

She nodded. It was a sound decision. The marquess had clearly loved Alban, and there was no sense disillusioning him more than was necessary. Alban was already dead, after all.

Never had Lily, nice Lily, thought she'd be glad for a man's demise. "Never say never," she whispered.

Rand slanted her a glance, then slowly opened the journal and flipped to the final entry. "'Nineteenth of August, 1677,'" he read aloud before looking up. "The day Alban died."

"We've got him," Kit said with a smile.

Lily dropped to her knees and buried her face in Rex's neck, wetting his fur with her tears. After a long moment, she got to her feet, reached for the bowl of meat, and set it on the floor.

"Thank you," she murmured.

SIXTY-SIX

*A*LL THE WAY back to Trentingham, Lily and Rand and Kit reminded one another that the journal might not reveal anything incriminating.

But they couldn't help but believe that it would.

It was late when they arrived, and Lily was exhausted. She'd hardly slept a wink those long nights waiting for word from Rand.

The rest of the family were already abed. After a yawning Parkinson let them in, Rand drew Lily close and dropped a kiss on the top of her head. "Go to sleep," he told her. "You cannot help with this, anyway. In the morning you'll feel better, and with luck I'll have good news."

She nodded and took herself off to her room.

Parkinson led the way up to the library, then lit a few candles and went back to bed himself. Rand and Kit settled at a round wooden table to decipher the diary.

No sooner had Rand opened the cover than Rose walked in, carrying another candle and wearing a white night rail with a red wrapper tied over it. Although the garments were concealing, their effect was undeniably intimate. She set down the candle and rubbed her eyes. "You found the journal?"

"We did," Kit said. "Would you like to help us decode it?"

Rand opened his mouth to protest, but before he could, she took a chair. "Of course. Lily asked me to help, because I'm good at that sort of thing."

She *was* good at that sort of thing. Inside of an hour, they had Alban's final entry translated, Rand and Rose doing most of the work while Kit sat back and watched.

Rand noticed that Kit mostly watched Rose.

"What does it say?" Kit asked.

"'I'm going to do it,'" Rose quoted. "'The time has come.'"

"It's not enough." Rand rubbed the back of his neck. "We need to find something that clearly implies murder. The rest of this entry's no more than a recitation of his day."

"Then we do the one before it," Kit said.

Rand sent him a wry glance. "We?"

"Hey, we all do what we can. I found the thing, didn't I?"

"With Rex's help," Rand conceded.

Rose went to a cabinet and poured them each a measure of Madeira, herself included. Then they went back to work.

Another hour passed, an hour of slow but steady progress.

"We're going to find the evidence," Rose said, adding to the ever-growing column of words they'd managed to decipher. "It's here. I know it." She looked up, her dark eyes troubled. "He was wicked, wasn't he, your brother?"

Rand nodded, afraid to be optimistic, but feeling Rose was right. They were going to find their proof. Then he'd just need to convince his father.

They puzzled out a few more words of an entry dealing with the sale of some cattle. "You're going to take care of my sister," Rose said while scribbling some notes. "And I expect you to be kind to her all your days."

He looked up. "I'll cherish her like no man has ever cherished a woman."

"You'd better," she said darkly, then jotted another word.

A smile on his face, Kit watched her and sipped his Madeira.

"'The date draws near,'" Rand read when the entry was complete. "'If I am to master her, steps must be taken.'"

"Not enough," Kit said. "He could be talking about a horse."

"But he isn't." Rose reached to refill his goblet. "He's talking about murder. Another entry. Let's get back to work."

She seemed tireless, and Rand was rarely tempted to sleep when faced with a puzzle. Especially one this important.

"Lady Rose," Kit started.

"Hmm?" She crossed out a word and wrote another.

"Rand led me to believe you were, ah, a mite antagonistic concerning his relationship with your sister."

"Well, that," she said, "was before I got to know the fellow properly. I didn't feel he was good enough for her at first. But now…"

Her soft smile said it all. Although she'd had other reasons to oppose the match than those she was willing to admit, Rand knew her change of heart was genuine. Miraculously, she seemed truly happy for him and Lily. And approving.

It would be an enormous relief for Lily, he knew, and for him as well. And now, when it seemed everything might work out after all, that seemed more important than ever.

Several hours and four entries later, at last they hit gold.

Rand sat back, staring at the page.

"Read it," Kit said.

"'Margery begged and begged,'" Rose read softly, "'but Hawkridge refused as always.'" She paused, glancing up at Rand. "He called your father Hawkridge?"

Rand shrugged. "Ours is not a warm family."

"You'll be warm now," she warned, "to my sister. Or—"

"Peace, Rose. I love Lily more than my life. Read the rest, will you?"

Kit laughed. At a time like this, he laughed. If Rand hadn't been so tense, he'd have reached over and slapped him. But in his present mood, he feared he might do his old friend permanent damage.

"'Hawkridge refused as always,'" Rose continued slowly. "'I followed Margery to Armstrong's place, her sobbing all the way. And there, they plotted to elope.'" She reached for her Madeira. "Here," she said, passing Rand their notes. "You do the rest."

He took a deep breath before reading, for the first time, the individual words they'd translated, all pieced together. "'When I overheard their plans, I felt I couldn't draw air. My heart swelled to such a size it filled my chest, squeezing my lungs, robbing me of sustenance. I cannot allow this to happen. Margery belongs to me. They leave in a week, and before that, I must kill him.'"

"There it is," Kit said admiringly.

"Yes, there it is," Rose echoed with a satisfied sigh.

"Thank you, Lord above," Rand whispered, closing his eyes.

After a moment, he heard Rose clear her throat. "You're welcome," she said archly.

When Rand laughed and opened his eyes, he realized his vision was blurred. "And thank you both, too," he said fervently, digging out a handkerchief to wipe his eyes. "From the bottom of my heart. If—when—Lily and I wed, I'll be silently thanking you as we recite our vows."

Dawn was breaking when they left the library. Rose had made peace with the fact that he'd chosen Lily over her, and amazingly, she and Rand were friends. But Kit, Rand was sure, wanted to be more than friends with Rose.

A shame she hadn't seemed to really notice him.

"Go to Lily," she told Rand. "Go tell her what we've found."

"Go to her in her chamber? You…you'll come along, won't you?"

"No." She flashed the sort of smile that only Rose could flash. "But if you're not out in five minutes, I'm coming in, and I'm bringing something pointy."

Rand didn't need a second invitation.

Lily looked like an angel, her hair a dark halo on her pillow. But her mouth was turned down in a frown. Her dreams, he knew, weren't sweet.

He leaned down and pressed a kiss to those pouting lips. They curved up, and her arms rose to wrap around his neck.

She smelled of sleep and lilies. "Rand?"

"Yes, my sweet. I'm here." Was it silly of him to be so glad she hadn't said someone else's name? He knew she was his, knew it as well as he knew which English words came from Latin.

Her eyes slid languidly open. "Could you read the journal?"

He smiled and sat beside her on the bed, his fingers playing idly in her hair. "Alban Nesbitt," he said, "has never contrived a code I couldn't decipher."

She sat up, suddenly wide awake. "What did it say, Rand?" Her hands twisted together in her lap, her fingers rubbing the faint scars. "What did it say?"

"It said he planned to murder Bennett Armstrong. I love you, Lily Ashcroft, and we're going to be married."

He would make it so. He hadn't come this far to fail now.

Before Lily rose for breakfast, he was riding hard for Hawkridge, the journal and notes in one hand.

SIXTY-SEVEN

*R*AND ARRIVED at Hawkridge to find the marquess and Margery at breakfast, sullen and silent.

His arrival took care of that.

"It's here," he said, striding in and waving his papers. "In Alban's own hand. His plans to kill Bennett Armstrong, here in black and white."

Margery's face lit like a full moon on a cloudless night. The marquess took one look at her and frowned. "Sit down, Randal. I haven't finished my breakfast."

Rand took some spice bread and a bowl of meat pottage from the leather-topped sideboard and carried them to the table. He sat and spread his evidence on the cedarwood surface.

The marquess deliberately looked away, focusing on his food.

Margery pushed her pottage around in her bowl, evidently too excited to eat. "What did you find, Rand?"

"The journal ended on the day of Alban's death." Ignoring the marquess's wince, Rand took a big bite of the fruited spice bread. He'd been awake twenty-six hours without taking any time to eat. "Here"—he rustled through the papers with one hand—"here's the crucial passage." He held out a page to Margery.

Her hand shook as she took it. Although it was a translation, not Alban's writing, the words on the paper were his.

As she scanned down the page, a soft gasp escaped her lips. Rand's father looked annoyed before she even began reading. "'I cannot allow this to happen. Margery belongs to me. They leave in a week, and before that, I must kill him.'"

The marquess snatched the sheet from her hand. His eyes narrowed before his gaze shifted to Rand. "This isn't Alban's hand. It's yours."

"Actually, that's Lady Rose Ashcroft's writing." Rand wasn't at all surprised the old goat didn't recognize his own son's hand. He'd never bothered to look at any of Rand's lessons. "Her writing is much tidier than mine."

With a flick of his still-nimble wrist, his father tossed the paper onto the table. "I'll never believe that's what the journal says. Do you think me a fool? You'd claim anything in order to wed that Ashcroft chit." He looked back down to his food, cutting a bite of ham with a fitful, angry motion. "Those aren't Alban's words. I know—I *knew*—my son."

Rand struggled for calm. "No, Father, you didn't."

The man's gaze jerked up from his breakfast. Rand hadn't called him Father in fifteen years or more. Staring at Rand, he stabbed blindly with his fork.

"You didn't know him," Rand repeated. "You knew the son you wished he was."

"Hogwash." Having managed to spear some ham, he stuck it in his mouth, taking his time to chew and swallow before continuing. "My son was incapable of premeditated murder."

"Are you aware that your son kept knives under his bed?

A collection to rival a museum's. Most of them stained with blood."

If Rand could judge from his expression, his father hadn't known. "There have been no murders in this district other than Alban's."

"Not of people," Rand agreed. "But I'd wager animals have been found senselessly slaughtered."

From the look on his father's face, he'd hit home. "What of it? It's no crime."

"It could be a small leap from beasts to humankind."

The marquess pursed his lips and shook his head, but his armor had cracked. Rand could see it in his eyes. He pressed his sudden advantage. "Come to Alban's chambers. I'll show you the blades. After you see the evidence, your imagination will fill in the rest." With that, he rose and strode out of the room, trusting the marquess would follow.

When he heard an additional set of footsteps as they crossed the great hall, he glanced over his shoulder. "Wait in the dining room, Margery. This isn't fit for a lady's eyes."

Lily had seen the knives—and worse, to Rand's regret. He had no intention of allowing another woman to witness his brother's depravity.

But Margery lifted her chin. "I'm no lady, as your father often reminds me. Only a mere miss. And seeing as I was supposed to wed the man, I feel entitled to view what I escaped."

By the time she finished her brave speech, they were all standing in Alban's bedchamber. Rand sighed and gave up.

"Where?" the marquess asked, clearly discomfited in the disarray that made it seem as though his eldest son were still alive. "I see no knives."

"They're under the bed." Rand stooped to pull out the box. They'd left it unlocked. He lifted the lid.

"Mercy me," Margery whispered, looking away.

Her hand went protectively to her abdomen, and Rand winced, hoping his father wouldn't notice the telltale gesture. He went to wrap an arm around her shoulders. "He's gone," he said softly. "He cannot hurt you now."

"Or anyone else." He felt her shudder, then straighten. "Or any*thing* else."

He looked to the marquess. "Well?"

The man's jaw looked tense enough to crack walnuts. "This proves nothing. Alban was an avid hunter, as you well know."

Margery's mouth dropped open. "Uncle William, those aren't hunting knives."

The marquess bent and drew one out. "This one is."

How could anyone be so blinded by stubborn pride? Rand felt anger boiling up from his gut, choking him. In frustration, he yanked the knife from his father's hand and tossed it back into the box. "Were you aware there's a secret space off this chamber?" he asked in a tight voice.

The one thing he'd vowed to avoid bringing into this. And in front of Margery, no less. But had he any choice? Better shocked and disturbed than married to the wrong man.

"Of course I know that," his father scoffed. "I built the place."

Though the room was flooded with daylight, Rand lit a candle. "Then I suppose you also know what's in it?"

"No, I don't. What Alban kept in his chambers was his concern alone." Though the marquess sounded adamant, trepidation laced his voice. His gaze flickered to the fireplace. "Will you never learn that a man is entitled to privacy, Randal? How many times did I tell you not to snoop in your brother's journals?"

Halfway to the fireplace, Rand whirled. "How many times did you beat me for it?"

"Too many to count," the man snapped.

"Yes, too many times I tried to show you who your son was, and still you continued to deny it." Shoving the candle into his father's hand, Rand knelt to work the latch near the floor. "Here, at last, is your proof," he gritted out. "Try to tell me I'm mistranslating *this* to my advantage."

He stood and swung open the panel.

The marquess stepped into the small space. And his face went white.

As though in a daze, Margery moved closer.

"No!" Rand reached to stop her and turned her into his chest. His arms went around her protectively. "Take a good look," he told his father over his shoulder. "Perhaps there have been no murders in the vicinity, but that only means he stopped short of killing. You won't convince me all those implements were meant for hunting. Or even animals."

Silence settled over the chamber, so profound Rand could hear both his own heart and Margery's. And the marquess's harsh breathing. Despite his convictions, the older man was clearly shaken.

Suddenly he stepped back and slammed the panel, the sound shattering the stillness. For a moment, he just stood in place, swaying on his feet as an odd sort of calmness settled over him. "This doesn't prove Alban meant to kill Bennett Armstrong."

"No," Rand agreed. "It only goes to show he was capable. His journal is the proof."

"I cannot read it. And I refuse to—"

"To take my word as to its translation? I'm not surprised, since you never have. But this time, I'm prepared to sit with you, for *days* if necessary, and demonstrate, step-by-step, how the code was broken and exactly what that journal says." To Rand's mortification, his voice broke. "You owe me the chance to do that, Father. All my life you've dismissed me, and you've already admitted that was a mistake on your part. *You owe me.*"

It didn't take days.

Four hours later, his father slumped in his chair and buried his face in his hands.

SIXTY-EIGHT

STANDING IN HER mother's perfumery, Lily gazed out the window and squinted into the distance. "Where on earth is he?"

On another day, Rose might have laughed, but she didn't. "Poor Lily. Give him time." She chose several cheerful yellow daffodils and added them to an arrangement. "He had to ride there and convince his father and then come all the way back…why, he likely won't be here for hours."

Mum plucked rose petals, tossing them into the clear glass bulb of the fancy distillery Ford had made for her while courting Violet. "Your sister's right, dear. Come and help me. It will take your mind off the waiting."

With a sigh, Lily walked to the table and idly picked up a rose. "I know Rand will convince his father," she said, as much to assure herself as them.

"Of course he will," Rose said. "If you'd seen that translation, you'd be even more certain. Rand's brother intended murder. The marquess won't be able to deny it."

"But that doesn't mean he'll allow us to wed."

That statement was met with silence, because, unfortunately, there was no arguing with it. No guarantees that proof of Alban's intent would lead to the marquess changing his mind.

"Tell me about Hawkridge," Mum said at last. "I've never been there myself. Is it beautiful?"

"Very." Lily absently plucked rose petals. "Much newer than Trentingham—Rand's father built it just before the war —and every room is exquisite." Except for Rand's, which was rather plain, but she didn't feel up to explaining that. "Why, the dining room even has *leather* on the walls, with designs stamped in pure gold. But the place is eerie, I think. Or perhaps it's just cold. It feels as though no one there has been happy for a long, long time."

"Perhaps they haven't," Mum suggested. "But that will change, of course. You and Rand will be happy indeed, and your happiness will rub off on everyone else. And I imagine that after you move there you'll be able to make improvements, make Hawkridge Hall feel warmer and more like home. If you cannot redecorate the whole house, you should at least have a say in the rooms assigned to you and Rand."

Picturing Rand's tiny chamber, Lily sighed. Maybe— assuming they were allowed to marry—they could occupy Alban's suite of rooms instead. But if that were the case, a complete overhaul would be necessary before she'd agree to sleep there even once.

Rose added several carnations to the colorful spray she was creating. "Will you live at Hawkridge after you marry, then? Will Rand have to give up his post at Oxford?"

"I don't know. As far as I'm aware, Rand and his father have yet to discuss any of those details." She tossed the last of the rose petals into the glass bulb. "All of their energies have been focused on the question of *who* he will marry."

Mum fitted the lid on the distillery. "Has Rand resigned himself to leaving his position?"

"I don't think he's had enough time to think about it. But I doubt he'll be happy leaving Oxford." Lily hoped he'd be happy just being with her, whether at Oxford or Hawkridge or somewhere else entirely. But she knew better. "He worked very hard to attain that professorship. And he enjoys that life. He's never fancied himself a baron, let alone a marquess."

Finished, Rose stepped back to eye her masterpiece. "I shouldn't think *that* would be hard to get used to."

Rose might have matured a bit, but she was still Rose.

"How about you?" Mum asked. "Will you be happy at Hawkridge?"

"I'll be happy wherever Rand is," she said, knowing it was true. "I'll have him, and my animals…"

Her voice trailed off.

Mum looked up sharply. "What is it, dear? Are you afraid Lord Hawkridge won't approve of your menagerie?"

"No," she said slowly. "He loves animals—more than people, truth be told. He raises mastiffs."

Mum smiled. "Well, then, it sounds like Hawkridge will be the perfect place to build your animal home."

Rose tweaked a few flowers, balancing the arrangement. "From what I saw, Hawkridge has plenty of space."

"No. I mean, yes, as you know, there are acres and acres of land." Lily took a deep breath and decided to come out with it. "But you might as well know that if the marquess blesses this marriage, it will be with the stipulation that my inheritance goes to him."

Rose gasped. "How dare he demand such a thing!"

"There was no demand. I offered of my own free will. Hawkridge was mortgaged during the war, you see, to provide funds for King Charles. The marquess was on the verge of losing it when Margery was dropped in his lap, along with her considerable fortune. Hawkridge would face bankruptcy without her land and money."

"Or *your* money," Rose said darkly.

"Exactly. Don't look so sour, Rose. It was my idea to offer my inheritance in exchange for the right to wed Rand, and I'll gladly do so, if only the marquess will allow it."

Rose plucked a daisy from the vase and pointed it at Lily. "All your life, you've dreamed of nothing but building a home for your strays." She shook the flower, emphasizing her words. "Maybe sometimes I've laughed at that, but I know how important it is to you. How can you give that up so cavalierly?"

"I'm in love," Lily said simply.

But she caught Mum's gaze on her and knew her mother hadn't missed the wistfulness in her voice.

SIXTY-NINE

*N*OT THE SORT of man to indulge in self-pity for long, nor to accept blame, the marquess had made an excuse and gone off to his study. Half an hour later, when Rand and Margery asked to talk to him, he readily—if gruffly—invited them in.

They sat in two chairs facing him, gazing up at him seated behind his desk on the raised dais. A few awkward moments passed before Rand cleared his throat.

"Father," he began, hoping calling him such might diffuse a bit of the tension, "we would like your assurance that, under the circumstances, you will no longer pursue the conviction of Bennett Armstrong for murder."

"Of course I won't. I'm a reasonable man when presented with persuasive evidence."

"Well, then, Margery respectfully requests permission to marry him."

"Does she?" the marquess asked with a raised brow. He shifted his gaze to his foster daughter. "I haven't heard such a respectful request."

"Uncle William..." Margery's voice shook, and she paused to control it. "May I *please* wed Bennett?"

"No," the man snapped. "I didn't agree before Alban's death, and nothing has changed between then and now. Marriage is primarily a business arrangement, and an alliance of Hawkridge with the Maybanks estates is best for both parties."

"You mean Hawkridge requires Margery's money," Rand said, struggling to remain calm. "As I've told you, Lily has ten thousand pounds that she's willing to invest in Hawkridge's future. Added to her dowry of three thousand, it should be a sufficient sum."

At Lily's name, the marquess's eyes had softened. It was amazing how much his father had apparently come to like her. He almost looked wistful.

But his expression swiftly hardened again. "I vowed on Simon Maybanks's deathbed that his daughter would wed my heir. Lady Lily's inheritance does nothing to mitigate that."

"Uncle William." Margery rose and walked over to him, stepping up onto the raised dais. She placed her palms on his desk and leaned toward him, her eyes pleading. "I was an infant when my father claimed that boon, and he was only attempting to provide for my future the best that he knew how. Don't you think he would have been thrilled to marry me to a baron with Bennett's vast lands and income? Most especially because I love Bennett so very much, and he loves me in return. You must agree that if my father had had any way of foreseeing such an opportunity, he would have given his blessing freely."

In the silence that followed, Margery backed down the step and returned to her seat. She folded her hands on her black-skirted lap. A clock ticked on the mantel, unnaturally loud in the stillness. The marquess blinked but said nothing.

"Father," Rand pressed, hoping the man's lack of response meant he was considering Margery's words, "you've told me that your treatment of me, in years gone past, was because you blamed me for my mother's death."

The marquess's lips thinned. "I've also told you I'm sorry."

"And I've accepted your apology—and your explanation." Saying the words, Rand suddenly realized he had. "But what I'm wondering now, or perhaps I should say what I'm assuming, is that you loved her very much."

"Of course I did," his father said, looking bewildered. "I loved her with all my heart."

"Then whyever would you wish to deprive your son and foster daughter of that same sort of love?"

The marquess blinked some more. Margery's hands clenched in her lap. The clock kept ticking. Rand prayed silently, harder than he'd ever prayed in his life.

"Marry whom you wish," his father said at last with a sigh.

Margery leapt up and rounded the desk to hug him. "Thank you, Uncle William, thank you! You've always been so kind to me, I knew in the end you'd choose for my happiness."

Rand's father just grunted.

Rand sat immobile, his entire body seemingly gone boneless.

He'd done it.

He was going to marry Lily.

"I must go tell Bennett!"

Rand had never seen Margery's eyes look so green, her face look so flushed. He smiled, picturing Lily looking that happy.

"I'll take you to him," he said, "on my way back to Trentingham. Lily will be anxious to hear this news, too."

"I'm going with you," his father said.

Halfway to rising, Rand dropped back onto his chair. "Pardon?"

"What sort of a man do you take me for?" the marquess asked, then apparently decided he'd best not wait for an answer. "Not only has your Lily saved my dog's life, she is also about to save Hawkridge from ruin. The least I can do is welcome her into our family."

Rand wasn't sure he was ready to think of himself and his father as a family—he suspected they might never truly be friends. But he grudgingly admitted that it seemed the man's heart might be in the right place.

Or getting there, anyway.

SEVENTY

*W*HILE **THE MARQUESS** rode around Armstrong House dismissing all the guards, Rand dismounted and walked Margery to the door. The butler answered and showed them both into a sitting room, then went to fetch Lord Armstrong.

Rand sat on a red velvet chair watching Margery walk aimlessly around the chamber, bouncing a little on the balls of her feet. She'd be happy here, he thought. Though the house was centuries older and much smaller than Hawkridge, it was well kept and richly appointed. Besides, he knew Margery would be happy anywhere so long as she was with Armstrong.

It was the same for him and Lily. Home would be where Lily lived, even if that was Hawkridge.

"Margery!" The baron rushed into the room, then stopped short when he saw Rand.

Rand rose from the chair. "She's yours, Armstrong."

Long-lost hope leapt into the man's eyes. "You mean…"

"Yes. My father has agreed to your marriage."

"How—why—"

"Margery will explain," Rand said. "Later."

She'd stopped roaming. Now she seemed simply frozen in place, gazing at the man she loved as though she couldn't believe he would be hers. When he took a step toward her, she came to life and rushed into his arms.

Their lips met, and Rand smiled. That would be he and Lily soon, and he knew their reunion would be even better. In fact, he couldn't imagine why he was standing here watching such a scene when he could be participating in one of his own.

"I'm leaving," he announced.

With a heartfelt sigh, Margery drew back—slightly. "Good-bye, Randy," she said, though it was Armstrong's eyes she was gazing into.

"I'm leaving you two alone."

"I know," she murmured, her mouth stretching into a wide smile.

"Be good," Rand said, knowing they wouldn't.

❧

*L*ILY'S FINGERS ran over the harpsichord keys in an unceasing pattern. "What time is it?" she asked.

"About five minutes after the last time I told you." Rose didn't bother to look at a clock. "I thought you found music calming."

"Well, today it's not."

"Perhaps it would help if you'd play something besides scales." Rose set down her needlework and pulled a droopy bloom from the flower arrangement beside her. "You're making *me* nervous."

"Sorry." The music stopped abruptly as Lily folded her hands in her lap. She closed her eyes, willing herself to be patient. "That it's taking this long, it's a good sign, yes?" She heard her sister rise and walk across the drawing room. "It must mean his father is listening."

"It must," Rose said in a soothing way.

But Lily heard laughter bubbling underneath. Her eyes popped open. "This isn't easy, you know. My entire life is hanging in the balance."

"Of course it's not easy." Rose plucked three browning leaves off some flowers on the wide windowsill. "But surely not your entire life. If it all ends badly, you'll go on—"

"You've never been in love," Lily said.

The leaves crunched in her sister's fisted hand. "No," she agreed, "I haven't. And given what you're going through, I believe that's just as well."

"You're wrong." Lily's voice came a whisper. "I wouldn't trade love for tranquility."

"Some of us," Rose said, "don't seem to have a choice."

"Oh, Rose." Lily's eyes met her sister's dark ones. "Someday..."

You'll find someone.

The words hung between them, unsaid, until Rose looked away and out the window. "Someone's riding up the road."

"Rand!" Lily jumped up and brushed at her sky blue skirts.

Rose frowned. "No, two someones. I wonder who they could be?"

"Two?" Lily pulled a few curls forward to frame her face. "How do I look?"

"He's not going to care," said the sister that took the most care with her own appearance. "Go to him, Lily."

As she hurried to the entry hall, Lily wondered if one of the riders was indeed Rand. After all, there were two, and he'd set out for Hawkridge Hall alone. As Parkinson opened the door, she braced herself for disappointment.

Rand stood on the other side, a wide smile on his face. Her heart leapt—until she looked beyond him.

"Lord Hawkridge. How, um, how very nice to see you."

"Lady Lily." Rand's father bowed, for once looking at a loss for words.

"Rand," her mother said warmly, glossing over the awkward moment as she appeared from seemingly nowhere. "Come in, please. And you," she said to Lord Hawkridge, "must be this young man's father. The resemblance is unmistakable."

Rand didn't look particularly pleased at that observation. Lily stared at him, caught in his compelling gray gaze, wondering…

"And you must be Lady Trentingham. I'm pleased to make your acquaintance," the marquess told her mother. "I've come to welcome your daughter into my family."

It took a moment for Lily to register those words, and when she did, she was embarrassed to feel tears spring to her eyes.

"Rand," she whispered.

His gaze flicked over to his father, then her mother, and finally Rose standing at the bottom of Trentingham's wide staircase. He stepped forward to take Lily's hand.

"Come," he said, "I feel a need to take a run." He glanced at her fashionable heeled shoes. "I mean a walk."

That old, rude habit, but Lily didn't care, so long as he wanted her with him this time. Her mother and the marquess would do fine—Rand's father might be on the curmudgeonly side, but Mum had never met a man she couldn't wrap around her finger.

Without saying a word, Rand hurried her through the house, out the back into the gardens, and along the paths to the summerhouse. He dropped her hand long enough to shut the door behind them, enclosing them in the cool dimness of the small, round brick building. Then he turned and gathered her into his arms.

"Rand, how did you convince—"

"Hush," he said as his mouth crushed down on hers.

She was hushed, very effectively, by a kiss so intense it rattled her to her toes. His lips slanted over hers again and again until she couldn't remember where his mouth stopped and hers started, until her knees were so weak she needed his arms to hold her up.

"When can we marry?" he asked, dropping little kisses on her nose, her cheeks, her chin. "When? Today?"

"No." She laughed, rising on her toes to allow him better access. He felt so very *good*—especially knowing that finally, miraculously, he was going to be hers.

"Tomorrow?" he asked, his lips dancing over her skin, slow and sweet.

"Not tomorrow."

"The next day, then. Or the day after that. Saturday. A perfect day for a wedding."

"No." She shivered, and not only from the sensual assault. "You and Margery were supposed to marry on Saturday."

"Her birthday. The day she'll wed Bennett Armstrong." His hand moved to cup her cheek.

"Oh," she breathed, "they must be so happy."

"Mmm." His agreement was muffled by his lips taking hers. "Margery will want us at her wedding," he murmured against her mouth. "So ours will have to be the day after that."

"No." Pulling back, she laughed again. "Two weeks. When Violet and Ford wished to marry in a rush, Mum insisted on two weeks to plan the wedding."

"Two weeks?" he said on a groan. "After all we've gone through, two more weeks seems a lifetime."

She smiled softly, basking in the candid sentiment. "Two

weeks is entirely survivable—as long as nothing else gets in our way." But it didn't seem real. "Even so, I don't think I'll believe this is happening until we're married. Until you're mine, heart, body, and soul, and no one can threaten otherwise."

The adoration in his eyes transformed to steel. "Nothing can endanger us, Lily. *Nothing*. We've survived a nightmare, and there is *nothing* I will allow to come between us."

"I know," she said. And she did. After too many hours and days when she'd thought he was lost to her, the agony was finally at an end. All would be well. She knew that.

She just couldn't quite believe it.

"Nothing," he repeated, that piercing gray gaze clearly seeing through her as usual. His hands came up to grip her shoulders. "Fate may send us dragons, but I'll slay them for you, fair Lily. Nothing will steal you from my side."

Watching her closely, he pulled something from his pocket.

His mother's pendant, on a delicate white gold chain.

"I've learned that my father gave this to my mother on their wedding day. I was planning to save it for our own wedding day, but I want you to have it now."

"Oh, Rand."

If this wasn't proof that he was certain they'd stay together, she didn't know what was. She heard beautiful music in her head as he clasped the chain around her neck. Looking down, she lifted the necklace, admiring all the diamonds and the beautiful enameled filigree design.

Her throat closed with emotion. "I'll cherish it always," she whispered.

It was all she could manage.

"Come, let's walk," he said, steering her out of the summerhouse with a hand at her back. "Perhaps if I tell you how this all came about, it will begin to feel more real."

They strolled across the wide lawn and over the bridge and along the Thames. As his story poured out, Lily held on to his hand, reminding herself that he was truly here.

"You were brilliant," she said when he'd told her everything.

"I was desperate." He squeezed her hand and smiled.

"And how has your father taken it?"

"We spent over an hour riding here—maybe the longest time alone together ever. He expressed regret that he'd never seen Alban for who he was. He seems…repentant."

"You like him more than you thought."

"I wouldn't go so far as to say *like*. We've a long history between us. But the idea of living with him isn't nearly as abhorrent as I would have thought last month."

Lily hugged that small victory to herself. It seemed there was hope for the Nesbitt family, after all.

"Will we have to? Live with him, I mean?"

He seemed surprised by the question. "Do you imagine we have a choice? He's certainly assuming we will. Hawkridge will someday be mine, and I've a lot to learn about handling it."

"But you, *Professor* Nesbitt, can handle anything you put your mind to. Your father has years left to live. Why should you give up the life you love now?"

He looked as though he wanted to believe her—but couldn't. "It's a matter of responsibility. Once I would have agreed with you, but now that I've been home…well, there's Margery—"

"Margery will be at Armstrong House."

"There's Etta and all the others. They're depending on me, and I cannot let them down. Oxford…" His voice turned wistful for a moment before he straightened his shoulders, his hand gripping hers tighter. "This is the way it must be."

"But your research, your house."

"There's nothing for it. I'll have to sell the house."

"After you worked months designing it with Kit? The two of you put your hearts and souls into that house."

He gave her a wan smile. "Kit liked some of my ideas so much, he's planning changes to his own home in Windsor."

"You cannot just sell it, Rand."

"Well, it makes no sense to keep it if I'll never be using it, does it? I can put the money into Hawkridge, help it recover from the loss of Margery's land that much sooner. Or...wait..."

A light had entered his eyes. "What?" Lily asked.

"The money can be *yours*," he said softly, looking pleased with himself. "For your animal home."

It would mean she'd have the best of both worlds—Rand *and* her dream—but she said, "No."

"Yes." He nodded emphatically. "It's my house, after all, built with income that had nothing to do with Hawkridge. My father and the estate have no claim on it whatsoever."

"No, Rand." She wouldn't—couldn't—let him give up his house in Oxford—and the life he'd made for himself there— for an old childhood dream. "I won't hear of it."

It was a silly dream, anyway, a childish dream for a child. Her strays had no need of a fancy, custom-built home and a staff of trained caretakers. She'd done just fine by them so far, all by herself with makeshift pens in a corner of a barn, and surely the marquess would have no objection to her doing the same at Hawkridge.

True, she dreamed of helping more animals—hundreds more, possibly even in several homes spread across the country—but who knew if she'd ever find such a large number of needful creatures? Her strays had always found *her*.

They'd reached the woods, and Rand apparently decided not to argue, instead pulling her into his arms. "Are you *really* going to make me wait two weeks?" he asked, lowering his lips to hers, for an unhurried, teasing, coaxing kiss.

She wasn't thrilled about the wait either. All she wanted was to know—no, to *believe*—that he was truly hers. He felt so warm and solid against her body, she could almost see them staying together forever.

She sighed against his mouth. "Let's go back," she said. "There's much to settle. Our wedding date, for one."

"And then?"

"And then maybe I'll believe it."

SEVENTY-ONE

THE NEGOTIATIONS took place over a dinner that had gone cold while waiting for their return.

"Two weeks," Lily told her mother.

"Two weeks! I cannot plan a wedding in two weeks."

"You did for Violet and Ford," Lily reminded her, and that was that.

Looking victorious, Lily turned to Rand's father. "Now I would like to discuss our living arrangements."

His gaze landed on the diamond pendant she wore. Though he'd granted Rand permission to give it to her, Rand still held his breath, waiting for a reaction.

At last the marquess nodded his approval, a small smile curving his lips. "I realize Randal's chamber is small," he told her. "Perhaps we can refurbish—"

"That would be nice, but I meant where we will live and when."

The man picked up his fork, his smile becoming a slight frown. "You'll live at Hawkridge, of course. Where did you think you would live?"

"Oxford, at least part of the year. Rand's position there is important to him. His research—"

"Lily," Rand started.

"He can research at home," his father cut in. "He'll be the marquess someday, which means he has responsibilities."

She smiled sweetly. "Certainly he does—"

"Lily," Rand interrupted.

"—but that doesn't mean he must be at Hawkridge all the time. Many landowners have more than one estate, and a man cannot be two or three places at once. Why, Father visits Tremayne but once a year, and it thrives quite well without his constant presence."

"Lily," Rand tried to put in.

But she wasn't finished. "Oxford has three terms a year of eight weeks each. Twenty-four weeks out of fifty-two. There are long breaks between those terms and the whole summer free...if Rand agrees to spend the remaining twenty-eight weeks at Hawkridge learning his responsibilities, surely you can survive without him during term times."

"Lily—"

"Just until he's needed at Hawkridge year-round," she said by way of conclusion. "But given your excellent state of health, we're both hoping that won't be for a long, long time."

She topped off her arguments with a sweet smile that the marquess apparently found bemusing, given he seemed to be frozen in place with his fork halfway to his mouth.

But Rand was not similarly charmed. "Lily," he repeated and paused for a moment, expecting her to interrupt. When she didn't, he sighed. "I truly want to sell my house so you'll have the money for your animal home. It's the least I can do after you so generously offered to save my family."

Rose clapped. Lady Trentingham smiled.

Rand's father came to life. "Animal home?"

"Lily's lifelong dream," the countess explained. "She's rather fond of animals—"

"This isn't news to me," his father said with a smile that looked out of place on his face.

"And she had planned, upon coming into her inheritance, to build a home where strays could be sheltered and, if necessary, nursed to health."

"With a staff," Lily added. "But truly, my lord, I don't mind investing in Hawkridge instead. It will be my children's legacy, after all. And I especially don't want Rand to sell his Oxford house. As proud as you are of building Hawkridge, he feels the same of his home. And—"

"Enough." The marquess waved his fork. "You will talk my ear off, child. Randal shall keep his house, and if his responsibilities at Oxford can be fulfilled in twenty-four weeks a year, they may have him for that time. But I get him the rest," he warned.

"Of course."

His jaw set, Rand shook his head. "No. I said—"

"She shall have her animal home," the marquess interrupted, "at Hawkridge. I have staff enough to spare, and if nothing else, it will ensure you two stay there on a regular basis. Now, if everyone's concerns have been addressed to their satisfaction, I had better be off. Margery's wedding day approaches, and although it surely won't be the extravaganza the countess has in mind for yours, there are details to which I must attend."

Half an hour later, Rand found himself dragged out of the house, drafted into helping his father, since, as Lady Trentingham pointed out, it wasn't term time at Oxford.

No sooner was he riding away than Lily's mother started a guest list.

～

"**WELL, DARLING,**" Joseph said that night, "that was very cleanly done, although I suspect the poor lad might die of longing if there were such a disease. And I don't expect our daughter was very happy, either."

"Nonsense," Chrystabel said as she climbed into bed. "They can survive two weeks."

"Two weeks entirely apart? I'd like to see someone try to keep me from you for that space of time. That someone would not survive long."

"They won't be *entirely* apart. We're all attending Margery's wedding on Saturday."

"Well then, we had better be especially vigilant that day, my pretty Chrysanthemum. They're bound to try to sneak away." Drawing her to him, Joseph kissed her soundly. "It's what I would do in their situation, after all."

Chrystabel knew he was right, but she put those concerns aside for now. Tonight she had no inclination to worry or plot. Tonight she could only thank God, from the bottom of her heart, that her daughter's happiness was secured at last.

SEVENTY-TWO

"**S**OON," **RAND** whispered, "it will be *our* turn."

Lily watched the starry-eyed bride and groom exit Hawkridge's grand red-and-gold private chapel as though they were walking on air. Tears had welled in her eyes more than once during the emotional ceremony. "I cannot wait," she whispered back, reaching up to touch the pendant Rand had given her.

The past few days without him had felt so empty.

Holding his hand, she walked sedately from the chapel, following the other guests to the great hall. Once there, she rushed to hug her soon-to-be sister-in-law. "The wedding was beautiful! You both look so happy."

"We are," Margery and Bennett said together, sharing a joyful smile.

Rand hugged Margery, too, while Lily watched, not at all jealous this time.

"Your gown is gorgeous," she told her.

"Thank you." Margery's fingers skimmed the pearls and embroidery that covered her pale green satin overskirt. "It's my best."

Standing nearby, the marquess narrowed his eyes. "What happened to the gown you ordered in Windsor?"

"Oh." Color flooded her cheeks. "Well. I—I...it wasn't quite ready, after all. You didn't give the seamstress much time, Uncle William."

"Hmmph," he said and walked away.

Rand waited until the man was out of earshot and then grinned at his foster sister. "You never ordered a wedding gown, did you? I suspected you were with Bennett that night."

"It's the vows that count," she said evasively. "Not the clothes."

Her groom laughed and gave her a kiss. As other guests pressed close to offer felicitations, Rand turned to Lily, a silvery glint in his eyes. "Come. I have something to show you."

He led her from the great hall, grabbing a pewter goblet off a sideboard and handing it to her as they went.

She sipped, then smiled when she tasted what was in it. "Your father poured the champagne my parents brought."

"He likes your parents." His shrug encompassed all the bafflement she knew he felt at his father's recent behavior. Beatrix appeared and padded at their heels as Rand entered the corridor that led to his room. But instead of turning left, he walked straight ahead into Alban's bedchamber.

Only it wasn't Alban's bedchamber anymore. It wasn't a bedchamber at all.

She stared. "What happened?"

"You'll be living here the week after next. I told my father we needed more room. He didn't argue, so I sent a message to Kit. The day after that, a crew of men showed up to begin the remodel. They'll resume tomorrow, once all the wedding guests go home."

The dark paneling had been stripped and was half refinished in a warm, honey tone that lightened the whole chamber. The door to the secret space stood open, and she could see it had been emptied. The rest of the room was empty, too.

"Even the bed is gone," she said.

"This will be our sitting room." The drapes had been removed, and soft summer rain blew against the naked windows. Taking her hand, Rand drew her into Alban's old sitting room, now dominated by a huge four-poster bed draped in yellow silk. "I had it brought from another chamber. Just until you choose a new one. Something without a history. I thought we could go to London, and—"

"Thank you," she whispered past a sudden lump in her throat. She knew Rand didn't care whether he slept in the same room that Alban had, or even in the same bed. He'd done this for *her*. "Where are Alban's things?"

"I had them sent to a foundling home. Every last item. I asked Father, and he didn't say yes, but he didn't say no, either. I think he wants to forget that Alban ever existed. He even had his portrait removed from the long gallery."

In an effort to steady herself, she took a sip of champagne. "Did he send that to the foundling home, too?"

"No." Again, that baffled shrug. "He burned it."

"Maybe he'll have one painted of you to replace it."

He gave a strangled laugh. "I wouldn't go so far as to assume that."

Beatrix followed them back through the sitting room and into Alban's old dressing room, and it was empty, too. The clothes presses were gone, the walls stripped and waiting to be finished. "Kit is arranging for someone to build cabinets." Rand took the goblet from Lily's hand. "Newfangled ones with drawers."

She turned to him. "It all sounds wonderful. I love it. I love you."

"And I love you." A smile lit his eyes as he sipped,

regarding her over the rim. Without swallowing, he bent and put his mouth to hers, giving her a sweet, cold, sparkly kiss as he shared the bubbly beverage.

She swallowed and laughed. "Eleven more days and we'll be together for good."

"Too long." He took another sip and gave her another effervescent kiss, the champagne still fizzing in her mouth when he pulled back to skim his knuckles along her cheek. Her skin tingled wherever he touched, and the champagne kisses were making her lightheaded.

When Beatrix began hiccuping, Lily bent to pet her soothingly. A distraction from Rand while she attempted to recover her wits. Looking up at him, she mustered a teasing smile. "Did you bring me in here to show me the renovations or to get me alone?"

"Both," he replied with a grin. When she straightened, he took another sip and leaned over to meet her lips once again. When his mouth moved to her neck, she sighed dreamily, licking the remnants of champagne off her lips. Delicious. Rand's kisses were delicious.

Beatrix suddenly began meowing emphatically.

"Ignore her," they whispered together.

Meow…

Lily felt Rand's warm hand settle on the small of her back while a chilled goblet touched the nape of her neck, making her shiver—and not from the cold. A thrill of excitement rolled through her, coupled with wonder that he would be hers. Not only today, but forever. Seeing Margery wed Bennett had made it all seem more real.

Her own wedding was next.

Meow, meow…

The mere thought made her giddy, made her heart beat wildly. She pressed closer to Rand, tilting her head until their mouths fit together perfectly.

Meow, meow, meeeoooow...

A knock came at the door. "Lily? Rand? Are you in there?"

"Goodness! It's Mum!" Lily sprung away from Rand, her pulse racing not with excitement now, but with something more akin to panic. "Beatrix was trying to warn us!" she whispered, straightening her neckline where it had drooped down one shoulder.

"Your mother?" Rand looked altogether unruffled.

More knocking. "Lily? Are you in there?"

Amusement lit Rand's eyes. "I'll get the door."

"Not yet!" Her hands patted her coiffed curls. "Is my hair all right?"

"Are you in there, dear?"

"You look fine. Irresistible, in fact." Apparently proving himself unable to resist, Rand gave her one last kiss before taking her hand and leading her into the sitting room to answer the door. Lily did her best to look composed. As the door swung open, revealing her parents, she plastered on a smile.

Mum's gaze flicked to Lily's bodice before settling on her face. "There you are!" she said brightly.

Too brightly.

"I was just showing Lily the rooms we'll be using when we live here," Rand said unconvincingly.

"We'd love to see them, too," her mother said and walked straight into the bedchamber.

As her parents passed, Lily looked down, mortified to find one of her stomacher tabs had somehow come unattached. She whirled away, fastening it surreptitiously before joining them in the other room.

"This entire home is magnificent." Mum crossed to a wall and ran a hand down the newly stripped paneling. "The grain is lovely."

"I thought to paint it white for Lily," Rand said. "But Kit suggested a pale stain might look nicer on this wood."

Mum nodded her approval. "What kind is it?"

Her husband pulled out his pocket watch and flipped open the lid. "Half past three."

"Maple," Rand said, clearly suppressing a laugh.

Joseph snapped the pocket watch shut, nodding vaguely at Rand. "I expect you'll be staying here the next week or so to supervise finishing this?"

Rand raised his voice. "The house in Oxford needs my attention, too, Lord Trentingham. Perhaps I can bring Lily along—"

"I think not," Mum interrupted. "The bride-to-be will be at home, busy with wedding plans."

Lily looked at her mother in surprise, having thought the arrangements more or less complete. "Mum, I think—"

"You'll be busy," she repeated. "If you weren't insisting on marrying so quickly, it might be a different matter. But I'll need your help. Now, I imagine Margery and Bennett are missing us, so let us end our little house tour here."

As they all returned to the great hall together, Lily exchanged a frustrated glance with Rand. Were they to be kept apart entirely until their wedding?

"Elizabeth!" Mum cried, waving to a neighbor and dragging Joseph in her direction. "I've found the perfect man for your daughter."

No sooner had her parents walked off than Rand swung Lily to face him. "Margery wasn't missing us." He aimed a pointed look to where his baby sister was half entwined with Bennett, blissfully unaware of any of the guests.

Lily nodded. "Mum is trying to keep us apart. I cannot figure why—"

"Does it matter why? She intends to make certain we don't see each other again until the day of our wedding."

A maid came by with fresh goblets of champagne. Rand took one and a bottle, too, meeting Lily's eyes in a way that made her certain he had an idea that involved the sparkling wine.

An idea Mum wouldn't approve.

Lily's lips tingled at the thought. She took the goblet from him and downed a bracing swallow.

"If this is to be our last evening together, we must make the most of it," Rand said, sounding as though he'd just assigned himself a mission. He cast a glance to Lily's parents and, seeing their backs momentarily turned, grabbed her hand. "Come along."

He hurried her into the adjoining dining room, where footmen were setting the long gatelegged table with Delft-ware dishes for the wedding supper. Lily glanced back into the great hall. "They'll just find us again."

"I wouldn't bet on that," he advised her, taking the empty goblet from her hand and setting it on the leather-topped sideboard. Still carrying the bottle, he led her into the next room.

Having peeked in here once, Lily recognized the tall, heavy oak bed. His father's bed.

She stopped short and gaped. "We cannot hide in here! What if your father comes in to get something?"

Laughing, Rand leaned a hand on the wall.

Lily was astonished to see a panel swing open. They slipped beyond it, and Rand closed it quietly.

"A secret passage?" she said in wonder.

"Not secret." Calmer now but no less determined, he guided her through a windowless corridor lit by plain lanterns mounted on walls painted a simple pale gray. "The house has these passages all through it," he explained, guiding her around a corner. Here, a longer hallway bustled with servants carrying dishes and linen. "Father didn't want the staff walking through one chamber to get to another, so corridors run behind. That way, they can duck in and out of rooms unobtrusively."

The floors were not painstakingly polished here, but covered with long rush mats instead. With no fire to warm it, the passage was chilly. "Do all the rooms have secret doors?"

"Most of them, but the doors aren't secret, either. They're designed not to be obvious, but you'll find them if you look for them."

Lily shivered. "If there's a door into our suite, I want it sealed."

She thought Rand smiled beside her, but the corridor was too dim to tell for sure. Rows of leather fire buckets hung overhead, making her think they must be near the kitchen. "Where are we going?"

"Out. Through the servants' entrance."

"Out? You mean outside? Into the rain?"

His hand squeezed hers. "No one will be coming out in the rain to look for us, will they?"

Summer rain blew in when he pushed open the door. They made a run for it, Rand holding Lily with one hand and the champagne bottle with the other. After crossing the courtyard to the outbuildings, they finally ducked into the dairy.

Though Rand shut the door against the rain, it still pattered on the roof and slashed against the dairy's diamond-paned windows, reminding Lily of their betrothal picnic in the summerhouse at Trentingham.

"I can hardly believe it," he said, shaking rain out of his hair. "I thought this day would never come."

"What day?" she asked.

He adopted a solemn tone. "The day I, Rand Nesbitt, outsmarted the incomparable Lady Trentingham."

Lily giggled, glancing around the small room. "Where are the dairymaids?"

"Inside, helping with the wedding. No one will interrupt us." He grinned. "Even Beatrix failed to make it out here."

The walls were plain and whitewashed. Lily turned in a slow circle, her shoes leaving wet prints on the red tile floor. Pails, pans, and strainers sat on a wide marble counter supported on legs that ended in cows' hooves. She hugged herself, smiling at the whimsy.

"Cold?" Rand asked.

"A little. There's no fire."

"I'll warm you up," he said, the tone of his voice leaving no doubt how he planned to accomplish that end. The champagne bottle landed on the marble surface with a definitive *clunk*.

He took her hands and raised them to his lips. Slowly he kissed the palms and the backs and the fine white scars.

"Don't flinch," he murmured when she did. Looking down, he traced the webbed patterns with a fingertip. "They're beautiful, because they're part of you."

Her throat closed with emotion, but she managed a shaky smile. "They remind me that I'm imperfect, which I suppose is not such a bad thing."

"It's a good thing you have one flaw." He kissed her nose and then her mouth, tiny damp kisses. "I'd feel too inferior living with perfection."

Something twisted in her heart. "There were times when I feared you'd never be living with me at all."

"Never say never," he murmured, raising the champagne bottle, as if in a toast. He tipped his head back and took a sip, then held the bottle to her lips. The champagne tickled as it slid down her throat.

He backed her against the counter, his hands coming around her waist to make a barrier between her and the cold marble. His lips were gentle and cherishing, slow and languid, as though they had all the time in the world.

The pitter-pat of rain blended with her sighs, blocking out everything but the two of them. Here and now, it seemed there was only she and Rand and their love.

It was a long time before he broke the kiss. But he stayed close, leaning his forehead against hers.

"This is a perfect afternoon," she whispered.

"We'll have more." He pulled back to look at her with those startling gray eyes, the first thing she'd ever noticed about him. With one gentle finger, he touched the dent in her chin. "A lifetime together."

Nothing would ever come between them again.

⚮

OR A LONG time Rand held Lily in his arms, humming a gentle lullaby that reminded him of his mother, his gaze drifting out the window. It struck him that he was happier here in this cold, austere dairy with Lily than he'd ever been, anywhere, without her. Beyond the glass, tall old trees danced in the blustery breeze, bright green against the dark gray sky, and farther beyond that, the red brick of Hawkridge Hall loomed majestically.

This estate—all of this—would someday be his. And he belonged here, as much as he belonged in a lecture hall or huddled over a cryptic passage of ancient text.

He'd spent his childhood here craving acceptance from a father who couldn't stand the sight of him and a brother who lived to torment him. Alban was dead now, his evil laid to rest. And as for the marquess...perhaps now he'd finally have a chance to get to know the son he'd turned his back on. Perhaps he'd even approve.

But to Rand it didn't really matter anymore. Because now he had Lily.

He tilted her chin up for a kiss. He would never get

enough of her, he thought as he grazed her eyes and her cheeks and her mouth, settling there to savor her soft lips. A kiss as gentle as the summer rain, a kiss for them both to melt into, a kiss to meld bodies and souls. And then another kiss. And another.

And another, until they heard a scratch and a peck and a tap against one of the dairy's windows.

AUTHOR'S NOTE

∼

DEAR READER,

Before I receive a bunch of letters claiming that mastiffs are gentle, protective, indoor, family-type dogs, I want to say that all of that is true—for today's mastiffs. But in days gone by, the mastiff was known as a fighting dog. Caesar mentioned mastiffs in his account of invading Britain in 55 B.C., describing the huge British dogs that fought beside their masters. Soon afterward, mastiffs were bought back to Rome, where they saw combat at the Circus, matched against not only other dogs but also bulls, bears, lions, tigers, and human gladiators. Marco Polo wrote of Kubla Khan, who owned five thousand mastiffs used for hunting and war. Henry VIII gifted Charles V of Spain with four hundred mastiffs intended for use in battle.

However, by the 1920s, mastiffs were disappearing from England. During World War I, people thought it unpatriotic to keep dogs alive that ate as much in a day as a soldier. By World War II, they were nearly extinct in England, but afterward, mastiffs were imported from Canada and the United States to start new kennels. Now they are well established again, but with a change: modern breeders have bred the mastiff for gentleness and companionship rather than fighting. In his *Knight's Tale*, Chaucer described mastiffs as large as steer, which sounds unbelievable until we remember that cattle were much smaller in those days. Today's mastiffs are the same massive size, but they're loving and sociable pets.

In 1680, Irish scientist Robert Boyle began selling coarse sheets of paper coated with phosphorus and wooden sticks with sulfur. A stick drawn through a fold of the paper would burst into flames. This device was the first chemical "match" and ultimately led to what we think of as matches today. In 1855, the first red phosphorus "safety" matches were introduced in Sweden, and paper "match books" were invented in the United States in 1889.

Bawdy songs have always been popular, and in the seventeenth century the English were more comfortable singing such verse than they tend to be today. Cromwell's Puritan Protectorate may have driven lusty singing underground, but with the Restoration, the ballad sellers returned. These early entrepreneurs sold single-sheet songs on the street, cheaply printed overnight to gain the most profit from each newly written piece.

In 1661, publisher and composer John Playford put together a collection of these songs and ballads and called it *An Antidote Against Melancholy*. In 1682, his son Henry expanded the collection and published it as *Wit and Mirth: An Antidote Against Melancholy*. By 1698, the book was so popular that Henry expanded it again, this time sold as *Wit and Mirth, or Pills to Purge Melancholy*. It proved so successful that after Henry's death it was published by others, and five further volumes were eventually added. By the time Thomas D'Urfey edited the final edition in 1720, the six-volume set contained more than a thousand bawdy songs.

Most of the homes in our books are inspired by real places you can visit. Trentingham Manor came to life after we saw The Vyne, a National Trust property in Hampshire. Built in the early sixteenth century for Lord Sandys, Henry VIII's Lord Chamberlain, the house acquired a classical portico in the mid-seventeenth century (the first of its kind in England) and contains a grand Palladian staircase, a wealth of old paneling and fine furniture, and a fascinating Tudor chapel with Renaissance glass. The Vyne and its extensive gardens are open for visits April through October.

Hawkridge Hall was modeled on Ham House, another National Trust property. Known as the most well-preserved Stuart home in England, Ham House was built in 1610 and enlarged in the 1670s. The building has survived virtually unchanged since then, and it still retains most of the furniture from that period. The house and gardens are open daily from April through October. Ham House was owned by the Lauderdales, one of the most powerful families in Restoration England, and a visit gives a wonderful picture of seventeenth-century aristocratic life.

Rand's house in Oxford was inspired by the house Edmond Halley (1656-1742) lived in while he held the post of Oxford's Savilian Professor of Geometry. If you visit Oxford, look for the house in New College Lane near the Bridge of Sighs. The building isn't open to tourists, but you can see the outside, including the rooftop observatory Halley added (although he never saw Halley's Comet from it, since it made no appearance during the years he lived in the house).

I hope you enjoyed *The Baron's Inconvenient Bride*! Next up is Rose's story in *The Gentleman's Scandalous Bride*. Please read on for an excerpt!

Always,

Lauren Royal

Read on for an excerpt from

The Gentleman's Scandalous Bride

Book 7 of the
Sweet Chase Brides series
by Lauren & Devon Royal

Determined to land a wealthy, titled husband, Rose Ashcroft heads off to Charles II's court to find love. And runs smack dab into Christopher "Kit" Martyn, the one man who could ruin all her plans.

～

Trentingham Manor, the South of England
September 1677

STANDING IN her family's small, crowded chapel, Rose Ashcroft shifted on her high Louis-heeled shoes, wishing she were in a cathedral so there would be somewhere to sit.

Wishing she were *anywhere* but here watching her sister get married.

"Randal John Charles, Baron of Newcliffe, wilt thou have this woman to thy wedded wife, to live together after God's ordinance in the holy estate of matrimony? Wilt thou love her, comfort her, honor, and keep her in sickness and in health; and, forsaking all others, keep thee only unto her, so long as ye both shall live?"

"I will." The confident words boomed through the magnificent oak-paneled chamber, binding Rand to Rose's sister Lily.

But Rose wasn't listening to the ceremony. Instead she heard *nineteen, nineteen, nineteen* running through her head. Nineteen and a lonely spinster...while both her sisters had found love.

Happy tears brightened their mother's brown eyes. She leaned close, bumping against Rose's left side. "They're perfect together, aren't they?" she whispered.

Rose could only nod dumbly, staring at her sister's petite figure laced into a gorgeous pale blue satin wedding dress embroidered with gleaming silver thread. Lily's hair, the same rich sable as Rose's, cascaded to her shoulders in glossy ringlets. Beside her, Rand beamed a smile, looking tall and utterly handsome in dark blue velvet, his gray gaze steady and adoring.

The two were so clearly in love, Rose knew they belonged together—and truly, she was happy for her sister.

If only Lily weren't her *younger* sister.

The priest cleared his throat and looked back down at his *Book of Common Prayer*. "Lady Lily Ashcroft, wilt thou have this man to thy wedded husband..."

Standing on Rose's right, her older sister Violet shifted one of her twin babies on her hip and gazed up at her husband of four years, Ford. Sun streamed through the stained-glass windows, glinting off her spectacles. "Oh, isn't this romantic?" she sighed.

Holding their other infant, Ford squeezed Violet around the shoulders. Seated cross-legged at their feet, their two-year-old son Nicky traced a finger over the patterns in the colorful glazed tile floor, obliviously happy.

Rose gritted her teeth.

Her friend Judith Carrington poked her from behind. "I cannot believe Lily's wedding is happening before mine," she whispered in a tone laced with dismay. "*I* was betrothed first!"

Rose couldn't believe Lily and Judith would *both* be married before she even received a proposal.

"...so long as ye both shall live?" the priest concluded expectantly.

In the hush that followed, even knowing it wasn't kind of her, Rose half wished Lily would fail to reply.

But Lily didn't, of course. "I will," she pledged, her voice as sweet as she was, ringing clear and true.

A few more words, a family heirloom ring slid onto her

finger, and Lily was clearly and truly wed now, the new Lady Newcliffe.

And Rose was clearly and truly miserable.

When Rand lowered his lips to Lily's, Rose turned away. Behind her, Judith was grinning up at her own betrothed— although only a little way up, since his stature was less than impressive. Lord Grenville was five-and-thirty to Judith's nineteen, and his pale brown hair was thinning on top, but Rose imagined that the way Judith looked at him made him feel like a king. And he looked down on her in a way that surely made pretty, plump Judith feel like a queen.

Rose wanted someone who'd make her feel like a queen. Gemini, a duchess or countess would do. Or even a lowly baroness...

As the years crawled by without a husband on the horizon, she was getting less picky. Most any man was acceptable to her now.

So long as he was handsome, titled, rich, and powerful.

The guests parted as Lily and Rand began making their way from the chapel. They'd taken but a few steps when a cat, a squirrel, and a chirping sparrow came to join them.

Rose moved to hug her sister. "It was beautiful," she murmured. "I'm so happy for you."

She was. Truly she was.

Lily leaned down to pick up the cat, straightening with a brilliant smile. "Your turn next."

A hurt retort came to Rose's mind, but she wouldn't snap at her sister on her wedding day.

"I'm happy for you, too, Rand," she said instead, rising on her toes to give her sister's new husband a kiss on the cheek. But not too far up on her toes, because Rose was tall. Too tall, perhaps, or too slim, or too quick-tongued...or too *something*.

There had to be some reason she had yet to marry.

Too intelligent, most likely. At one point, she'd thought

Rand might be the one for her. Handsome, titled, and a professor of linguistics at Oxford—surely a good match for Rose, given her own exceptional command of foreign languages. But he'd chosen her little sister.

"I'm the luckiest man in the world," he said now, making Rose feel the unluckiest woman.

She'd had better days.

Lily must have noticed her dejected expression, because her fingers stopped stroking the cat's striped fur. Concern clouded her lovely blue eyes. "You *will* be next," she said quietly.

"Undoubtedly so, since I'm the only one left," Rose quipped. "Unless, that is, Rowan manages to find himself a bride before I find a groom."

They both swung to look at their ten-year-old brother where he stood with Violet's young niece, Jewel, their dark heads close together as they whispered animatedly.

"He may have found himself a bride already," Rose added dryly.

Lily's giggle rang through the chapel, echoing off the molded dome ceiling. "Surely someone will claim you long before Rowan gets it in his head to wed. Why, you're the prettiest of us all!"

Rose had always thought Lily the *most* pretty, but she knew she was pretty, too. Yet beauty, she'd learned, was not enough to hook a husband.

Well-wishers pressed closer. Rose began moving toward the drawing room and found Judith by her side. Forsaking her betrothed, Judith clutched Rose's arm. "Who is *that* charming fellow?" she whispered conspiratorially.

Rose slid a glance to the fellow in question, a friend of Rand's whose gaze suddenly found hers, then skimmed over her in a way that might have made her heart skitter…if she were at all interested. "That's Mr. Christopher Martyn—Rand calls him Kit. He's an architect," she added dismissively.

Judith frowned. "The name sounds familiar…"

"King Charles recently awarded him a contract to renovate Whitehall Palace," Rose admitted. "Among other commissions." She happened to know that Windsor Castle and Hampton Court were also on Kit's account books. But she didn't want Judith to go getting the wrong idea. That he was someone of importance.

But Judith's blue eyes grew round with awe. "He must be of great consequence to work for the king. And intelligent, too—no need to play the featherbrained country maiden for him."

"I've no interest in playing *anything* for him. And I've never acted featherbrained." But perhaps now was the time to start.

Her recent efforts to entice a certain gentleman—very well, to entice Rand—through intellectual conversation had failed. Hideously. So hideously that the object of her affection was at this very moment marrying her sister. What could be more hideous than that?

Nothing. Which was why she wouldn't be making the same mistake again.

Unfortunately, where Rand was concerned, Rose's mistakes had multiplied. Desperation had driven her to proposition him in a most unseemly manner, and when that hadn't worked, in vexation and despair she'd attempted bribery and trickery of the worst kind.

She couldn't imagine what had come over her that day and had feared she'd never be able to look Rand in the face again. But to her utter relief he seemed at ease with her, as though he'd graciously forgotten that humiliating episode.

"You cannot tell me," Judith whispered, dragging Rose

back to the present, "that you don't think Mr. Martyn good-looking."

Rose slanted Kit another covert look. Dressed in forest-toned velvet, he was tall and lean, his hair dark as jet, his eyes a startling mix of brown and green. She shrugged. "I suppose he's handsome in a typical sort of way."

Judith sighed. "He looks ever so nice. Do you think he's nice?"

"He's nice enough." Except for those unusual eyes, which were decidedly *not* nice. *Roguish* would be a better description.

"And good Lord, he's building things for the king! I'm certain he has money—"

"Money," Rose interrupted pointedly, "does not make up for lack of a title."

Her sister Violet walked up, sans children for once. "Who needs a title?"

Judith crossed her arms. "Lady Rose apparently wishes to become Lady Something-Higher."

"Oh, well." Violet sent Rose an indulgent smile. "That's only because she has yet to fall in love."

Rose smiled in return. "And given that it's as easy to fall in love with a titled man as one without, I've decided to concentrate on the former."

Violet and Judith exchanged a glance that set Rose's teeth on edge, then left her, to return to their respective —*titled*—men.

Since Lily had given their mother barely two weeks to plan the event, the wedding party was small. Still, there were more than enough guests to fill the drawing room and spill out onto the Palladian portico and into the exquisite gardens. Trentingham Manor was known for its gardens, thanks to Rose's father and his passion for flowers and plants.

But it was a warm, sunny day, and Rose feared for her creamy complexion, so she opted to stay indoors. She wandered the crowded drawing room, sipping from a goblet of the new and frightfully expensive champagne her parents favored for special celebrations. Although she enjoyed sharing a word or two with various relatives and neighbors, she was generally feeling at loose ends, not quite sure what to do with herself.

Until, that was, she heard her father's voice and turned to see him addressing Kit Martyn.

"...one of those newfangled greenhouses," Father was saying. "On the east side of the house, I'm thinking, to catch the morning sun. Since autumn is nearly upon us, I'd be much obliged if you could start it immediately."

Rose couldn't believe her ears. It was the second time her father had asked the esteemed architect to build him a lowly greenhouse.

Half tempted to ball up the lacy handkerchief she had tucked in her sleeve and stuff it into her father's mouth, she hurried to join them. "Mr. Martyn builds things for the *king*, Father! Palaces, for heaven's sake. He hasn't—"

"Well, not quite palaces," Kit corrected her. "Renovations to palaces, additions to palaces, but I've yet to build an entire—"

"See?" Rose met her father's deep green eyes, speaking loudly and slowly to make sure he could hear her over the hubbub of the celebration. "Palaces. He hasn't the time to build you a greenhouse."

Kit sipped from his own goblet of champagne, then grinned at Rose's father. "Oh, I think I might find the time," he disagreed, his words infused with a hint of laughter. "In exchange for a dance with your lovely daughter."

He shifted to look at Rose, making it clear which daughter he meant. His green-brown gaze swept her lazily, almost as though he were mentally assessing her...and Rose wasn't certain she liked being assessed.

Lord Trentingham frowned. "My chubby doctor?"

Kit looked confused, and Rose knew she should remind him that her father was hard of hearing at the best of times—and in a crowded room, he was all but deaf.

But she couldn't seem to speak. The impertinence—thinking he could trade a building for her company! Surely her father would never—

"I'll be most pleased to build your greenhouse," Kit reiterated a bit louder, "if your lovely daughter will grant me a dance."

"Plant what in grass?"

Understanding dawned in Kit's eyes. "A dance," he shouted. "May I have the honor of a dance with Lady Rose?"

"Oh, yes. Of course," her father said. "Now, about that greenhouse—"

"I'll do a preliminary design before I leave," Kit all but bellowed.

"Excellent." Lord Trentingham turned a vague smile in Rose's direction. "Run along, my dear. Enjoy yourself."

Her mouth dropped open, then shut when she found herself propelled from the drawing room by a warm hand at her back. Then she was stepping out onto the covered portico, which had been pressed into service as a dance floor.

Three musicians in one corner were playing a minuet, a graceful dance that facilitated conversation. The wedding guests chatted and flirted, their shoes brushing the brick paving in unison. Though the dance was already in progress, Kit handed both their champagne goblets to a passing maid, took Rose's hands, and swept her into the throng.

She'd never touched him—certainly not skin to skin—and the contact reminded her of her reaction to him the first time they met. The mere sight of him had set her nerves to jangling inside her, and she was not a nervous girl. But that, of course, had been before she'd discovered he was a plain mister. Since then, seeing him had had no effect on her at all.

So it was disconcerting to find that touching him now seemed to make the champagne bubbles dance in her stomach.

"Lovely Corinthian capitals on the columns and pilasters," Kit noted, ever the architect. "Do you know who carved them?"

She pliéd and stepped forward with her right foot at the same time she finally found her tongue. "Edward Marshall, who also carved the Ashcroft family arms in the pediment. And in future, please keep in mind that there's no cause to seek my father's permission for a dance. Ashcroft women make their own decisions."

"So Rand has told me," Kit said, breezing over the implication that she might have refused him.

They rose on their toes, and when he pulled her closer, she caught a breath of his scent. A woodsy fragrance with a base of frankincense and myrrh. It smelled nice, she thought, wondering if she could duplicate it in her mother's perfumery.

"Your family is an odd one," he said. "I don't allow my sister to make her own decisions. Not the important ones, in any case."

She felt sorry for his sister. "Our family motto is *Interroga Conformationem*."

He looked at her blankly.

"Question Convention," she translated. What sort of educated gentleman didn't know Latin? Certainly not one she'd ever consider husband material.

It was a good thing he wasn't in the running.

They dropped hands to turn in place, then he grasped her

fingers again. "Is it true, as Rand said, that your father allows his daughters to choose their own husbands as well?"

She noticed Lily and Rand dancing together—much closer than the dance required. Surprisingly, envy didn't clutch at her heart this time. She only smiled. "Yes."

"In future, I'll keep *that* in mind," Kit responded with a disarming grin.

Ignoring his impertinence, Rose gazed across the wide daisy-strewn lawn toward the Thames. Just then, her brother Rowan raced onto the portico, looking like a miniature version of their father in a burgundy suit, his long midnight hair streaming behind him.

A quite ordinary-looking man followed more sedately, but as he wore red and white—the king's livery—he attracted more attention.

The musicians stopped playing, and the dancers ground to a halt.

"There he is," Rowan said, pointing to Kit in the sudden silence. "Mr. Christopher Martyn, the man you seek."

∼

AVAILABLE NOW!
Learn more about *The Gentleman's Scandalous Bride* **at**
www.DevonAndLaurenRoyal.com

ENTER FOR A CHANCE TO WIN
a sterling silver replica of the pendant that Rand gives Lily in this book!*

Visit the Contest page on Lauren & Devon's website
at www.LaurenandDevonRoyal.com
and answer a question to be
entered in the monthly drawing.

No purchase necessary. See complete rules on the site.

*Please note: Depending on when you enter, the prize may be another piece of jewelry associated with one of Lauren & Devon's books. The authors reserve the right to discontinue this promotion at any time.

ABOUT LAUREN & DEVON ROYAL

~

LAUREN ROYAL decided to become a writer in the third grade, after winning a "Why My Mother is the Greatest" essay contest. Now she's a *New York Times* and *USA Today* bestselling author of humorous historical romance novels. Lauren lives in Southern California with her family and their constantly shedding cat. She still thinks her mother is the greatest.

DEVON ROYAL is the daughter of romance novelist Lauren Royal. After attending film school, she wrote an award-winning TV comedy pilot and worked in digital video production before turning her focus to fiction writing. Devon lives in Southern California with her husband and son. She also thinks her mother is the greatest.

ACKNOWLEDGMENTS

OUR HEARTFELT THANKS:

To Ayn Rand, for the concepts behind Violet's philosophical musings on love at first sight.

To all the honorary Chase cousins in our Chase Family Readers Group, for their enthusiastic support.

And, last but certainly not least, to all of our wonderful readers, especially those of you who send emails and post about our books on Twitter and Facebook.

Thank you, one and all!

CONTACT INFORMATION

～

Newsletter

littl.ink / News

Facebook Readers Group

facebook.com / groups / ChaseFamilyReaders

Website

www.DevonAndLaurenRoyal.com

Email

royall.ink / Email